J.P. O'Connell is a writer and editor who lives in South London.

Hotel Portofino

VOLUME I

J.P. O'Connell

**SIMON &
SCHUSTER**

London · New York · Sydney · Toronto · New Delhi

First published in Great Britain by Simon & Schuster UK Ltd, 2021

THE WRITERS' ROOM

Written by J.P. O'Connell. Based on scripts by Matt Baker.

1 3 5 7 9 10 8 6 4 2

Simon & Schuster UK Ltd
1st Floor
222 Gray's Inn Road
London WC1X 8HB

Simon & Schuster Australia, Sydney
Simon & Schuster India, New Delhi

www.simonandschuster.co.uk
www.simonandschuster.com.au
www.simonandschuster.co.in

A CIP catalogue record for this book
is available from the British Library

Paperback ISBN: 978-1-3985-1175-0
eBook ISBN: 978-1-3985-1176-7
Audio ISBN: 978-1-3985-1372-3

Typeset in Bembo by M Rules
Printed and bound by CPI Group (UK) Ltd, Croydon, CR0 4YY

MIX
Paper from
responsible sources
FSC® C171272

1

It was so satisfying, Bella thought, readying the rooms for new guests. After some discussion with Cecil, she had decided to put the Drummond-Wards in the Epsom Suite. Not only did it have a sea view, but it was light and airy with solid mahogany beds and the sort of delicate floral wallpaper that didn't overwhelm.

Too much pattern was always a mistake. A person might be tempted to stop and stare; to try to work it out, by its interplay of lines and shapes. But sometimes – in life as well as decor – it was better not to notice patterns at all.

In any case, Bella didn't have time to stop. She had too much to do.

She crossed the room to where Francesco and Billy were struggling to turn a mattress.

'You're a strong lad,' she said to Billy, who was red in the face and panting. 'Give it another go.'

'But it's so heavy, Mrs Ainsworth!'

'It's the horse hair,' Bella explained. 'That's what makes it so comfortable to sleep on.'

'There's metal in there, too. I can feel it.'

'Those are springs, Billy.'

As Billy shook his head in disbelief, Paola hurried in with a pile of crisp, freshly-ironed sheets. The linen had come from London – Heal's on Tottenham Court Road no less! True, the British Store in Bordighera sold bed linen alongside such staples as Gordon's Gin and Huntley & Palmer biscuits. Many expat families were happy to buy from there.

But for Hotel Portofino, only the best would do.

And that meant soft cotton with a thick yarn. The type of sheets that snapped when you fetched them off the washing line.

The mattress duly turned, Billy sloped off to help his mother in the kitchen. Paola set to work making the bed, while Francesco moved a vase of iridescent purple irises onto an occasional table.

Bella liked to stock the bathrooms herself. At Hotel Portofino, the better suites had their own bathrooms. She and Cecil had invested in the very latest hot water technology. People expected to be able to take a bath nowadays, without the fuss of servants standing around to feed logs into a stove. And some of the old systems were frankly dangerous. Everybody knew the story of the exploding geyser at Castle Brown. Some hapless English tourist had turned it off at the wrong moment and – well! – they were still redecorating the place three months later.

Padding across the polished mosaic tiles, Bella placed a fresh white towel by the hand basin and a scented candle on a ledge beside the giant claw-foot bath. The suite's previous tenants back in April – an elderly couple, awful fusspots from Guildford – had complained about a smell. Bella hadn't been able to detect anything amiss. But she wasn't going to take any chances where the Drummond-Wards were concerned.

By the time she emerged, Paola had finished with the bed and was standing beside it, awaiting Bella's judgement. Paola was a war widow from the village. She had large, dark eyes and curly, raven hair tied back so that it trailed glossily down her neck. As attractive as she was reliable. But Bella had noticed a change recently. A new wariness combined with something more primal and suggestive. It was hard to put a finger on it, but if Paola had been a man, Bella would have said she swaggered.

The bedspread needed only the smallest amount of titivating. Stepping back, Bella nodded her approval of the maid's handiwork.

'*Eccellente*,' she said, with a smile. Paola smiled too, avoiding her employer's penetrating gaze.

Why am I worrying? Bella asked herself. *Why can't I relax?*

Her rational side knew the answer was obvious. There was such a lot at stake this summer. Not just the hotel's reputation but Lucian's future and – admitting it upset her, but there was nothing else for it – her marriage to Cecil. It sometimes felt as though it hung by the slenderest of threads.

At least where staff were concerned she was lucky.

Betty, their cook, and her son Billy had been with them in London and in Yorkshire before that. They were like family and Bella trusted them implicitly, though goodness knows they were still finding their feet in this new, alien world. She had high hopes of Constance – Lottie's new nanny, recommended by Betty.

Paola, by contrast, remained an unknown quantity. An hour in her company had Bella wondering if she understood Italians at all. And yet she wanted to, so very much.

From a young age, Bella had been obsessed with Italy. At boarding school, she had hung beside her bed reproductions of famous Italian paintings and been quietly furious when the nuns who ran the place asked her to take down Botticelli's 'The Birth of Venus' on the grounds of obscenity. For Bella, Italy stood for truth, beauty and goodness. It was a beacon high on a promontory, radiating shafts of pure Mediterranean light which cut like razors through the gloom of damp, smoggy London.

Cecil liked Italy, too. He said so, anyway. But it had been Bella's idea to honeymoon in Portofino.

She sighed now at the memory of those carefree days. Strange to think the daughter conceived on that holiday was now a widow, their son a wounded veteran of the worst war anyone could remember. Stranger still that it was now 1926 and she was forty-eight years of age.

The years had passed like a shadow.

There was another loss too, of course. But she pushed it down, as far as it would go. If she allowed it to get a purchase, she would never think of anything else.

What she *really* struggled with was the fact – and it was a fact – that she and Cecil had once been young and in love;

had spent soft, persuasive nights staring out at the glittering water before swimming naked in the bay at Paraggi as the sun rose over the mountains.

On that first trip to Portofino, there had been deep kisses in the moonlit silence of back streets and a welter of new tastes and sensations – salty, chewy prosciutto and figs so fresh they burst on her tongue.

While Cecil played tennis at the hotel, Bella had taken herself off, following ancient mule tracks up to hill farms and olive groves. She'd glanced through locked gates into gardens radiant with flowers and wondered who might live there – and if it would ever be her? She had watched the lace-makers in the town square, then lain on warm rocks, drinking in the sunshine as lizards scampered over her bare legs.

Of course, it had been a more formal age – when a woman on her own drew tuts and raised eyebrows. But Bella hadn't let this stop her. Why on earth should it? She was a New Woman like the ones she read about in novels, and she was glimpsing a new reality.

One day, attracted by its striped façade, she had climbed up to the church of San Martino, high above the harbour. Apart from an old woman in black with a crocheted shawl over her head, she had been the only person there. As she inhaled the incense, dipped her fingers in the holy water and crossed herself – she wasn't Catholic, but it seemed the right thing to do – she had felt as if she were acting as well as participating, and this had struck her as revelatory, something she could file away and use later.

So much of life depended on ritual and performance, especially now that she was running a hotel, filling the roles of both manager and concierge. It felt foolish to call what she did a vocation. But there was a religious dimension to it. She was good at it, too – she knew that. Which made the memory of Cecil's initial scepticism all the more hurtful.

'Open a hotel? In Portofino?' They had been in the drawing room of their tall, thin house in Kensington, Cecil topping up his glass of single malt. 'Why on earth would we want to do that?'

He knew exactly how to crush her. But on this occasion she had refused to submit.

'It would be an adventure,' she said, brightly. 'A new start. A way to forget the war and all the awful things it's done to our family.'

'Running a hotel is donkey work. Imagine the nonsense you'd have to concern yourself with. Buying the right sort of chairs for the terrace. Organising day trips to museums. It's all so . . .'

'Middle-class? Suburban?'

'Well, yes. Not to mention,' Cecil's mouth curled as he searched for the *mot juste*, '. . . prosaic. Which would be fine except that you, Bellakins, are never prosaic. It's the reason I married you. One of them, anyway.' He sank into his favourite armchair with a sigh. 'Besides, there's so much competition nowadays. If, that is, you're hoping to attract a better class of tourist.'

There was no denying the truth of this. Every November

saw the annual migration of the British upper classes to sunnier climes where they remained until winter passed. Some swore by Cannes, others preferred the Venice Lido or the health benefits of Baden-Baden. Biarritz came into its own as a sanctuary when the heat on the French Riviera grew unbearable.

The Italian Riviera, by contrast, was relatively undiscovered. There was a British colony here, of course – where in the world *wasn't* there one? – and the larger hotels even had tennis courts and swimming pools.

But this wasn't the market Bella hoped to attract.

'I see this as a summer hotel,' she said. 'Not a refuge for Society flotsam.'

Cecil pretended to gasp. 'Now, now! Inverted snobbery is never becoming.'

'I'm not being a snob, inverted or otherwise.' Bella tried to keep the anger she felt out of her voice. 'I just want it to appeal to interesting people. People I might actually want to talk to.'

'Like artists.'

'Yes.'

'And writers.'

'I'd hope so.'

'People with *radical opinions*.' Cecil's sneering tone was unmistakable.

'Not necessarily.'

'People who aren't posh like me.'

At this Bella's patience snapped. 'Don't be ridiculous.'

7

'Or poor like me. I assume your father will be funding this venture?'

'He'll be happy to help us out, I'm sure.'

Cecil raised his glass, mockingly. 'A toast, then – to his bountiful majesty!'

Over the years, Bella had trained herself to ignore Cecil's sarcasm, knowing it to be a cover for insecurity. It wore her down. But now she concentrated on involving him, encouraging him to look out for property advertisements in newspapers and magazines while she sifted through piles of agents' brochures. That way he would feel as if he had a stake in the plan. And besides, he could be surprisingly resource-ful – inventive, even – when he put his mind to it.

There was no shortage of houses on the Riviera coast. But nothing they saw in the brochures was quite right. The prop-erties were either too big or too small, or they were in the better-known but overdeveloped resorts of Santa Margherita and Rapallo when Bella had set her heart on Portofino, which was on a more intimate scale.

They had been looking for several months and were on the verge of giving up when, one winter evening, Cecil casually produced that day's *Times* from beneath his arm, directing Bella's attention to an advertisement he had circled in his favoured burgundy ink:

Historical villa in Portofino, set in elegant grounds with delightful sea views. Close to town and beach. Would make an excellent 'pensione'. Serious enquiries only to: 12 Grosvenor Square, Mayfair.

Three days later they had found themselves in Italy, buzzing with excitement but nervous that after all their efforts – the journey out had been a nightmare of seasickness and missed connections – the house might be a disappointment, or at least less perfect in reality than it had looked in the photographs that the vendor, an elderly Victorian reeking of talcum powder, had produced for them over tea.

A gravelled drive lined with palm trees led to a large, pale-yellow villa with a stocky tower like a fifteenth-century farmhouse. Oddly Tuscan, as Cecil observed, but beautiful – so beautiful. Relief flooded through Bella's body like an opiate. She would never forget the momentous silence as the heavy oak door swung open and they stood for the first time in the cool marble entrance hall.

Vi piacerà, vedrete, the agent had insisted. You will like this. And here they now were!

From along the corridor, Bella heard a door open and a man clear his throat. Lucian's friend, Nish; short for Anish. He had been here a few weeks already, a gentle, scholarly soul who had saved Lucian's life after the war, no doubt about it.

But as Bella descended the staircase, another sound flooded out – female voices raised in anger, or at least consternation. Alice rushed from the kitchen, almost bumping into her mother at the foot of the stairs. She looked agitated.

'It's Betty,' she cried. 'She's having one of her fusses. Will you help me calm her?'

The two women headed into the kitchen, where an abundance of copper pans glinted in the sunlight streaming through the open door to the courtyard. The smell of baking bread tormented Bella. In her distraction, she'd forgotten to eat any breakfast that morning.

Betty was standing by the stove, her ruddy face creased in a grimace. Bella went over and spoke to her. 'What is it, Betty? What's the matter?'

'Nothing, Mrs Ainsworth. I'm making do.'

'Making do?'

Without turning, Betty gestured to a joint of beef resting on the table behind her. 'It's not like any cut of meat I've cooked before.'

'But it's beef?' Bella beckoned Alice over. Together they peered at the joint.

'Oh, it's beef all right. *Italian* beef.'

'And is there a problem with *Italian* beef?'

'There's no fat on it,' said Betty, matter-of-factly.

Alice piped up. 'And is that . . . a bad thing?'

Betty stared, as though Alice were a fool. 'I'll have no dripping! For me puddings! Or the potatoes! Talking of which, you've never seen the like.' She fished one out of a saucepan and held it up between thumb and forefinger. 'Waxy little bullet-like things. Not like proper spuds at all.'

'I'm sure you'll manage splendidly,' said Alice. 'You always do, Betty.'

'I'll try my best, Mrs Mays-Smith.'

Alice wandered off, leaving Bella alone with Betty. Not for the first time, Bella was struck by how overwhelmed the older woman seemed and felt a pang of guilt. Persuading Betty to uproot from London and follow the Ainsworths to Italy had not been easy, especially as she had only moved down from Yorkshire a few years earlier. Not only had Betty never been abroad before, but she still regarded London as dangerously foreign.

This move was her life's biggest, boldest undertaking and Bella had lavished Betty with praise for it. But she worried sometimes that her encouragement shaded into coercion. And she didn't want that. She wanted always to be kind, especially to someone like Betty.

Like so many people, Betty was still recovering from the war. She had lost two sons on the Western Front. Two sons! She still had Billy, of course – but how must she have felt every time she laid eyes on Lucian? It would be like getting a fragment of glass in your foot, day after day.

The hardest thing had been explaining Italy's appeal, which for Bella was self-evident. She'd resorted to showing Betty some of the postcards she had picked up on her honeymoon. Hand-tinted, redolent of sun and happiness. The strategy seemed to work – to reassure Betty that Italy was a safe, civilised place for her and her fatherless son, despite some news reports to the contrary.

'What about the food?' Betty had asked, full of suspicion.

Bella plucked a book from her bag. Betty ran a plump hand over the soft green cloth before squinting at the title: '"Science in the Kitchen and the Art of Eating Well" by Pellegrino Artusi.'

'It will tell you everything you need to know,' said Bella. 'No one writes better about Italian food than this man.'

Betty smiled. She was rightly proud of her literacy. 'I'll get reading this very evening.'

Betty's early efforts had not counted among her greatest culinary achievements. An attempt at minestrone was particularly notable, for all the wrong reasons.

'What on earth is this?' Cecil had asked, stirring the soggy vegetables.

Bella tasted the soup cautiously. Its pungency startled her and she stifled a cough with her napkin. 'She's used wild garlic, I think. Quite a lot of it. Oh, well. It doesn't matter.' She placed her spoon down. 'We must be encouraging, Cecil. Besides, she won't be cooking Italian food every day. Many of our guests will prefer steak and kidney pie.'

Within weeks, however, it was a different story. Betty was hard-working and competent. As for Billy, he had grown into an impressive, trustworthy young man who was going to make a splendid bell-boy. Soon Bella was planning to teach him how to wait tables – the fine art of observant hovering.

Now, Bella gripped Betty's shoulder softly. 'You're doing a wonderful job,' she said. 'The food you produce. It's out of this world.'

Betty flushed with pleasure. 'You're very kind, Mrs Ainsworth.'

'And Billy is helping you, yes?'

Betty nodded. 'I've just sent him off to fetch some cream for the lemon pudding.'

'That's good. And don't forget you'll have Constance here soon. She'll have plenty of time to lend a hand in the kitchen when she isn't looking after Lottie.'

At this, Betty turned to face Bella. Her body seemed to turn entirely rigid. 'What day is it today?'

'Thursday.'

'Oh no . . .' The older woman's hand flew to her mouth.

'What is it, Betty?'

'It's today. Constance is arriving *today*. On the Genoa train.'

'But that's the train Lucian is meeting. The train the Drummond-Wards are on.'

'Oh, Mrs Ainsworth.' Betty looked as if she was about to burst into tears. 'And you trusted me to make all the arrangements. On account of Constance being a family friend . . .'

'Don't panic, Betty. It's possible Lucian hasn't left yet. In which case he can collect Constance too.'

She was trying to sound confident and upbeat. But the situation was far from ideal. From what Bella knew of her, Julia Drummond-Ward was not the sort of woman who would react well to sharing a carriage with a servant. In any case, Lucian was almost certainly halfway to Mezzago station by now. Bella had spoken to him earlier while he was waiting for Francesco to harness the horses. That would have been the time to mention Constance . . .

Rushing out into the entrance hall, Bella called Lucian's name – more in hope than expectation. Her voice was still echoing off the walls when Nish emerged from the library.

'He isn't here, Mrs Ainsworth. He set off about an hour ago. He was worried about being late for Rose.'

'And Rose's mother,' Bella reminded him.

'Of course. Her too.' Nish smiled. 'Can I help with anything?'

'No, no.' Bella waved him away. 'You relax and enjoy yourself. You're our guest here.'

'But this is a big week for the hotel. A big week for you.'

This much was undeniable. Guests had started to arrive on the Monday – first Lady Latchmere and her great-niece Melissa, then Count Albani and his son Roberto. By the weekend the hotel would be full.

Bella had been particularly excited to receive the Count's booking. His endorsement was a signal to the wider world that Hotel Portofino was for Italians too. Cecil wasn't sure this was a signal they should be sending, but then Cecil's presence around the hotel was increasingly a fleeting, unpredictable thing.

Where on earth was he now? Would he be back by the time the Drummond-Wards arrived? Bella didn't want to be on her own when she met Julia for the first time. She was aware of Julia and Cecil's history. She couldn't deny that she harboured powerful, complicated feelings towards the woman. Curiosity, envy – even fear. What was a husband for, if not to reassure her in such a situation?

'Are you all right, Mrs Ainsworth?' Nish's voice disrupted Bella's reverie.

'I was just worrying about Constance,' she said. 'The

new nanny. She's on Lucian's train, apparently. But there's nothing we can do now. She'll have to find her own way here.'

'She'll be fine, I'm sure,' said Nish. 'I couldn't move for hollering taxi-drivers when I got to Mezzago.'

Bella laughed. 'Why does that not reassure me?'

*

Bayonet fixed, Lucian planted one foot firmly on the firestep, the other on the rickety ladder leaning against the trench wall. He rested his head against the top rung, closed his eyes and whispered a prayer.

Was God listening? He couldn't see much evidence of it.

Dusk had settled heavily, merging sky and land into a shapeless grey mass. Icy rain pricked Lucian's face like needles. His feet and hands were frozen but sweat was still pouring down his back. The muffled thunder of the guns encircled him. When had there last been a lull in this racket? Lucian had stopped keeping track. By now, he'd become used to this world of cold, sick fear.

Perhaps a part of him had always been used to it. At school, waiting to be caned for some trivial misdemeanour, Lucian had perfected a coping strategy. He'd shrunk so far into himself that he became incapable of registering pain.

He tried the same tactic now, willing himself to focus on his breathing and the pounding of his pulse in his ears. But he couldn't ignore the howitzer's distant boom, the whine and crash of shells. Each second ticking by felt like an eternity.

And then it came – the ghostly chorus of whistles along

the line. Barked exhortations to prepare. Lucian gripped at the muddy banks to steady himself. Frozen solid. When a shell burst, tiny particles flew like splinters of masonry.

A sudden blast of whistle pierced his left ear. It meant only one thing. That it was his turn. His turn to do his bit and climb over the top . . .

Lucian's eyes sprung open, unprepared for the sight that greeted them: a thick-set, moustachio-ed man in a red peaked cap and long, brass-buttoned coat. He was bearing down on Lucian and barking in Italian: '*Signore! Il treno da Nervi sta arrivando!*'

But then the man stepped away cautiously, his hands raised in supplication.

Lucian sat up slowly, his heart pounding.

It had happened again. He must have fallen asleep. And so often when he slept, he dreamt of Cambrai. Awful dreams that took him right back to the front line.

The noise came again and Lucian flinched, gripping hold of his seat. Where was he? His glance darted around – and he was reassured immediately by the terracotta tiles and bright posters, the sun streaming in through the windows.

Of course.

The waiting room at Mezzago station.

The panic drained away.

The station master's bulky frame filled the doorway. Taking the whistle from his mouth, he looked across at Lucian and gestured at the stopped train with his thumb. Lucian rose and followed him out onto the platform. The man's resemblance to his old sergeant-major was uncanny. Then again, these ghosts seemed to pop up everywhere.

The sudden wall of heat felt glorious, restorative. He took a deep breath and inhaled the scent of jasmine and hot asphalt. The platform was crowded with passengers and porters, steam and voices. He wove his way through the crowd towards the First-Class carriage.

He was here to collect his father's old friend Julia Drummond-Ward and her daughter. Old friend ... Lucian knew what that meant, though it was rarely discussed above stairs.

'Have I met Mrs Drummond-Ward before?' he'd asked his mother.

'Only once, when you were small.'

'So, how will I recognise her?'

She had smiled enigmatically. 'I imagine there'll be limited scope for confusion. Though if you're worried I'm sure your father has an old photograph tucked away somewhere.'

The platform was narrower than Lucian remembered. A large group swarmed forward, blocking his view. It took a while to thin out but once it had Lucian saw, in the distance, the statuesque figure of a woman he knew immediately and unmistakably.

Mrs Julia Drummond-Ward.

She had clambered down from the carriage and was standing on the platform clutching a parasol, trying to appear composed. '*Scusi!*'

Quickening his pace, Lucian approached her and offered

her his hand. But she did not take it. Instead her eyes flicked from his tanned face to his collarless white shirt and rolled up sleeves.

'My daughter,' she said, gesturing back towards the train.

And that was when Lucian saw Rose for the first time: standing by the carriage door, poised to descend, wearing a long-sleeved lace dress with a sash that accentuated her slim waist. A wide-brimmed straw hat struggled to contain a mass of curly auburn hair. If she looked a trifle weary from the journey, it didn't detract from her extraordinary natural beauty. In fact, it enhanced it – made it more natural, if that were possible.

She caught him looking at her and returned his smile. Lucian's stomach dipped. He felt shy and – an unusual sensation – inadequate.

The older woman's eyes were on him still. She said suddenly '*Nostri bagagli*' and pointed toward the baggage car. Then just as loudly but more slowly, as if to a child: 'Our baggage. There are eight cases.' She held up six fingers and two thumbs. '*Otto.*'

Lucian suppressed a laugh as the truth dawned on him. Mrs Drummond-Ward had no idea who he was. And fair enough, he did look swarthy, as she would probably say.

Well, if she thought he was Italian, Italian he would be. He gave a little bow. 'Signora,' he said.

'And don't lose any of them!'

He dipped his head. 'No, Signora.'

Lucian turned on his heel and walked up towards the

baggage car. Relieved to see the ladies' luggage already piled up on the platform, he oversaw its loading onto a trolley. After that, he walked studiously close to the porter back through the station and out onto the piazzetta.

Several taxi touts were plying for trade. After agreeing what seemed a reasonable fee, Lucian loaded most of the bags into the least dangerous-looking fly. The remainder would travel with the Drummond-Wards in the Hotel Portofino's own carriage, which Lucian had refurbished himself and driven to Mezzago in his unofficial capacity as hotel coachman.

Lucian walked back to where the women were waiting. He was conscious of walking not quite like himself – more how he imagined an Italian peasant might walk. A jaunty strut, or as much of one as his broken body could manage.

They had found some shade under an awning. Even so, Mrs Drummond-Ward was scowling and fanning herself. Her wool outfit was much too warm for the weather. Rose seemed less concerned. She was gazing in wonder at her new surroundings. Goodness, she was beautiful. Lucian had never seen anything like her – not up close, in the flesh. She was like something out of a cinema magazine.

On the one hand, Lucian longed to say something – to stop playing the ridiculous game he had set in motion. But it was hard to know how to do this without giving offence. It would also, he had to admit, be amusing to see if the game could be sustained; if, in fact, he could win the game, because it had without doubt become a competition. Not between

Lucian and Rose – nothing could compete with her – but between himself and her proud, sour-faced mother.

Within five minutes, Lucian had installed the pair in the carriage. There had been a certain amount of fuss from Mrs Drummond-Ward about the hardness of the seats, but she settled down soon enough and, having made herself comfortable, proceeded to talk continually.

They set off along the cobbled streets that led to the coast road. Sitting up front, Lucian longed to turn round and address his passengers as a native driver would. *Ecco la famosa chiesa! Attenta al vestito, per favore . . .* This would also give him an opportunity to snatch glimpses of the divine Rose. But his Italian was rudimentary, and in any case Mrs Drummond-Ward was not to be diverted.

She talked and talked. And if, during a rare lull in the stream of snobbish gossip, Rose failed to respond quickly enough she would say, 'Do pay attention!' and Rose would reply, 'Yes, mama' with a blankness bordering on defiant.

The road straightened after a succession of hairpin bends and Lucian found his mind wandering. But then the conversation turned to his own family and his ears pricked up.

'They're one of the oldest families in the county,' Mrs Drummond-Ward was saying. 'I've known Cecil since I was a girl.'

'And what about Mrs Ainsworth?' An innocent question, innocently asked.

'Goodness, no. She's quite a different sort.'

'A different sort?'

'Don't be so dim, Rose. You know perfectly well what I mean.'

'I'm not sure I do, Mama.'

'She's the sort of woman who thinks there's nothing strange in opening a hotel.' She dipped her voice. 'Her father owns a leather factory. And he doesn't care who knows it!'

*

The trick with her mother, Rose had discovered long ago, was not to rise to her provocations. If you did, the result was anger quickly followed by sulking. Much better to be placid and docile. Which wasn't the same as passive, not if you were doing it deliberately. What surprised Rose was how hurtful she still found her mother's remarks, even though she was now a grown woman in her twenties.

Soon – please, let it be soon! – she would be married. So why couldn't she shrug off Mama's slights and put-downs?

A good example had come on the train earlier. As it was pulling into the station, Rose had leant out of the window, the better to see the darling little platform and all the bustling people. But Mama had been so disapproving. She had prodded – yes, actually prodded! – her in the side with her wretched parasol. 'Come away from the window, Rose! You'll get smuts all over your dress.'

There had been nothing for it but to do as she'd been asked.

If only she, Rose, could have come to Italy alone. How wonderful that would have been! But, of course, it was out of the question. It was always out of the question. A young lady must be chaperoned. And that chaperone must be ... Mama.

But why? Mama hated 'abroad', as she called it. Her enthusiasm for this trip had peaked early, the moment she and Rose arrived at their first port of call in Rome.

She and Rose had stayed a few days in a respectable boarding house near the Spanish Steps. This was Rose's first time in Italy, and she was trembling with nervous excitement, longing to eat spaghetti and try out her Italian, painstakingly gleaned from an old grammar book she had found in the library. But her mother, on the few occasions she agreed to accompany Rose on sightseeing expeditions, was even more grudging and unimpressed than usual. So frustrated did Rose become that she decided for once to voice her disappointment.

Of course, Mama had dismissed Rose's concerns, which fell from her mouth as nervous, feeble protests. 'You're too ready to romanticise the place. As a girl, I made my Grand Tour, so I know Italy well – perhaps too well. Never forget that this is, by and large, a country of illiterate farmers.'

'Dante was Italian,' Rose objected. She hoped she was right. It sounded about right.

Mama had laughed coldly. 'What do you know of Dante? Dante won't help you find a suitable husband.'

Now, Rose felt as if she were wrapped in a heavy cloak. She couldn't move, she couldn't breathe. She wanted so much to cast it off and ... be herself. Whatever "herself" was. Perhaps she would do that, be that, at the Hotel Portofino.

For they would be there soon, surely. While Mama expounded in her right ear on the horrors of social housing – 'None of it here, you'll notice. In Italy the poor are poor and happy to be so' – Rose drank in the unfamiliar sights of the villages they passed through. There were dark-browed girls craning from upper windows, old grandmothers knitting outside their houses while children played at their feet. It was all so utterly charming. *To understand Italy, one must look at the people as well as the art.* Where had she read that? She couldn't remember. She had a terrible memory, Mama was always complaining.

Rose was especially transfixed by the back of the carriage-driver's head. Curly tendrils of dark-brown hair crept down his neck. It was impossible not to notice his broad shoulders, the muscles all too visible beneath his white collarless shirt, stained in the centre with a broad patch of sweat.

Rose willed him silently to turn round, but of course he wouldn't, couldn't. He had to watch the road, which was barely a road at all, more a rutted track hacked out of the hillside.

Even so, she thought. Even so. It would be rather nice to see his face.

*

They reached Portofino just as the worst of the heat was draining from the day. The carriage followed the climbing, twisting road in a flurry of loose stones and dust.

Off to the left was a grove of orange trees – or to be exact *chinotto*, the bitter baby oranges used to flavour Campari, one of Lucian's favourite tipples.

The sight of them had amazed Lucian on his first trip to Liguria, buttressing his sense that sun-drenched Italy stood somehow for the opposite of war. In France during that terrible winter of 1917 a fellow officer had shown him two frozen oranges stuck together. 'Look at 'em! Hard as cricket balls!'

Well, there were no frozen oranges here.

One of the first things Lucian did, once he had been discharged from the Convalescence Depot and recovered sufficiently to concentrate for more than ten minutes at a time, was read his mother's ancient Baedeker travel guide to Italy. He adored its plans and maps, the sweeping, scathing judgements of this restaurant and that hotel.

He resolved to go to Europe and paint like his hero David Bomberg. Because that's what he was – a painter – and to hell with his father! Lucian wouldn't tolerate lectures from a man who had never done a decent day's work in his life.

All his friends were plotting their escape from an England that felt mean and diminished. The best writers and artists had cleared off already, especially the ones who'd seen action in the war. After all, what was there to stick around for? A lot of patriotic bluster served with a chaser of almost total ignorance about what had actually happened in the killing fields of France and Belgium.

'England is a philistine country,' Nish was always saying, 'but it doesn't realise it. It has no cultural power at all. That's the reason its empire is doomed.'

Good old Nish. You always knew where you were with him.

24

Now, Lucian stopped the carriage before the final descent, to give the horses a rest and his passengers a chance to take in the view: the tall, pastel-coloured houses curving around the bay and the boats bobbing gently in the perfect azure water. He assumed they would want this – that it would be as momentous a sight for them as it had once been for him. But while Rose reacted with a tremulous gasp, Mrs Drummond-Ward was nonplussed.

'Why has he stopped?' he heard her ask.

'I don't know. To show us the view, I expect.'

'But I don't want to stop.' Lucian felt a tap on his shoulder. 'Walk on, please.' To Rose: 'How do you say, "Go to the hotel?"'

'I'm trying to remember,' she said.

'Say it, then. To the driver.'

'*Vai in albergo*?' Rose held her breath . . .

'*Certo*,' replied Lucian. For the first time since leaving the station he turned round in his seat and caught Rose's eye. The brief smile they exchanged lifted his heart. *She's twigged who I am*, he said to himself. *Or if she hasn't, she strongly suspects.*

Grinning, Lucian turned back to the front and coaxed the horse into motion, down the hill and towards the hotel.

2

Billy came hurrying down the hall, pulling at his jacket, his shiny black shoes click-clacking on the marble. 'When do they arrive, Mrs Ainsworth?'

Bella was waiting for him by the door. 'Any time now, Billy. Is the uniform troubling you?' She lowered her voice as if the question might embarrass him.

'It's the collar.' He dug a finger beneath the starched cotton. 'I can't get it to sit right.'

'Let me help you.' Bella leant forward and adjusted it. For good measure, she tucked in his shirt tail and straightened his tie. Ever since he was small, she had had this curious impulse to mother him. Standing up mock-straight she said, 'Remember, Billy. First impressions.'

His face broke into a grin. 'First impressions. Yes, ma'am!'

Heralded by the crunch of wheels on gravel, the carriage pulled up outside the porticoed entrance. Billy rushed out to help Francesco with the luggage. Bella opted to greet the Drummond-Wards on the front steps, rather than from behind the reception desk. She saw Julia opening her purse and sprinkling a few coins into Lucian's hand.

'*Grazie,*' she heard her say. 'For your assistance.' It seemed a curious thing to do and she made a mental note to ask Lucian about it at the earliest opportunity.

For now, though, she was on duty.

She stepped forward. 'Mrs Drummond-Ward. Rose. Welcome!'

'Mrs Ainsworth?' Julia extended a gloved hand, which Bella shook warmly.

'Please,' she said, 'call me Bella. I hope I may call you Julia?'

Julia gave a small nod of assent.

'How was your journey?'

'Long,' Julia replied, flatly. 'And exceedingly tiresome.'

'Well, then. We must do our best to make it all seem worthwhile.' She gestured towards the villa's façade, which gleamed in the bright sunshine. 'Welcome to Hotel Portofino!'

Rose seemed more smitten with the building than her mother. Her face shone with delight as she angled her head back to take in her new surroundings. 'How utterly charming,' she said.

Bella seized the initiative, intertwining her arm in Rose's. 'I hope Lucian gave you the rundown. On the way here from the station.'

'Lucian?'

'Yes.'

Julia caught up with them. 'The man driving us was Lucian?'

'Of course.'

'But I thought . . . *We* thought . . .'

'What?' Bella looked around, hoping to find Lucian so that he might come to her rescue. But he was nowhere to be seen.

*

Melissa put down her book to watch the Drummond-Wards' arrival from the window of the Ascot Suite's living room. They were charming to look at, so poised and glamorous. All the rumours about the girl's beauty were true.

Melissa became pleasantly lost in her contemplations. How many outfits had the Drummond-Wards brought with them? Would they be staying all summer?

But then her great aunt called out from the adjoining bedroom: 'Melissa! What is that dreadful racket?'

'I believe some guests are arriving.'

'They are? Oh, dear. I knew we should have rented a villa.'

This had become a perennial lament. Melissa looked around at the ample, exquisitely furnished suite. 'I very much doubt it would have been as comfortable as this,' she said.

Lady Latchmere appeared abruptly in the doorway, as though from a concealed trap-door. 'But a little more private, perhaps?'

What a curious woman she was. Her greying (but only just) hair was piled high, her commanding frame draped in a black velvet gown with a frilly collar. Melissa had no idea of her age and no easy means of finding out: none of the few people who might know would react well to being asked such an impolite question. But she was intrigued by the mismatch between Lady Latchmere's sluggish deportment and the evident robustness of her physique; and between her old-fashioned clothes, which frankly belonged in a fancy-dress shop, and her smooth, unlined skin.

Melissa's job here in Italy, however, was to indulge Lady Latchmere's whims, not query them. She smiled brightly. 'How are you feeling, Aunt?'

'Simply ghastly!'

'Shall I let them know you won't be down for dinner?'

'Goodness no, dear. I need to keep my strength up.' Lady Latchmere came slowly forward, leaning on the stick Melissa suspected might be a prop; she had seen no evidence of infirmity. 'So, tell me.' She peered out of the window. 'What's your impression of the Drummond-Ward girl?'

Melissa started. She hated being put on the spot like this. 'I don't know, Aunt.'

'Come, come. You must have formed *some* sort of opinion.'

'Of her appearance, yes.'

'Let's hear it, then!'

Melissa chose her words carefully. 'Well,' she began, 'she has beautiful hair. And she's certainly up with all the latest fashions.'

'Do you think the boy Lucian will like her?'

'I've no idea,' said Melissa. 'Why do you ask?'

Lady Latchmere sighed. 'Really, Melissa. You need to pay more attention.' She leant forward and stage-whispered. 'Their parents intend for them to marry!'

*

29

They called it the Epsom Suite, which made Rose smile.

Bella, who had been so friendly and welcoming, said that her husband – Mama's special friend from her younger days – had had the idea of naming each suite after a famous racecourse. This one consisted of two rooms with two shallow-balconied windows overlooking the sea.

It was a spectacular view. But a bit boring, if Rose was being honest with herself. The sea didn't *do* much, after all. It was just . . . the sea. It looked the same wherever you were in the world.

First, Rose and her mother had rested after their arduous journey. Then, after a stand-up sponge wash, Rose had slipped into her new gown – a silk Chanel number tricked out with metallic lace and rows of overlapping sequins – while Julia readied herself in the bathroom.

An hour later, she was *still* readying herself in the bathroom.

Honestly, thought Rose. Who was she intending to impress?

Feeling exploratory, she opened a drawer and found a muslin pouch of dried lavender. How she loved all these little touches! It made the old Roman pensione seem very drab, when only a few days ago it had struck Rose as the utmost glamour.

'Mother!' she called.

'What is it?'

'Look how dear and delightful everything is. Do you think Mrs Ainsworth does it all herself?'

Her mother's voice carried over from the bathroom. 'I'm

sure she enjoys getting her hands dirty. It runs in the family.'
She appeared in the doorway. 'Are you ready to go?'

'I've been ready for ages.'

Julia bustled towards Rose. 'Let me look at you.'

Rose stood placidly while her mother adjusted the dress,
plumped her bosom and pinched colour into her cheeks.
After what seemed an eternity of fussing, she pronounced
that Rose would do. She spun the girl round so that she faced
the long, gilt-edged mirror and together they examined
her reflection – Rose not sure what she was supposed to be
looking for, her mother all too certain. Julia straightened her
shoulders and signalled to Rose that she should do the same.

'Posture,' she said. 'It's all about posture. Remember what
your old dance teacher used to say.'

There was a long pause, filled only with male laughter
from the room below.

Rose asked casually, 'Do you think Lucian will be
at dinner?'

'Who knows? I must say I found his conduct this afternoon
extraordinary.'

Rose decided to risk an argument. 'You did mistake him
for an Italian. You *addressed* him as if he were an Italian.' The
memory made her smile.

'And he had ample opportunity to correct me. But for
some reason he chose not to. There's clearly a good deal of
his father in him.' Julia frowned. 'Where *is* Cecil anyway?'

So, that's it, thought Rose. *That's what's making you even
more snappish than usual.*

Slowly and with fastidious care, they processed down the stairs.

'I shan't be eating much,' whispered Julia, 'so I advise you to do the same.'

'But I haven't eaten all day.'

'Hunger matters less than keeping your figure.'

Bella greeted them at the door to the dining room. The space was only half full but no matter, Rose felt the eyes of the seated diners settle on her as she followed her mother through the low buzz of chatter to a table near the open doors to the terrace.

The attention of others turned the pang of emptiness in her stomach into a warm glow.

A breeze stirred the room, making the chandelier shudder. Bella stood and watched over a maid – dark-skinned, Italian – as she poured them each a glass of sparkling wine. Rose's mother hadn't said anything about Bella being beautiful. She was quite stunning – in a natural, unadorned sort of way. Her chestnut hair fell in great curls down her shoulders, though Rose fancied she saw sadness in her enormous greyish-blue eyes.

'Champagne,' observed Julia. 'How lovely.'

It was the first positive thing Rose had heard her say since they'd arrived. She looked up at Bella, to check the remark had registered with her.

Bella acknowledged the compliment with a smile. 'It's Prosecco, Julia. Lighter and fruitier. From a local vineyard.'

Julia took a sip, holding the taste on her tongue for a few seconds. 'It's rather sweet. But not unpleasant.'

Bella didn't seem to notice the insult — or if she did, she was a good actress. 'I'm pleased you think so. How are you finding your rooms?'

'A little smaller than we're used to.'

Rose interjected: 'But so exquisitely decorated! We were wondering if you did it all yourself? Weren't we, Mama?'

'Dearest Rose,' said Bella, her face creasing in a smile. 'I hope all my guests are as sweet and observant as you.'

'Are we among your first?' Julia managed to give the question an admonitory edge.

Bella didn't miss a beat. 'We've been open since Easter. But things have only really started to get busy in the last month or so.'

From the other side of the room came a sudden violent commotion. A woman wearing old-fashioned clothes was scolding the Italian maid who had, it seemed, attempted to pour her a glass of Prosecco. Excusing herself, Bella walked over to where another woman — Lucian's sister? — was attempting to intervene.

An intrigued hush descended on the room.

'Is there a problem, Lady Latchmere?' Rose heard Bella ask.

'I never touch alcohol,' replied the woman. 'How many times must I remind you?'

The sister — Alice, Rose remembered she was called — gestured to the maid to remove the glass. 'I'm very sorry, Lady Latchmere,' she said. 'I promise it won't happen again.'

Rose was watching all this with interest when her attention

wandered to the door. Two Italian men were entering the room – one middle-aged and rather regal in bearing, the other more casually dressed and significantly younger, closer to her own age of twenty-three. The physical resemblance suggested they were father and son.

Rose tapped her mother's arm. 'Who are they?'

Julia had noticed them too and was keenly tracking their progress across the room. 'I don't know,' she said. 'Let's ask.' She beckoned Bella. 'And that is?'

Their hostess glanced over. 'Count Albani.'

'And his son?'

'Yes. He's called Roberto.'

Julia frowned. 'I understood the guests were all to be English. Your advertisement was quite specific about it. "A very English hotel, on the Italian Riviera."'

'English or English-speaking,' clarified Bella. 'Count Albani is an Oxford man.'

Julia pointed at a dark-skinned young man sitting alone at a table in the far corner. He was reading a book. 'What about him?'

Rose cringed. Mama could be so blunt.

'Mr Sengupta is a friend of my son,' Bella explained.

'I see,' said Julia, uncertainly.

At that moment, Lucian appeared in the doorway. He had smartened himself up since the afternoon, though his previous handsomeness had drawn some of its power from his ruffled hair and artistic air of creased disorder. Rose felt her cheeks reddening and looked down at the table. She was not used to emotions of this nature and had not yet acquired the ability to keep them in check.

Seeing Lucian, Bella became animated. 'Speak of the devil, Lucian! Come and redeem yourself. Tell Julia and Rose all about Portofino.'

Lucian had been making his way towards Nish's table, but altered his course when he heard his mother's voice.

'If you'll excuse me,' said Bella and straightened up to leave.

On his way to their table Lucian stopped the maid, who was passing with a tray, and helped himself to a glass of Prosecco. He winked at the maid, which Rose thought endearing – though she hoped her mother hadn't noticed.

'Well,' he said, taking a seat at their table, 'I hardly know where to start.'

'With an apology?' suggested Julia.

Lucian grinned – a disarming, schoolboy grin. 'I'm sorry,' he said. 'It was a foolish thing to do. It gave completely the wrong impression of the kind of person I am.'

'Which is?'

The question seemed to catch Lucian off guard. There was a distinct pause before he answered. 'Serious. I'm a serious person. With serious ambitions.' He glanced across at Rose, as if imploring her to believe him.

'To be what?'

'An artist.'

'Goodness.' Julia raised her eyebrows. 'Is that even a profession?'

'Start at the beginning,' said Rose, eager to steer the

conversation into more convivial waters. 'How does an English family like yours come to be here in the first place?'

Lucian took a large gulp of his Prosecco. 'That's easy. Mama fell in love with the place. On her honeymoon.'

Was it Rose's imagination or did her mother blanch slightly at the word 'honeymoon'?

'That's to be expected. But what made her decide to *move* here?'

'She thought we needed a fresh start.' Lucian made it sound so simple. 'A new adventure after the war. Her, Alice, Lottie, me. Even Papa.'

Julia butted in. 'And is your father going to grace us with his presence this evening?'

For goodness' sake, thought Rose. Why did she always have to be so direct?

'He sends his apologies, I'm afraid,' said Lucian, his face flushing. 'He's been unavoidably delayed in Genoa.'

Paola placed a tray laden with crostini in the centre of the table. Too hungry to wait, Rose took one and popped it in her mouth. 'Delicious!'

She waited for her mother to tell her off. But Julia didn't seem to have noticed.

*

By ten o'clock all the guests had finished their meals and left the dining room in search of other amusements. Some sat out on the terrace smoking. A small party headed by Lady Latchmere was playing bridge in the library. Nish had retired to his room to read.

Bella took advantage of the lull to sit down for a few moments in the dining room while Alice busied herself laying the tables for breakfast. The evening was over and Bella realised that she'd been bracing herself for weeks for the arrival of Julia and Rose. Now, they were finally here.

Julia was rather chilly; Bella had expected that. As for Rose, she was certainly beautiful, if a touch thin. Would Lucian take to her? She wasn't wholly convinced.

Images from the day passed before her like slides in a magic lantern. The back of Cecil's head as he lay beside her in bed. That stray cat with the damaged ear, curled up in front of the kitchen range. Julia's pendulous earrings, so like the ones Cecil had once bought for her.

Despite Betty's worries the food had been exceptional. She had roasted the Italian beef in herbs with sweet wine – most probably an idea from the Artusi book, though Bella had seen Betty talking to the local butcher, who spoke some English. It had tasted, in Count Albani's words, 'like heaven itself'.

Julia had enjoyed the Prosecco. As had Lucian – perhaps too much. At one point, he had signalled to Francesco to bring him some more, an entire bottle. Francesco had looked to Bella for guidance, and she had shaken her head. It was expensive, for one thing. Not for everyday family consumption. And she knew only too well the damage alcohol could do, the way it made some men behave.

She prayed every night that Lucian hadn't inherited his father's weakness.

Alice was putting zigzag folds into the napkins to make

them fan-shaped. It was a boring job and Bella tried to cheer her up.

'That seemed to go as well as could be expected,' she said.

'Dinner?' Alice looked up.

'Yes. And the introduction to Rose.'

Alice said nothing.

'She's very pretty,' observed Bella.

'I suppose so. Not that it matters.'

'You're right. Character is what counts.'

At this Alice gave a snort of horrid laughter. 'Oh, Mama. Her father's six thousand acres of prime arable land is what counts.'

Bella was shocked by the force of this barb. But was that fair? Perhaps Alice was only articulating what she herself dared not. 'Don't be cynical, Alice. It's unattractive.'

But Alice was not to be deterred. 'It's the truth! She could look like the back end of an omnibus and Father would still be mad keen for Lucian to marry her.'

'Alice!'

'I don't believe he'd put one tenth of the effort into finding a new husband for me.'

Bella didn't have the energy to argue. Besides, there was truth in what Alice said. They finished laying the tables in tense silence, then Bella went down to the kitchen, where Betty was untying her apron.

'Still here, Betty?'

'I was just going, Mrs Ainsworth.' She paused. 'Do you want something, ma'am?'

'Perhaps a cup of mint tea.'

Wearily, Betty started putting her apron back on.

'No, please.' This wasn't at all what Bella wanted. 'Please. I can manage.' She padded across to where a bunch of fresh mint was sitting in a jar of water and tore off a handful of scented leaves. 'Thank you, by the way. For dinner.'

Still, Betty said nothing.

'Count Albani sends his compliments.'

At this a tired smile crossed Betty's face. 'Did he just?'

'Particularly for the beef.'

'Well, I never.' She looked as if she might levitate with pleasure.

Betty dragged herself upstairs to bed. Bella took the kettle from the shelf above the stove and carried it to the sink to fill. She was about to turn on the tap when she noticed an open bottle of white wine tucked behind some bottles of olive oil. She only hesitated for a second before rewarding herself with a small glass at the end of what had been a long and exhausting day.

From the pantry she took the petty cash box. Also, a breakfast roll and a jar of tapenade. A small snack would sustain her while she checked the accounts – something she tried to do at the end of each day, because really, who else was going to do it? Cecil?

She sat down at the empty kitchen table. But no sooner had she opened the book, when there was a knock at the rear kitchen door.

Who on earth could be outside?

The hinges grated as Bella unlocked the door and dragged it open. On the doorstep stood a slight girl of about twenty with wide, imploring eyes and ash-blonde hair tied back beneath a straw boater. She was carrying a small suitcase and looked half-crazed with fatigue.

Bella stared at her, taking in her scuffed shoes and coarse linen dress. 'Can I help you?'

'Please ma'am,' said the girl. 'I'm Constance. The new nanny.'

*

It had been years – many years – since Constance felt as tired as she did right now. Despite being mostly downhill, the last half mile had been an agonising walk. Her feet were sore and blistered and her dress damp with sweat.

Constance only possessed two outfits in the whole world. This rough, weighty dress, shrunk from excessive washing, was one of them. The other was her Sunday-best frock which she had been nervous about wearing on the journey in case it got torn or soiled. Her dream was to save enough from her wages to buy some new clothes. But she already knew that it was a forlorn hope. Most of what she earned here in Italy she had promised to send home to her mother and the baby.

Perhaps Betty would know a local shop, somewhere not too dear? They made lace in Portofino, didn't they? Did that mean lace was cheap there? Or that it was expensive? She wished she knew, wished she didn't always feel her lack of education rise so close to the surface.

Betty had been so kind, recommending her for this post.

Constance was determined not to let her down or be any sort of burden. So, it was good that she had arrived at Mezzago at exactly the right time.

She had waited on the dusty platform, watching the bustle of busy, incurious strangers and porters pushing carts loaded with luggage. Bright red flowers burst from rust-coloured clay pots. A young man rushed past – a rather attractive man, actually. He was obviously on his way to meet someone important. At Genoa, she had watched a well-dressed English mother and daughter get into a First-Class carriage, all the while bickering. Perhaps, she thought idly, he was meeting them.

But then the crowd started to thin out, until Constance was the only passenger left standing.

No matter, she thought. Perhaps whoever the hotel had sent was waiting out at the front? Betty had said it would be the owners' son, Lucian, meeting her. She unfolded the letter and read it again.

Wait on the platform. You can't miss Lucian. He is tall and good-looking with dark brown hair.

Mezzago station was tiny compared to Genoa, where there was a covered hall with lines of omnibuses waiting to take travellers to their hotels. A straggle of unkempt men milled around by the entrance, smoking foul-smelling cigarillos. Cab drivers. They stared at Constance as she passed. One of them whistled at her, but she ignored him.

A thorough search of the station turned up nobody who fitted Betty's description of Lucian.

Possibly, the manager had forgotten she was arriving. Or Lucian had been delayed. Either way, Constance urgently needed to get to Hotel Portofino before the end of the day.

Panic surged in her chest. She fought to suppress it the way she always did – with careful, deliberate breathing to slow the world down and stop her heart from pounding; and by using her brain, which she had always been told was a good one.

She didn't have enough money for a carriage. She couldn't speak Italian. But she was a strong, resourceful person who had been in worse predicaments than this. If the worst came to the worst, she could always walk. Mezzago couldn't be *that* far from Portofino. Growing up in West Yorkshire, it had only been a three-minute walk from Menston station to her house . . .

She made a beeline for the first person who looked vaguely official – an elderly porter in a peaked cap. 'Excuse me,' she said. 'Do you speak English?'

'No,' he replied, without looking up from his newspaper.

Charming.

Next, she tried the ticket office. The clerk couldn't have been much older than her. He had almond-shaped eyes and a neatly trimmed moustache. Something about him put Constance in mind of one of her mother's expressions. *If he was made of chocolate, he'd eat himself.*

'Good afternoon,' he said. 'You are a beautiful girl.'

'Thank you.' Constance deflected the compliment with

the briefest of smiles. 'Perhaps you can help me. I need to get to Portofino.'

'Portofino? Why Portofino?' The clerk spread his arms wide. 'Is very nice in Mezzago!'

'It is,' Constance agreed. 'But my job – my *work* – is in Portofino. I need to get there today. And I have no money.'

'No money?' He looked shocked.

'None at all.'

'But you are English, no?'

'Yes. But we don't all have money.'

The clerk thought for a moment. He rose from his seat. 'Wait here,' he said, raising a cautionary finger. 'Maybe I solve problem.'

He walked briskly out of the station and into the square at the front. 'Carlo!' he called. Hearing his name, an elderly man with close-cropped white hair looked up. He was standing beside a cart laden with fruit and vegetables. The pair spoke for a moment, then the clerk beckoned Constance over.

The mid-afternoon sun was hot and still dazzling. Sweat beading on her forehead, Constance crossed the square to where the cart was parked, in a patch of shade outside a tobacconist's shop. The single horse attached to it had seen healthier days.

'This my friend,' the ticket man explained. 'He take you to Portofino.'

A relieved smile broke across Constance's face. 'Thank you so much,' she said. 'It's a hotel I want. Hotel Portofino?'

'Yes, yes.'

'Your friend knows it?'

'Of course!'

Constance climbed up onto the cart beside Carlo, placing her suitcase in between them. She tried not to notice the smell of wine, or the way Carlo was swaying gently from side to side. As the clerk waved them off, she caught him winking surreptitiously at his friend. *'Buon viaggio!'* he called.

Carlo brought down his whip on the horse's thin rump and the cart lurched forward, out of the square and along the main road out of the town.

Despite the intense heat, Constance soon settled into the journey. After about ten minutes, however, Carlo's swaying became more pronounced and the cart's progress more erratic. Indeed, he was having trouble steering a straight course.

The sound Constance had imagined to be the brisk rattle of revolving wheels turned out to be coming from Carlo's open mouth.

He was snoring.

The cart veered sharply to the left, narrowly missing a tree. Terrified, Constance grabbed the reins from Carlo's hands and tried to bring the horse under control. Her action roused Carlo from his slumbers. Seizing the reins back with an indignant holler, he brought the cart to an abrupt standstill.

'You fell asleep,' Constance explained. 'We nearly crashed.'

But Carlo was not to be placated. He started shouting at her in Italian, his craggy face puce with anger. Constance couldn't understand what he was saying, but his hand gestures were less than friendly, and it became clear that he wished her to get out of his cart and continue her journey on foot.

Constance's moorland upbringing meant she was used to walking long distances. But not in this sort of heat and certainly not without a map. Still, what choice did she have?

Clutching her suitcase, she followed the curve of the road as it climbed uphill, trusting her instinct that this was the right way, the only way. At least the scenery was beautiful. The sky above her was a cloudless blue, the banks on either side of the road a riot of purple anemones and yellow oxalis. Several times she walked past shrines with candles and little framed pictures of the Virgin Mary. She wondered why they had been put there, and for whom.

She was beginning to feel uncomfortably thirsty, when the rotund figure of an elderly peasant woman hoved into view on the opposite side of the road. She wore a bright-red scarf around her neck and was carrying on her head a basket containing bottles of some dark golden substance and several loaves of bread.

When she drew level with Constance, the woman stopped. She smiled, looking her up and down. Constance smiled back. And then a remarkable thing happened. As if intuiting Constance's needs, the woman produced a wicker flask from the belt around her waist and held it out to her. '*Bevi un po' d'acqua*,' she said.

Constance took several large sips – she didn't want to seem

greedy – before handing it back. '*Grazie*,' she said. It was the only Italian word she knew.

The woman seemed delighted by this. '*Prego*,' she said.

Constance walked on. As the sun sank behind the mountains, the road grew steeper and more precipitous. A few carriages passed her and on one occasion a motorcar, but no one stopped to offer her a lift, or even acknowledged her presence. She started to feel lonely, even tearful; homesick, both for Yorkshire and her family, especially little Tommy.

Her first glimpse of the sea, steely grey in the soft dusk, suggested Portofino might be close. The sharp smell of thyme assailed her nostrils. In the hills above, large villas were visible behind massed ranks of pine trees. One of them must be the hotel. But which one? All Constance knew – all Betty had told her – was that it was a yellow villa, very beautiful, with gardens sloping down to the coast.

Eventually, she came to a white wrought-iron gate set in a low stone wall. The brass plate on the gate post confirmed that this was indeed Hotel Portofino. When she pushed on the gate and it opened, Constance nearly burst into tears of relief.

The house reared up before her, its façade a wash of soft, warm yellow.

Even in the low light, it looked magnificent. Constance had seen plenty of grand houses during her years in service. But this one was different – welcoming rather than forbidding, its vast size offset by a disjointed stockiness that made its height hard to gauge. None of the windows seemed to be on the same level. To the left was a tower with a flat roof like a squashed hat. But on the other side, beyond a row of green-painted shutters, a sort of corridor was exposed to the elements.

Constance couldn't quite make sense of it.

What happened when it rained? Or did it not rain in Italy?

Nervous of ringing the bell at the front door and waking the household, she followed a path round to the side and saw a light on in what she assumed was the kitchen.

There was a door, which she rapped on sharply.

'Can I help you?' asked a woman, who was tall and handsome and presumably Mrs Ainsworth.

'Please,' she said. 'It's Constance March, ma'am. The new nanny.'

A smile broke across the woman's face as she stepped back. 'Come in, come in. How on earth did you get here?'

'I walked, ma'am. I got a lift on a cart for the first few miles.'

'There was some confusion over when you were arriving. You should have sent a telegram from Genoa.'

Constance was tempted to point out that she would have had no idea how to do this even if she could have afforded it; also that there should not have been any confusion – she had been perfectly clear in her reply to Betty's letter. But she couldn't say any of this. Her job was to be capable, willing, reliable. 'I didn't want to waste the money, Mrs Ainsworth.'

'I would have reimbursed you.'

'It's generous of you to say so.'

Constance looked around the large, cool kitchen and caught sight of Bella's bread on the table. She must have been staring at it with particular intensity because Bella asked, 'Are you hungry?'

Constance had never been hungrier. But she didn't want to make a fuss. 'I'll manage until breakfast, ma'am.'

Bella was not to be deterred. 'When did you last eat?'

'This morning, ma'am.'

'And you've walked all this way?'

Constance nodded.

Shaking her head, Bella disappeared into the pantry, returning with a roll and a glass of water, which she placed on the table. They sat down opposite each other. As Constance drained the glass, Bella pushed a small bowl towards her. 'Try some of this,' she said. 'You spread it on the bread.'

'What is it?'

'It's called tapenade. It's made from olives and capers. Here, use this knife . . .'

Constance scooped a mound of tapenade on to the bread and ate it hungrily, enjoying the explosion of saltiness on her tongue. On the face of it this was a strange situation – sharing a table with your employer, being served rather than serving. But there was no awkwardness at all. She kept sneaking glances at Bella's face, though it was difficult because of the way the older woman was watching her. There was something angelic about her, Constance decided, with her mass of curly hair. Something still and stone-carved.

'Do you like it?' Bella asked.

Chewing, Constance nodded. 'Very much,' she said once she had swallowed her mouthful. 'It tastes of . . .' She paused, searching for the right word.

'What?' Bella sat back, smiling. She seemed genuinely curious.

'Sunshine,' said Constance. 'It tastes of sunshine.'

*

A pillow propped behind his head, Nish lay on his bed and reviewed what he had written in his journal.

Over the last decade or so this stretch of coastline has developed beyond all recognition. The jewel in the crown, so to speak, is the village of Portofino, which nestles around a harbour on the landward side of a small promontory. Elegant villas with lavish gardens perch upon the flanks of the surrounding hills. For its pervading air of sober Edwardian luxury, we must thank the English, who have always loved Portofino and who continue to holiday here in their unthinking droves.

He snapped the book shut and bit his thumbnail, a habit since childhood. On the one hand, he didn't want to sound harsh and ungrateful. But on the other, this idyll needed interrogating by someone who wasn't a part of it – someone who, like him, would always be an outsider.

Sometimes he convinced himself that he was the man for the job. He had always loved books and dreamt of writing them. But his training was medical. That had been his family's wish. And he did love medicine too, he couldn't deny it – the thrill of mending broken bodies, not to mention the discipline and teamwork involved.

Nish had enjoyed people-watching at dinner. But he had hoped to see more of Lucian; that Lucian might sit and eat with him as he usually did. When Lucian walked over to Rose's table, Nish had felt the desertion like a slap. He'd tried to shrug it off. It was ridiculous, after all, what he felt for the man. The only correct thing to do was suppress it. Yet, time and again, he felt compelled to create situations in which something might happen. To try to force moments to a crisis.

The journal was a distraction, perhaps even an evasion. Certainly, it contained little flavour of the personal so far – and might never.

He gazed around the attic-floor room, so English and understated in its decor. Bella had lavished care even on the smaller rooms, which were not rented out but reserved for servants and family friends. He had customised this one, he realised with a smile. Turned it from a showpiece into a shabby undergraduate's study, with its cloistered airlessness and tottering towers of novels – Conrad, Wells, that Indian one by Forster from a few years ago. Nish had been saving that up for this summer.

There was a soft knock at the door. Nish opened it a crack to see Lucian standing there. Without saying anything, he beckoned his friend inside and closed the door quietly.

Lucian said, 'Sorry about earlier.' He made a wincing face.

'There's nothing to be sorry about.'

'Duty called.'

Nish gestured to the journal on the bed. 'My work kept me company.'

'I thought you might fancy a swim.'

Nish laughed. 'It's very late. Way past Lady Latchmere's bedtime.'

Lucian picked up a towel from the back of a chair and threw it at Nish. 'Paraggi or the rocks?'

'The rocks,' said Nish. 'It's nearer. More private.'

They crept down the stairs and out of the front door, then followed a curving path to where some shallow stone steps led to a padlocked gate in the wall. Beyond it lay the private stretch of beach they called "the rocks".

Nish stripped off quickly and waded naked into the surf, relishing the feel of the cool night air on his body, the limpid black water as it swallowed him up. He turned to see Lucian following him. As usual, he had kept his undershirt on. Nish swam out for perhaps a hundred yards then headed back, mindful that Lucian might be finding it hard to keep up with him.

By the time he reached the shore, Lucian was towelling himself dry, still wearing the undershirt.

Nish felt an uncomfortable mixture of concern and desire. 'Take the shirt off,' he said. 'It's soaking.'

'So? I'm hardly going to catch cold.'

'Don't be such a baby. I've seen it before. Hundreds of times.'

Lucian looked unconvinced so Nish tried again. 'Seriously. Take it off. I'd like to see how it's healing.'

Reluctantly, Lucian peeled off the undershirt and turned his back. Nish knelt and peered closely at the large scar that stretched from Lucian's waist all the way up the left side of his body to his neck. He reached out an experimental finger and touched it. It was a tender gesture but he felt Lucian flinch.

Nish pulled his hand back. He understood Lucian's demons. He remembered the state he had been in the first time he ever saw him – on a stretcher, his uniform soaked in blood.

Lucian asked, 'What's the prognosis?'

'Just a scratch,' said Nish, and they both laughed. It was an old joke. 'Does it bother you?'

'Hardly at all. It's been eight years now.'

'You're doing well,' said Nish. He meant it, too. In most other respects, Lucian was a picture of health. 'Italy suits you.'

Lucian smiled shyly. Not for the first time, Nish wondered how much Lucian suspected; whether he even knew it was possible for men to love other men. Surely, he must? Lucian had been to boarding school and everyone knew what went on in those places. Also, he was a painter who had started to move in what people euphemistically called 'artistic circles'.

Nish longed to open up to his friend, but he lacked the courage. There was a code of silence where inversion was concerned. And if you breached it with the wrong person, at the wrong moment, well . . . It didn't bear thinking about.

'So,' said Lucian, 'what do you think?'

'Of what?'

Lucian burst out laughing. 'Of the girl, you ass.'

The girl. Of course. 'First impression? She's a bit of a peach.'

'You really think so?'

'Absolutely. Although it was hard to tell from five yards away. And with you drooling all over her.'

Lucian bent over and scooped up a hand of sand to throw in Nish's direction. 'I was not drooling!'

'I'm sure the two of you will be very happy.'

'Nothing's decided.' Lucian took another swig from the bottle of whisky Nish hadn't noticed he'd brought with him until now. He offered it to Nish, but he shook his head. He didn't like Lucian's drinking.

They walked back to the hotel. Lucian had his own key. He opened the door and stood back to let Nish into the darkened hall. 'I'll say goodnight here.'

Nish felt a crushing disappointment. 'You're not coming up?'

'I thought I'd take a turn round the garden.'

'Do you want company?'

Lucian shook his head. 'You go ahead.'

Nish watched Lucian walk off into the dark.

He hesitated for a moment, then decided to follow him.

Wedging the front door open with a rock, he crept past the flower beds and banks of hedges to the stable block the Ainsworths had converted into accommodation for the

Italian servants. He crouched behind a piece of statuary, trusting the dark to obscure him.

So, it had come to this. Spying on his friend.

Lucian stopped outside what Nish knew to be Paola's window. Her shutters were closed but cracks of light were clearly discernible around the edges. He watched as Lucian knocked lightly on the shuttered door.

For what seemed like an age there was no response. Lucian had turned, ready to walk away, when he heard the rustle of shutters being unfastened from within.

A faint beam of light spilled out into the courtyard. Through the half-open shutter, Nish could see Paola standing, imperfectly wrapped in a white sheet. There was no concealing the swell of her heavy breasts or the dark blur of hair between her legs. She turned away from the window into the room. Lucian glanced around in a futile bid to ensure he had not been seen, then followed her inside.

Ah, thought Nish. *So we all have our secrets.*

3

The box had belonged to Bella's mother. It was wooden with a floral mother of pearl inlay, and Bella kept it in the bottom drawer of her dressing table, hidden beneath a layer of black velvet on which a variety of tubes and pots jostled for space.

The box could be locked – and was, always. The drawer could not be, but this proved helpful. It allayed suspicion. If a drawer was unlocked, it stood to reason that it could contain nothing secret.

Cecil would never bother looking in an unlocked drawer.

After their impromptu meal, Bella had shown Constance to her room. She was a sweet girl, open and ingenuous. Pretty, too, in her way. Bella had outlined the rudiments of Lottie's morning routine, stressing that no one would be expecting Constance to take charge tomorrow, but it was clear she was far too tired to absorb information.

'Get some sleep, child,' she'd said, and Constance had nodded. 'We'll talk properly in the morning.'

Bella had walked back along the corridor to the suite she shared with Cecil, though "shared" wasn't quite the right word. They kept separate rooms and, the odd red-letter day excepted, slept in separate beds.

Where on earth was Cecil, anyway? Perhaps he was going to pull an all-nighter, as he would say.

At least, then, she would have the relaxing privacy of solitude – for a little while, anyway.

Bella opened the drawer and removed first the deterrents – the pots, the velvet – then the box in which she kept her most intimate possessions. Placing it on the bed, she unlocked it with the tiny key she kept around her neck. Inside, was a stack of letters tied neatly with ribbon.

She went straight to the one she wanted and was surprised by the way her hands shook as she unfolded it.

My darling Bella, it read. *How your last letter thrilled me. How I wish I could be there, by your side, to experience all the wonders that Italy has to offer.*

*

Cecil didn't mind admitting that he was drunk. Not to himself, at any rate. To Bella – well, that was a different story. It was the Fernet Branca that tipped one over the edge. Horrible stuff. You should never mix it with brandy. But it did steady your nerves during a poker game.

Cecil had made sure to be out when Julia arrived. It was too much to cope with at once. Bella's fussing *and* Julia's icy composure. Like two weather systems meeting. Better to stay away. Though that said, he was looking forward to seeing Julia again after so many years. Perhaps the old flame could be rekindled?

As for the daughter, the one they'd earmarked for Lucian, everyone said she was a looker. Though – good God! – imagine having Julia for a mother! Poor girl.

The front door was always locked, which was irritating. The key was huge and Cecil could never be bothered to take it out with him. This meant that now, he had to pick his way in the dark round to the kitchen door, which had a smaller key. Actually, it was so small he kept losing it . . . Where was it now? After some frantic rummaging he found it. There it was, in the pocket of his jacket.

He flicked on the light. On the kitchen table was a smeared plate. Tapenade? Cecil sniffed it and took an experimental bite. Yuck. He spat it out in disgust.

Then he saw the cash box and ledger. He reached for the lid and found that it was unlocked. Well, well.

He glanced around. There was no one in sight.

Grinning, he opened the box, selected the largest note he could find and stuffed it in his jacket pocket. *What's yours is mine*, he thought.

Bella must already be in her bedroom. He would surprise her. She liked surprises – or, at least, used to.

Night diminished the villa, he thought as he climbed the stairs. Without the heat and the view you could be any-where – just with more mosquitoes.

He entered Bella's room without knocking, as was his wont.

She startled and spun round from where she sat on her bed. She looked flushed, Cecil thought.

'What are you doing?' The question sounded more accusatory than Cecil had intended.

'Removing my make-up,' said Bella, quickly. 'You're very late.'

'The train was delayed.'

'How was Genoa?'

'Oh ... you know.' For a moment, Cecil forgot his own cover story. 'Genoa was Genoa.' He stared at Bella. She was still beautiful. Too bad she never let him near her. Most of the time, he could tolerate this. He had other outlets, as it were. But when he'd had a few drinks, it was hard to resist the urge. Trying not to sound desperate, he asked, 'Should I come to you?'

She sighed. 'Not tonight. It's been rather a long and stressful day.'

'Ah, of course. How was it?'

'Julia was put out that you weren't here to greet her. And Alice's nose is rather out of joint. Otherwise, it went well.'

'And the girl?'

'Rose is charming.'

'And pretty? Will he go for her?'

Bella rolled her eyes. 'Looks aren't everything, Cecil.'

'No. But they do help sugar the pill.'

*

Cecil didn't linger for long, at least. One of his virtues, Bella sometimes thought, was that he knew when he wasn't wanted. Still, she waited for him to start snoring before locking the door connecting their rooms – a door to which only she possessed the key.

Cecil had come perilously close to discovering her secret cache. But Bella had been careful, replacing the box in the drawer as soon as she'd removed the letter. She took that same letter now from the pocket in her night-gown, where she had stuffed it upon hearing Cecil. She opened it back out to read again, paying special attention to the last lines:

There is still no other who is dearer to me.
Yours, forever faithful, in love. Henry. X

The words, and imagining Henry writing them, made her stomach dip. They weren't enough on their own to awaken her; to make her feel what she needed to feel.

Bella crept over to the bookshelf and removed a Bible. She flicked through its tissue-thin pages until she found what she was looking for – a posed photo of a dark-haired young man with soft lips and warm, inviting eyes. She stared at the image, drinking it in, fixing it in her memory.

Were she truly alone, she would bring the photo to bed with her, along with the letter. But it was too dangerous, even with Cecil asleep and the door locked, so she returned them to their hiding places before climbing into bed.

It was a hot night. She threw off the heavy covers, enjoying the way the single remaining sheet tickled her skin. She let her hands glide over her body, reacquainting herself with its hidden creases and folds, giving in to the thoughts that had been flitting so distractingly through her head all day.

Her throat ached with pleasure. She imagined Henry putting his arms around her and giving her nape gentle kisses. She imagined him taking her hand and guiding it to where he wanted it to go.

A long, low moan echoed through the room.

At first, Bella imagined its source to be her own lips. But the closer she listened, the more she realised it was coming from the corridor outside – and that it was a distinct moan of pain, not pleasure.

She sat bolt upright, frustration giving way to alarm. Her dressing gown was hanging on the back of the door. As she padded across the room to retrieve it, she noticed that she had forgotten to close the shutters properly. A movement outside in the courtyard caught her eye. The door to Paola's room in the old stable block had opened and someone was leaving. Bella squinted in the faint light.

When she saw who it was, she reeled back from the window.

It was Lucian, shoes in one hand and an empty bottle in the other.

Her hand went automatically to her mouth. *Of course*, she thought. *It all makes sense.*

But as another moan pierced the silence Bella gathered herself. There was no time now to dwell on this unwelcome turn of events.

The corridor was lit dimly by electric lamps mounted on the wall. Bella paused for a moment and listened. The cries were coming from the Ascot Suite – Lady Latchmere's rooms.

Melissa, the great-niece, answered the door, looking pale

and exhausted. 'Oh, Mrs Ainsworth,' she said. 'Her Ladyship is in great pain.'

'Which part of her?'

'She doesn't seem able to say.'

'We need a doctor,' Bella decided. 'Only it's so late.' Then a thought occurred. 'Nish.'

'Who?'

'Mr Sengupta. My son's friend. He was a medic in the war. He saved Lucian's life.'

Nish took a few minutes to rouse. He looked dishevelled and smelled of the sea. Bella explained the situation, but he was nervous about involving himself. 'I'm a little out of practice,' he cautioned.

Bella rushed to reassure him. 'Please, Nish. It would be the absolute end of us, before we'd even got started, if something were to happen to Her Ladyship.'

The attic floor felt cramped and stuffy. Unvisited by paying guests, it was Bella's least favourite part of the house – the only part she felt still needed work. She waited outside the door to Nish's room while he threw on some pyjamas and a cardigan, then together they made their way down the stairs and along the corridor to the Ascot Suite where, after sensing fresh doubt in Lady Latchmere, Bella stressed once more Nish's impeccable medical credentials.

Melissa's anxiety was awful to witness. She genuinely believed that Lady Latchmere was about to die, not least because Lady Latchmere herself believed this – and her belief was loud enough to be infectious.

In the pale light cast by the standard lamp it was easy to miss the still, prone figure on the bed. Only the groans it periodically emitted suggested it lived and breathed.

Bella followed Nish and Melissa to the foot of the bed. Her lower half concealed by a sheet, Lady Latchmere wore a nightdress of white lace and, on her head, the sort of silk nightcap that even Bella's grandmother would have rejected as old-fashioned. Her perfect hands were folded across her chest.

Nish turned to Bella nervously. 'Perhaps it would be better if you left me alone with her?'

Bella nodded.

Melissa stared at Bella imploringly. 'Will she be all right?' she asked. Her freckled face looked so adorably young.

Bella smiled. 'She's in very good hands.' She took the girl's hands in hers. 'Would you like a cup of tea? Or something a little stronger?'

Melissa nodded, laughing through her tears.

*

The next thing Bella knew it was morning and Nish was gently shaking her awake. She was curled up on an armchair in the suite's sitting room, a half-empty glass of whisky beside her. Important to tidy *that* away before Lady Latchmere saw it . . .

'Did you sit up all night?' he asked, clearly as amused as he was surprised.

'I told Miss De Vere I'd make myself comfortable here,' Bella remembered. 'In case her great aunt took ill again.'

Yawning, she stretched out, surprised by how sore her muscles were. Sleeping in armchairs was an activity for the young and flexible. 'What happened?'

'Nothing very much.'

'Do I need to call for a doctor?' She corrected herself. 'Another doctor, I mean.'

Nish dismissed the accidental slight. 'I'm not a proper doctor and no, I don't think so. I've relieved her immediate symptoms. But,' he grinned, 'you might want to serve prunes for breakfast.'

'Oh!' Bella returned Nish's smile.

'And may I suggest a digestif for Her Ladyship. After every meal.'

'Did you have something in mind?'

'Perhaps a little of that excellent Limoncello you served last night?'

'Lady Latchmere doesn't drink alcohol.'

He grinned. 'Then tell her it's Italian lemonade.'

Bella let rip a peal of delighted laughter. This was a delicious conspiracy.

Lady Latchmere and Melissa were still asleep in their bedroom. Bored with the dark, Bella threw open the sitting-room shutters, savouring the first faint breeze of the day as it came off the sea. The room would be light and alive for them when finally they awoke.

An image flashed unbidden into her head – of Lucian leaving Paola's room the previous night. The bottle swinging in his hand.

'Tell me, Nish,' she asked. 'How do you find Lucian?'

'Like he's finally starting to heal. Physically, at least.'

'And otherwise?'

Nish shrugged. 'What he went through will always cast its shadow.'

'I know, I know. I just wish . . . 'She stopped and tried again. 'He used to be so full of schemes and plans. And purpose.'

'He will be again,' Nish assured her. 'Give him time.'

Bella looked at her wristwatch. Half-past six – a good time to be up and about. She washed and dressed, trying to ignore the stiffness in her back.

No sooner had she got downstairs than Alice approached her, brandishing the ledger and the petty cash box like trophies. 'You left these in the kitchen last night,' she said. 'Betty was most put out.'

She opened the box so that Bella could immediately see what had happened.

With a flush of heat to the face, she saw that money was missing – again.

'Thank you, Alice,' she said, stiffly.

'I do think—' Alice began.

'I said thank you. I'll deal with it from here.'

Fuming, Bella withdrew to the small room next to the kitchen that she used as an office. Taking advantage of a few minutes' solitude, she addressed an envelope for the letter she planned to write later to Henry.

She had just finished when Cecil barged in. He had an annoying gift for looking rested, even when he had been drinking the night before. Bella's industrious father, no fan of the aristocracy, would have said it was because complacency had been bred into his bones. 'Morning,' he said, flatly. He picked up the envelope from the desk. 'And who is Henry Bowater Esquire?' He tried to make the name sound comical.

'One of my father's accountants.' Bella said it so confidently she almost believed it herself.

'From the textile factory?'

'From his private estate.' She watched her husband closely. 'I'm writing to him about our cashflow.'

The word had the desired effect of making Cecil back away, like a vampire from a crucifix.

'Ah,' he said. 'Well. I thought I might stroll into town later. Would you like me to post it?'

'I'll find you when it's finished.' In fact, Bella's plan was to ask Paola to post it. You could trust Paola to do a job properly – though not, it seemed, to leave her son alone.

'Jolly good.' Cecil turned to leave.

Before he got a chance Bella said, 'I know what you did, Cecil.'

He paused and turned back round. 'Then you're one up on me.'

'It's bad enough you took the money,' she said. 'Please don't lie to me, as well.'

He closed his eyes, as if this was all very hard for him. 'I was going to tell you.'

'Really? When?'

'When I had the means to pay you back.'

'What about your money from the family trust?'

He shrugged. 'Spent every last sou, I'm afraid.'

Just as she'd feared, not that there was any consolation in being right. Her anger swelled. 'I can't run the hotel on credit. I need all the cash I can get.'

Cecil barked a hollow laugh. 'Me too, sweet-heart. Me too.'

*

Constance had set her alarm clock for six o'clock.

After making use of the bathroom she shared with Lottie – which was bigger than the entire ground floor of the family home back in Yorkshire – she put on her Sunday-best dress, picked up the parcel she had brought for Betty and wandered downstairs to the kitchen.

The door she had knocked on so desperately last night stood wide open. She paused on the threshold and inhaled the cool morning smells of pine and wild thyme, grateful to feel her enthusiasm for Italy returning.

The sound of someone else entering the room made her turn abruptly.

A round, dazed face beamed across at her. 'Is that you, Constance? My goodness ...' Betty – at least, Constance guessed it must be her – rushed over and enveloped her in a warm embrace. Then she released her and stood back. 'Let me look at you. I've not seen you since you were a nipper. My, you're a sight for sore eyes.'

Constance felt embarrassed beneath the scrutiny. 'I can't quite believe I'm here,' she said.

'You'd have been here sooner if I hadn't got my dates all muddled. When did you get in?'

'A little after midnight.'

Betty gave a squawk. 'Please tell me you found a carriage from the station.'

Constance smiled. 'I found a carriage from the station.'

'Well, that's something.' The cook's eyes flicked to the clock on the wall which showed the time as a quarter past six. 'You're up at the crack of dawn, at any rate.'

'Old habits die hard.'

'They surely do. How are you finding Portofino?'

'It's magnificent. I can't stop looking at the view.'

'It can have that effect on you. Though if you ask me, Whitby's just as handsome in its way.' She winked, then looked down at the brown paper parcel Constance was pressing into her hands. 'What's this? You didn't bring this all the way from England?'

'It's just a few oddments. Mam thought you might like them. There's a letter, too.'

Betty carried the parcel to the kitchen table and ripped open the package. When she saw its contents she smiled broadly. 'Oh, thank the Lord. Marmalade! And some proper English mustard.' Then she took the letter, holding it close so that she could read her name on the envelope. 'Who'd have thought it . . .' Constance saw tears in her eyes and moved to comfort her, but Betty shook her head. 'Who'd have thought that when me and Fanny Gray was girls in service together, that I'd be standing here – more than thirty years

67

later – with her daughter.' Smiling, she hugged Constance. 'In Italy, of all places!'

But there was no time for reminiscing. There was too much to do; too much for Constance to learn.

Her borrowed apron fastened tightly, Constance helped Betty with the breakfasts, chopping fruit and loading up plates with scrambled eggs and bacon to take out to the guests. Two of the female guests she had served – one middle-aged and unfriendly, the other beautiful but vacant: Rose, was she called? – had been rather demanding, sending the coffee back for being too bitter and the fruit for being 'squashed'. But, on the whole, people had been kind.

She was washing up in the enormous butler's sink – it was the size of a bath! – when Bella came into the kitchen and declared that now would be a suitable time to talk Constance through her duties.

'Of course, Lottie will be your priority,' she said. 'But there will be other jobs as well. Helping Betty, as you did this morning. Cleaning if needed. We'll need you to muck in.' She gave a smile. 'Though you certainly seem to be doing a good job so far.'

'I'll be happy to turn my hand to anything, Mrs Ainsworth.' Constance meant it. She was happy simply to be here.

'Wonderful! There's a uniform in my office which you should wear when you're not looking after Lottie.' Bella handed her a stack of menus. They were hand-written in a fancy script. 'You can start by taking these to the dining room. And be sure to answer any questions the guests may have.'

Constance glanced at the top menu. She must have looked confused by all the foreign terms because Bella asked: 'You can read and write, child?'

She wasn't sure how to reply. She had no idea how to pronounce 'stracciatella' or even what it was. What English girl did? 'I get by, ma'am,' she said, cautiously.

Bella took the menus off her. 'We can do better than get by.'

Constance was about to protest, or at least clarify, when a prim-looking young woman appeared at the door. Bella beckoned her over. 'Alice! This is Constance March, the new nanny. Constance, this is my daughter and Lottie's mother, Mrs Mays-Smith.'

'Pleasure to meet you, ma'am,' said Constance and curtsied. Somehow the woman looked older than Mrs Ainsworth. Pinched and worn.

'There's no need for that,' said Alice, more sharply than Constance thought strictly necessary.

Turning to Alice, Bella asked: 'Would now be a good time for her to meet Lottie?'

'No time like the present,' said Alice. 'I'll bring her down.'

Constance sighed with relief as both Alice and Bella left the room. She felt as if she had passed some unspecified test. Sensing her mood, Betty came to her side and placed a pudgy hand on her arm. 'Don't mind Mrs Mays-Smith,' she said. 'She's not a bad sort.' She lowered her voice. 'I found a few moments just now to look at the letter. I don't mind telling you, I wept buckets while I were reading it.'

Constance could guess at the reason. 'Bless your kind heart.'

'When your mother wrote to me and asked me to find a place for you ... Well, I never dreamt why.'

'You weren't to know.'

'You've had a terrible time of it. You poor little thing. I can see now why you jumped at the chance to come here. For a fresh start. Somewhere far away.' Constance nodded. She felt her eyes filling with tears. 'So that's what we're going to give you. A new beginning! A chance to put all your troubles behind you.' Betty took Constance's face in her hands, running her thumbs over the tear-streaked cheeks. 'Time heals everything, sweetheart. Time ... hard work ... and good food.'

*

Half way between Alassio and Portofino, Jack's brow furrowed above the ridge of his driving goggles. Coaxing the gear from third to second was a delicate manoeuvre which required careful concentration.

Claudine watched him, smiling. Not for the first time, it occurred to her that Jack drove the way he made love: smoothly and confidently, with careful regard for his passengers' enjoyment. The trade-off was how much he relished being in control – and how certain he was that he alone knew the way.

Motorcars had never been Claudine's thing. But it was

hard not to be wowed by this one. Its power matched its beauty. Other vehicles groaned and rattled as they negotiated Italy's twisty mountain roads. But the Bugatti could cope with anything.

She and Jack had spent the whole summer driving around the French and Italian Rivieras. Starting in Cannes, they had followed a glittering chain of parties, concerts, blackjack games and villa retreats eastward along the coast, stopping at Nice, Monte Carlo, San Remo and Alassio. Their next port of call was Portofino, the most beautiful town of them all, or so people said.

It was almost a year now since Jack had come to see Claudine's show in Paris. 'You sing like an angel,' he had said, in his soft Texan accent.

Claudine had just come off stage. She had been hot and tired, not quite in the mood. But although Jack was clearly nudging fifty and not strictly her type – he was portly, with receding sandy hair and a too-neat moustache – he had won her over with his old-fashioned charm and air of calm competence.

'It would be an honour to take you to dinner,' he had said, bowing graciously. 'We Americans in Paris must stick together.'

'All right,' she had replied, smiling. 'But I get to decide where.'

She had taken him to La Coupole on the Boulevard de Montparnasse. She always felt comfortable there among the expatriate flotsam who made up its clientele, many of them artists and writers. She was also reassured by how often she saw other Black folk there.

Jack knew what Claudine did. She had told him all about her residency at the Lido in Venice, how Cole Porter himself had recommended her to the producers at the Théâtre des Champs-Élysées. But what did *he* do?

'Oh, you know,' he replied, tucking into his Choucroute à l'Alsacienne. 'This and that.'

'I need more detail, Jack.'

He gazed at her with a hazy, undecided expression. 'What if I told you I was a *commissionaire d'objets d'art*?'

Claudine raised an eyebrow. 'Is that true?'

Jack smiled. 'Let's just say it isn't untrue.'

As she had soon learnt, that remark summed up her lover perfectly.

Jack existed somewhere between truth and untruth, honesty and dishonesty. But this didn't really trouble her. At least, it hadn't – until now.

Why not? Because the last thing Claudine had expected was for the relationship to last. The problem was that it had proved remarkably resilient. Also, the longer it endured, the more conscious she became of needing more from it than Jack seemed able to supply. Not commitment exactly, but security; a confidence that, should they return to America as a couple, Jack would remain as happy to be with her – and as happy to be *seen* with her – as he'd been in Europe's eternal playground.

Jack loved to travel. But if you travelled constantly you stopped noticing where you were. Life became boring and mechanical, a vague procession of new towns and new people. For the first time in her life, Claudine yearned to put down roots. But where? And with whom?

The coastal road wound endlessly around the rocky headlands, beneath towering rocks and steeply sloping hillsides. As the sun blazed down, the scent of thyme filled the air. Claudine lowered her sunglasses, the better to observe the scattered villages and pine forests.

It was hard to talk over the noise of the engine. But it was so long since either of them had spoken that it was becoming uncomfortable. Leaning across, Claudine shouted into Jack's ear, 'Tell me about Hotel Portofino.'

He grinned. 'It's a hotel,' he shouted back, eyes fixed on the road ahead. 'In Portofino.'

'Very funny.' She punched his arm gently.

'I don't know much,' Jack conceded. 'Only that it hasn't been open long. Less than a year. It's very comfortable, apparently. Big suites. Modern bathrooms. Great views over the town and bay. It's run by an English couple, Cecil and Bella Ainsworth. He's some sort of aristocrat, but on his uppers, like most of them nowadays. All the money is hers.'

'How unfortunate,' said Claudine. 'For him, I mean.'

Jack laughed. 'I'll say.'

'How do you know all this?'

'Cecil is a friend of a friend of a friend.'

Now it was Claudine's turn to laugh. 'With you, everyone is a friend of a friend of a friend.'

Jack shrugged. 'It's the best way to be.' He glanced across

at her and winked before turning back to face the road. 'You've got to stay connected, baby. If you want to succeed.'

*

Rose was standing by the railing looking out to sea when Lucian approached. She had been waiting, hoping for him to find her, confident that in the outfit her mother had chosen – a cream shift dress with lace sleeves, enhanced by a low-slung pearl necklace – she looked close to her best. Alluring, but modest. Fashionable, but not frighteningly so.

It gave her a thrill to realise that Lucian must have been thinking along the same lines. 'There you are!' he cried, in a tone of jokey irritation.

She gave him a shy smile. 'Here I am,' she said, then turned back seaward. She sensed him taking a moment to appreciate her beauty, the one aspect of herself in which she had total confidence. Beauty was something she had always possessed, to the point where she had never stopped to wonder what else might be needed in life.

The morning was warming up nicely. They stood for a moment and stared out at the sea, grateful for the breeze that rippled their hair.

'Such a pretty view,' Lucian said, then paused awkwardly. 'Perhaps, we could go down to the beach later? It cools off a bit in the late afternoon. Or we could take a boat trip. You do know how to swim?'

'I'm not sure I do.'

'Then it will be my pleasure to teach you.'

Rose wasn't sure about swimming. It meant getting wet,

and no one looked their best when they were wet. 'I don't know,' she said. 'I should see what Mama says.'

Lucian looked at her with amusement, evidently wondering why she would need her mother's permission to do something so straightforward. 'There are so many wonderful things to see and do here, Rose,' he said, coaxingly. 'Florence and Pisa are a day away. Genoa is just up the coast.'

'I know. We caught the train there.'

'And there are small marvels closer to home. Every church seems to house a treasure. It's like living in a museum.'

Rose couldn't imagine anything worse. She made a face and said, 'I do hope it's not too stuffy.' The remark was supposed to be a joke but it landed flatly and Lucian didn't seem to know how to react. Rose remembered that she wasn't very good at jokes. Why was that?

She was thrown all over again. Not just by this awkward conversation, but by the realisation that the attractive cart-driver whose beautiful neck she had stared at so intensely hadn't been an anonymous Italian – but Lucian. Now, confronted by the *real* Lucian – the Lucian her mother hadn't stopped talking about – she didn't know how to behave. Did she find him attractive? Did she even like him? These questions seemed impossible to answer. And yet they weren't difficult in themselves.

A strange noise derailed her train of thought. 'What's that?' she asked, looking around.

'What's what?'

'That awful throbbing hum.'

Lucian made an exaggerated play of listening. 'Ah, the cicadas.'

'The what?'

'They're a type of insect. A bit like a grasshopper.' He looked around at the bushes and shrubs surrounding them. 'Here. Let me see if I can spot one for you.'

Rose squealed. 'No, Lucian! Please! Don't! I really can't abide bugs.'

She glanced up at the window where, beyond the glass, she could see the erect, unyielding figure of her mother watching her.

This was no surprise; she was used to that. But who was the man who had suddenly appeared beside her? Mama must have heard him, but rather than turn round she closed her eyes. As she did so a curious look came over her face. An expression of serenity, Rose thought. Or was it desire?

*

Julia knew it was Cecil without turning round. When he entered a room its whole atmosphere seemed to change. He even smelled the same as he always had done – the musky aroma of eau de Cologne and tobacco. She had always found it rather alluring.

He crept up to join her at the window and peered over her shoulder, standing far too close. 'Trouble in paradise, I see.'

She didn't move. 'Where did you spring from? Have you been avoiding me?'

'As if I could. Or would. Is my son making himself agreeable?'

'Let's just say we didn't get off to the best of starts.'

'So I heard.'

'You thought it was funny, I suppose.'

'A little, I admit. What about the girl? Will she go along with our plan?'

'Oh, Rose is entirely biddable,' she said, as if the question were absurd. 'She'll do whatever she's told.'

*

Bella happened to glance into the library as she was passing, when she saw Julia and Cecil in intimate conversation by the window. Her chest tightened. What silly mischief was he up to?

Well, he was welcome to Julia. Goodness, but she was a piece of work. Bella had bumped into her and Rose on their way from breakfast. She asked how they had slept, genuinely keen to know after all the effort she had put into their rooms.

Julia's reply had been calibrated to wound. 'Adequately. The room was hot. And rather cramped, I'm afraid.'

'I'm sorry to hear you think so.'

As usual, Rose rushed to undo the damage. 'I slept like a baby. It's more like a wonderful country house than a hotel.'

Eager to get away, Bella had gestured them towards the dining room. But Julia had held her ground. 'I was wondering whether you had anything a little more spacious.'

'All our rooms are booked,' Bella had replied, careful to keep her tone measured and calm.

'But not occupied. Perhaps I should speak to Cecil.' Julia had glanced around her. 'If he's about.'

'No, no. I'll see what I can do.' The last thing Bella needed was Cecil's blundering, unhelpful involvement.

Perhaps that was what the pair were discussing now.

But any thought of intervening was banished by a loud, cheerful klaxon from outside.

Of course, she thought. *The Turners are arriving this morning!*

Bella didn't know much about motorcars beyond the terrible noise they made. Even so, it was hard not to be impressed by the gleaming red machine that crunched to a halt as she strode out into the sunshine.

'Goodness!' she exclaimed. 'What a splendid entrance!'

The driver removed his goggles and grinned broadly. In a marked American accent he said: 'Jack Turner. At your service.'

A small crowd was gathering around the motorcar. 'A Bugatti,' observed Count Albani, approvingly. 'Nice.' But within seconds, everyone's attention had shifted entirely towards the elegant woman emerging from the other side of the vehicle, the tight curls of her hair catching in the breeze.

'Thank you,' she said, as Billy approached her to help. She too had a strong American accent.

Billy was agog at her clothes – a man's suit, tailored to showcase her figure to stunning effect. Betty, who had rushed out from the kitchen to see what was going on, gave him a sharp nudge. 'Stop gawping, lad. Just fetch their bags!'

Bella led the new arrivals into the hall and asked them to sign the register. 'Here, please,' she directed, handing Jack a pen. 'On behalf of you and . . .' She darted a discreet glance at the woman's hand, bare of rings. 'Mrs Turner.' Jack signed without speaking, then gave his companion a knowing look.

She smirked minutely. 'You can call me Claudine,' she said.

*

Something Lucian had discovered during his convalescence was the importance of keeping busy. It had been his doctor's idea, actually – to cut to a minimum any rumination or reflection. It hadn't taken much in those early days to coax the Black Dog out of his kennel, and the attacks had felt all the more violent for their randomness. Lucian might have been walking across a field on a perfectly pleasant summer's day when suddenly, for no apparent reason, a hole would open in his soul and he would fall in.

Over time, he'd learned to banish these moods with a paintbrush. For painting took Lucian out of himself. Not just the repetitive, automatic act of daubing oils on canvas, but the all-consuming focus on something external, be it a bowl of fruit or a railway bridge.

The problem was, Lucian's faith in his art was being chipped away by the very people he believed should be supporting him. One of the attractions of Italy – the reason he had swallowed his pride and followed his parents out here – was how paintable its landscape was.

Such was his father's hostility to artists, however, that whenever Lucian raised the subject of pursuing this as a career, he found it impossible to state his ambitions without sounding feeble or deluded. This spilled over into his private thoughts, so that even when he talked to himself, his voice had an edge of mockery.

His family had poisoned his attempts to build his own future happiness. All they cared about was marrying him off.

Another trigger for his bad mood had been his conversation with Rose. How could someone so beautiful be so empty? Dreaming on the way back from the station, he had conjured into being a quite different Rose – sharp, poised and independent. This initial elation had given way to a sort of torpor as he realised how unfounded it was. The real Rose was a promise too lavish to believe in; so much under her mother's thumb that she was like one of the squashed figs he kept finding in the garden.

Pleased to discover the library empty, Lucian plucked a book from a shelf and stood flicking through it desultorily. Trollope. As if any sane person would come all the way to Italy and think, 'I know, I'll read *Barchester Towers*.' He made a mental note to share this observation with Nish. He would think it was funny, too.

He was still chuckling to himself when his mother entered the room. 'Where is everyone?'

'Sleeping, if they've got any sense.'

'You didn't fancy a siesta yourself? You were up rather late last night.'

So, she knew about the swimming. He looked up. 'Why are you here? Did you want me for something?'

She walked over to where he was standing. 'I was just wondering how you were. You weren't among the crowd witnessing the Turners' arrival.' She made it sound like the opening of a gallery.

Lucian shrugged. 'Guests come and go. It is a hotel, after all.'

'There's no need to be rude.'

'Did Father send you?'

'Lucian!' She sounded genuinely shocked.

'What? He's been chivvying away at me every chance he gets. Tell him, he doesn't need to worry.'

A motherly hand grasped his arm. 'It's me that's worried.'

'About this blasted wedding?'

'About *you*!'

He looked at her and could see that this was true. It was there in the dark circles beneath her eyes, in the vein throbbing gently on her right temple. 'You needn't be,' he said.

'But I am. You hardly seem yourself.'

'What does that even mean?'

'It means you seem to be frittering your time away. In a rather unhealthy fashion.'

Lucian looked stung. 'You sound just like him. "Go home. Get a job. Get married."'

'I don't care a fig what you do. Just do *something*.'

'You wanted me here.'

'I *do* want you here. Of course I want you here. That's not what I'm saying.'

A sullen silence descended on the room. Lucian decided to break it. 'And what about you?'

'I have *my* passion project.' Bella gestured around her.

'And does it keep you fulfilled?'

'That and motherhood.'

'And marriage to Father?'

'Of course,' she said, uncertainly. 'That as well.'

'Can you find your purpose in loving someone?'

'If you truly love them, yes.'

'But if you don't?'

Bella was about to answer when Cecil burst in. 'What are you two skulking around in here for?' He had smartened himself up, Lucian noticed. Put on a suit. He obviously wanted to impress someone. He stared at his father's once-handsome face.

The way Bella answered, it was as if she actually hated him. 'We were talking about love,' she said, her eyes fixed on Lucian.

Cecil grimaced. 'Ye Gods,' he said before turning and walking out into the corridor.

*

To please Lucian, Bella had hung a selection of his paintings on a discreet patch of wall behind the staircase. Cecil was taken aback to find Jack Turner, the new American guest, examining them with every appearance of interest.

The sight of Jack's car in the drive had led Cecil to believe he might be a useful person to know. So, he had set out to find him.

Thankfully, it hadn't taken long.

'Not bad are they,' he called out now, strolling towards Jack. In truth, he had no idea whether the paintings were any good.

'A lot better than "not bad",' said Jack.

Cecil thrust out his hand. 'Cecil Ainsworth. I imagine you've already met my wife.'

The other man shook his hand, with an annoyingly limp grasp. 'Jack Turner,' he said, and turned back to the painting he was contemplating – a portrait of a woman in a satin gown holding a yellow rose. 'Is it a local artist?'

'You could say that. It's by my son, Lucian.'

Jack raised an eyebrow. 'He has talent.'

'Perhaps, but keep it to yourself. The last thing I want him thinking is that he can make his living as a painter.'

They shared a low conspiratorial laugh.

'Are they for sale?' Jack asked.

The question baffled Cecil. 'They might be,' he said. It wasn't something he had ever thought about. 'Are you a collector?'

'Not really. But I know a few.'

Cecil was about to ask more questions when he heard the sound of slippered feet descending the stairs. They belonged to Jack's companion – wife seemed unlikely, he thought – the Claudine everyone was talking about. Beneath her silk kimono Cecil could see a bright-red swimsuit, cut high in the leg. Her skin was a rich brown.

'Baby, this is Mr Ainsworth,' said Jack, without looking around. He seemed to know exactly who was standing there, just from the lightness of her step.

Claudine didn't remove her sunglasses or hat, but she did hold out her hand for Cecil to kiss. 'Enchanted,' he said, kissing it. Then he turned to Jack. 'Any grand plans for the day?'

'We thought we'd walk down to the beach,' said Jack.

Cecil walked a little ahead of them, for once enjoying playing the role of attentive host. 'Then allow me to open the door for you. This is much the best time for a bathe.'

*

No sooner had Melissa watched Jack and Claudine leave, than she walked back out onto the terrace where Lady Latchmere was snoozing in a chair. Creeping up to her, she whispered: 'Aunt! Wake up! You have to see this!'

Lady Latchmere did a little turkey-gobble, as if shaking herself awake. 'What?' She batted at Melissa's head, which dodged quickly out of range. 'Calm down, dear. Don't flap.'

'But, look!'

She pointed towards Claudine, who was making her precise, catwalk-perfect way towards the path leading down to the beach. Jack was in tow, carrying her bag and parasol.

Lady Latchmere craned forwards, straining every calcified sinew in the pursuit of gossip.

'Good heavens!' she said, catching a glimpse of the red swimsuit. She fell back in her chair and started fanning herself. 'I feel quite unsteady.'

Melissa was anxious. 'Shall I fetch Mr Sengupta?'

'That won't be necessary. But perhaps I might take another glass of that Italian lemonade I had at breakfast?'

'I'll see what I can do,' said Melissa.

*

The *caffès* were expensive in Portofino. They had the same tin tables and white porcelain cups as the ones in Genoa, but with an extra thirty per cent slapped on for the privilege of watching English matrons paddling in the surf. Occasionally, just occasionally, you might strike lucky and get a sighting of a proper English rose disrobing . . .

There were a couple of roses staying at Hotel Portofino, mused Roberto. The younger one was literally called Rose. How funny was that? She had skin like cream, smooth and delicate. A bit on the thin side, but then English girls often were. They needed feeding up like geese.

English Rose came with a mother attached. Roberto smiled wolfishly at the thought of the older woman. She was fierce! She watched over her daughter as if she were still a toddler.

Don't go here!

Where have you been?

All day, every day. He didn't know how the girl stood it.

Roberto sipped his Campari soda. Someone was coming down the path from the hotel. A man of medium height, clutching a parasol. Striding before him, a tall Black woman with the most incredible figure Robert had ever seen.

They reached the beach, whereupon the woman slipped off her kimono to reveal . . . Goodness! This had been worth waiting for. Roberto removed his sunglasses, in order to get a better view. The problem was, he wasn't the only person to have noticed. A small crowd was clustering on the beach, inching its way closer to where the man had spread out a towel on the sand.

People! Blocking his view!

Roberto stood up and craned his neck. As he did so, a man approached his table. With him were two younger men. They hung back with their arms folded and trunk-like legs slightly apart. The older man had close-cropped hair and bowed shoulders. His clothes were smart but cheap. He held out a hand.

'Danioni,' he said. His accent was coarse and rustic. It wasn't even Genoese.

'It's a pleasure to meet you,' said Roberto, trying to conceal his irritation as his glance was torn from the beach.

Danioni stood back. 'I apologise for interrupting your ... observations. But I'm interested to know. Are you a party member?'

'I'm thinking about joining.' Roberto kept his accent clipped and refined.

Danioni followed Roberto's gaze across to the woman stretched out on the beach, drawing attention to herself. 'A foreigner?'

'Could she be anything else?'

'Are you staying at the English hotel?'

Roberto nodded and lit a cigarette.

'I hope you're watching your back.'

Roberto grinned. 'My father is staying there, too. He loves the English.'

Danioni hoiked up a gobbet of phlegm and spat it so that it landed by Roberto's feet. 'He didn't fight in the war, then.'

Roberto stared at the quivering yellow mass. Slowly, he allowed his glance to travel to Danioni's sallow, hangdog face. 'I understood that the war was over,' he said.

'Did you?' Danioni lifted his eyebrows. He glanced round at his two companions who smiled obediently. 'That's funny. I hear it hasn't even started.'

*

Bella's parting shot to Lucian at the end of their argument – or, should she say, disagreement – had been that if he wanted to do something useful rather than mope about, he could teach Constance to read.

'Who's Constance?' he had asked.

'The new nanny.'

'That girl I saw earlier in the kitchen? Wearing a maid's uniform?'

'She'll be doing a bit of everything.'

'Poor Constance.'

Bella's smile had been conciliatory. 'Are you having a "radical spasm"?' This was an allusion to a notorious row Lucian had had with his father.

'I might be.' Lucian paused. 'I just don't see why we can't hire a nanny *and* a maid, if we need both.'

Bella sighed. Lucian, Cecil, even Alice – they had no idea how costly it was to keep this show on the road; or if they did, they didn't care. 'Because we're not made of money,' she snapped. 'Anyway, good servants are hard to find these days. And I think she's going to be special.'

*

Lucian found Constance perusing a battered copy of *The Iliad*.

'Ah,' he said. 'What's that? Trollope?'

She closed it with a snap, her face blushing. 'I beg your pardon, sir?'

'Never mind. Private joke. Show me?'

Constance held up the book like a shield, but Lucian took it from her nevertheless.

'It might be wise to start with something a little less ambitious than Homer, don't you think?' He handed it back.

Nodding, she hurriedly returned it to where she had found it.

Lucian said, 'I understand you need some assistance with your letters.'

'I couldn't read the menu, that's all. It was written funny.' She had a strong Yorkshire accent. It was charming, really charming.

'Well, my mother was insistent that I should help you.'

'I know, sir. It's why Mrs Mays–Smith has been good enough to give me an hour off.'

Taking off his jacket, Lucian began to make himself comfortable at the writing table. Constance remained where she was, by the bookcase. Was it him or was she sulking? He cast her an impatient glance. 'Look. I don't want to be here any more than you do. But we should try to make the best of it.'

After a moment of hesitation, Constance walked across to the table. She pulled out a chair and sat down. 'All right,' she said. 'Sir.'

'Please, call me Lucian.'

'Lucian.' She wrinkled her nose. 'It sounds funny. Not the name,' she added, hastily. 'Hearing myself say it.'

Lucian smiled. What a sweet girl she was. 'Let's start with the alphabet,' he said.

From a leather satchel, he took a child's primer, a sheet of paper and a pencil. These he placed on the table, evenly spaced as if the very neatness of the arrangement was supposed to teach her a lesson.

'See how you get on with these exercises,' he said. 'And holler when you've finished.'

As she made a start on the task, Lucian sank deeper into his favourite chair – the red leather one with the studs – and tried to concentrate on his newspaper. He read about the General Strike back home, which he knew was something he should take an interest in. But he couldn't stop sneaking little glances at Constance. She wasn't conventionally pretty, not like Rose. Her eyes were close-set beneath heavy eyebrows. Of course, her clothes were worn and shapeless. Still, there was something about her.

He must have nodded off, because the next thing he knew she was clearing her throat.

He looked up, shuffling in his seat to distract from the fact of his dozing. 'Have you finished?' he asked, faking efficient interest.

'I have to go now,' she said, glancing at the library door. 'I'm needed.'

'Let me have a look, then.'

She handed him the paper, which she had carefully folded in two.

'Same time tomorrow?' he suggested.

Constance hesitated. 'Let me talk to Mrs Mays-Smith.'

'Or I can?'

'I'll do it. She's my employer.' A respectful pause. 'If there's nothing else, sir?'

'Nothing at all,' said Lucian.

She left the room, but watching her departure, he had the oddest desire to summon her back – just so that he could experience again the delicate sensation of sharing space with her. But he had no plausible excuse, and it would have been the worst kind of power play. Having servants in the first place was shameful enough, and not something Lucian mentioned in front of his artistic friends – even the ones who'd had their own staff at home, growing up. Which was most of them, now he came to think of it.

When he had finished this rumination, which he knew did not show him in the best light, Lucian unfolded the piece of paper Constance had given him.

What he read made him burst out laughing.

I may not know an Eggs Benedict, but I do know my ABCs!

*

Cecil passed the new servant on his way to the terrace. She was leaving the library and smiling in that delightful minx-like way girls like her smiled. What was she? Lottie's nanny or something? Bella had chosen well.

He had a bottle of brandy, and he was on a mission – to

seek out Jack and have a proper conversation. He had spotted him on the terrace, formally dressed and without Claudine. Which was a disappointment in some ways, useful in others.

He grabbed a couple of glasses from the sideboard in the dining room before sidling up to the table.

'Mind if I join you?'

Jack glanced up. 'Be my guest.'

Cecil poured two generous measures. Then he removed a silver case from his pocket, which he opened with a theatrical flourish to show a row of plump cigars. He offered one to Jack but the American hesitated.

'Don't worry,' Cecil reassured him. 'They're imported. There are certain things you don't rely on the Italians for.'

Smiling, Jack took one and accepted a light. A few minutes passed in comfortable silence as they puffed away.

Cecil said, 'You were telling me about your connections in the art world.'

'Was I?'

'I can tell you have an eye for it. Is it your line of work?'

'I buy and sell a bit.'

'You have a gallery?'

Jack shook his head. 'Private clients.'

Cecil paused before asking the question to which he most wanted an answer. 'And you think they might be willing to purchase some of Lucian's work?'

'My interest was entirely personal,' replied Jack, flatly.

'Oh.' Cecil tried not to sound disappointed.

Jack went on. 'There's not much money to be made

from anything painted this century. Unless you're Matisse, of course.'

'Of course.'

'Now, the Renaissance ...' Jack said, his face suddenly alight. Cecil noticed that he pronounced it 'ree-naaay-suns'. Bloody Americans. 'That's a whole different ball game.'

'Really?'

'It's what paid for the Bugatti.'

Cecil felt a stirring in his chest. A rush of animal excitement. 'The Old Masters?'

'They're selling like hot cakes in the States. Museums. Old Money. Wall Street bankers. They just can't get enough of 'em.'

'How fascinating.'

'Of course, the smart money is in authentication. If you're paying a hundred grand for a Tintoretto ... Well, you want to be sure you're getting what you've paid for.'

'They pay for your seal of approval?'

'Not mine, buddy.' He glanced at Cecil, peering between threads of cigar smoke. 'But I have the best guy in the business.'

*

Of course, Danioni told himself, it was a very smart place, this Hotel Portofino. There was no denying the English understood the market. Understood it better, perhaps, than some Italian hoteliers.

Take this bell pull, he thought, as he tugged at the rope by the front door. How many hotels nowadays would have an old-fashioned bell like this? They would have electric bells and be proud of it. 'See my new electric bell! Press the button and marvel.' The English, however ... They did things the old way, said that this was the best – and people believed them.

He wondered, as he introduced himself as Mr Danioni from the Communal Council, if Mrs Ainsworth had noticed the badge on his lapel – a National Fascist Party badge with the Italian tricolore and the Roman 'fasces'. He thought he saw her eyes dart in its direction, but it was hard to be sure.

Having ascertained that she spoke some Italian, he asked if there was somewhere they could speak in private.

She looked taken aback. 'My husband isn't here, I'm afraid,' she said. 'He'll be back later.'

Danioni had been obliged to tell her that it wasn't her husband he wanted to speak to. It was her.

She led him into the room she called a library on account of its bookshelves, where a young lady and a girl of around six were reading. The look on Mrs Ainsworth's face must have communicated the gravity of the situation, because the other two left the room abruptly.

'Your daughter?' he asked.

'Our nanny.'

'Ah. The Great British Nanny. The rock on which an empire is built, no?'

Mrs Ainsworth ignored this comment. 'What can I help you with, Mr Danioni?'

And so, to business. He reached into the inside pocket of his suit jacket. He took out a letter – her letter to the man she called Henry – and laid it on the table. 'It is a delicate matter.'

Mrs Ainsworth looked at the envelope warily before picking it up. He could sense her fear. 'Who gave this to you?'

Danioni shrugged. But, of course, he knew very well. He had intercepted Paola as she walked to the post box. She was a sensible woman – such a shame about her husband – and knew better than to withhold anything from him. Why bring unnecessary problems upon yourself and your family?

'There is nothing here in this place I do not know about,' he said now.

'This is a private letter.' Mrs Ainsworth was becoming agitated.

'Indeed. Full of private sentiments. It will be *una grande disgrazia*, no? If this . . . how you say? Falls into the wrong hands.'

He had expected her to crumple. Instead, she drew herself up to her full, considerable height and said, 'Then I must thank you, Signor Danioni. For returning it.'

Danioni rose too, acknowledging her attempt to terminate the interview. She led the way to the door, but as she showed him out, he spoke again. 'I hope . . . the many letters you write, that they have reached their destination.'

At this Mrs Ainsworth brought the door shut behind her. She stood before him with her arms folded. 'What exactly is it that you want?'

A smile spread across Danioni's face. He loved the moment of comprehension. Some people took longer than others.

'What we all want, Signora Ainsworth.'

4

Bella sat at her dressing table in her nightgown, brushing out the tangles.

The night before, while Cecil slept like a dead man, she had crept to her room and opened the shutters – to let out evil spirits, she told herself – and inhale the fresh scents of the Italian night.

Then she had slipped back into bed beside him, knowing he would be withering if, after one of their rare nights together, he didn't find her there in the morning.

The shutters were still open, but this time they let in the glaring sun and the racket of cicadas. A fly crawled sleepily up the wall before coming to a halt at the cornice. Bella watched it, half hypnotized. Then her eyes drifted back to the mirror. The reflection showed Cecil, naked, looming behind her like a shadow.

'Are we friends again, Bella?'

In her dream daze, she didn't quite hear him.

'I said, "Are we friends again?"'

'Yes, Cecil.' Reluctantly, she turned to face him.

'So, say it.' His voice was pleading.

She held back a sigh. 'We're friends again.'

'Good. You know I can't stand it when I'm in bad odour with you.'

He placed a cigarette in his mouth and prepared to light it. Bella grimaced. 'Must you?'

Making a show of mastering his displeasure, Cecil complied.

As she opened the top drawer to return her brush, Bella saw with alarm that a letter from Henry was sitting there. She had thrust it there in haste, intending to lock it in her box when she had a spare moment. She just had time to pat the drawer shut – ever so casually – before Cecil wandered across and started caressing her shoulder, kissing her neck.

Their eyes met in the mirror.

'It was nice, Bellakins, wasn't it?'

'Very nice.' She meant it too. He was a good lover, solid and dependable.

'Then why do you look like such a wet weekend?'

'I don't know. I have things on my mind.'

Cecil sighed and dropped his hand from her shoulder. 'Don't tell me.'

She couldn't bear the expression on his face. 'I know you hate talking about money.'

'I don't hate talking about it. I hate all the unpleasantness that comes from not having enough of it.'

Bella rose, intending to go to her dressing room, but he stopped her, taking her in his arms. 'Of course, there's an easy solution to this, sweetheart.'

She shook her head. 'There's nothing easy about asking my father for money.'

'There you go again.'

'He's been incredibly generous. More than generous, in fact.'

'He's paid out precisely what was agreed in our marriage settlement. Not a penny more or less.'

'But none of which has come to us.'

At this Cecil let go of her, exasperated. 'Don't start that. You can't blame me for blasted death duties. The estate, the house, everything . . . It will all come to Lucian in the end.'

'Assuming he ever wants to go back.'

And why would he? she thought. It was a horrible place. Like a mausoleum.

Cecil tried another tack. 'Your father . . . You're all he's got. He adores you. Only wants you to be happy. He doesn't begrudge a brass farthing you spend on this place.'

'I can't keep going cap in hand to him.'

'That's utter foolishness.' His voice was raised now, his face red. 'He has money coming out of his ears!'

'What's foolish about not wanting to be indebted to someone?'

'But you already are! He paid for every cushion and candlestick in this bloody place.'

'And I've promised to pay him back.'

'He's not expecting to see a penny.'

'Which is why I'm determined he will.'

They had reached the same impasse as always. So, it was fitting, Bella thought, that Cecil should respond as he always did – dramatically, as if it were he who had triumphed, not her.

'Swallow your damned pride, Bella.' He spat out the words with full-blooded contempt before leaving the room and slamming the door behind him.

Why? she thought, perching on the edge of the bed. *Why can't he be kinder? The way he was when I first knew him?*

*

Nish was strolling through the gardens, looking for somewhere to have a quiet smoke, when he saw Claudine – the woman everyone had been talking about.

She was sitting cross-legged on some sort of rattan mat, wearing loose-fitting silk pyjamas. Embarrassed to catch her unawares, he was about to retreat when he realised she had noticed him. She clasped her palms together and made a little bow.

Nish hadn't been among the crowd who witnessed her arrival. But he had heard all about the scene from Lucian.

'She's a singer, I think,' he had said. 'Or maybe a dancer. She knows how to make an impression, at any rate.'

'Namaste,' she said now.

The word made Nish jump. 'I'm sorry?'

A cloud of alarm passed over her face. 'Did I say it wrong?'

'No! No, please. Not at all. It's just the first Hindi word I've heard in … quite a time.'

'Well, it's the only one I know.' She smiled. 'That's all he taught me.'

She resumed her yoga pose as Nish took a seat on the garden bench beside her.

Nish asked, 'And who is he, if I might enquire?'

'The Maharaja of Jaipur's brother.' She didn't look round, her back straight.

'You've been to Jaipur?' This was more than Nish had, he realised with a flush of shame.

'Hell, no!' She still didn't move. 'He came to see my show.'

'In America?'

'In Paris.' Claudine finally broke her pose, eased herself into a standing position. She came over to sit beside Nish, silk spooling across the bench. Her toenails were painted bright red. Her skin, several shades darker than his own, was smooth and shiny. Without asking, she plucked the cigarette from his fingers and took a long drag before blowing a perfect smoke ring into the air. 'I haven't been home since the war.'

'Neither have I.'

She handed the cigarette back with a smile. They were both enjoying the faint but gleeful air of truancy.

'And how do you find Italy?'

She laughed. 'You mean, how does Italy find me? Italy would like to arrest me on the spot. They just haven't got round to passing a law against me.'

Nish gave an inward shudder. 'I have a feeling they soon might.'

She rose and hoisted herself into a downward dog, her long legs and arms stretched out perfectly straight. 'It isn't just Italy, though, is it? Let's not kid ourselves.' Her voice came out muffled. She paused in her pose and glanced naughtily up from beneath her armpit. 'I'm sure you don't any more than I do.'

It was odd, Nish thought. Most men – or so he assumed – would be driven wild by proximity to this extraordinarily lithe body. He could see that it met all the traditional criteria for attractiveness. And yet here he was, his senses absorbed instead by the solid blue of the sea and the dry rustle of the wind through the palm trees.

Claudine nestled back down, crossing her legs. 'He was my mentor, in case you're wondering.'

'The Maharaja's brother?'

'He offered me a pearl as big as a duck egg. But I wasn't able to oblige him. So, he had to settle for giving me yoga lessons instead.'

'That was very honourable of you,' Nish conceded, dipping his head. Even though he wasn't attracted, it was still fun to flirt.

'Me, honourable?' Claudine laughed. 'That's a good one.' She nodded to the ground at her side. 'You want to join me, honey?'

'It's not really my thing.'

'Come on.' She beckoned him. 'You'll catch on soon enough.'

Nish hesitated for one last moment, then in a burst of spontaneity slipped off his spats and gingerly got into position on all fours. He was worried about marking or ripping his trousers, which were new.

'Something I noticed in Cannes,' she said, 'is how they all want skin like ours.'

'"They"?'

100

'White folk.' She glanced at her own skin. 'It wasn't the fashion, but now ...' She shrugged. 'Now it is, or seems to be. Women lie there, grilling like steaks, covered in oil and dyes. When they get up to eat, all they talk about is how brown they are or how much browner someone else is. They're so desperate to tan that they burn themselves. One night, Jack and I went to the Restaurant des Ambassadeurs. The woman at the next table had raw red patches on her arms and bandages on her legs. I said to her, "That looks painful". And do you know what she said in reply?'

Nish shook his head.

'She said, "It's all right for you."'

They both laughed.

'My grandmother died a slave,' Claudine continued. 'And there's a reason my skin isn't darker. But hey, it's all right for me.'

'They want to be brown,' said Nish. 'But they don't want to be us.'

She nodded. 'Exactly.'

If Nish could have chosen the most propitious moment for Lucian and Rose to appear, it would not have been now. But here they came, walking side by side.

Love's young dream.

Rose was dressed sportily, in a golf-jersey with a woven straw satchel dangling from her arm and a patterned blue scarf in her hair. Nish thought dismissively of a child rummaging in a dressing-up box.

'What's this?' Lucian asked, arriving beside them. 'Callisthenics?'

Nish rolled his eyes. 'It's yoga, you fool.'

'Room for two little ones?'

Claudine smiled. 'The more the merrier.'

Lucian looked at Rose. 'What do you think?'

Before she could answer, Julia's voice rang out like a bell at a funeral. 'Rose? Where are you?'

'I'd better not,' she said.

'Really?' Claudine's tone was politely incredulous.

'Yes.' She turned to walk inside.

'I'll be here every morning,' Claudine called after her. 'In case you change your mind.'

*

It wasn't clear to Constance why Julia and Rose were moving out of the Epsom Suite. It looked beautiful to her. The wallpaper was clearly new, but its delicate patterning – which a person had to go close up to notice – gave the impression that it had faded over the course of decades in the slow-turning sunlight. As a result, the room felt warm and homely despite its grandeur. It hadn't been designed to shut her out like so many of the rooms in grand houses she had worked in. Such rooms she had generally seen from a low vantage point – on her knees, clearing out and laying the fire first thing in the morning.

Not anymore.

Bella had asked her to accompany her so that she could learn how to ready a room. Constance wondered aloud if the Drummond-Wards were leaving.

Bella had replied, 'Goodness me, no! They've just asked to be moved to another room. Although I'm not quite sure why.'

Constance looked around. 'I've never seen a room quite so beautiful, Mrs Ainsworth.'

'Thank you, Constance. Let's hope Mr and Mrs Wingfield agree with you.'

Alarmed by the pained expression on Bella's face, Constance rushed to reassure her. 'I'm sure they will,' she said.

Paola was already changing the bed as they arrived. When Bella greeted her, she responded by bobbing an inelegant curtsey. Constance found herself transfixed by the other woman's curly black hair and heavy, voluptuous mouth.

What was it about her?

Paola's confidence in her body expressed itself in behaviour that looked defiant but was simply blithe and unselfconscious. It said, *This is me and this is how I live.*

For the first time in her life, Constance understood that she had been bred to lack confidence. That was what it meant to be in service, to be working-class in England at this moment in history. Absolutely no confidence.

Paola was a widow, Bella had explained earlier. Constance wondered what she had been and done when her husband was alive. Had she been a servant then? Or did a whole other life stretch out behind her? She didn't look old enough to have done very much.

Bella spoke to Paola in Italian, then translated for Constance. 'I've told her that you'll be helping her. She seems to like the idea. I'm not sure how much English she understands. But, you never know.'

As soon as Bella left the room Paola looked across at Constance and winked emphatically. 'You never know,' she said, in thickly-accented English.

Constance's mouth fell open. 'You *do* speak English!'

'A little. Signor Lucian . . .'

'Master Ainsworth?'

'He give me . . .' She paused, searching for the right word. 'Lessons?'

'*Si*. English lessons.' She giggled and Constance found herself laughing too. There was something infectious about Paola's humour.

But then things took an odd turn, and Constance remembered something her mother had said to watch out for – that Italians could be very changeable, like April weather.

Constance had taken hold of one corner of an eiderdown and was helping Paola to shake it out when she said, 'I have lessons too.'

Paola stopped and looked at her sharply. 'Lessons?'

'*Si*.'

'With Signor Lucian?'

'*Si*.'

The atmosphere chilled. Paola frowned and gave the eiderdown a disapproving tug – so hard that it almost fell out of Constance's hands.

'I don't understand,' said Constance, gazing across the expanse of the bed. 'What did I say?'

But all of a sudden Paola's English had dried up.

*

Lucian felt obliged to follow Rose inside. But he was starting to tire of this unusual situation.

If you knew you were being coerced and belittled, why would you tolerate it? However placid Rose was on the surface, he thought, she must have been fuming inside.

Certainly, it was no surprise, upon entering the drawing room, to see her standing forlornly by the window, her tennis outfit hanging loose off her tiny frame. She was staring out onto the garden, where Claudine and Nish were still chatting and laughing over their yoga lesson.

Julia was sitting at a low table, reading a travel guide.

Her reptile eyes flicked up. 'You look flushed,' she said.

'I've been having a yoga lesson.'

'Yoga?' She managed to make the word sound both whimsical and grotesque.

'It's a sort of . . . stationary gymnastics,' Lucian explained, suspecting Julia knew this full well. 'The Indians have been at it for centuries.'

'Mr Sengupta has been teaching you?'

'Mrs Turner, actually.'

As if on cue, the sound of Claudine's laughter drifted up from outside.

'She seems a woman of many talents,' Julia observed.

'Apparently so.'

She looked back down at her book, but Lucian had more to say. 'If I may be so bold . . .'

'Yes?'

'I was thinking . . . hoping . . . that with your permission,

Rose might accompany me to look around the town later. And perhaps visit the beach afterwards. For a painting lesson.'

Julia's head swivelled to where Rose was standing at the window. 'Is this something you've discussed?'

'No, Mama.' She sounded panicked.

'You'd be very welcome to join us,' offered Lucian.

'I would insist upon it.' She closed her book. 'But won't it be ridiculously hot?'

'There's always a breeze by the sea. And plenty of shade.'

'I should want tea there. A proper tea.'

Lucian nodded. 'That can easily be arranged.'

'And staff to serve it.'

'Of course.'

Julia frowned, as if she were weighing up options. 'Perhaps the child would enjoy it.'

'Rose?' Lucian frowned, confused.

'I meant your niece. Lottie.'

'Ah. Of course. It's a kind suggestion. I'll talk to my sister.'

'Rose will enjoy it too, I'm sure. Though I fear your efforts will be wasted. She's completely devoid of artistic talent.'

At this jibe, Rose flushed with anger. Watching her thin fingers flex, Lucian braced himself for what he hoped would be a defiant riposte that put Julia squarely in her place.

The reply, when it came, was measured. But there was method in her restraint. 'You always say I should take every opportunity to improve myself, Mama.'

'I do,' Julia acknowledged.

'So, then. I think I should go. I think I *shall* go.' She looked at Lucian. She was doing this for him.

The silence that followed this statement was tense and expectant. It seemed to last an eternity, long enough for Lucian to feel uncomfortable, for in truth he disliked witnessing other people's rows, having endured so many of his parents' as a child.

Rose shifted her gaze to her mother. The two women stared at each other. Rose's lips tightened and an obstinate line formed between her eyes.

Julia's scrutiny held Rose's face as if in a spring of steel. Then, quite suddenly and with a dry smile, she yielded and looked away, over towards the clock on the mantelpiece. 'Very well,' she said. 'You are an adult woman. You must seek improvement where you think best.'

'Wonderful,' said Lucian. 'Then, that's sorted.'

Grateful for an excuse to leave the room, he made straight for the cupboard beneath the stairs where he stored his painting equipment.

As he shuffled the crate towards him, tugging at it on either side, he bumped his head against the low door frame. 'Damn it,' he said, then looked up to see his father watching him from the stairs above. In his crisply ironed cream linen suit he looked faintly absurd – the oldest dandy in town.

'Father,' he managed. 'It's you.'

'It's me.' Cecil looked from the easels and paints to his son. 'You know this nonsense will have to stop sooner or later, don't you?'

'Nonsense?'

Cecil gestured to the paintings on the wall. 'It's not worth a penny. Any of it. I have it on good authority.'

'They're worth something to me,' said Lucian, then regretted it because it sounded so weak and ineffectual. Just the sort of thing his father expected him to say. 'I'm taking Miss Drummond-Ward for a painting lesson. At the beach. I thought you'd be pleased.'

Cecil pondered this information, rubbing a hand over the polished mahogany of the bannister. 'That's something, I suppose. Well, then. You'd better not keep the lady waiting.'

*

The eggs bobbed gently in the frothing water. Constance put the lid back on the saucepan. *Another few minutes*, she thought.

She had spent much of the morning with Lottie, being shown toys and books and oddments such as a moth she had caught in a jar. Lottie had held it up so that Constance could see its huge wings closed over its furry body.

'You need a hole in the lid,' Constance told her. 'Otherwise, it can't breathe.' She'd shown the child how to hammer a nail into the lid, borrowing equipment from Francesco.

'This is just an ordinary moth,' Lottie had said. 'Next, I want to capture a hawk moth. They're huge, like humming-birds! And they have a skull-and-crossbones pattern across their wings.'

She was a sweet, likeable child, round-eyed and healthy, not especially demanding. Children like Lottie were used to seeing little of their parents. And, of course, she had no siblings – which was freeing for her but also confusing, like being queen of an unknown country.

Constance wondered what it must be like, having a whole room to yourself at that age. A whole house like this to roam around in. Would you grow up thinking you had a God-given right to space and freedom, no matter what?

The mother, Alice, was a funny one. Chilly and brittle. Perhaps she'd warm up over time.

The kitchen was cool, like a furnished vault. She was glad of it, unaccustomed as she was to the Italian heat. Humming to herself, Constance slipped one foot rhythmically back and forth across the polished red-tiled floor. She checked the eggs again. Nearly ready.

She had enjoyed spending time with Lottie – it didn't feel too much like work – but inevitably it made her sad, because it set her thinking about Tommy. Kitchen duties were a welcome distraction. She remembered Betty's remark about hard work and good food restoring you to health. That was true, and really meant something coming from Betty, who had been through so much. Constance's mother had always said, 'I don't know how Betty has coped. What we've been through, it's nowt in comparison.'

Betty was cutting thin, even slices from a loaf she'd baked earlier in the morning.

'What are you putting in the sandwiches, Betty?' Constance called over.

'Good question. *La lingua di . . .*' Betty hesitated. 'Now, wait a minute. Mrs Ainsworth wrote it down for me.' She fished into her apron for a shopping list, producing it with a flourish. '*La lingua di . . . vitello.*'

'And what's that when it's at home?'

'Veal tongue. It's a local delicacy.'

'We have tongue at home sometimes. Not veal, though. Ox.'

'I like a bit of ox tongue,' said Betty. 'Tell me, are you excited? To see the beach?'

Constance shrugged. 'I'm only there to fetch and carry.'

'You might get to dip a toe in.'

'I'm sure Mrs Drummond-Ward will keep me far too busy.'

Betty sliced the crusts off the sandwiches. 'She's a proper dragon, that one.'

'Betty!' Constance put a hand to her mouth to catch her laughter.

'What? She is! The way she bullies that poor girl.'

'Rose is very beautiful.'

'Well, that's as may be. Silly little ninny. She wouldn't say boo to a goose.' She wrapped the sandwiches in greaseproof paper, then held the packet up for Constance's inspection. 'Still, I should hold me tongue. No pun intended!'

She burst out laughing at her own joke – so raucously that Constance quickly succumbed too.

As she started work on the scones, however, Betty's mood became more reflective. 'She'll be boss of us all soon enough.'

'Rose will be?'

'Haven't you worked it out? Her and Master Lucian?'

'They're in love?'

Betty snorted. 'There'll be plenty of time to worry about love. After they're married.'

Constance fished the eggs from the pan with a slotted spoon and placed them in a bowl of cold water to stop them cooking any further. 'It's all agreed, then?'

'No. But it will be before summer's over. If Mr Ainsworth's got anything to do with it, at any rate.'

*

Cecil strolled purposefully, taking care not to scuff his shoes on the cobbles or tread in anything unpleasant. He had chosen what to wear with care. Clothes communicated so much, after all. Take that, new nanny. She was pretty enough in a pointy-faced sort of way, but her dresses looked as if they were made out of sackcloth.

He pushed his way through the narrow, surprisingly crowded streets of Portofino town until he reached the telegram office, which was just behind La Piazzetta in a squat, single-storey building the colour of crumbling shortbread. A sign on the door said 'Chiuso' but in Cecil's experience, closure in Italy was often a starting point for negotiation, especially if you had a wallet full of notes. He knocked loudly, but nobody answered.

Edging back to avoid the pigeons flapping on the stone steps, Cecil lit a cigarette and pondered his next move.

Italy's backwardness could be infuriating. Obviously, the Italians were addicted to their after-lunch nap, their siesta. They justified it on the grounds of heat, even though everybody knew it was only an excuse to do nothing for several hours. But – he checked his wristwatch – it was still morning. Twenty-past eleven!

This was the kind of thing his friends in the colonial service were always complaining about. In these parts, it was impossible to get what you wanted, when you wanted it. Absurd!

A woman walked past him. Middle-aged, Italian. Some sort of gammy leg. Cecil said '*Telefono*?' and mimed putting a receiver to his ear, but she ignored him. So bloody rude.

It was then that he saw a wiry little man standing in the doorway of the municipal building across the way. He was fingering his cufflinks. Something about him looked familiar. Had he been up to the hotel for some reason? Cecil wasn't sure. The man raised his hat in greeting and Cecil noticed two younger men hovering behind him, taut muscles clearly visible beneath their black shirts.

'Mr Ainsworth,' the man called out. 'You require *assistenza*?'

'I was hoping to find a telephone,' he called back.

The man laughed and gave an exaggerated shrug. 'We are poor Italians. We marvel at you English and your inventions.'

'Try telling that to Mr Marconi,' said Cecil. It always paid to flatter the natives. He tipped his hat and started to turn away.

But the man was nothing if not persistent. 'One moment, Signore.' Cecil turned back reluctantly to see the man gesture towards the open door of the building. 'If you come with me, I may be able to help.'

Tipping his hat to the black-shirted heavies, who remained outside, Cecil followed the man up the stairs and into his office, which was surprisingly spacious, with a table and desk and a large fan on a stand. A row of pot plants wilted on the windowsill. On the wall facing the desk was a framed photograph of Benito Mussolini. As usual, the Italian Prime Minister looked slightly deranged, with his clenched fists and proud, jutting chin.

'Ah,' said Cecil. 'The great man himself.'

'A great man indeed.'

'I don't suppose you'd lend him to us? To crack some English heads together?'

The man looked at him blankly.

Cecil shuffled. 'Perhaps not.'

On the desk stood a shiny black telephone. 'Please,' said the man. 'Take as long as you need.'

Cecil eased himself into the chair behind the desk. 'You're very kind. I'll pay you, of course.'

The man made a show of taking offence at such a suggestion.

'But I insist,' said Cecil.

'And I insist. Also.' With a click of his heels he produced a card which he laid before Cecil. 'Vincenzo Danioni. At your service.'

'Cecil Ainsworth. At yours.'

They shook hands, then Danioni left the room. Cecil gave him a few moments to scarper before producing a calfskin pocket book and finding the telephone number he needed.

After the usual rigmarole with an operator, the butler picked up the receiver. And after what felt like hours it found its way into the hands of Edmund, his brother – Viscount Heddon, to give him the formal title he dined off, because honestly, what else did he have?

'Cecil? Is that you?' The line was hissy, his brother's voice faint and subaquatic.

'It's me.'

'From Italy?'

'Yes, Edmund. All the way from Italy.'

'Well, I'll be damned.'

Cecil leant back in the chair and put his feet up on the desk. 'How is the old place?'

'Oh, you know. Creaking under the strain a bit.'

'And Margot?'

'Happy when she's in the saddle.' Edmund paused, clearly bemused by the unexpectedness of the call. 'To what do I owe this pleasure?'

'I'll get straight to the point.'

'I wish you would.'

'Do you still have Grandpapa's Rubens?'

'The large blonde with the mirror? In the West Wing sitting room?'

Cecil examined his fingernails. 'The very same.'

'Still gathering dust among the ancestors, last time I checked.'

'Well, then. Crate it up and send it over, there's a good fellow.'

'And why would I do that?'

114

'Because I may know someone who wants to buy it.'

'For more than it costs to send?'

'Much more. Enough to keep the tax man off your back for a year or two.'

Cecil was enjoying this – being in a position to dispense largesse. It didn't happen very often.

'Of course,' Edmund pointed out, 'we only have the old chap's word for it. That it's a Rubens.'

Cecil had been expecting this. 'Not for very much longer, I hope.'

'What do you mean?'

'I've found an American. He knows about these things.'

'Well, well,' said Edmund. 'Keep me posted.'

Cecil assured him he would.

He was about to replace the receiver – his brother had already terminated the call at his end – when he heard a curious clicking sound on the line.

Faulty connection, probably. Nothing to worry about.

On his way out, he looked for Danioni so that he could thank him again for his generosity. But he didn't seem to be anywhere, so Cecil headed to the bar on the corner.

A celebratory snifter was definitely in order.

*

In the middle of the hall sat a neat pile of items needed for the expedition to the beach. Alice noted the spade and bucket and thought how nice it would be for Lottie. Then she took in the easels and canvases, the brushes and pencils and sketchbooks, and her mouth flattened. Such a lot of . . . paraphernalia.

She shared her father's ambivalence towards Lucian's painting. It was a louche, ill-bred habit; acceptable as a form of therapy, but nothing more. At the same time, she was self-aware enough to suspect that this indicated failings on her own part – both the lack of any equivalent talent and a rigidity that increasingly had the accent of a dogma. Unable to unclench herself, she had made a virtue of her shortcomings, ascribing the bitter, ungenerous results to grief. She knew she looked older than her years, so she dressed older, so she looked older . . . It was a circular conundrum.

Turning, she saw Lady Latchmere bustle out of the drawing room rather faster than anyone might have expected. Alice felt sorry for her, despite her rudeness at dinner. She sensed they had a certain amount in common. Respect for etiquette. Impatience with faddish new ways of doing things.

She would reach out to her, she thought, and surprise everyone by securing the older woman's involvement in activities no one would expect her to tolerate.

She called out to her: 'Lady Latchmere!'

Lady Latchmere stiffened and turned. 'Yes? What is it?'

'Would you like to come on the trip to Paraggi beach this afternoon? It's a wonderful beach, I hear. The only sandy beach in the vicinity.' In fact, Alice had never been to Paraggi and had resisted all Lottie's entreaties to take her.

A look of horror came over Lady Latchmere's face. 'Gracious, no. I can't abide sand.'

Alice smiled sympathetically. 'Perhaps a visit to church on Sunday might suit us both a bit better.'

But the reaction this provoked was even more extreme. Lady Latchmere's voice rose a whole octave. 'To church? In Italy?'

Alice was mortified. 'I'm sorry,' she said. 'I assumed . . .'

'I have no greater consolation than religion, dear. But only if it's the right sort. All that smoke and popery!'

Claudine, arriving in the hall in a state of expensive undress, had evidently overheard the end of their conversation. 'Any port in a storm, I always say,' she said, winking at Alice.

Alice decided to ignore this over-familiarity, which she had read was a feature of Americans. 'Are you a regular churchgoer, Mrs Turner?'

'Nothing about me is regular, honey.' Claudine looked very deliberately at Lady Latchmere. 'But a spot of confession. That's always good for the soul. Right?'

Afraid of how Lady Latchmere might respond to this provocation, Alice wandered outside to where Constance, Paola and Francesco had started loading the boxes and various loose items into the carriage. Lucian was supervising, being typically fussy about the way the easels were laid. Off to the side stood Julia and Rose, with their parasols and impatience.

'Who's this, then?' asked Constance, wiping the sweat from her forehead and nodding towards the end of the drive where another carriage had appeared. The whole hushed and brooding group turned.

The carriage drew up neatly. Then the driver dismounted and opened the door. Out tumbled an athletic-looking young man, with a shock of black hair offset by piercing blue eyes. Then a woman emerged – his wife, Alice assumed. Her high, sharp cheekbones contrasted oddly with the plainness of her red dress.

Francesco broke away to fetch the bags as the couple rushed inside before any onlookers had a chance even to say hello. They had an air of being put-upon, like movie stars harassed by photographers on the Croisette.

'So those are the Wingfields,' said Alice, who remembered seeing their name in the bookings register.

Out of everyone, she thought, Lucian seemed the most impressed. To a baffled Rose and Julia he exclaimed, 'I can't believe it's him! Plum Wingfield!'

'Who?' asked Rose.

'Is he one of the Suffolk Wingfields?' wondered Julia.

'I haven't a clue,' said Lucian. 'I only know he's a tennis player. A terrific one at that.'

Julia and Rose looked as nonplussed as Alice felt. Lucian was such a boy sometimes. Did anyone really care about tennis? No, yet on and on he droned.

'He nearly won the Davis Cup for us a few years back!'

'I'll take your word for it,' said Julia.

*

At least the Wingfields seemed happy with the Epsom Suite.

'This view is stupendous,' said Plum, leaning out of the window. He had impeccable Etonian manners and the politician's habit of looking deep into your eyes when he spoke to you.

'Isn't it?' said the wife, who had introduced herself as

Lizzie. She was harder to read, Bella thought; possibly older than Plum. She seemed tired from the journey, whereas Plum was bright and bouncy. 'And this room ...' She glanced around. 'It's so beautifully done. There's everything one could want.'

'There's probably a drinks cabinet,' said Plum, 'if you look hard enough.'

Lizzie said nothing. Bella pretended she hadn't heard. Which was easy, because she had glanced out of the window and been entirely distracted by the sight of Cecil walking up the drive in the company of that Italian man, Danioni. She felt a surge of panic. How on earth had they found each other? No good could possibly come of such an alliance.

'If you'll excuse me,' she said, 'there's someone I urgently need to speak to.'

'Don't worry about us,' said Plum. 'We'll make our own fun.'

* * *

Cecil and Danioni were on the terrace by the time Bella found them. She hated Danioni being here, in the hotel. He felt like a pollutant.

'There you are,' said Cecil. 'May I introduce Mr Danioni.'

The Italian removed his hat with an ostentatious flourish that put Bella in mind of Uriah Heep. 'It is my honour, Signora Ainsworth.'

She gave the merest acknowledgement civility demanded. 'If you'll forgive me, Mr Danioni, I need to ask Cecil something.' Indicating to Cecil that she wished to speak to him alone, she left the terrace and waited in the dining room.

119

J.P. O'Connell

When finally Cecil joined her, Bella hissed, 'What is *he* doing here?'

'Danioni? He's really being most obliging. I thought the least we could do was show him some hospitality in return.'

'Hospitality?'

'You know. Tea. A sandwich or two. A bit of Betty's cake. Let him think he's an Englishman for an afternoon.'

She looked out at Danioni, who was pacing up and down the terrace, pretending not to be the least intrigued. 'Has he ... asked you for anything?'

'Not a sausage. He let me telephone home entirely free of charge.'

'You know he's a ...' She raised her eyebrow, but Cecil looked blank. 'He's a fascist, Cecil.' She tapped a finger on her lapel where a badge might be, one featuring the tell-tale symbol of a bundle of sticks and an axe.

'Well, yes. Possibly. But you know what I always say – better than the damned reds.'

'We agreed we should do our utmost to stay out of local politics.'

He looked dismissive. 'You never know. He could prove useful.'

'Lady Latchmere might come across him!'

'They probably have more in common than you think. So, then.' He clapped his hands together. 'Tea, it is! Will you put in an order?' She turned away. 'Oh,' he added, 'and Bellakins. Ask Albani if he'd like to join us. It might jolly the conversation along a bit.'

120

Bella realised she hadn't seen Count Albani recently. She resolved to seek him out, but hoped than when it came to Danioni he would decide to keep himself to himself.

*

The heat on the beach was truly unbearable. Only the occasional gust of wind provided any relief as Constance, Francesco and Paola worked to set everything up for the picnic party. Each item of furniture had required a separate trip down from the road where the carriage had dropped them off.

They unfolded the table and chairs. Constance held the beach umbrella in place while Francesco dug a hole for it in the sand. Then Paola made a nest of rocks at its base to keep it upright. By the time they started laying the table for afternoon tea they were exhausted.

Lucian had taken Julia and Rose into Portofino to show them the sights. She imagined them wandering through rose-filled gardens before stopping to admire a street artist; exploring cool, shadowy churches smelling of candles and ancient prayers. Would Rose enjoy such things?

Sweat was beading on her forehead. Paola was fanning herself with her hand. Clearly, she thought it absurd that English people wanted to picnic on the beach in the full heat of the day.

The others soon arrived, picking their way stiffly down the path, Lucian leading them.

'Goodness, I'm hot!' exclaimed Rose from beneath her parasol. Then she noticed the laid table with its silverware sparkling in the sun. 'How delightful. All this tourism has made me hungry.'

'I wish I could say the same,' said Julia, waiting for Paola to seat her. 'I find the sun suppresses my appetite.'

Lottie ran up to Constance. She was beaming with excitement. 'Are you going to eat with us?' she asked. 'Will you sit beside me?'

'Not just now,' she whispered. 'I'm on duty.' She winked.

'It's rather irregular,' Julia observed, 'having a nanny who is also a maid.'

'Is it?' Lucian sat back, while Paola poured him a glass of lemonade. 'Why maintain these old distinctions?'

'So that we all know where we are,' said Julia. 'And the servants know where they are.'

Constance felt a surge of anger. Betty had been so right about this woman.

'We went up to the church,' Lottie told Constance, slipping a hand into hers. 'Inside, it was cold and smelly. What's that funny sweet smell in churches?'

'Incense,' said Lucian.

'Why don't we have it at home?'

Julia sipped her lemonade, grimacing at its tartness. 'Because at home there are episcopal restrictions on its use.'

Lottie frowned. 'What does that mean?'

'That we're not Catholics,' said Lucian. 'Now let's get started on the sandwiches.'

*

After helping clear up tea, Constance played with Lottie on a damp patch of sand. Lucian set up two easels next to each other. The idea was to paint watercolours of the seascape – the glistening sea, the boats silhouetted in the distance, the green-tufted headland.

Rose sat beside him, holding a brush as if it were a loaded gun. He had to keep leaning over and showing her what to do. Constance overheard him giving her tips. 'We sketch in pencil first, then colour it in with a wash of paint. The sky will need a faint cobalt, then – here – a more neutral tint will help the foliage to breathe a little . . .'

'It all sounds very complicated,' said Rose.

Lottie threw a ball so that it landed just behind the easels. As she went to collect it Constance sneaked a look at Rose's sketch and saw immediately that she had no eye, no eye at all. What, she had produced was crude and naive, like a child's drawing.

Constance had expected this knowledge to give her pleasure or at least a dull satisfaction. But to her surprise she found that it did not.

Meanwhile, Julia was sitting like Lady Muck, watching a small fishing boat at anchor a short distance offshore. Paola brought her some water, which she accepted without thanks. Julia asked, 'What are they diving for?'

Lucian followed her gaze out to the boat. 'Scallops? Sea urchins, maybe?'

The divers emerged from the water and dumped their catch in the boat. Constance watched them too, and noticed something. She turned and called to Lucian, 'Isn't that Billy?'

Lucian looked through his binoculars. 'I don't believe it! I wondered where he'd been all day.'

Hoots and laughter drifted across from the boat. Billy

wrestled one of his companions before diving into the water with him. It looked great fun and Constance wasn't surprised when Lottie, who had also been watching, asked Lucian if he would take her swimming.

'Not now, Lots. I'm busy.'

'Aw.' Lottie looked as if she was about to cry.

Constance stepped in. 'How about a paddle instead?'

Lucian gave her a grateful look as she dropped down and started to untie her shoelaces.

*

Back at Hotel Portofino, Cecil's tea party in honour of Danioni was in full flow. Bella hated the atmosphere, which felt curdled and false. It also felt overpoweringly male, like some horrible Pall Mall club. Cecil was in his element, smoking one of the foul cigars he reserved for special occasions. He had just told a joke, probably an off-colour one, and was guffawing loudly with Count Albani.

Ironically, it was Danioni who was the first to notice her. He rose to greet her, despite her protestation that he should stay seated, and when Count Albani saw her, he too stood up and asked if she was joining them.

'Sadly, no,' she said. 'I just came to check you were being well looked after.'

'As always,' he said. 'Danioni has been in raptures over the scones.' He indicated the plate, which was empty apart from a scattering of crumbs.

Danioni asked him in Italian, 'What do the English call them?'

Count Albani answered pointedly in English. 'A Fat Rascal, I believe.' He looked to Cecil for confirmation.

But Cecil just said, 'How apt.'

Danioni kissed his fingers at Bella to show his appreciation. '*Squisito*,' he said.

Bella acknowledged the compliment with a thin smile.

'He reckons we could make a bundle, serving afternoon tea to the locals,' said Cecil.

Count Albani nodded. 'I have to agree with him.'

Bella rushed to close the idea down. 'Betty has her hands full, catering for our guests. But I'll be sure to pass on your compliments. Now if you'll excuse me, gentlemen.'

*

Lucian had sketched the basic lines and was now laying down paint, little dabs here and there, building up shade and texture. He was aiming for something gauzy and heat-soaked to evoke how he felt now, which was parched – they had run out of water – slightly burnt and in awe of the elements. Every so often he would break off and study the scene through his binoculars. The shadows creeping across the hillside. The band of white where the sea met the blue sky.

Julia clicked her fingers. 'May I borrow those?'

A please would be nice, thought Lucian. But he handed them over, wiping his hands first to remove the worst of the paint. She had abandoned her shady spot beneath the parasol and was standing up, seemingly intent on examining the other end of the beach.

Lottie had gone off with Rose. Lucian couldn't help

feeling sorry for her. She was clearly thrilled by this profusion of adult playmates and would be devastated when the day ended.

Constance came up behind him. She smelled of sea and sweat. He became conscious of her gazing at his painting, so intensely that he felt suddenly embarrassed.

'Not much to look at,' he said. 'Not yet, at least.'

She said, 'I'd die happy if I could do anything half as well as that.'

The ferocity with which she said this intrigued him. Indicating his sketchbook and a box of pencils he said, 'You're welcome to have a go.'

She was about to say yes, he was sure, when a bare-footed Lottie scampered up the beach towards them with Rose in tow. As she approached, Lucian felt something, a sort of pain in his abdomen, and realised with a shock that it was disappointment.

'Look,' called Lottie. 'Look what Rose found!' He crouched down and she put into his hand a beautiful mother of pearl shell.

'Gosh,' said Lucian. 'It must be worth a fortune, Lots.'

As he handed it back, he and Rose exchanged a knowing smile. He indicated the easel. 'Ready to resume?'

'I suppose so,' she said, without enthusiasm.

'You're doing well,' Lucian heard himself insist.

Rose blushed. 'If you say so.'

Constance backed away. 'Come on, Lottie,' she said. 'Let's leave Lucian and Rose to get on with their painting.'

At that moment there was a cry from Julia. 'My word!'

Alarmed, Lucian put down his brush. 'What is it?'

She beckoned him over and handed him the binoculars. What he saw at the far end of the beach was a small but cluttered tableau. Claudine reclined on a deck chair, limbs arranged in a languorous posture, surrounded by a crowd of onlookers.

'Do you think she needs rescuing?' asked Lucian, lowering the binoculars.

'Heavens, no,' said Julia. 'She'll be selling tickets in a minute.'

*

There was no doubt Claudine looked the epitome of cool in her low-cut swimsuit and Foster Grant round-framed sun-glasses. She was used to attracting attention. It came with being Black and a woman, especially in places like this. So, why not play along? Get something out of it?

She had been doing her best to ignore the crowd that had formed around her. But now, feeling thirsty, she beckoned over two boys in the front row. Lowering her sunglasses had the desired effect of terrifying them. Evidently, they were more comfortable being passive voyeurs.

'It's OK,' she said. 'I won't bite.'

They looked nervously at each other before approaching her.

She fished two coins from her bag and gave them to the taller of the two boys. He had the faint beginnings of a moustache and black hair pushed back over his forehead. '*Due limonate*,' she said. She pointed to herself, then to both of them. '*Una per me. Una per voi.*' One for me. One for you.

The boy nodded and led his companion away, up the slope to the shops.

She had pushed her sunglasses back up her nose and was about to lie down again when she noticed Roberto, the young Italian from the hotel, standing on a wooden diving platform some way out. As she lowered her glasses to get a clearer view of his lean brown body, clad in briefs that left nothing to the imagination, he swallow-dived into the clear blue water.

He stayed beneath the surface for a long time, long enough for Claudine to grow worried. She sat up, bringing her knees up to her chest. But then – miraculously, or so it seemed – he resurfaced. He hauled himself on to the platform and stood there, running his fingers through his wet hair, letting the water drip off him.

He knows I'm here, she thought with a smile. *And that I'm watching him. The question is, what am I going to do about it?*

5

Bella watched through the window as Cecil and Count Albani said their protracted goodbyes to Danioni. Their clubby baritone laughter repulsed her. Why was it that men changed so much – became so coarse and excluding – when you put them together?

Cecil had always been proud of his talent for ingratiation, which arguably exceeded his talent for anything else. Count Albani's civility she excused on the grounds that Danioni was his fellow countryman. All the same, she was disappointed that he hadn't given the sneaky blackmailer the wide berth he deserved. She liked to think he was better than that.

The Count was the first to come inside. He must be so hot, Bella thought, in his charcoal herringbone suit – cut in Savile Row, he had told her proudly. But he never seemed to break a sweat.

'You don't much care for Danioni,' he said, joining her at the window.

'Was it that obvious?'

'Your manners were impeccable.'

'Italy would be heaven if it weren't so full of petty bureaucrats.'

'It would,' he said with a smile. 'Still, you would be wise to tolerate him.'

'Because of his politics?'

'Because men like him enjoy nothing better than making a thorough nuisance of themselves.'

'I'm beginning to realise that.'

Cecil blundered in, puncturing the atmosphere of solemn intimacy. 'So,' he said, cutting across her nerves like a saw, 'how about next Thursday?'

'Thursday?' Bella frowned.

'For our first public tea party. Danioni's promised to drum up some custom.'

'Really, Cecil! That's awfully presumptuous.'

This was exactly what Bella didn't want – Danioni's cronies pouring into the hotel. But Cecil seemed hell bent on making it happen.

'Nonsense,' he said. 'What do you think, Count?'

'The whole town will beat a path to your door. We Italians pretend to despise the perfidious English. But we aspire to be just like you.'

Cecil winked at Bella. 'Just as I thought.' He turned to Count Albani. 'Care to join me for a drink?'

'Perhaps in a little while.' Count Albani had a way of making no sound like yes. It was enough to satisfy Cecil, who wandered off without noticing the way the other man lingered solicitously around his wife. Turning to Bella, the Count asked, 'Have I said the wrong thing?'

'No, no. It's a wonderful idea,' she said, faintly.

'I would be delighted to assist with your little project.'

'Your advice is always most welcome.'

'Perhaps Mrs Mays–Smith and I might plan the menu between us?'

She followed Count Albani's rapt gaze through the open door to the reception desk, which was being manned by Alice, her face pale and serious as she filled in the latest batch of forms required by the Italian government. Bella had always prided herself on being attentive where her children were concerned. How had she failed to notice what was going on here?

Her brain whirling, she managed to reply, 'I'm sure Alice will enjoy that.' Though, in truth, she had never been good at predicting what Alice might enjoy. Noticing something was not the same as being able to fix it.

'It will be a perfect union of Italian *gusto* and English refinement,' declared the Count.

Bella tried not to show her unease. 'I can hardly wait,' she said.

*

Julia was snoring in a deckchair, her mouth hanging open. Constance smiled to herself, remembering another of her mother's sayings, 'You'll catch flies like that'. How odd that sleep could transform someone so; rob a forceful, frightening person of all her power and influence. The only time Rose got any time to herself must be when her mother was in bed.

Constance was sitting at Julia's feet sketching Lottie, who had also fallen asleep but on a towel under a beach umbrella with a doll clasped to her chest. She looked across to where Lucian was standing behind Rose, gently guiding her hand as she daubed the canvas with her brush. Then, her gaze shifted to Paola, who was clearing up the tea things in a cross, clattery way. Something was going on here, something she had missed. She felt it must be connected to Paola's reaction the other day, when she had told her about her own lessons with Lucian.

Was Paola sweet on Lucian?

The idea troubled her, even though she barely knew either of them.

Best banish it. Think about something else.

She had turned back to her own sketch, trying to capture the way locks of damp, sandy hair were shading Lottie's forehead, when the drowsy tranquility was shattered by an exclamation.

It came from Rose. 'Bother it!' she shouted, leaping out of her chair.

'Rose,' said Lucian. 'I'm so sorry.'

A bright red mark was clearly visible on the sleeve of Rose's dress. Rose stared at in horror, and for a second Constance wondered if it was blood. 'It's ruined! It will never come out.' She held out her arm accusingly.

The noise roused Julia. Her eyes snapped open. 'What is it?'

'Paint, Mama.'

'I told you to be careful!'

Lucian stepped forward. 'It was my fault, Mrs Drummond-Ward. Her sleeve brushed my palette.'

Quite suddenly, Rose burst into tears – proper tears which streamed unstoppably down her crumpled china-doll face. Constance felt embarrassed for her. It was such an undignified display, like a child's tantrum.

'It will come off, I promise,' said Lucian. He reached into his paint box for a bottle of turpentine and tried to dab some of it on Rose's sleeve. But the second she saw the stained old cloth approaching she recoiled in horror.

'I feel faint,' she said – and there was no denying that her face looked even paler than usual. Constance hurried forward and helped her back into her chair.

'We had better go back,' said Julia, emphatically.

Lucian agreed. 'Of course.'

'I mean immediately.'

They came to an arrangement. Francesco would take the Drummond-Wards back to the hotel in the carriage with Paola and the tea things. Constance would stay behind with Lucian and Lottie and help pack up the painting equipment, after which the three of them would make their own way back on foot.

The easels were lightweight 'plein air' ones. Constance carried them under one arm, leaving her hands free to hold the box of paints, which was like a small suitcase, and the bag containing the sketchbooks and canvases.

The worst of the heat was now over. Still, they followed the road at a gentle pace, Lucian clutching a drowsy Lottie to his chest. Constance felt a pang of tenderness at the sight of the girl's little sandalled feet hanging down, the thick screw of dark hair. But she felt concern too for Lucian, who was more out of breath than she might have expected.

His mood was sullen and weary. 'What a fuss,' he said, as if to himself. 'Over a bit of paint.'

'She did seem very upset.'

'Who wears a silk dress to the beach?'

Constance felt an almost sisterly urge to defend Rose. 'She just wanted to look her best,' she said.

'I shall be in the dog house.'

'I'm sure Rose will forgive you.'

'I don't mean with Rose. I mean with my father.'

Constance wasn't sure how to respond. Sensing her discomfort, Lucian said, 'I'm sorry. It isn't fair of me to involve you.'

'I don't mind. Really.'

He indicated the paint box and easels. 'Are you managing those all right?'

'Oh, yes. Don't worry about me. I'm sure they're lighter than Lottie.'

'You should know.'

She smiled. 'I haven't had cause to lift her yet.'

'You're very good with her.'

'Thank you.'

'Have you had a lot of practice? At looking after children?'

It was an innocent question, affectionately asked. Perhaps this was why Constance felt a lump in her throat and tears well up in her eyes. She prayed Lucian wouldn't notice, but her silence attracted rather than repelled his attention.

'I'm sorry,' he said, looking at her. 'I didn't mean . . .'

She turned her face away, not wanting to be looked at. 'It's quite all right. It's the sun and the salt. It irritates my eyes.'

A moment passed before he asked gently, 'It's more than that, isn't it?'

Again, it was kindly meant. But it was wrong, all of this, all wrong – not what Constance wanted to be talking about. Her job here depended on her *not* talking about it. So she had no choice but to lie. Except she hated lying. People did it too often, too casually. She knew this from experience. And it always rebounded on you in the end.

'Would you mind if we changed the subject?' she said.

*

Lucian lay on the bed, playing idly with a loose thread on the bedspread while his mother dressed for dinner. Visiting his mother as she performed this uncanny transformation was an old habit forged in early childhood – one neither Lucian nor Bella was ready to break just yet.

The evening light cast by the window was lambent and mysterious. When Bella turned, it caught her hair at such an angle that it seemed to flame out softly.

I must paint her, he thought. *Paint her the way Rembrandt painted his mother.*

But thoughts of painting only reminded him of the afternoon and its epic frustrations.

On returning to the hotel, he and Constance had gone their separate ways – she to bath Lottie (who woke up just as they reached the gate), he to rinse the brushes and tidy away all the painting paraphernalia. He'd kept the sketch book by his side and brought it with him to Bella's when he realised that what he really needed was motherly counsel.

In one long, rambling outburst he told her about Rose and the dress and how she and Julia had gone back early. He was careful to say nothing about his conversation with Constance.

'It wasn't a complete success, then?' Bella was patting her hair in front of the mirror.

'You could say that.'

'Don't worry, darling. Paola will work her magic.'

Panicking, he said rather too sharply, 'What are you suggesting?'

Bella looked down so that their eyes met. 'Only that she'll clean the dress.'

'Right.' Lucian changed the subject. 'Has my father said anything?'

'About what?'

'The marriage.'

'I've not spoken to him,' she said. 'He's been drinking with Count Albani.'

'I need a clearer idea of what he wants.'

Bella spun round. 'How many times do I have to tell you? What he wants isn't important!'

'Have you tried telling him that?'

'All that matters is you and Rose. And whether you think you could be happy together.'

He nodded, unconvinced.

'Is there any chance you might?' She paused. 'You know, be happy together?''

Lucian sighed. 'It's pretty hard to form any kind of impression with her mother looming over us like some awful gooseberry.'

Bella smiled. 'She does seem rather formidable.'

He laughed. 'I must say, it's hard to imagine her and Father as an item.'

'They were very young. Too young to be serious.'

'Then they weren't engaged?'

'Not formally. Or so I believe.'

'I'd rather imagined they were. It would explain why he's so hellbent on Rose and me getting hitched.'

Bella frowned. 'I don't understand.'

'You know – righting the wrongs of his past. He and Julia failed to bring the two estates together through marriage. But now he's got a second chance with Rose and me.'

'Well, if that's the case he certainly hasn't confided in me.' She rose from her stool and held out her arms. He stood and let her embrace him, lowering his head to her shoulder, inhaling the jasmine and sandalwood scent of her perfume, which always reminded him of his childhood. 'Give it time with Rose,' she whispered, and he nodded.

As they separated, slightly awkwardly, Lucian's sketchbook slid off the bed and onto the floor. Bella stooped to pick it up. She flicked through it, politely interested, before her thumb stopped at a picture that particularly pleased her. 'At least she's got an artist's eye,' she said, nodding at the page. 'That's something, surely?'

'Hmm?'

She placed the open book in Lucian's hands and returned to where she had been sitting in front of the mirror.

He looked at the drawing and saw at once what his mother could not – that the drawing was not Rose's work at all.

Rose had no eye. Whoever had drawn this was clearly untrained but had the natural gift of seeing objects in three dimensions and knowing how to capture them. The shading, especially, was extremely well done.

Constance, he thought. *Constance did this.*

The knowledge shocked and excited him in equal measure.

Taking the book with him – he decided to keep it in his desk drawer from now on – Lucian went back to his room to change.

On the way back down, he stopped to collect his mother as they had agreed, and together they made their way out to the terrace, where the guests were starting to assemble. The evening had turned out balmy and pleasant. Bella was waylaid almost immediately by Lady Latchmere, who had a Limoncello clasped between thumb and forefinger.

Smiling, Lucian edged his way through the crowd to where Francesco, dapper in his uniform, was mixing Bellinis at a low table. Nodding his appreciation, Lucian took one and drained it at once, savouring the way the sweet, viscous liquid fizzed on his tongue. He helped himself to another, then went over to Plum and Lizzie, who were standing on their own at the far end of the terrace.

'I hope I'm not interrupting,' he said, after introducing himself properly.

'Not at all.' Plum was a slim, supple man who radiated charm and plausibility.

'I saw you play at Queens in twenty-three,' said Lucian. 'You beat an Australian. Tom something or other.'

'Todd Phillips.'

'That's the fellow. Six-two, six-four, six-two, I think.'

'Six-three in the third.' Plum smiled regretfully in acknowledgement of a nice try. 'But what's a game between friends?'

'You barely missed a ball!'

'And now he barely hits one.' This tart observation came courtesy of Lizzie, who was standing by Plum's side looking blank and, it must be said, bored.

Lucian changed the subject. 'What brings you to Portofino?'

'I played in Monte Carlo last week,' said Plum, brightly.

'He lost in the first round,' Lizzie added.

Plum gave Lucian a put-upon, all-men-together look. 'I'm heading to Milan at the end of the week. The local Championships start the Monday after.'

'Which means we'll be taking the train home on Tuesday, with any luck.' Lizzie drained her glass.

Lucian felt suddenly awkward and ill-at-ease. He glanced around, searching for someone else to talk to, any sort of escape route. But he couldn't see one. Nish was talking to Count Albani. Rose hadn't appeared yet – she was probably arguing with her mother somewhere. Claudine and Jack were heading into the dining room . . .

Claudine and Jack. Claudine was good value. Jack he hadn't spoken to yet, admittedly – but he must be interesting if he was with Claudine.

After asking the Wingfields to excuse him, he followed the American couple into the candlelit hush of the dining room.

Seeing his father, he froze suddenly. The old man had made a beeline for them. They were halfway to their table and unable to avoid him, poor souls.

Not wishing to share the Turners, Lucian turned and headed back out to the terrace, trying to look casual – as if he had left his glass somewhere and was on a mission to find it. But he couldn't help wondering . . . Why was his father so interested in the Americans?

*

Cecil had been hovering outside the dining room for several minutes when he heard Claudine say, 'I don't know about you but I'm famished'.

As a result of the telephone call he was buzzing with excitement about the painting and needed to set his plan in motion – a plan that required Jack's discreet involvement.

He managed to make the meeting look accidental. 'Ah, Jack! How good to see you.'

'Cecil.'

The men shook hands. Cecil bowed to Claudine. He turned on the full beam of his charm. 'I'm just on my way outside, but can I offer you a nightcap later?'

Claudine noticed at once that Cecil was looking at Jack

and not her. 'He means "you" singular, not "you" plural,' she said, and walked away, over to their table.

Jack too tried to wriggle away. 'No offence. But I think I'll pass.'

'Perhaps tomorrow?'

'Perhaps.' He made to follow Claudine.

'Oh, well,' said Cecil. 'It can wait.'

'What can wait?'

'The story of Grandpapa's Rubens.'

Jack stopped in his tracks. *I've got your attention now, you little weasel*, Cecil thought. 'Your grandfather owns a Rubens?'

'Owned not owns,' Cecil clarified. 'He kicked the bucket when the old queen was still on the throne.'

But Jack's interest was piqued. He'd turned back round, food suddenly forgotten. 'So, where is it now?'

'Still hanging up back home.'

'And you're sure it's a Rubens?'

Cecil laughed. 'I rather thought you might tell me.'

Around them, the room began to fill as guests trickled in from the terrace and stood in little groups talking. The faint scent of cigarette smoke and perfume grew stronger. Jack looked across to his table where Claudine was sitting with her back to him, touching up her lipstick.

'Tomorrow,' he said. 'Let's talk tomorrow. It'll be easier.'

The two of them were like patients in the same hospital ward, Cecil thought, taking comfort in each other's sickness.

'Very good,' he said. 'Tomorrow it is.'

*

Bella woke late with a slight headache, the result perhaps of the Bellinis she had permitted herself last night. How many had it been? Three? Or four?

Oh well. She had enjoyed them.

She washed and dressed and was on her way downstairs when, passing the door to the Ascot Suite, she heard a clamour. Her first thought was that Lady Latchmere had been taken ill again. But then the door opened to reveal a flustered-looking Melissa who said no, it was a quite different problem and perhaps Bella would like to come in?

Lady Latchmere was sitting up in bed with a breakfast tray in front of her, her chest rising and falling in agitated gasps. *Don't tell me*, Bella thought. *Someone has given her apricot jam instead of marmalade.* But this wasn't the problem either. No, the problem seemed to be the bread, a buttered slice of which Lady Latchmere was waving in the air like a toy flag.

'Completely inedible!' she said. 'I nearly broke a tooth on it.' To ease the almost-pain she took a generous sip from the glass of Limoncello without which no Ascot Suite breakfast order was now complete. The long, thin fingers twitching on the stem reminded Bella of a daddy-long-legs.

'I'm terribly sorry, your Ladyship,' she said, genuinely horrified. 'I'll send someone up with a fresh tray. Straight away.'

The stairs rang to Bella's descending feet. By the dining room door stood Lucian looking puzzled, as if he had been waiting for her. 'Is there a problem?' he asked, frowning.

'Good morning to you, too,' said Bella. 'What problem? Why do you ask?'

'There doesn't appear to be any breakfast.'

Bella's hands grew clammy with panic. What was going on?

In the kitchen, Betty was sitting at the table, head resting on the pillow of her arms. Constance was crouching beside her, apparently trying to comfort her while an exasperated Alice looked on. Upon seeing her employer Betty said weakly, 'Oh, Mrs Ainsworth.'

Bella turned to Alice for explanation, but her daughter shrugged. 'I can't get any sense out of her.'

Bella placed the basket of inedible bread on the table in front of Betty. Gently but sternly, she said: 'We agreed when you took the job, Betty. Only the best at all times.'

'It's not her fault,' said Constance, fiercely.

Alice glared at her. 'Hold your tongue!'

But Constance persisted. 'She can't make breakfast from thin air.'

'Thin air?' asked Bella.

'There's no food, Mrs Ainsworth. See for yourself. Nothing's delivered. No bread, no milk, no eggs.'

'The cupboard's bare!' Betty lifted her head to wail, before dropping her head back into her arms.

The door to the outside opened. Billy rushed in and deposited two large loaves and a round of cheese on the table. Then he started emptying his pockets of eggs.

'Oh,' said Betty, seeing this. 'You little beauty. Put them in here ...' She took a bowl from the shelf behind her and put it on the table.

'It's the best I could do, Ma,' said Billy. Betty brightened and started to busy herself. 'Nobody would sell me nowt, Mrs Ainsworth. I had to beg what I could.'

'It must be a misunderstanding,' said Bella.

'Begging your pardon, but no, ma'am. I don't think so. They shut the door in me face!'

'It doesn't make any sense. We're not behind on any payments as far as I know.'

Bella fell silent as she pondered the matter. *The power that Danioni man must have*, she thought. *To intimidate an entire town into doing his bidding.*

There was something truly frightening about it, something that went far beyond Hotel Portofino and its inability to serve breakfast.

Alice asked, 'What is it, Mama?'

'What time does the service start?'

Alice looked at the clock. 'In two hours.'

'It sounds odd,' said Bella, 'but I think the answer might lie in church.'

She had learned soon after their arrival in Portofino that churchgoing in Italy was even more important than it was in England. Of course, the congregation here was more devout, and instances of actual belief higher. But as in Tonbridge or Leeds, services were predominantly social events where business was discussed and gossip exchanged. Love it or hate it, the church bound society together. You could no more ignore its endless feasts, processions and firecracker festivals than you could a shopkeeper, or a troublesome local councillor.

It was Bella's idea to present a united front; to rally the troops, as she put it. She enlisted Lucian to quickly write a notice in his best copperplate, informing guests about the morning service and recommending they attend on the grounds that Mass represented 'a golden opportunity to observe Italians in their natural habitat'. This Bella framed and placed on the reception desk in the hall.

Nish drew Claudine's attention to it, explaining the context. She consented to join the party but said there was no point asking Jack, so Bella did not. Count Albani assured Bella he would come, despite some issues with the wording – '"Natural habitat"! What are we, elephants?' Alice and Lottie agreed readily, as did Melissa. To Bella's chagrin, though not her surprise, Lucian refused point blank. He had brushes to clean, he said.

Even less surprising was the response of Lady Latchmere, who said the very thought of attending a Catholic Mass made her feel ill: 'I wouldn't have chosen to stay at Hotel Portofino if I'd known it was a den of papist iniquity.'

After a while, they set off for San Martino together – a loose, stuttered procession along the cobbles and up the steps, which were not designed for smart shoes. When they reached the mosaic terrace outside the church an assortment of tourists, local townspeople and what Count Albani called 'rural poor' was waiting on the steps.

In the midst of this throng stood Danioni, who was holding forth like a barrister at trial. When he saw the Count he removed his hat and bowed low, which infuriated Bella and hardened her resolve to have it out with him – at a time of her choosing. For now, she would fire a shot across the bows.

She made a beeline for him, gripping Lottie's hand so hard the girl complained. 'Signor Danioni!'

He turned, breaking off from his conversation with a short, balding man Bella recognised as the town pharmacist. 'Ah, Mrs Ainsworth.' He managed an oily smile. 'I did not know you were a religious woman.'

'Don't worry,' she said. 'I'm not going to make a scene in front of the whole town. At least, not *before* Mass.'

As he tipped his hat she saw his eyes flick away from her and on to Claudine and Nish as they walked up the steps and into the church. His distaste for them was glaringly apparent.

*

'Did you see that?' asked Nish. He and Claudine were following Alice to a pew with enough seats for them all.

Claudine looked around. 'No. What?'

'That man. The way he looked at us.'

'Oh, him. You know what, honey? I don't even notice it anymore. If I did, I'd be noticing it all day long. And that's tiring.'

Nish sat at the end of the row, like an usher. As the service got underway he was surprised by how much he enjoyed the sonorous but empty mystery of the Latin liturgy in all its reassuring familiarity. He was used to Mass from his Catholic boarding school, where he had been expected to attend regardless of his true religion. The atmosphere here couldn't have been more different from the freezing chapel at Stonyforth. Children wandered freely carrying toys and votive candles, oblivious to the weeping and imploring of the old women hunched together at the back, as dry and grey as cinders.

On their way out, Alice came rushing over. 'Thank you so much for coming, Nish. I wasn't sure if church would be ...'

'My thing?'

'No.' She blushed. 'Only because ... Well, Lucian has become so *anti* all of this.'

'He says God died in the trenches. A lot of people I served with feel the same way.'

Claudine asked, 'You were at the Front?'

'Indian Medical Service.' He gave them a tiny salute.

'And do you think God failed to come back from the war, Mr Sengupta?'

Nish considered. 'England's God, maybe. Not mine.'

Alice and Claudine walked on. Nish stuck his tongue out and crossed his eyes at a young boy who was staring at him. He had intended to amuse him, but the boy seemed genuinely terrified and buried his face in his mother's side. Feeling guilty, Nish looked quickly away before the woman had a chance to notice and upbraid him.

Outside the church, he waited with Melissa and Claudine for Bella and Carlo to appear. A well-dressed woman of aristocratic bearing emerged with a female companion. Alice called out: 'Lady Caroline!' But the woman merely glanced in Alice's direction before wandering off.

'Well I never!' Alice seemed very put out.

'Perhaps she didn't see you?' Melissa suggested.

'Or didn't choose to,' said Claudine.

Clutching her hat, Bella joined them. 'What is it? What's funny?'

'I think I've just been snubbed,' said Alice.

Melissa added, 'By Lady Caroline Haig!'

Claudine looked confused. 'Should I know who that is?'

Melissa explained that she was the Earl of Harborne's daughter and they were renting a villa in the hills.

'We called on them when they arrived,' added Alice. 'They were perfectly civil then.'

Claudine's brow creased. 'I hope she didn't ignore you on my account.'

'I'm sure not,' said Bella, a touch too emphatically. 'There must be a perfectly reasonable explanation.'.

On the far side of the terrace, Lady Caroline was making small talk with Count Albani. He rejoined the hotel party to find them looking at him expectantly. 'Did I miss something?'

'We were talking about the Haigs,' said Bella.

'Apparently you know Lady Caroline,' said Alice.

'I was at Oxford with her uncle,' the Count explained.

But Bella was looking distracted. She had spotted someone, Nish noticed – the weaselly man who had stared at him and Claudine before the service. 'Will you excuse me?' she said and eased her way towards him through the milling crowd.

'What's that all about?' asked Nish.

But nobody seemed to know.

*

It was funny, thought Cecil, how things changed. One minute, someone didn't want to talk to you. And then, quite suddenly, they did. Take Jack, for example. He had come upon Cecil reading the newspaper in the library and greeted him heartily, without any of the wary hesitancy of their earlier meetings. Everyone else had left for church. Cecil never bothered with such things and evidently Jack didn't either because when Cecil raised the subject he said, 'I only kneel at the altar of Mammon.' Which, as it happened, was precisely Cecil's sentiment.

Grinning, Jack produced the key to his Bugatti and dangled it in the air. 'I wondered if you might like to join me for a spin?'

'Now that,' said Cecil, folding up his newspaper, 'is an excellent idea.'

The motorcar handled the bends admirably, though the road was narrow and Cecil terrified of what might happen if they met another vehicle. But he kept his fear to himself. Besides, Jack seemed to know what he was doing.

They parked by the side of the road between Rapallo and Camogli. From the cliff edge, they looked out over the ragged profusion of red pantiled roofs and down to the crumbling castle on the foreshore.

'First-rate tennis courts in Rapallo,' observed Cecil, not that he had ever made use of them. He had only pretended to like tennis to impress Bella on their honeymoon. 'And there's an English library, I'm told.'

'You people get everywhere,' said Jack. He smiled. 'Then again, so do we.'

They turned and walked back to the motorcar. Jack leant against the bonnet smoking while Cecil traced a finger along the hot metal. 'This must have cost a pretty penny.'

'A thing of beauty is a joy for ever.'

'So I'm told.'

'It's a Type 35,' said Jack. 'It has alloy wheels and the springs go through the front axle. Bugatti won the Targa Florio with it last year. The guy's a genius, I tell you.'

Cecil knew nothing about motoring, but was prepared to take Jack's word for it. Still, he felt a glow of patriotic jealousy. 'A bigger genius than Walter Bentley?'

'Bentley?' Jack laughed. 'Do you know what Bugatti calls Bentleys? "The world's fastest lorries." He's right, too.'

Cecil fought back. 'Perhaps. It's a shame the Eye-ties didn't have decent kit like this in the war. They might have fared a little better.'

'You served?'

'Not last time.' He paused, contemplating the spectre of his brief, undistinguished military career. 'My fighting days ended a few miles outside Ladysmith at the end of last century. What about you?'

Jack shook his head and looked down. There was a story there, Cecil sensed. But Jack wasn't prepared to tell it. Not yet.

Perching beside Jack on the bonnet, he fished out a ragged piece of paper from his inside pocket. 'About this painting,' he said, smoothing it out.

Jack squinted at the paper. 'That can't be it.'

'Of course not. I tore this out of one of Lucian's books.'

Jack took it and held it up, studying it carefully. 'Venus with a mirror.'

'That's the girl. It took me quite a while to work it out.'

'She's quite a common theme in Renaissance art,' said Jack, airily.

'If you say so.' Cecil disliked people who flaunted expertise he didn't share.

Jack sniffed. 'So your Rubens isn't titled?'

'No. And not signed either. Unfortunately.'

'Hmmm.'

'Will that be a problem?'

Jack gave a little shrug. 'It's not unusual for the period.'

'Which is presumably where fellows like you come in?' Cecil was growing impatient. He wanted answers, not ponderous equivocation.

Jack handed him back the scrap of paper. 'There's no way of knowing. Without getting my guy to take a look.'

'Of course,' said Cecil. 'I understand that. It's why I'm having it sent over as we speak.'

This news had the desired effect of surprising Jack. 'You're really serious about this?'

'I'm always serious when it comes to making money. Aren't you?'

151

Jack fell silent. Then he said, 'If it's not what you say it is, it's a hell of a lot of trouble to go to. For both of us.'

Cecil produced a hip flask from his pocket. 'Don't worry, old man.' He took a swig before handing it to Jack. 'I'm sure we can find a way to make it worth our while.'

*

Was it Bella's imagination or did Danioni shrink back as she approached? Like all bullies, he was a coward at heart and did not enjoy confrontation for its own sake. 'Signore,' she said, empowered by the crowd around her, the fact that this was happening in public. 'A word with you, please?'

Bowing his acquiescence, he excused himself from his companions, who exchanged knowing looks.

'I take it I have you to thank for this morning's wonderful surprise,' said Bella.

'I do not understand, Signora.'

'Oh, I think you do. You said it yourself. Nothing occurs here without you knowing about it.'

He tilted his head. 'Perhaps.'

'Then perhaps you can tell me what it will take to resolve this difficulty. I cannot run my hotel without the town's supplies. Or its goodwill.'

He turned away. Bella followed his gaze back towards the church and saw a woman in a blue dress standing on the steps. She was watching them closely. Danioni raised a hand to acknowledge her and she raised one back. 'My wife,' he said.

'Does she know you're blackmailing me?'

He winced. 'Such an ugly word. We do not believe in blackmail in Italy, Signora.'

'Then what do you believe in?'

'*Furbizia*.'

'I don't understand.'

'Shrewdness. It is what puts food on our table. And buys dresses for our wives.' He looked back at his wife, then at Bella again. 'Pretty dresses. And jewellery. Like *zaffiro*.'

'Sapphires?'

He looked at Bella's hand, where a sapphire ring sparkled.

'Si. *Zaffiro*. My wife, she likes them very much.'

*

Constance and Betty were by the sink when Bella walked into the kitchen. They were laughing and fooling around, Constance manipulating the jaws of the fish she was holding so that it appeared to be talking. They stopped and stood to attention when they saw Bella, though wrinkles of laughter still showed on their too-solemn faces.

'I'm glad you've recovered, Betty.'

'Thank you, Mrs Ainsworth. I'm feeling much more meself.'

At first Constance worried that something was bothering Bella. Her expression was fretful and distracted and she kept fiddling with the middle finger of her right hand. The woman had a lot on her mind, she told herself. All that business this morning with the deliveries – as if running a hotel wasn't hard enough.

Anyway, she seemed to brighten when she saw the

glistening mounds of fresh fish on the table. 'Someone's been busy,' she said.

'It were Billy, ma'am,' said Constance.

'Gracious. Did he catch all this himself?'

'No, Mrs Ainsworth. There's some lads he knows down the harbour. They help each other out.'

'You must thank him for me. It will make a splendid dinner.'

'I'll pass it on, Mrs Ainsworth.'

'Thank you, Constance. And Betty, I'm assured deliveries will resume tomorrow morning.'

'Very relieved to hear it, ma'am.'

Bella was about to leave when she noticed the fish they had been laughing at earlier. 'Goodness, he's an ugly fellow!'

Constance picked it up. 'He's the spit of my Uncle Albert,' she said. He was, too.

'I hope he tastes better than he looks.'

'I were just wracking my brains for what I could do with him,' Betty confessed. 'I was going to have a look in that book ...'

'Artusi?'

'That's the one.'

While everyone was talking, Paola had been going to and from the kitchen store cupboard fetching brushes and dusters. She was on her way back outside when something she heard made her ears prick up. 'Artusi? Pah!' She blew out through her cheeks and shook her head, a slow swing heavy with the weight of English ignorance.

Bella asked her in Italian for her views on Artusi, then translated her reply for the others' benefit. It turned out Paola disliked Artusi because he was a 'foolish old man who knows nothing'. She added that the fish Billy and his friends had caught was gurnard – good to eat, especially in a stew.

'Paola's keen to try something,' said Bella. 'If you don't mind, Betty?'

The cook made a sweeping gesture of welcome with her arm. 'Not one bit.'

At Bella's signal, Paola put down the box she was carrying and started rummaging through the fish, one by one, examining each slippery specimen for signs of damage and decay. From her approving hums and grunts all assembled deduced that she must like what she was seeing. Only a very few fish were found wanting and tossed aside.

Bella and Betty exchanged a look.

'Perhaps a sous-chef would be useful this evening?' Bella suggested.

'I was thinking just that, ma'am.'

'Shall I ask her?'

'It doesn't look as if she'll take much persuading.'

'Wonderful.' Bella clapped her hands. She looked thrilled. 'It will be a special dinner. We can bill it as "a taste of Italy".'

Constance always helped to serve dinner after she had put Lottie to bed. Her previous employer had trained her in silver service, but while Bella mostly favoured a scaled-down version of this, the plan tonight was for Betty to serve up in the kitchen and for Constance and Billy to carry the plates through to the dining room.

Lottie had heard all about the fish stew and was furious that she wasn't allowed to stay up for it. 'Italian children all get to stay up,' she complained to Constance.

'But you're not Italian,' Constance had pointed out. 'We do things differently. Besides, your mother can't have you running around getting in the way while we're serving the guests.'

'I won't run around,' said Lottie, her eyes watering.

In the end Bella agreed that Lottie could help to prepare the dining room. The little girl looked adorable in a sky-blue linen dress with white piping around the collar. She and Alice and Constance spread out the crisp white table cloths, laid out the cutlery and side plates and placed bowls filled with flowers in the centre of each table. Alice showed her daughter how to fold the napkins.

As they worked, someone – Lucian? – put a record on the gramophone. The music drifted serenely through the house. It was what Constance had always thought of as posh people's music: opera. She had heard bits of it before on the wireless but it had never made sense, never struck her as something anyone would listen to out of choice. Now, for the first time, and despite the language being mysterious to her, she felt as if she understood the drawn-out yearning and melancholy, the uplifting expression of tumultuous emotion. Her heart aching for all that she had left behind, Constance had to work hard not to let these feelings get the better of her.

Paola had been cooking all afternoon. Betty stood beside her, watching and taking notes, trying not to get in the way. 'She's good, she is,' she kept saying. 'She's putting paprika in it and everything.'

It was unusual for all the guests to be present at dinner. Often one or two chose to eat elsewhere, for there was no shortage of good restaurants in Portofino. But word had got around that tonight would be special – a taste of Italy like no other.

By eight o'clock, the diners had finished their cocktails and taken their seats. The mood was restless and expectant, an added piquancy being that nobody knew what to expect, the precise contents of the meal having been kept a secret; though in truth the delicious smell from the kitchen had permeated the hotel all afternoon.

Paola ladled generous portions of the stew into large, shallow bowls which Constance and Billy carried carefully into the dining room. Her first delivery was to Roberto and Count Albani. As she set the bowls before them, the Count inhaled the rising steam before touching her lightly on the arm and saying, 'Now, my dear. You must tell me what this is.'

Constance had been expecting this and knew exactly what to say. 'It's a Ligurian fish stew with gurnard, red mullet and scallops.' She didn't know how to say 'langoustines', so she omitted to mention them.

'Excellent,' said the Count. 'And do I detect the aroma of fennel?'

157

'You do, sir.'

'Tell me ...' He beckoned her close and dropped his voice to a whisper. 'Is this Signora Betty's work? Or Signora Paola's?'

'It's what you might call a joint effort, sir.'

He roared with laughter. 'Such a diplomat! An invaluable asset, I am sure, in a hotel such as this.'

Billy drew the short straw of serving Julia and Rose, though they seemed to find the stew to their liking. Constance saw Rose fish a whole langoustine out of her bowl and show it to Julia, whose eyes widened in shock.

Lady Latchmere, on the other hand, looked deeply suspicious as she raised her spoon to her mouth. But her expression resolved into one of unexpected pleasure as she took her first mouthful.

Towards the end of the meal Constance had gone into the kitchen to change her apron when she spotted Billy sneak out of the door and into the night. Off to meet his new friends, probably. She hoped they weren't leading him astray. He struck Constance as very young. She'd known his type at home. Village boys. Always up for adventure, but without the wisdom to know when enough was enough.

Mind you, she thought, people probably used to say that about her.

Despite having done most of the cooking, Paola helped with the washing up, which was good of her. She, Betty and Constance washed and dried in weary but contented silence until Betty hung up her apron and said, 'Right. I'm away to bed.'

'*Buona notte*, Elizabetta,' said Paola.

Betty beamed. 'You did us proud tonight, love.'

It was obvious Paola didn't quite understand, but she gave Betty a hug.

It was just the two of them now and there was a new coolness in the air. Clearly, Paola thought something was going on between Constance and Lucian. But it was all based on a misunderstanding – because there wasn't, was there?

'*Buona notte*, Paola,' said Constance, preparing to go upstairs.

But Paola said nothing.

Up in her room, Constance sat at her dressing table in her night-gown. In the mirror she examined her face with a severity of judgement others would have said was undeserved. But she had always found it easier to detect flaws than virtues; or perhaps it just felt more fitting to be brutal, as if she didn't deserve anything more. Not after what had happened. Though it hadn't been her fault. It really hadn't.

Taking care not to damage the clasp, she removed the locket she always wore on a chain around her neck and opened it. Inside was a tiny photograph of Tommy, taken when he was six months old. They had gone to Keighley especially and he had cried the whole time, the little scamp. She smiled, kissed the tiny photo, then – despite the tiredness in her bones – she started writing the letter she had been planning all day.

My dearest Ma, I have so much to tell you . . .

*

159

Bella was in the bathroom removing her make-up with a soft cotton cloth. Cecil was out somewhere. He alone had missed out on the fish stew. Once upon a time, he would have enjoyed it. It would have been a pleasure they could share.

All of that was in the past. She had no wish to share his current pleasures, poker and brandy. But what infuriated her more than anything was the way his behaviour cast her in a role she had no desire to play – a sour-faced Mrs Temperance, forever lecturing him about the demon drink like some figure from an eighteenth-century cartoon.

She jumped in her skin when a sound came from below, interrupting her thoughts – a violent crashing from somewhere close to the kitchen.

Her mind immediately flew to Cecil. What was he doing this time? When he didn't appear after a few minutes, she slipped on her dressing gown and padded downstairs to investigate.

The kitchen was pitch black. She snapped on the light and her first impression was that the room was spotless. The girls had done a superb job of clearing up. She was about to flick the switch off and head back to bed when she heard something.

It was, unmistakably, a groan.

Her heart stopped, then began to beat so violently she felt sick. 'Who's there?' Arming herself with a large metal ladle, she took a few tentative steps further into the room. 'Is that you, Cecil?'

She stepped forward decisively, holding the ladle over

her head, ready to strike – when she saw a cowering form beneath the table. She looked closer. It was two cowering forms, only one of which she recognised.

'Billy!'

'I'm sorry, ma'am.' He had a bruise on his cheek and his clothes were torn. In his lap, he was cradling the head of a boy of around his age. It was covered in blood, the hair matted and sticky. His whole face was bruised and swollen, the eyes thin slits.

'What on earth?' she asked, in shock.

'Please don't be angry with me,' Billy pleaded. 'I didn't know what else to do.'

'But what's he doing here, Billy? What's happened to him?'

'Oh, Mrs Ainsworth,' he said, his voice cracking. 'It's the Fascists. They've beaten him senseless.'

6

That night there was a violent storm. Rain clattered in the palm trees and poured from the gutters. Long barbs of lightning plunged into the hills, illuminating the landmark of Castle Brown as brilliantly as if it were on fire.

Constance wasn't frightened exactly, but this was like no storm she had ever witnessed and she found it impossible to sleep. With every bang the hotel shook and the windows rattled. She lay on her side, debating whether to open the shutters and watch the firework display. In the end she decided against it. She was about to turn over and try once more to doze off when there was a sturdy rapping at the door.

It was Billy, in his ordinary clothes, holding a candle up to his dirty, bruised face.

She gasped. 'Billy! What on earth's the matter?'

His voice was blank with the effort at control. 'Mrs Ainsworth says you're to come to the stables, now. Bring a basin of hot water with you. And towels.'

He turned away before she could question him further.

Constance tied her hair back and pulled on her dressing gown. As she crossed the courtyard the rain was still falling, the air hazy and vaporous. The moon cast a trembling silver light on the wet cobblestones. She almost collided with Nish, who was responding to the same peremptory summons. One hand held a brown leather doctor's bag; the other was fastening a recalcitrant button on a shirt that had plainly been thrown on in haste.

'What is it, Mr Sengupta?' she asked. 'What's happened?'

'I don't know,' he said, wearily. 'But I must say, I dream of an unbroken night's sleep.'

'What do you mean?'

'I seem to be less a guest here than a doctor on permanent call.' He corrected himself quickly. 'Not that I'm complaining, of course . . .'

Billy walked ahead, leading them towards the old stables where the carriage horses were kept. As another clap of thunder broke above their heads, a low male voice cried out in terror.

Nish was the first to recognise it. He stopped and said wonderingly, 'Lucian?' He and Constance turned as one towards the source of the sound – the servants' accommodation on the far side of the courtyard. 'He hates the thunder,' Nish explained, suddenly looking embarrassed. 'It reminds him of France.'

Yes, thought Constance. And that must be awful, intolerable. But what was Lucian doing in the stable-block in the middle of the night when his room was in the main house?

She almost asked Nish this question. But no sooner had she framed it in her head than her heart tightened, for she realised she knew the answer perfectly well. It had been staring her in the face and she had been too foolish and naive – too trusting, she supposed – to recognise it. No wonder Paola hated her!

Still, there was no time now to dwell on such things because Bella was calling softly but urgently from the doorway. 'Please! Come quickly.'

They went through to the first stall, where a boy of around Billy's age was prone on an improvised bed of straw.

The boy was groaning in pain. Willing herself to stay calm, Constance knelt beside him. She soaked a cloth with water from the bucket. His skin and clothes were sticky with blood, his pale face swollen so badly it would, she thought, be hard to identify him except from his tatty jacket and close-cropped brown hair. He lay perfectly still, as if any movement at all was the purest agony. Gently, Constance dabbed at his face with the cloth, trying to clean off the worst of the blood. But every time it touched his skin, he yelped in agony. It was all utterly heartbreaking. How could someone do this to a young boy?

'Wait for a moment,' said Nish, crouching next to her. 'Let me give him something for the pain.' From his bag he produced a hypodermic syringe, which he filled from a bottle. 'Roll up his sleeve and hold his arm steady.' He looked up at Bella, as though asking for permission. 'I'm giving him morphine. A quarter of a grain.'

'Do whatever you need to,' she said.

The boy's arm tensed as the needle pierced his skin. In a matter of minutes, the groaning stopped and Constance resumed her work cleaning his face. When she had done what she could, she stroked his hair soothingly. It felt furry, like a cat's.

She stayed with him for what might have been an hour, it was hard to be certain; until Bella called her over and whispered, 'You've done enough now, child.'

The storm had passed. Birdsong drifted down from the hills. They gathered outside the stable door – Nish, Constance and Bella. Bella had sent Billy to the town to notify the boy's family.

Now, she turned to Nish. 'How is he?'

'More stable, but still weak. He's lost a good deal of blood.'

'Will he be all right?'

'He's young and strong. Although I suspect his sight may be damaged.'

As Nish was speaking, Billy hurried into the courtyard leading two middle-aged Italian men pushing a handcart. It rattled across the cobblestones. After tipping their hats to Bella in thanks, they made their silent way into the stable, pushing past Constance.

'Who are these people?' asked Bella.

Billy said, 'Better for you if I don't make no introductions, Mrs Ainsworth.'

Constance followed the men into the stable. They spoke to each other sharply in Italian. And then they were lifting the sleeping youth, lifting him roughly by the feet and shoulders so that his broken body sagged in the middle. Despite the morphine, he cried out with pain as the duo loaded him onto the rusty cart. Constance shouted out, 'Be careful with him!' But they ignored her and covered him with tarpaulin, as if he were already dead.

The sight affected Nish, too. 'He must see a doctor,' he said to Bella. 'Tell them it's essential. Please!'

She spoke to them and they gave some impression of listening. One of them nodded, which was hopeful. Then he and his companion wheeled the cart away as unceremoniously as they had brought it.

Bella turned to Billy. 'Go and get cleaned up,' she said.

'Yes, ma'am.'

'And then I would like to see you and Constance in my office. You have a lot of explaining to do, young man.'

Billy sloped off. Constance gathered the bowl and flannels, straining to hear Nish and Bella's whispered conversation. She felt a nervous fluttering in her chest. Why did Bella want to see her too? What had she done wrong? She had only been trying to help ... Hadn't she come as quickly as she could?

'Has Billy said anything else?' Nish was asking. 'About how the boy got injured?'

'Only what I told you. It was Mussolini's thugs.'

'In this sleepy little town of all places!'

'Oh, Nish!' she said, exasperated. 'Don't you understand by now? They're everywhere!'

*

Bella's office had the tense, expectant atmosphere of a court room. With its lime-washed walls and tall, thin filing cabinet, the room felt thoroughly English and reminded Constance of

166

all the housekeeper's offices she had ever known. It seemed to deflect the Italian world outside; to stand obscurely for rules and money and buttoned-up emotion, so that the way the sun strained to make an impression through the small casement window felt sadly apt.

The realisation struck her suddenly. *Bella isn't happy when she's in here*. But this was presumptuous. It wasn't her place to judge the force and scope of Bella's relationships – to her family, the hotel and Italy.

Constance thought back to that initial moment of connection, the two of them sitting at the kitchen table, Bella pushing the tapenade towards her. She realised that her own controlling desire was for all this formality to dissolve. For Bella to disclose her whole self to her in a single, secret gesture.

As if she were Bella's equal, not her servant.

She and Betty stood at the back of the room while Bella, seated at her desk, tried to determine what exactly had happened the previous night. Her controlled patience was more frightening than outright anger would have been.

'Why did you bring him here, Billy?'

'I suppose I panicked, ma'am.'

'You were being chased?'

'Yes.'

'By whom?'

'Some lads. Three or four of 'em.'

'Do they know you work here?'

'No, ma'am.'

'That's something, at least.' Bella fell silent for a few moments, as if working out how best to respond. Finally, she said: 'I know you did what you did with the best of intentions, Billy. But it mustn't happen again.'

Billy hung his head. 'I promise it won't, ma'am.'

'The situation in Italy is very complicated and we can't be seen to be taking sides. Do you understand?'

He nodded.

'All right. You can go.'

On his way to the door, he glanced at his mother. 'I'm sorry, Ma.'

But Betty was cold and impassive. 'I can't bear to look at you.'

Constance's heart went out to both of them, but especially Billy. He was only a child – the child Constance still felt herself to be on those mornings when all she wanted was to run and dance and throw something up in the air. To forget that she was twenty years old, and already a mother.

An absent mother, at that.

After Billy had closed the door, Betty said, 'I don't know what to say, ma'am.'

'You don't have to say anything, Betty. It's not your fault.'

'His brothers used to give him a clip round the ear if he stepped out of line. But now ... Well, it's hard for a woman on her own. To know how to handle a lad of his age.'

Bella's tone softened. 'Billy's a credit to you, Betty. He's desperate for adventure, that's all.'

As Betty left the room Constance braced herself. It was her turn now.

She was used to being shouted at in these situations. Still, she felt an unreasoning shame that she had, without realising it, disappointed Bella.

Or, had she got things round the twist? The smile being directed at her from across the desk – and it was a smile, no question – was warm and inclusive.

'I want to express my gratitude to you,' Bella said.

Constance could not have been more astonished if Bella had stripped naked in front of her. 'It were nothing, Mrs Ainsworth,' she managed.

'And ask for your discretion.'

'You can trust me, ma'am.'

'Of course, you understand, I can't abide injustice.' Bella glanced out of the window. 'Especially the sort that's enforced with a boot or a fist.'

'No, ma'am. Me, neither.' This was an odd conversation, Constance thought. Where was it heading?

'In any other circumstance, I'd be down at Mr Danioni's door in a heartbeat. And be holding his feet to the fire.'

'I'm sure you would, Mrs Ainsworth.'

'But I've put everything into the hotel. Into making a success of it. And if it failed, or was taken away from me, I don't know how I'd cope.'

'No, ma'am.'

For a moment Bella looked as if she might cry. 'Heavens!' She laughed uneasily. 'What must you think of me? Confiding my troubles. And the two of us little more than strangers!'

'Don't mention it, ma'am.' In truth, Constance was thrilled by how quickly the formality between them was eroding.

'Thank you, Constance.' Bella rose, signalling a shift in atmosphere; the introduction of a brighter, more frivolous tone. 'Now, let's go and see about this tea party. Count Albani is most insistent that we have one. To show off our English cakes to the locals.'

*

They found Betty talking to Alice in front of the kitchen range. The two of them were apportioning roles and working out the menu. Constance hoped she might be sent into town to buy something. Any form of mission was enjoyable and besides, she felt a need to be on her own – to think over what Bella had said to her and asked of her, which was echoing in her head.

When Alice saw Constance she said, 'Where's Lottie?'

'I don't know. I've been ...'

'You're her nanny, aren't you? Why are you here?' She looked her up and down. 'And wearing your dressing gown?'

Bella came to her rescue. 'She's been helping me, Alice. Helping me very much, as it happens.'

'Oh, well.' The wind went out of Alice's sails and Constance had an insight into the morose, dissatisfied child she would once have been. 'The thing is,' Alice went on, 'I'm wondering whether a tea party is even a good idea?'

'It will add another string to our bow,' said Bella.

'But Betty's rushed off her feet, as it is!'

'I'm always happy to have a go,' said Betty, mildly affronted. 'You know how much I like baking.'

Alice pulled a face. 'You didn't seem very happy the other day.'

'I could lend a hand,' offered Constance, quickly. 'I mean, I'm not in Betty's league. But I can bake biscuits. Or even a bit of Parkin at a push.'

Alice said nothing, but Bella smiled encouragingly. 'I'm not sure the good burghers of Portofino are ready for Parkin. But thank you, Constance.'

'I'll take all the help I can get, love,' said Betty.

Bella turned to Alice. 'So, you'll take charge?'

'Yes, Mother.'

'And talk to Count Albani? About what we should serve?'

Alice sighed. 'Is that *really* necessary? I'd rather make my own decisions.'

'He was most insistent about wanting to be involved.'

'It's hard to imagine his interest in cake extends much beyond eating it.'

'Well,' said Bella, 'maybe it's not cake he's interested in.'

The silence that followed felt cavernous – the sort you might get lost in without the right thread to guide you out. It was broken by Betty trying to stifle a laugh with her hand. Constance wasn't sure where to look, so she looked at her fingers, which were still crusted with the Italian boy's blood.

Blushing deeply, Alice withdrew from the group, edging back so that she was leaning against the table, dusty with flour from Betty's earlier efforts at making *gnocchi*.

It was as if Bella had forgotten that there were servants

present. Or perhaps, thought Constance with a thrill, she simply didn't care.

*

Both Lucian and the poor old carriage-driver had been waiting a good half hour for the Drummond-Wards. Finally, they emerged from the hotel in a flurry of bags and parasols, both blaming the other.

It was Rose's obsession with her hair . . .

No, it was because her mother had brought the wrong shoes . . .

Privately, Lucian wondered at the wisdom of embarking on a sightseeing expedition to Genoa with only a Baedeker for company. He had offered his services as a guide but been rebuffed. Mother and daughter wished to experience 'the real Italy' by themselves; though Lucian suspected this was the Italy of shops and salons rather than his preferred one of galleries and museums.

Never mind. He had waited to wave them off, like the dutiful son-in-law his parents wanted him to become.

'You should try to visit the Palazzo Bianco, if you have time,' he said, helping Julia up the steps and into the carriage. 'It has an extraordinary Caravaggio.'

Julia was finding it hard to contain her boredom. 'We have a lot of errands to run. Rose has nothing suitable to wear for this tea party everyone keeps talking about.'

But Lucian ploughed on. 'The Doge's Palace is worth a look, too. From the outside, at least.'

Rose frowned, her nose scrunching up delightfully. 'What's a Doge?' she asked.

'A sort of elected king.'

Her eyes widened. 'Genoa had its own *king*?'

'In its day, it was the most feared Republic in the Mediterranean,' said Lucian, delighted to have provoked a sliver of interest. 'Old Joe Green even wrote an opera about one of Genoa's most famous Doges, if memory serves.'

Julia looked at him sceptically. 'My husband keeps a box at Covent Garden, Mr Ainsworth. And I've *never* heard of Joe Green, young or old.'

'Giuseppe Verdi?'

The penny dropped. 'Ah,' she said, unembarrassed. 'A witticism.'

'I don't understand,' said Rose.

The carriage stuttered away, leaving Lucian with a hangover of panicky irritation.

Rose, on her own, he could take pleasure in, because if he grew bored he could always look at her.

Julia, on her own, he could tolerate, because he had met many such women over the course of his life and so acquired a degree of immunity.

Together, however, they were exhausting.

He turned back towards the hotel just as Plum was emerging from the front door. Plum, his sporting hero! Here, now, bounding across the gravel towards him. At any other moment, he would have been thrilled.

'Ainsworth! Just the man I was looking for. I don't suppose you could organise a ride for me?'

'On a horse?'

'Good grief, no! A bicycle! I was an infantryman, not a donkey walloper!'

'My mistake,' said Lucian, puzzled by Plum's touchiness.

'I thought I might take a training ride. Pump some power into the old leg muscles. For the battle ahead.'

'I'll see what I can do.'

'Good man.'

Lucian thought of something. 'And perhaps you might lend me a couple of rackets in exchange?'

'Rackets? Happy to, old chap. More than happy. I always travel with an oversupply.'

They walked back into the hotel, Plum's animation dipping after Lucian admitted he didn't play tennis much these days. Not that he went into the details, which involved shattered bones and experimental plastic surgery. People rarely wanted to hear about all that.

'I want to have a knockabout with my niece,' he explained.

'A *knockabout*?' Plum started, as if he found the concept abhorrent. His attention switched to Bella, who was at reception sorting through a pile of guests' post she had brought from her office. 'I don't suppose there's anything for me, is there?'

'I'm afraid not.' She smiled. 'Were you expecting something?'

'A letter from home.'

'I'm sure it will turn up. Although the post here is not the most dependable. To put it mildly.'

Plum had an odd knack of looking at you closely when he

spoke to you, as if you were a magician concealing a trick. He was watching Bella now, Lucian noticed, as she placed the office key in a drawer behind the desk.

'Not to worry,' he said. 'Perhaps it'll turn up tomorrow.'

'I'm sure it will.'

As he wandered off, Bella handed Lucian a letter – 'One for you' – and flicked through the others. 'And one . . . two . . . *three* for your father.' One of them had words embossed on the front: *Casino di Sanremo*.

They looked at each other knowingly.

'Allow me,' said Lucian and took them from her.

'Don't get into a fight.'

'Why would I? What's the point?'

He found his father in the library, reading the paper.

Cecil looked up and frowned. 'What is it?'

'Mama asked me to give you these.'

He had placed the letter from the casino at the top of the pile. It gave Lucian pleasure to watch Cecil take it from him – take it in full awareness that his son knew what it was.

But Cecil chose to keep up the pretence that nothing was amiss. He slipped the envelopes casually into the inside pocket of his jacket.

'Thank you,' he said. 'Don't let me keep you.'

*

Bella distributed the rest of the post herself, leaving the most intriguing till last. It was addressed to Alice – a cream envelope, thick and weighty, the address written in an exquisite copperplate even neater than Lucian's. As if that weren't tantalising enough, the postmark was local.

She found her daughter in the drawing room, sitting with Melissa and Lady Latchmere. They made a curious trio, all of them wearing an identical sombre expression that reminded Bella of a bust she had once seen on a tomb in St Paul's Cathedral.

Alice's face, at least, brightened when she saw the letter. 'My goodness,' she said, clutching it like a sacred relic for what seemed an eternity.

'Aren't you going to open it?' said Bella.

'Don't rush me,' Alice snapped.

She unpeeled it slowly, delighted by the audience she had acquired and was still acquiring – for Count Albani had appeared in the doorway and was watching her keenly.

Alice's eyes scanned the tidy, compact writing. 'It's from Lady Caroline!' She stood up, barely able to contain her surprise and excitement.

'What does it say?' Melissa was practically squealing. 'Oh, don't keep us in suspense, Alice!'

'"Dear Mrs Mays-Smith. Please forgive my unpardonable rudeness for not having written before now to thank you for calling at the Villa Franchesi the week before last."'

'We don't need every word, darling,' said Bella.

Alice skimmed the rest of the letter, her eyes darting from left to right. 'Her mother is inviting us to a light supper!'

'All of us?' asked Melissa.

'You, dear Melissa. And your aunt . . .'

'Gracious!' said Lady Latchmere, uncertainly.

'And Mama and Papa. And Count Albani. And the Drummond-Wards.'

'Do I know these people?' asked Lady Latchmere.

Patiently, Melissa explained that Lady Caroline was the Earl of Harborne's daughter.

'The Countess looks forward to making your acquaintanceship, your Ladyship,' said Alice.

'Hmm,' said Lady Latchmere. 'Is it far?'

'A short carriage ride into the hills,' said Bella.

'Only I cannot be expected to travel any sort of distance after dark.'

'Oh please, Aunt!' There was desperation in Melissa's voice.

Count Albani stepped forward. 'Perhaps I might be permitted to ride with you, Lady Latchmere. And offer you my personal protection.'

'Your protection?' Lady Latchmere made a soft grunting noise. 'Well . . .'

'And when is this grand occasion?' asked Bella.

Alice looked again at the letter. 'The twenty-first.' She gave a little scream. 'That's Thursday!'

'Well,' said Bella, who couldn't remember the last time she had seen Alice so animated, 'you'd better go and warn Betty so that she doesn't prepare unwanted food.'

'And we should decide what we're going to wear,' Alice added.

The effect of the letter was extraordinary, Bella thought. Alice and Melissa rushed out of the room arm-in-arm, almost bumping into Count Albani, who was smiling and stroking his chin with his long, tapering fingers.

Suddenly understanding, Bella shot him a playful look. 'Do we have you to thank for this, Count?'

'It is Lady Caroline you should be thanking.'

'Is that so?' She continued to stare at him, daring him to meet her gaze – but he refused to play along. 'Well, whoever is behind this has made someone very happy.'

'Then, I am happy also.' He smiled and bowed his head before leaving the room.

Now, only Bella and Lady Latchmere remained.

The older woman was still fretting. 'Am I safe to entrust myself to him? You know what they say about Italians.'

'I'm not sure I do, Lady Latchmere.' Really, this woman held some peculiar opinions.

'They're notorious for it, I'm told.'

'Notorious for what, your Ladyship?'

'Goodness me, Mrs Ainsworth! Don't make me spell it out for you!'

Bella bit her lip, trying not to smile. 'Count Albani is certainly attentive. But also, very proper. At least, I've always found him to be.'

'And is there a Countess Albani?'

'He's a widower.'

'Ah,' said Lady Latchmere, darkly. 'Then *that* explains it.'

*

When Constance came downstairs after changing out of her nightdress, she felt suddenly exhausted after her broken

178

night. But she resolved not to be consumed by it. A servant never should be. As her mother always said, 'They're not paying you to be tired.'

This morning she was on 'Lottie duty', as she thought of it. It was always her favourite stretch of the day.

The first person she saw was Lucian, through the kitchen window. He was out in the garden, attaching a length of twine to two canes embedded in the ground. Beside him stood Lottie, bouncing a ball on some sort of tightly strung oval-shaped hoop. She looked rather practised at it.

Wandering outside, Constance asked her where she'd got hold of such a thing.

'Mr Plum,' she said.

Lucian laughed, though Constance could see tell-tale dark shadows beneath his eyes. 'She means Mr Wingfield. He lent us two rackets. To say thank you for finding a bicycle for him.'

Constance wasn't absolutely sure who Mr Wingfield was. She hadn't yet met the latest influx of guests. 'So, what are you doing, then?'

'This is going to be the net,' he said, tying a knot in the twine.

'The net?'

'You know. For tennis.'

She had never heard this word before. 'Tennis?'

Lucian looked as confused as she felt. 'Good God. Don't tell me you don't know what tennis is?'

'Not really. Not at all, in fact.'

J.P. O'Connell

'What about Wimbledon?'

She shook her head.

Lucian narrowed his eyes. 'This isn't some elaborate jape is it, Miss March? Like that business with your reading?'

'I swear on my life.'

His face brightened. 'Well, then. Here's something I really can teach you.'

He showed Constance how to hold the racket – as the oval-shaped hoop was called – and how to serve. He told her why it was important to keep her arm relaxed and her knees a little bent. He kept coming up to her and adjusting her stance, and she found herself looking forward to this – to the light, respectful touch of his fingers on her bare arm.

Lottie's whoops and hollers were thrilling to hear. Constance brushed a strand of hair from her sweaty forehead. How wonderful it was to be outside in the vital, sparkling heat – and for this to be her job.

They kept hitting the ball back and forth. Apparently, this was called a rally. Or was it a volley? At one point she hit the ball incredibly hard, and it hit him in the head, much to Lottie's amusement. 'Fault!' she said and jabbed her finger at Constance. 'Fault! Fault!'

Constance had no idea what her young charge was talking about.

But she wasn't to be deterred. She was starting to get the hang of this!

Next, she attempted something called a reverse forehand,

but the ball went sailing over Lucian's head and through the kitchen window . . .

There was a bright tinkling sound as the window smashed.

'Oh no!' Waves of panic coursing through her body, Constance dropped the racket and ran towards the kitchen door.

'Don't worry,' called Lucian, catching up with her. 'And don't apologise. I'll cover for you.'

By the time they reached the house, Betty was already sweeping up the broken glass while Alice watched.

'Well,' Alice said, arms folded. 'That wasn't very clever, was it?'

'Please be careful,' Constance said to Lottie, who had run in after them and who was about to walk across the kitchen floor in bare feet. She grabbed the girl's hand and held it tightly.

They stood, briefly shocked into silence, watching the broom as it gathered the shards of glass into a tidy pile.

But then Bella appeared, breathless, followed by Alice, who had gone to fetch her from her office. 'What on earth is going on?' She looked from face to face.

'We broke a window,' said Lucian.

'I can see that!' She handed him the offending ball.

'We were playing tennis,' Lucian explained.

'Who's we?'

'Lottie and me.' He paused. 'And Miss March.' He looked across at Constance, who wanted nothing more than for the ground to open up and swallow her. 'It was an accident.'

'A costly and avoidable one.'

Lottie started to cry. 'It wasn't me, Nana Bella!'

At that moment, both Lucian and his sister spoke simultaneously.

'It was me!' from Lucian.

'It was Constance!' from Alice.

Constance felt herself start to shake. Had Alice seen what had happened?

'It was my fault,' repeated Lucian, more firmly this time. 'I was messing about. Things got a little out of hand.'

Bella's hand flew to her mouth – and Constance fancied she saw tears in the older woman's tired eyes. 'As if I don't have enough on my plate!'

'I'm sorry, Mama,' said Lucian. 'I'll fix it.'

'Please see to it that you do.'

She turned and swept out. Constance looked at Lucian, trying to communicate gratitude, but he was chasing after his mother, grabbing the green baize door before it slammed shut. She was left alone with Alice, who glowered at her. Constance got the impression that if Lottie had not been there Alice would have said awful, unforgivable things. All Alice managed, because it was all she could get away with, it being vague enough not to attract Lottie's attention, was: 'Remember your place.'

*

Bella's office was unusually messy. There were bills strewn across the mahogany desk and the rug was rucked up. Beneath his anger, Lucian felt concern for her.

'Is something wrong?'

'I'm fine.' She was collecting up the bills, stacking them in neat piles.

'You don't seem to be.'

'I'm fine, Lucian! Please!' She looked flustered.

'Is this about money?'

Her face darted up. 'Why would you think that?'

'You seem to be making an awful fuss about a few lira for a broken window.'

Bella said nothing.

His glance travelled to his mother's hands. 'And I couldn't help noticing your ring was missing. I thought perhaps you might have felt obliged to sell it.'

Her left hand instinctively covered her right – far too late. 'What a vivid imagination you have! My fingers have swollen in the heat, that's all. I didn't want it to get stuck. So, I removed it.'

The force of the lie hit him hard. 'I saw the letter from the Casino this morning. You handed it to me, so I can't help thinking that some part of you wanted me to see it.'

His mother's face grew pinched. 'We're a little short of ready money, that's all. There's been a lot of expense upfront. And I've been hit with a demand I hadn't anticipated.'

Worried now, Lucian softened his tone. 'Will it be all right?'

'I expect so. If we can get through to the end of the season.'

'Can grandfather help out?'

'Oh, Lucian. Not you as well. You know I can't abide a freeloader.'

183

'Forget I said it.' He felt embarrassed to have made the suggestion.

'I told you opening the hotel would fulfil me. But that's only true if I can get it to pay for itself.'

Lucian sat down. As silence gathered around them, he grew gloomy. 'Perhaps Father's right. Perhaps it *is* time for me to go home and get a job. And do whatever else is necessary.'

But Bella shook her head. She held out her arms to him. He reached across and took her hands in his. 'No, no. No one is going to force you to do anything before you're ready.'

'Maybe I'm as ready as I'll ever be.'

'I'll be the judge of that,' Bella said, her tone and face finally softening. 'After all, I am your mother.'

*

As the morning lengthened, Paraggi beach filled with tourists. Men stood in groups chatting, while the women wedged their fringed rush hats under rocks and pulled on their bathing dresses to run laughing into the sea. It was hot and windless, the sky vast and empty above the burning sand.

Claudine was lying on a lounger, listening to the lazy flopping of the waves. Next to her, lay Lizzie. They had met by chance in the foyer. Lizzie had asked Claudine if she minded her tagging along. Claudine had said not at all, meaning it, too. She had left Jack back at the hotel.

To be honest, she was one of the few people at the hotel who knew who Plum Whitfield was, having overheard a good many conversations about tennis on her travels, and she was as keen on gossip as anyone. But Lizzie seemed anxious, discontent, as if the heat was a surprise to her. She wasn't the world's best company, if the truth be told.

'I'll look like a lobster if I'm not careful,' she said.

Claudine produced a silk, tassled wrap from her bag and draped it on the other woman's shoulders. 'There,' she said.

'Don't you feel it?' Lizzie asked.

'What?'

'The sun.'

'Sure. If I stay out too long.'

'But do you ... you know ...'

Claudine knew where the question was leading. 'Go darker?'

Lizzie nodded.

'We *all* change colour in the sun, honey.'

'You don't mind me asking?'

'Hell, no. I've been asked worse than that!' And much less politely, Claudine thought. She was prepared on this occasion to overlook the naivety of Lizzie's questions. That the English woman was respectful in how she asked them counted for a lot.

Lizzie giggled, then stopped abruptly, her glance travelling coolly and deliberately along Claudine's face and body. 'It must be hard,' she said.

'Sometimes,' Claudine conceded. 'And sometimes not.'

Lizzie absorbed this – the complexity of it, Claudine hoped, rather than the apparent simplicity. Then she said: 'I think I'll go and have a wander. Maybe get a drink.'

As she was saying this, Claudine found herself distracted by the sight of Roberto. He was standing on a cluster of fat rocks that made her think in some childish way of dinosaurs drinking together at a pool. 'You go ahead,' she said. 'I'll join you in a bit.'

'Right you are,' said Lizzie.

When she was sure Lizzie was far enough away not to notice, Claudine lowered her sunglasses, the better to observe Roberto's stupendous physique.

An idea formed in the basest, most reckless part of her brain. It made her mouth dry and her pulse quicken.

She waited for him to dive in again. Then she rose and waded into the lapping waves, submerging herself quickly so he wouldn't see her. After the initial shock of immersion, she felt blissfully safe and serene. What some people get from church, she told herself, I get from the sea – the sense of suspension in something bigger and grander than yourself.

She was a strong swimmer and made it to the rocks in a few moments, hauling herself up so that she was already standing by the time his head broke the water. She stared down at him, confident and imperious, perfectly aware of how she looked and how this caused men like Roberto to react.

He grinned. '*Ciao*,' he said, and climbed out to stand next to her.

'*Ciao*.'

'Signora Turner?'

Claudine nodded. 'I've seen you at the hotel.'

He pointed to himself. 'Roberto. Roberto Albani.'

'Pleasure to meet you, Roberto Albani.' She held out a dripping hand, which he kissed.

'My English is . . . little,' he said.

'*Parlez-vous Français?*'

He looked confused.

'Don't worry, honey. We don't need to talk.'

They stood there, each appraising the other. Roberto mimed a dive. 'You like?'

'Sure, I like.'

Claudine swallow-dived perfectly into the sea. She kept on swimming, staying underwater for as long as she could. Long enough to worry him, hopefully, and so ensure that he was tempted to dive in and rescue her.

She came up for air and looked around, treading water. He was no longer on the rocks. So where was he?

Finally, he bobbed up, several yards away. Wiping the water from his face, he spotted her and grinned broadly.

Laughing, she swam away, confident that he would follow. Her previous explorations had revealed the existence of a sheltered, sandy cove not far from where they were now. She headed towards it, shifting from crawl to breaststroke before giving up and allowing the waves to lift her weightlessly onto the shore.

Once there she propped herself up on her elbows, waiting as Roberto strode from the azure sea. He stopped in front of her, his face backlit by the sun, then fell on his knees. She allowed herself to relax into the sand, silently inviting him to cover her body with his.

Roberto was above her now, his sinewy arms encompassing her; his broad, hairless chest mere inches from her breasts. A dry, intoxicating heat seemed to radiate from every pore on his skin. She put an arm around his neck to pull him closer. He pushed his mouth towards hers and then they were kissing – kissing so insistently that it felt helpless, even shocking. The softness of his lips, the taste of his tongue – it was all as she had hoped, and as she had wanted.

As they pulled apart, gasping, Claudine slid her hands along the taut ripples of his back and beneath the loose band of his briefs.

She smiled up at him, her skin prickling in anticipation.

'*Bene*,' she said. '*Molto bene.*'

7

The first thing Lucian and Nish did when they reached Portofino was visit the *tabaccaio* on Via Roma so that Nish could stock up on his favourite Caporal cigarettes.

They had decided a walk would be head-clearing. Well, it had been Lucian's idea – but Nish had agreed enthusiastically.

At times Lucian worried he was being insufficiently attentive to his old friend. But he had been trying to focus on Rose, and on himself. Work out what he wanted from life. This entailed a certain selfishness. Besides, he thought, Nish was a self-contained sort of chap, with his books and his politics. He didn't need Lucian fussing over him.

On their way down, they had passed a long-legged English child from one of the hotels further up the hill, reading as she walked. She had ignored, or perhaps hadn't heard, Lucian's 'hello' and he had realised with unease that he envied her – her freedom to escape so utterly into a book that all she had to think about were the simple satisfactions of a story.

Nothing yet was expected of her, though it soon would be. That was the English way. Lucian wasn't sure Nish understood how boxed in he was by family forecasting, the teeming mass of assumptions about whom he should marry and how he should earn a living. Which was ironic, considering how similar their predicaments were.

They had talked about their families a lot during Lucian's convalescence. Nish's father wanted him to return to India – marry a suitable girl and practice as a doctor in the British medical tradition.

Nish didn't want that. As it was, he felt ambivalent about the Indian Medical Service, believing it to be an instrument of empire. 'I mean,' he'd argued one evening, long ago, while changing Lucian's dressings, 'what are people like me even doing? Fighting a European war based on European geopolitics?'

Nish wanted to be a writer as fiercely as Lucian wanted to be a painter. And so, they had a common bond of sympathy. At least, Lucian had always assumed as much.

After leaving the shop, the pair stood chatting on the kerbside, waiting for the traffic to pass before crossing. There was a smell of dry heat and drains. A dog ran by like a shadow, barking at something it had seen. Outside the *drogheria* an old woman was sweeping the steps in slow, methodical strokes.

A motorcycle approached, its rider a mechanic of some sort – judging by the oil on his hands and face. As the vehicle drew close, a Blackshirt stepped out from nowhere and stood in front of it, forcing it either to stop or mow him down.

Lucian and Nish took advantage of the moment to cross the road. Nish nodded an acknowledgement, trying as always to be polite. But the Blackshirt just stared at him. Then he muttered something to his companions, and they laughed mockingly.

One of the men, a burly fellow with slicked back hair, asked: '*Cosa stai fissando?*' What are you staring at?

Lucian started to square up to him, but Nish pulled him away. 'Don't, Lucian.'

'But he insulted us.'

'It isn't worth it. Believe me.'

Another voice called out: '*Ehi! Negretto!*' Hey! Darkie!

They walked briskly down the street, radiating efficiency rather than panic, or so they hoped. Whenever they glanced back, the men were following them, grinning malignly.

'*Venite qui, bei ragazzi.*' Come back, pretty boys.

Lucian looked at Nish. 'They don't give up, do they?'

Nish shook his head.

They sped up, pushing apologetically past pedestrians before breaking into a run as soon as they had a clear stretch of pavement.

A *gelato* cart emerging from a side street bought them valuable seconds by blocking their pursuers' progress. Edging round it, they ducked into an alleyway and flattened themselves against the wall. Seconds later, the Blackshirts passed in a flurry of raised voices and laughter, their quarry apparently forgotten.

Panting, Nish sank slowly into a crouch. He wiped his face with a handkerchief. 'I sometimes wonder when this will stop. If it will ever stop.'

Lucian, too, was exhausted. He rested his hands on his knees.

Then they heard a voice – deep, Italian. 'Signori? May I be of assistance?' A dark-haired man in his early twenties was walking towards them out of the shadows.

'It's all right,' said Lucian. He grabbed Nish's arm protectively. 'We don't need help.'

The man raised his hands. 'Do not worry. They will not harm you in daylight. Perhaps just humiliate you.'

Lucian looked at him with suspicion. 'And who are you?'

'My name is Gianluca.' He signaled that they should follow him. 'Please. This way. If you want to be safe.'

They followed him trustingly, silently, past balconies festooned with drying clothes and windows, from which seeped the reassuring sounds of babies crying and couples arguing. After about five minutes, they emerged from this warren of narrow, unfamiliar back streets onto the seafront, bustling with well-dressed tourists. Lucian felt sweaty and shabby, as if everyone was looking at them.

'The hotel is that way,' said Gianluca, pointing.

Lucian said, 'How do you know where we're staying?'

He laughed. 'Everyone knows where the English live.'

'I'm not an Englishman,' said Nish.

'Then you only behave like one.' Nish looked offended. Noticing this, Gianluca rushed to clarify. 'My friends met you at the hotel this morning. There is no one else in Portofino who fits your description.'

Of course. The men with the cart.

Nish's compassion and curiosity eclipsed his resentment. 'How is the boy?'

Gianluca made a face, as if to say, *Not good*.

'Has someone examined him?'

'The doctors here ... They are not for people like us.'

Lucian couldn't resist asking, 'And who are "people like you"?'

'The ones who fight.'

From the pocket of his trousers, Gianluca produced a small leaflet, which he handed to Nish. On the front, it had a skull-and-crossbones motif but with Mussolini's head in place of the skull. Lucian took the flimsy bit of paper from his friend and looked at it before giving it back to Nish.

'We've both seen what happens when men fight,' Nish said. 'The horror of it.'

Gianluca looked unimpressed by this. 'So, what will you do? When they come for you?'

'There are no *Fascisti* in England,' said Lucian, confidently.

'Of course there are, my friend. They just have not put on the shirt yet.' Gianluca looked steadily at them. His eyes were clear – a hard, metallic blue – but something in the depths of them glittered and shifted.

*

When they got back to the hotel, Nish went up immediately to his suite. He washed in the second-floor communal bathroom – which for once was unoccupied – before allowing himself the luxury of a short nap.

When he awoke, he worked on his journal. He felt angrier and more political than he had the last time he picked up his pen. Less inclined to let Italy, or English tourists, off the hook.

Several years have passed now since the March on Rome. And English visitors to Italy, secure within their luxury hotels, convince themselves that fascism has nothing to do with them. But they are mistaken. Fascism has penetrated all aspects of life in Italy. *Squadrismo* violence continues to be perpetrated in all provinces against anyone Mussolini's Blackshirts deem subversive, because of their socialist views. Or because their skin happens to be a different colour.

If you ask me how I know this, I will tell you.

Because it's happened to me.

He kept thinking about Gianluca. The clench-fisted salute he had given before he ran off. His blue eyes and aquiline nose. The thick knots of muscle at the top of his arms. He wondered what he would look like naked.

Stop, stop. Ridiculous thought. Unhelpful.

The leaflet taunted him from his desk. He picked it up, relishing the seductive danger of its message and the feel of the cheap paper between his fingers, paper that had been touched by Gianluca.

The writing was in Italian. Nish wished he could under-stand it properly. He could pick out the odd word and his Italian-to-English dictionary wasn't bad.

Better, though, to get a proper idiomatic translation by someone who had spent time in Italy.

He closed his journal and shrugged on his jacket.

But Lucian was not in his room as he had said he would

be. The trail of his sonorous voice led Nish downstairs, to the library.

Nish hovered outside the door, listening. Constance was reading to Lucian, carefully, falteringly. He was giving her a lesson of some sort.

'Then the fair Helen chose a prince, whose name was Men ... Men ...'

'Menelaus,' corrected Lucian, kindly.

'The brother of Aga ... memnon, who reigned in ... ugh!'

'Mycenae. Keep going. You're doing brilliantly.'

Nish knocked lightly on the door. 'I'm sorry to interrupt.'

'Don't be,' said Lucian, glancing up. 'We're reading Homer.'

'The children's version,' added Constance, looking slightly sheepish.

Lucian kept his gaze level. 'Did you want something?'

'It can wait.'

But Lucian had clearly spotted the leaflet in his hand. 'That looks familiar.'

Nish dared another step into the library. 'I thought you might be able to tell me what it says.'

Lucian snapped his fingers. 'Throw it here, then.' Squinting at the tiny text, he read out loud: '"For lovers of justice and liberty! We disclaim any solidarity with fascism and its crimes ..."' He read on, translating in his head, before summarising. 'There's a meeting tomorrow night. In a workshop. Somewhere off the road to Rapallo.' He flipped it over, squinting at the caricature of Mussolini on the front. 'All a bit schoolboy, isn't it?'

Nish reached over and snatched it back.

Lucian frowned. 'Don't tell me you're thinking of going along?'

'Are you mocking me? For wanting to inform myself?'

'Of course not. Don't be so touchy.'

'You think Mussolini is a joke?'

'I think all politicians are contemptible. Whatever their stripe.'

A typical Lucian answer. Confident but vague. Uncommitted. They glared at each other. As they did so the room seemed to tilt, the furniture shrinking back into the corners, and Nish was seized by a suspicion of being alien, unwelcome, alone.

It meant he was the first to crack. 'I'm sorry. I thought it wouldn't hurt to know a little more about what's going on here, that's all. It's not worth falling out over.'

Lucian shook his head. 'No, no. It's me who should apologise. For being such a dilettante.' He stood up and embraced Nish, patting him on the back as they separated.

Constance shifted in her seat. Nish had quite forgotten that she was there. 'I'm sorry,' he said to her. 'I've spoiled your lesson.'

'Not at all,' she said. 'We'd almost finished.' She began to gather her things. She looked unembarrassed, which was a relief.

'Please don't go on my account,' said Nish.

'I have to. Alice will be needing me to take over with Lottie. Then there's dinner to prepare.'

'You mustn't think much of us,' said Lucian. 'Arguing over nothing.'

'It didn't sound like nothing to me.' Constance paused. 'My brother, Arthur . . . He says there's a fascist lurking in all of us.'

'He sounds like a wise man,' said Nish.

'Not really. He emigrated to Canada. And he can't stand the cold!'

They all laughed.

Lucian asked, 'You have a big family?'

'Not anymore. There's only Mam left at home. And little Tommy.' There was a perceptible catch in her voice as she spoke this name.

'It must have been hard for her,' said Nish. 'To let you go.'

She responded with a directness that surprised Nish. 'What about you, Mr Sengupta?'

'Me?'

'Yes, you.'

'I haven't seen my family for nearly ten years.'

'Ten years!' She gasped.

'His father packed him off at twelve,' explained Lucian. 'To be educated like an Englishman.'

'And how long does that take?' wondered Constance.

Nish laughed. 'I'll let you know when I find out.'

*

'Where have you been?' snapped Alice. 'If I've rung the bell once I've rung it a thousand times.'

'I'm sorry. I was with Master Lucian. The lesson ran late.'

'It certainly did.'

Alice and Francesco were emerging from the kitchen when Constance bumped into them – Alice carrying a folding washing stand, Francesco a basin containing a jug of hot water.

'Here,' said Alice, handing her the stand. 'Take this and follow Francesco to the Turners' suite. Mrs Turner is complaining that someone is using the communal bathroom and she can't get in. Honestly,' she sighed, 'not every suite can have its own bathroom. This isn't the Savoy.'

The door opened almost at once to reveal Claudine wearing a silk slip that clung so tightly to her body it might as well not have been there.

'Wonderful,' she said, observing the servants' load. 'Put them over there. The wash-stand by the vanity table, please.'

Averting his gaze from Claudine, Francesco carried the heavy jug unsteadily towards the chest of drawers. Before Constance had had a chance to arrange the basin on the wash-stand, he scuttled hotly from the room.

'Someone's in a hurry,' Claudine noted. She had gone to perch on a velvet stool in front of her dressing table, holding a sponge in her left hand. 'Can you help me?' She held out the sponge and indicated to Constance that she wanted her to bathe her neck and back. 'I've grit everywhere. I got a little overexcited on the beach.'

Claudine lowered her head, keeping still as Constance washed her neck with slow, soft sweeps of the sponge, her eyes drawn to the mirror and the reflection of the older woman's figure beneath the sheer slip. Claudine leant her head to one side and suddenly looked up. Constance blushed and dropped her gaze.

'It's all right. No harm in looking.'

Constance smiled shyly, resuming the sponging. 'I didn't mean to be rude.'

'You haven't seen skin like mine before, have you?'

Constance shook her head. 'I imagine Helen of Troy must have looked a lot like you.'

'And who's Helen of Troy?'

'A woman in my book. They fought a war over her. The Greeks and the Trojans.'

Claudine burst out laughing. 'Then I'll do my best not to start another one. Wars are bad for business!'

Gently tugging the slip loose, Constance pushed the sponge down between Claudine's shoulder bones, following the bumps of her spine. She started to relax, to enjoy Claudine's easy company. 'Can I ask you something, Mrs Turner?'

'Sure. But first things first, I'm not "Mrs" and I sure as hell ain't "Turner".'

'But I thought . . .'

'Of course, you did.' She smiled. 'I'm Claudine Pascal. At least I was, in Paris.'

'But now?'

'I'm still Claudine, I guess. Most of the time.'

Well, that's clear as mud, thought Constance. She squeezed out the sponge and started patting Claudine dry with a towel. 'Your life sounds so dramatic.'

'It does,' Claudine conceded. 'Drama is overrated, though. Don't you think?' As she said this a sad, reflective look came over her face and Constance decided not to press further.

When they had finished, Claudine rummaged in her wardrobe for something to wear while Constance collected up the jug and bowl.

'I'll send Francesco up later, Miss Pascal.' She smiled and Claudine smiled back. 'To fetch the wash-stand.'

'One moment.' Claudine rummaged through a bag on her bed, producing a handful of coins which she held out to Constance.

She shook her head. 'There's really no need.'

'Take it, child.'

'I couldn't.'

Claudine must have noticed her eyes flicking towards the array of lipsticks on the dressing table. Smiling, she said, 'You prefer one of these?' She reached across and picked out a gold tube engraved along the sides with a leaf pattern. On the top were the initials 'P&T', encircled by a wreath.

'It stands for Park & Tilford,' Claudine explained. 'It's an American brand.'

Constance held the tube nervously. 'I wouldn't know what to do with it.'

'It's easy enough. Let me show you.'

She mimed pursing her lips, encouraging Constance to follow her example, then told her to keep still while she applied a generous coating of brownish pink lipstick to her mouth. On each of Constance's cheekbones she placed an almost imperceptible dab of rouge.

'Now for the eyes,' she said. 'You know what they say about eyes, don't you?'

'What's that?'

'That they're the windows to the soul.'

Constance smiled, trying not to move as Claudine experimented with different shades of eyeshadow. 'Do you believe that?'

'No,' said Claudine, without pausing. 'Eyes can deceive. I know *your* soul is good from the way you talk. The way you conduct yourself.'

She took Constance by the shoulders, angling her slightly, and together they examined the results in the mirror. Constance didn't recognise the person staring back, but Claudine seemed to like her. 'Never mind them fighting over me. You've got everything it takes to start your own damn war.'

Constance felt herself blushing. She looked away. 'No one notices me.'

'That's because you're hiding! You can't be shy to show them what you've got. Or what you want.'

Gently, she lowered Constance down into the seat and started to unpin her hair. It was golden brown, blonde in places where the sun had caught it.

'Are you sure?' Constance had been enjoying this pampering, but worried things were getting out of hand. 'Mrs Mays-Smith won't like it.'

Claudine looked at her incredulously and laughed, her

hands gently squeezing Constance's shoulders. 'But, honey,' she said, 'it isn't Mrs Mays–Smith we're aiming to please.'

*

'What are you two doing?' Bella popped her head round the door of the library to see Lucian and Nish looking through a stack of gramophone records. 'Careful with those. They're fragile, you know.'

'We're reliving our misspent youth,' said Lucian.

'This one!' said Nish, pulling the disc from its paper sleeve. 'Put this one on!'

Lucian looked at the label. 'Oh God, please . . .'

Bella mock-frowned. 'Language, Lucian.'

Smiling, she left them to it. Evening was approaching. Time to light the lamps. As she walked to the drawing room, there was a crackle and then the music started up, the unmistakable strains of 'For He Is An Englishman' from *HMS Pinafore*.

Bella hummed to herself as she went about her business. Like most of its rivals, Hotel Portofino was wired for electric light. But Bella – and, she suspected, most of the older guests – preferred the atmosphere created by oil lamps, which gave off a diffuse autumnal glow.

She was adjusting the wick on one especially recalcitrant lamp when out of the corner of her eye she saw something that made her jump.

It was Lady Latchmere, sitting in the green chair by the window. She looked disorientated, as if she had just woken from a dream-filled, unrestful sleep.

'I'm sorry, your Ladyship,' said Bella. 'I didn't see you there.'

'I was about to dress for dinner,' said Lady Latchmere. Her voice was flat and affectless.

The music continued to play.

'I can't help smiling when I hear this song,' said Bella.

'Indeed.'

'The Italians gave us opera and we turned it into this. What a funny nation we are. At least we have Elgar, I suppose.'

She was about to resume her lamp-lighting when Lady Latchmere said, 'I saw them perform it.'

Bella turned. 'Yes?'

'*HMS Pinafore*, at the Savoy. Before the war. With Ernest.'

She fished a locket from her dress and opened it, beckoning Bella closer so that she could see the photograph it contained. Bella pulled up a chair and sat beside her, dimly conscious that the music had stopped. She took the proffered locket. The photograph showed a handsome young man wearing an officer's uniform.

'He was my eldest,' said Lady Latchmere. 'He stepped on a landmine. Somewhere called Mont Sorrel. Nine years ago, tomorrow.' She paused. 'He'd only been there five minutes.'

Bella handed the locket back. Then she surprised herself by producing the one she wore around her own neck. She had never shown it to anyone before, let alone a woman like Lady Latchmere. But Bella felt strongly that it was the right thing to do. In fact, the urge to disclose was so powerful that it was indistinguishable from a need.

The photograph inside was of a young boy dressed in a sailor suit. 'This is my youngest. Laurence,' said Bella. 'He would have been fourteen next month.' Lady Latchmere held it up, scrutinising it. 'The influenza took him,' she added. 'He's one of the reasons we came here.'

'To start afresh?'

'Somewhere with no memories.'

The clock ticked soothingly. Soon it would chime the half hour.

Lady Latchmere folded the locket back into Bella's hands, enclosing them with her own, and said: 'I wish I had your courage, my dear.' At that moment Bella had a sudden intuition that the other woman was not so much older than she was; that there were perhaps five years between them, maybe fewer.

The difference was that Lady Latchmere had frozen in time. Even worse, the past had gathered up inside her as if in a great box and continued to exist for her so that each day, from morning till night, she was compelled to live through it without ever moving beyond it.

Bella couldn't imagine a greater torture.

*

Dinner that evening was another Ligurian classic: chicken braised in white wine with rosemary, pine nuts and tomatoes, served with sautéed spinach.

'Now that were a tasty one,' Betty said to Constance as she placed a heap of dirty plates beside the sink. 'It weren't complicated either.'

Constance felt like observing that the recipe had only seemed uncomplicated because Paola had once again helped to cook it. But she bit her tongue.

To Constance's mild annoyance, neither Betty nor anyone else seemed to have noticed the subtle but significant transformation wrought by Claudine on her face.

Betty handed Constance a tray laden with glass bowls containing a thick creamy-brown mixture.

'What's this?'

'Tiramisu. It's the Italian version of sherry trifle, but with Amaretto instead of sherry. Take 'em through, there's a good girl.'

Constance pinned her shoulders back, took a deep breath and strode into the dining room.

Perhaps it was something to do with the way she was carrying herself, but this time there was a palpable difference – she felt it like the static shock from touching a doorknob.

As she passed Billy – he was on his way back to the kitchen – he gave a low whistle of appreciation and she shivered inwardly even though he wasn't her target, if that was the right word. She put the tray down on the sideboard and turned for instruction to Bella, who was busy checking the desserts.

Bella didn't notice anything different. But then she wouldn't. She was in her own world sometimes. A right Mrs Dreamy.

The tiramisu was ready for serving. As Constance approached Claudine's table the older woman winked at her. Mr Turner looked up briefly, but there was a quizzical expression on his face, as if he both did and did not recognise her – understandable really as she hadn't had much to do with him.

Roberto was the one. The real noticer of women. He was sitting with his father and Cecil, bored by the conversation they were having in English, which of course he didn't understand. He straightened in his seat as she approached, smiling lasciviously as he took in the sight of her. She nodded and smiled back, then moved on quickly to Nish's table. Roberto wasn't someone she wanted to encourage. Though he did have nice eyes.

Nish was sitting on his own, watching Lucian, who was sitting with Julia and Rose.

'Left on your own again?' she asked.

'It seems that way.' He watched her closely as she put the bowl on the table. 'Something about you – it's different.'

She smiled, but turned away without comment.

Her next and most important stop was Lucian's table.

He and Rose were huddled together, examining a selection of art postcards she had bought on her trip to Genoa. Snatches of their conversation, or rather Lucian's commentary, wafted across. 'It's easy to disregard the Genoese School, but Strozzi especially is fascinating ...' Rose was nodding, spellbound. Or was she bored? It was hard to tell.

Only Julia looked up as she put the desserts on the table. Constance hesitated for a few seconds, hoping Lucian would notice and acknowledge her.

He did not. He continued to talk, as if he were frightened to stop. But Rose's mother stared at her and kept staring with a bored malice that was frightening because it was so casual.

Her look said: *Oh, for goodness' sake.*

At home, this sort of treatment would have aroused in Constance some useful instinct of self-defence. But here she felt foolish and exposed. She wanted nothing more than to escape, before the tears welling in her eyes became notice-able. Slipping the tray under her arm, she rushed from the room. Once outside, with the back of her free hand, she wiped the lipstick roughly from her mouth.

*

The next day Cecil woke early, mindful that he had more to do than usual. After a light breakfast of eggs and several cups of the strong, bitter coffee he had grown to love, he wrote some letters – including one to the casino thanking them for their bill and assuring them payment would be forthcoming.

The main thing was to avoid getting bogged down in tedious domestic dramas to do with Bella or the servants.

To that end, Cecil went for one of his walks. He wandered up to the Albergo Delfino, a rival hotel approached via a steep, narrow pathway along which old local women sat at intervals making lace on pillows. One ignored them, of course.

The Delfino was an old, rambling house not dissimilar to Hotel Portofino, with a terrace overlooking the quay. It was popular with Germans and while naturally one was sceptical of Germany, there was no denying the comeliness of the young women one saw staying there, some of whom were rumoured to sunbathe naked – *O tempora, o mores!* – or the magnificence of the view from its windows across the blue sea to Chiavari and Sestri Levante further up the coast.

He considered walking on to Faro di Portofino but decided against it. He had never understood the appeal of the lighthouse, which had sprung up in the years since he and Bella first came to Portofino and struck Cecil as something of a blot on the landscape. Useful for ships, though.

No one had asked him directly to help organise the tea party, but seeing as it had been his idea, he assumed his input would be appreciated.

By the time he got back, however, most of the hard work had been done. Wasn't that always the way? Francesco had mowed and swept the lawn and was now, with Billy's help, erecting a large white tent, hammering staves into the ground with a soft chock-chock.

Cecil went to the cellar and rooted around for something to serve those for whom tea might be insufficient. He was proud of his wine collection, which included several bottles of Petrus from 1915 and a Chateau Margaux from 1900.

Danioni and his friends were bound to want something Italian, which suited Cecil fine.

He found a couple of cases of Piedmontese plonk – inexpensive but acceptable – and summoned Billy to drag them up to the kitchen.

The hotel felt busy and alive. It was a curious thing, but as preparations for the party got underway, the more nervous

Cecil became. Crowds made him uneasy. And there was the additional worry of the painting, which was supposed to be arriving today. Would he miss its delivery? Would it even *be* delivered? There was no way of knowing in a place like Italy.

While Paola swept the terraces, plates of sandwiches and jugs of lemonade appeared on tables set up under garden umbrellas. People were changing into smart clothes and Cecil realised he had better do this too, so he went upstairs and put on his favourite cream linen suit with a new shirt and collar. He trimmed his moustache, then tinted it using the silver nitrate he applied every other day with a toothbrush.

The faint wind from the sea was ticklish. Cecil looked down from his window at the sun-dappled lawn, the billowing clouds of roses and agapanthus. At such moments, he felt a swell of pride at Bella's achievements and frustration with himself for not being more appreciative.

He resolved to try harder; to be a better husband. Not that he was a bad one. He knew how bad men could be – it was something all men knew. A secret, shameful knowledge passed down through generations. He wasn't *that* bad, if he did say so himself.

The weather stayed wonderful. He heard Bella remark that they could not have had a better day for a tea party if they had ordered it.

At around three o'clock the guests started to arrive.

He was just combing his hair when he heard the door to the Drummond-Wards' suite opening. Rose's voice flared out, leaving a trail of panic. She didn't have a hat. What hat should she wear? Then, Julia, an octave deeper: 'The one you wore on Sunday.' No, no, she couldn't wear that one, it was marked. Honestly!

Cecil waited upstairs for as long as he could, gathering his nerves, then came down to find Count Albani – who had rather taken charge – introducing Alice and Lucian to a group of local dignitaries, headed by ... Danioni.

Betty and Constance emerged every so often like cuckoos from a clock, carrying teapots and plates heaped with cakes and scones. There were Italian pastries too, included on the menu at the Count's insistence. But Cecil didn't care much for those.

He poured himself a glass of the Piedmontese wine. Knocked it back. It was thin and acidic and made him cough.

The groups were fragmenting and reforming. On the far side of the lawn was Bella, looking beautiful in the Jeanne Lanvin pastel *robe de style* he had encouraged her to buy last year. She stood at the centre of a circle that included Danioni, Danioni's deputy and a man from the electricity board. Their Director of Backhanders, probably.

Bloody Eye-ties. Always on the make.

Nish was talking to Alice. Rose, sitting beside her mother at one of the tables, was chatting to Lucian. Apparently she had never seen such darling sandwiches.

He heard Julia cut in. 'They're only for decoration. You're not supposed to eat them.'

Cecil smiled. But he felt frustrated. He wasn't enjoying the party, despite having done so much to initiate it. He stood apart from everyone else, clutching his empty glass like a prop.

He checked his pocket watch. Half-past three. It should be here by now. Come on, come on.

Five minutes later, the tinkle of polite chatter was drowned out by the sound of an engine pulling into the forecourt. 'If you'll excuse me,' he said to no one in particular, before quickly disappearing.

He reached the forecourt just in time to see two burly Italian men emerge from an open-backed truck.

'Ah,' he said, suddenly hearty. '*Buongiorno, amici miei.*' Without ceremony, they removed the covering from a large, flat package. Excitement surged in Cecil's chest.

The men carried it inside. Cecil followed them and asked them to prop it against the wall in the library.

He was just showing the men out when he saw Jack coming down the stairs. The timing couldn't have been better!

'Ah,' said Cecil. 'Just the man.'

'I saw the truck through my window.' Jack was rubbing his hands together in anticipation. 'All in one piece?'

'Seems to be.'

'Mind if I take a look?'

'I thought I'd leave the grand unveiling for a while if you don't mind,' said Cecil, playing down his elation. He gestured towards the outside. 'The tea party and all that. I shall be missed.'

'You go ahead.'

'I'm sure it will be worth the wait.'

At that moment, Plum came bounding down the stairs. He had obviously forgotten about the party as he wasn't dressed for it. Maybe he was going along anyway. He had the costume of his celebrity, after all.

'Sorry, chaps. Bit of a rush!'

Jack moved to one side to allow him to pass.

When he had gone Jack said, 'Do you think he heard us?'

'What, Plum? No. And even if he did, his mind's on higher things than art. Like winning tennis matches.'

'I guess so,' said Jack. But he sounded unconvinced.

Cecil closed the library door, then headed outside to find Danioni talking to one of the delivery men through the window of the truck. *Damn it*, he thought. *What's the blighter up to now?*

Danioni looked up when Cecil appeared. 'You had a delivery, I hear.'

'That's right.'

'From England?'

Cecil stiffened. 'I'm not sure what business it is of yours.'

Danioni smiled. 'Everything is the business of the Consiglio Comunale, Signor Ainsworth. Police. Licensing. Taxes . . .' He paused. 'On imports, for example.'

'I appreciate that,' said Cecil. 'Even so, I can assure you there's nothing to concern you here.' He fumbled in his jacket pocket for his silver cigar box, proffering it to the Italian as he tried to ignore the sweat prickling his armpits. 'Fancy a smoke?'

*

Betty was taking a tray of Fat Rascals out of the oven as Constance entered, bearing two empty sandwich trays.

The cook looked up at her. 'All the sandwiches gone?'

'Every last one.'

'That were quick.'

'They wolfed them down!'

'I had to beg every cucumber within three miles for those.'

Constance put the empty trays in the sink. 'Count Albani had most of them. I lost count at seven.'

'I love a man with a good appetite. There's plenty to hold on to!'

'Betty!'

They both burst out laughing.

Betty said, 'It's hard to imagine him with that slip of a girl.'

Constance looked confused.

'You haven't noticed, then?'

'Noticed what?'

'Him making eyes at Mrs Mays-Smith.'

'Alice is half his age!'

'Aye, but she could do a lot worse. I bet he'd put a smile back on that sourpuss face of hers.'

Constance loved it when Betty spoke like this. Said the things she herself thought but dared not say.

'I meant to ask you – what happened to Lottie's father?'

'The same as happened to the rest.'

The good humour of a moment ago gave way to something more sombre and reflective. The two women fell silent.

Then Betty shook herself. 'Come on,' she said. 'Let's plate these up. There's nowt so sad as a cold Fat Rascal!'

*

The tea party had broken up. Guests wandered in little groups, admiring the graceful solemnity of the gardens and the view across the glistening sea.

Feeling the heat in her light but formal dress, Bella was heading back inside when she saw Danioni with one hand cupped against the glass of the library window, trying to see into the room. She called out, 'Are you casing the joint, Mr Danioni?'

He stepped away from the window. '*Non capisco*,' he said.

'Are you looking for something else to steal?' With a new flush of fury, she held up her bare ring finger for his inspection, the skin white where the sapphire ring had once sat.

'Please.' Danioni pretended to look disappointed. 'We must be friends.'

'Friends don't blackmail one another.'

'Again! This word!' He held up his hands in mock offence. 'You have given me a gift for my wife. And I have given you custom for your hotel. This is how it works between friends.'

'Give and take,' she said, icily.

'Yes. Give and take.' He gestured towards the hotel. 'But let us both remember – some have more to give than others.'

Danioni tipped his hat and walked away up the drive.

As she watched him go, it occurred to Bella that Danioni was not wrong. Some *did* have more to give than others.

At the same time, she thought, she would do almost anything to get rid of him.

*

The promise of whatever might be lurking in the library had quite spoiled Plum's enjoyment of the party. He hadn't been able to stop thinking about it. As a result, he knew that his behaviour had been odd. Twitchy, even, Lizzie would say.

He'd left her in their suite. She'd drunk too much, never mind that it was supposed to be a *tea* party, and was complaining of a headache. She'd asked Plum to request some aspirin. Of course, he'd said. He'd ask Bella; he absolutely intended to.

But first, he went into the library, closing the door soundlessly behind him.

Something was going on.

He hadn't got where he was today by overlooking small details.

He crossed the room and tried the desk drawers. He'd noticed that Cecil used this desk; also that he lacked his own office, which said something about the balance of power between him and his wife.

Most of the drawers were locked. But one at the bottom wasn't. There was a letter in it too, from the casino in San Remo. He smiled. He could guess what that was all about.

Hands shaking – an unfortunate new development – he pulled the note out of its envelope. A bill. His eyes went straight to the bottom of the sheet: '*Totale dovuto*: 20.530 lira.'

Well, well. Naughty Cecil. Smacked wrists all round!

The sound of voices in the hallway made his chest tighten. When they finally receded, he looked around the library once again.

What had he missed?

Then he saw it – propped against the wall, wrapped in cloth and partially concealed by a chair. Quite a small thing, really. Still, his heartbeat quickened. He went over to lift a corner of the cloth, but at that moment Jack's booming voice surged as the door opened.

Damn it!

He just had time to duck beneath the desk, his heart hammering, before two men entered the room.

Jack and Cecil.

'Sorry about that,' Cecil said. From what Plum could see, he was carrying an easel. 'The party, I mean. Ghastly business. My wife ordered a three-line whip!'

Cecil walked across and picked up the painting. Plum cringed beneath the desk, hoping against hope that he wouldn't be spotted. Bella's husband whipped away the cloth, which fell to the ground, then placed something on the easel, which had been opened out on its three legs. At least, Plum assumed this was what Cecil was doing. Honestly, he couldn't see much more than a pair of shoes – brown Oxfords, slightly scuffed.

'First impressions?' said a voice. Cecil's.

A pause as Jack examined the painting. 'It's smaller than I expected,' he said, finally.

Another pause. 'Is that a problem?' Cecil's voice had

acquired an edge. Plum's own interest heightened. This was turning out to be a very interesting conversation.

'You don't sell art by the yard.'

Plum shifted beneath the desk. He could feel the first tinglings of cramp in his left leg.

There was the sound of someone taking a step back. 'Hmmm,' Jack said.

'Well?' Cecil sounded impatient.

'I'm not the expert.'

'But what's your instinct?'

'It's certainly his style.'

Cecil clapped delightedly, like a child watching a magic show.

'But, hey,' Jack cautioned. 'He had a workshop churning out hundreds of these things. Some he painted himself. Some he painted a little. Some he supervised. It's more likely "school of Rubens" than Rubens.'

'But it could pass?'

'It could pass.'

'And how much to authenticate?'

'A few hundred dollars, maybe.'

'No. I mean ... How much would it cost to *ensure* it's authenticated.' A new pressure had entered the conversation. 'Oh ...' Jack paused. 'Forty per cent if it makes over one hundred thousand. One per cent less for every two thousand beneath?'

'Let's start at twenty-five, shall we?'

'Thirty.'

'Done.'

'It goes without saying,' said Cecil, 'I'll need a copy of the letter of authentication. And a down payment. Before I hand it over to you.'

'Of course.'

There was a silence. The final shaking of hands? Plum dared to peer out and saw that this was indeed the case. Then the two men walked out of the room, leaving the painting sitting there on the easel for anyone to steal, should they so wish.

When he was sure they'd gone, Plum extricated himself from his hiding place. He stretched out his legs and arms and strolled up and down, practising behaving casually for the benefit of anyone who might suddenly walk in.

But he couldn't help staring at the painting.

A large blonde woman looking into a mirror.

Plum didn't know anything about art. But it seemed incomprehensible to him that this painting could be worth so much. Worth more than him, a sportsman at the top of his game.

He brushed himself down.

Cecil would be back soon to remove the painting.

It was time for one of Plum's patented sharp exits.

*

Claudine had not been asked to the light supper at the villa. But Jack had received a sudden surprise invitation after Rose, the Drummond-Ward girl, came down with a migraine.

Too much sun, probably. And not enough water. Anyway,

Nish had given her powders and now she was lying in her suite with a cold compress on her forehead.

Cecil had become Jack's new best friend. Which didn't surprise Claudine. They were peas in a pod. Chancers. Cecil had asked Jack to take Rose's place, but made it clear there was only space for one ...

'A great shame,' he had said, apparently, 'as I know Lady Caroline would love to meet ... Mrs Turner.'

Claudine didn't particularly want to go. But the idea of Jack going without her unsettled her. There was a word for what she thought – no, knew – was going on here. Racism. And it was tiring, the everyday grind of it. White people had no idea.

There had been less of it in Paris because there were more Black folk in that city – painters, dancers, musicians. Writers, too – like her good friend Langston. The creatives. At the Grand Duc, partying with Ada 'Bricktop' Smith and Florence Jones, she had felt truly at home. Here, well ... It was always going to be a different story.

'You don't mind?' Jack had asked, tying his tie in front of the mirror.

'I'll say it again,' she said, tiredly. 'I don't mind.'

'Ainsworth says this Harborne guy's got a massive pile in London. Packed with art, apparently.'

'He sounds quite the catch.'

She hadn't meant it to sound quite so sarcastic. But Jack picked up on her tone and came over to offer his special kind of consolation, the kind that consoled him more than her. She turned away as he tried to kiss her.

'Come on, baby,' he said. 'Don't be mad. You know I'd much rather be here with you.'

'I've hardly seen you. The whole goddamn time.' The force of her resentment surprised her.

'You know I have to take care of business.'

'No, Jack. You have to take care of *me*.' She moved things up a gear. 'You don't want to be seen out with me. Is that it?'

He turned away, exasperated. 'I told you! There was only room for one.'

Her sceptical look told him she wasn't convinced.

He tried again. 'Look. I brought you here, didn't I?'

'Sure you did, honey.' She leaned up on her elbows. 'But I'm beginning to wonder why.'

*

At some point, Rose peeled open her eyes and realised that the thumping pain behind them had gone. Even better, it had been replaced by a glorious lightness, the sort she remembered from her childhood when she really had felt light and free – a pristine sort of alertness.

There was music playing somewhere. It drifted up from downstairs. A tinny rasp but magical, like fairies singing at the bottom of the garden.

Calf-like, she stood and made her way slowly to the door. Opening it amplified the music and revealed new sounds – of laughter and conversation. They were coming from the drawing room.

She recognised the music. Why, she loved this song! It was 'Sweet Georgia Brown' played by Django Reinhardt.

She descended the stairs, clutching the banister. There were people in the drawing room. But everything was different from normal. The atmosphere was different. She could see through the open door that the carpet had been rolled up to create a dancefloor. Lizzie, the tennis player's wife, was there. Claudine and Roberto and some other people. They were sipping Prosecco and dancing.

What on earth was going on? She stood outside, watching and listening.

'God, I wish I could dance like you,' Lizzie was saying.

'Don't you know a professional when you see one?' Claudine's voice.

'You dance for a living?' Lizzie was incredulous.

'Among other things.' Claudine gave an exaggerated twirl. 'My name's in lights.' She used her hands to draw a picture. 'Claudine ... Pascal.'

'What a fabulous name. It sounds so French!'

'Well, I'm not going to cut it as Louella-Mae Dobbs. In Paris of all places.' Claudine burst out laughing.

Roberto whirled her away to dance with him. Lizzie indicated to Lucian that he should dance with her. He was there, too! Lucian!

'Where's your husband?' he asked her.

'He's gone to bed. He's awfully boring when he has a tournament.'

Finally, Lucian noticed Rose in the doorway. He hurried over, almost marching. 'Rose! Your mother said you had a migraine ...'

'I feel much better now.'

'Are you sure?'

'Absolutely.'

Claudine called out: 'Then come and join us. Nobody here's going to tell you "no".'

Lucian held out his hand. After a moment of doubt, Rose made up her mind that she would be ruled by caution no longer. Everyone else was enjoying themselves, so why shouldn't she?

How she loved the evening. She had the sort of fun she had never imagined. In her precious, cosseted world no one behaved like this, ever. Songs she had never heard before did unexpected things to her. They took her out of herself and placed her back energised. The result was a wonderful unsteadiness. Or perhaps that was the Prosecco.

'What's this one?' she asked Claudine.

'"Pine Top's Boogie Woogie". We danced to this in Paris. It was wild.'

'It's marvellous!' she cried.

'I know!' said Claudine.

Roberto poured the last of the Prosecco into Claudine's glass and indicated to Lucian that he should fetch more, which he did, handing a large glass to Rose. Roberto was dancing wildly, throwing shapes and showing off while Claudine and Lizzie watched, nudging one another and giggling. Lizzie drained her glass, holding it theatrically over her head.

Rose gulped at her Prosecco. Lucian was asking if she

was all right and she was nodding. Laughing, having fun, becoming more high-spirited by the minute.

This was so much better than a stupid light supper at a boring villa.

At some point, Nish turned up and joined in – leaping around, twirling and tumbling.

Everyone Rose liked was here. All the nice, good people.

Someone changed the music to The Charleston.

'I know this one!' Rose shouted and everyone cheered. 'I know this!'

The music became louder and faster. She was feeling Lucian's eyes on her. The way he pulled her close, the way he held her, as if she were made of clay and he was shaping her into a better, more serious person – someone who knew things. She wanted him to kiss her. She didn't think she had ever wanted anything so much.

Later, she reflected on how different things might have been if Mr Turner's Bugatti hadn't pulled up in front of the hotel at that precise moment.

If her mother hadn't been sitting beside him and Bella in the back.

If Julia hadn't heard the music and laughter and, after exchanging an alarmed look with Bella, hurried out to investigate.

If she, Rose, hadn't been the last one dancing, flushed and ecstatic, high on life itself.

Until the music stopped.

'What's happened?' She looked over at Lucian, who had

taken the needle off the record. He was staring at something behind her, a terrifying apparition.

She turned, her chest heaving, her fine clothes damp with sweat.

It was her mother, in the doorway, with Bella behind her.

'And what,' asked Julia icily, 'do you think you're doing?'

*

Nish found Lucian in the garden, looking flushed. Dazed, a little drunk.

'That was unfortunate timing,' he said.

They looked up towards the lighted windows of the drawing room, where Bella, Alice and Constance were clearing up.

Lucian asked, 'Did you see Rose?'

'Oh yes.' Nish laughed. 'She's having a strip torn off her by her mother. Several strips, I'd imagine.'

Lucian winced. 'What about *my* mother? Did she say anything?'

'She's clearing up with Constance and your sister. I offered for us to help, but she suggested it might be better to go to bed.'

'"Suggested".'

'All right, instructed.' Nish laughed.

'I won't sleep,' said Lucian. 'I'm too ... energised.'

'Me too.' Nish produced the pamphlet from his pocket – the one Gianluca had given him. 'So, what do you think?'

'The meeting? I think it's a long way to walk.'

'We don't have to walk. Not when there's a bicycle.' He

indicated the sit-up-and-beg contraption Billy had procured for Plum. It was leaning against the wall behind them, one of the hotel's monogrammed hand towels still strapped to the rear pannier rack by a couple of elasticated bands.

'Go on, then,' said Lucian. 'If we must.'

They wobbled along the twisty, unlit road to Rapallo, Lucian perched on the handlebars, laughing as they sang the chorus of the socialist anthem 'The Red Flag' in bad Italian.

After about fifteen minutes, they came to a juddering halt in a courtyard outside the only building readily identifiable as a workshop – a stuccoed barn-like building the size of a church hall. The voices emanating from within told them they had got the right place.

They knocked and were let in by an elderly fellow guarding the door. They stood at the back. On a raised platform before the packed, rapt audience stood Gianluca. He was speaking passionately in Italian, slapping the back of one hand into the palm of the other.

He had looked up, momentarily tense, as the door opened but relaxed visibly – even smiled a little – when he saw who was entering.

And then, it happened. The event the whole room must have been dreading but knew in their hearts was inevitable. People factored in the risk when they decided to attend.

The first anyone knew of it was the dull drone of engines, gradually rising in volume until it became a roar. By that time, it was too late to take any evasive action. The canvas blinds were already glowing yellow from the headlights. Car doors already slamming.

The lookout shouted: 'Carabinieri!'

There was pandemonium as the lights were hurriedly dimmed and the audience scattered, some fleeing the building, others hiding beneath furniture or scurrying up the fire escape and onto the roof. A ragged queue formed chaotically by the back door where the lookout was standing.

Lucian froze, not knowing what to do. He was about to join the others when Gianluca grabbed his arm and hustled him and Nish into a side room, pushing them forward.

'Andiamo, andiamo . . .'

Someone pushed aside some old burlap and bits of wood to reveal a hidden trap door. Tiles had been laid on top so that it blended in with the rest of the floor.

Gianluca pulled on a handle, and it opened easily, releasing a cold, earthy smell and a cloud of dust. There was a rope ladder going down.

'Quick,' he said. 'In here. Now!'

8

Nish stumbled along the street, trying to keep pace with Lucian and Gianluca. His head was pounding, and he was exhausted after the long trek from the workshop.

The journey had proceeded in fits and starts, with regular breaks waiting watchfully to ensure they weren't being followed. The most important thing had been to get off the main road.

Nish was concerned about the bicycle, which they had had no choice but to abandon. But Lucian just shrugged. 'I wouldn't worry,' he said. 'Someone will recover it.'

They scrambled down a steep, rocky slope and across a stream until they reached a small oak forest. From there, guided only by the moonlight, they picked their way from terrace to terrace between lines of olives until they came to a little white house standing alone in a grove of peach trees.

Its tenants, an elderly couple, were evidently friends of Gianluca – friends and allies. Although it was nearly two o'clock in the morning they were still up. Or, perhaps, they never went to bed. Gianluca spoke to the man, who was tiny with a shock of white hair and the merest snub of a nose. Nish made out the word '*cantina*' – at which the man smiled and nodded, as if he knew the very place where they had crouched, terrified, for more than two hours until the lookout rapped on the trapdoor to signal that the *carabinieri* had gone.

'He says to wait,' said Gianluca, turning to the others. 'His wife will check the road into town. Make sure it is safe for us.'

An old woman appeared and beckoned them into a low-ceilinged *salotto*. It was spotless, creamy-pink walls hung with plates and wicker baskets, a vase of bright flowers on the dresser. On the mantelpiece stood a framed chromolithograph of a bearded man Nish recognised at once as the Russian revolutionary anarchist, Mikhail Bakunin.

The woman was bird-like, oddly raven-haired. She walked slowly, with a slight limp. As she left the cottage, the man produced thimble-sized glasses which he filled messily with grappa. He handed them round, raised his glass and proclaimed, '*Alla nostra*'.

Nish, Gianluca and Lucian echoed him, then followed his example by downing their drinks in one.

Lucian turned to Nish. 'Are you all right?'

'Fine.'

'What about your feet?'

'It's nothing. Really.'

'And your head?'

'It's just a twinge. The grappa will relax me.'

It was odd, Lucian being concerned for Nish's health

rather than the other way round. At first, Nish had coped well. He was young and fit, after all. But about an hour into the journey, his unsuitable shoes had given him blisters, which made walking an agony.

He had been worried, and continued to worry, about letting the others down – being the weak link, the liability who gets everyone caught. Which would be infuriating, given everything they had been through since the raid. The worry made him anxious, and the anxiety gave him a migraine, as it had in France where he had sometimes had to make difficult decisions. To amputate or not to amputate; to patch up or leave for dead.

The old woman returned and murmured a few words to her husband.

'She says all is clear,' said Gianluca.

They set off, bleary but buzzing.

But it was not clear. No sooner had the trio reached the outskirts of Portofino, where the Via del Fondaco shades into the Piazza della Libertà, than they heard a whistle behind them.

The street, which had been supernaturally quiet, suddenly stirred into life. Lamps were lit and shutters opened as its inhabitants sought the source of the noise. Somewhere up ahead, a dog started barking.

Terror gripped the men. They stopped, each performing the same calculation, weighing up what was and was not possible.

'Do we hide?' asked Lucian. 'Or run?'

'Hide,' said Nish. 'I can't run.'

'Me neither,' said Lucian. 'But we've got to.'

'I say run,' said Gianluca.

And so, they ran – through streets so narrow a person could span them with outstretched arms, shadows leaping in the weak light thrown out by street lamps.

Nish was sweating now, a wave of nausea rising inside him. The cobbles were agony and because of the migraine he was disorientated, straining in the semi-darkness to work out where they were heading. He found it impossible to keep up even with Lucian, who had not been able to run properly since the war.

Gianluca was the first to notice that Nish was struggling. Later, Nish wondered with a twinge of guilt if the Italian had hung back deliberately out of a desire to keep close to him. He heard Gianluca call out to Lucian, who was some way ahead.

'Don't stop! Keep going!' Lucian must have looked conflicted when he glanced back, because then Gianluca added: 'If they catch you, they deport you.'

Gianluca waited for Nish to catch up with him. 'Come!'

'I can't.' His heart felt as though it was bursting out of his chest.

'You must.'

Another blast from the whistle. The police were closing in. Gianluca grabbed hold of Nish and forced him onwards, half-carrying him through the dim maze of streets until somehow they reached the harbour.

The sight of the boundless sea lifted Nish's spirits. It stood, as always, for escape and possibility. But the pastel houses looming up on either side possessed none of their daytime charm. Rather, they felt menacing, as if they were standing sentry. By the quay, the topsides of the moored yachts glowed ghostly white in the moonlight.

Where was Lucian? Nish felt an urgent need to find him. 'Lucian,' he said.

'Lucian is safe.' Gianluca squeezed Nish's arm. 'Now, wake up! Help me find a hiding place.'

A row of fishermen's boats lay beached and overturned on the pebbles. 'There,' Nish said, pointing. '*Le barche.*'

They crawled beneath one of the overturned boats and lay on their backs, their chests heaving. There was a smell of wet wood, of salt and fish. Gianluca placed a hand over Nish's mouth to quieten his breathing. For a glorious moment all was still, the darkness reassuring, the only sound the soft rattle of the shingle as the waves lapped the shore.

But then the whistle came again, as they knew it would. Through the narrow gap between the sand and the gunwale, they saw torchlight sweeping the beach.

There were three men in total. Two of them had wandered off to the far end. But the one with the torch was approaching the fishing boats.

Danioni.

He walked with a confident slouch – torch in one hand, lit cigarette dangling from the other. He stopped to inhale, close enough now for only his bottom half to be visible through the gap. Nish noted with satisfaction the rip in Danioni's trousers, where he had evidently caught them on some brambles.

But then Danioni took a step closer, and something changed. Fear, so far kept in check, spread out suddenly like fog so that it was impossible to believe Danioni couldn't see it wafting out from their hiding place. Gianluca's hand tightened on Nish's mouth.

Danioni stood there for perhaps half a minute, watching and listening. Then there was another blast of the whistle and a voice shouted, '*Da questa parte! Hanno trovato qualcosa.*' This way! They've found something.

Danioni turned and walked towards the voice. At one point, he looked back towards the boat. But whatever had troubled him couldn't have been very compelling, because his glance rested on their hiding place for only the merest second.

Nish and Gianluca lay like tomb effigies, listening as the voices and footsteps faded into silence. Finally, Gianluca removed his hand from Nish's mouth. Perhaps it was a nervous reaction, but Nish started to laugh. Not noisily, but loudly enough to alarm Gianluca because suddenly the Italian was silencing Nish again, pressing a finger against his lips and saying softly: 'Shhhh.'

'But they've gone,' whispered Nish.

'For now.'

The two men stared at each other. Something passed between them, urgent but unsayable. Then Gianluca leant forward, his face slipping across Nish's to plant a kiss on his mouth. The softness of his lips was a surprise and Nish's instinct was to listen to what his body was telling him and reciprocate.

But he didn't. He couldn't.

He turned his head away so that Gianluca's lips smeared across his cheek. 'Not now,' he said.

Afterwards, they walked slowly up to the hotel in silence. Nish's head was clearing. Though the pain in his feet still made him wince, the memory of what had happened on the beach was a stronger analgesic than even opium. He was about to speak, to explain. But Gianluca got there first.

'I understand,' he said. He smiled regretfully and extended his hand for Nish to shake.

'You don't,' said Nish. Stepping forward, he took Gianluca's face in his hands, pulled it close and kissed him passionately, pushing his tongue into his mouth, letting all his inhibitions go. Gianluca reciprocated, grabbing Nish by the buttocks then working his right hand round his waist-band to the front of his trousers.

Nish could feel his heart beating. A simple but momentous change had occurred, one he had been waiting for all his life. He had never done this before, never talked about it or seen it described anywhere. But he was doing it now, for the first time – and it felt like the most natural thing in the world.

*

Plum sat on the bed in his silk pyjamas, enjoying the silence and the superior, new-born feeling of being awake when everyone else was sleeping. He had been woken by a noise from outside – pounding footsteps and shouting, the sound of pursuit. But it had receded quickly enough and actually he was glad to be awake.

He had things to do. A plan he wished to execute. And this was the perfect moment, one he could not have engineered better, even if he'd planned it meticulously in advance.

A parallel with tennis suggested itself. Where the game was concerned, people tended to downplay the importance of chance in achieving success. Those wishing to bet on tennis stars were encouraged to consider more concrete variables: the frequency with which players hit an ace; the frequency with which they broke an opponent's serve; the number of unforced errors they made.

But sometimes things happened that you could never predict. Things that often had nothing to do with tennis.

Back in February, Plum and Lizzie had been among the lucky few who secured tickets to watch the so-called Match of the Century at the Carlton Club in Cannes between the era's preeminent female tennis players – Suzanne Lenglen and Helen Wills.

Lenglen was the older, more experienced player and her eventual win wasn't a surprise. But Wills played exceptionally well and most observers had thought the 20-year-old Californian had it in her to thrash the Cognac-swilling French drama queen Lenglen – both at this year's French Championships and at Wimbledon.

Then disaster struck. Wills got appendicitis and withdrew from both tournaments. Lenglen won at the French

Championships. But at Wimbledon *she* withdrew from her Third Round match because her family had run out of money and because stories in the newspapers that she had offended the Royal Family caused spectators to turn against her, affecting her concentration.

Plum chuckled to himself. He would never make the mistake of believing tennis was everything. After all, there were much easier ways to get rich.

After checking Lizzie was still asleep, Plum slipped into his dressing gown and padded in stockinged feet towards the door. He paused in the corridor for a moment before creeping down to the foyer.

It was the reception desk he was interested in. Some hotels manned them all night. But Hotel Portofino was a family affair, cheerfully amateurish in more respects than it cared to admit. The drawer where he had seen Bella hide the key to her office wasn't even locked. Finding this key – a whole bunch of them, in fact – would take a matter of seconds.

The office door unlocked quietly and easily. Using his cigarette lighter as a torch, Plum rifled through the drawers of Bella's desk and found the petty cash box. He tried one of the keys in the box's lock and could barely believe his luck when it opened. This was too easy!

The box was stuffed with cash. He grabbed a handful of notes, then put everything back as he had found it.

He had returned the keys to the reception desk and was about to head back upstairs when he heard someone enter the hall from the kitchen. A voice called out, 'Nish?'

'It's Wingfield,' said Plum, in a tone of righteous surprise. 'Who's that?' He sparked his lighter and held it up.

'Ainsworth,' said the voice, unmistakably the boy Lucian's.

'Funny place to meet,' observed Plum. 'Feeling thirsty?'

'Something like that. You?'

'Something like that.' He let the flame go out. 'Well, goodnight then.'

'Goodnight.'

He walked up the stairs, feeling Lucian's eyes on his back, cursing himself for not being more careful. His only consolation was how awful Lucian had looked, sweaty and dishevelled. And why had he thought Plum was Nish? It was most mysterious.

Wherever Lucian had come from, it was clearly somewhere he shouldn't have been.

Something else had happened tonight, after the illicit but utterly tame party certain of his fellow guests had got so worked up about.

The question was, what?

*

In the morning Bella rose early and went out to the garden. She picked an assortment of flowers, mostly roses and camellias, and arranged them carefully in a crystal vase. Taking a plain card, she wrote 'For Ernest' on it and tucked it among the blooms before placing the whole assemblage on Lady Latchmere's table.

At eight o'clock it was already warm enough to open the doors to the terrace. She asked Paola to get a broom and sweep up the leaves and other detritus, then busied herself supervising Constance, who was on breakfast duty and was serving coffee from a large Bialetti pot to Rose and Julia. As Constance poured, Julia sat ramrod straight, daring anyone to sneak so much as a glance in their direction. Rose stared down at the plate in front of her.

Bella couldn't help but smile.

On the other side of the room, Lizzie was hiding behind a pair of dark glasses, looking queasy as Plum wolfed down a plate of scrambled eggs. She refused the bread roll Paola offered her with a wordless shake of the head.

Unusually, Lady Latchmere arrived on her own, without Melissa. She manoeuvred herself into her seat with her usual stiffness, but her face brightened when she saw the flowers and even more so when she read the card.

Her eyes roamed the room, seeking out Bella. When they found her – easily, for Bella had been watching her, expecting this moment – she raised her hand minutely in a covert signal of thanks. Bella nodded, then turned her attention elsewhere.

She watched Lucian spreading marmalade onto a slice of toast. He looked exhausted. As Paola cleared his table he looked up at her, trying to get her attention, but she ignored him. The old spark and rapport between them had palpably disappeared. But why?

Nish, on the other hand, looked content for once despite the fact that he was, as usual, sitting on his own. What a funny boy he was. A mixture of strength and weakness, neediness and independence.

After breakfast, Bella took her turn behind the reception desk. She was sorting through the box of dropped-off room keys when Lady Latchmere appeared in front of her.

Bella knew by divination that something had changed – no, yielded – in Lady Latchmere. The old hardness and ferocity had disappeared completely.

At the very moment Bella nodded her greeting, there was a clipped stomping. The source turned out to be Julia marching Rose out of the dining room and up the stairs. Both Bella and Lady Latchmere swivelled to watch.

After their departure, Bella cleared her throat. 'I hope you weren't put out by last night's high jinx, your Ladyship.'

The older woman merely smiled. 'They seem to have had a much gayer evening than we did. I only wish Melissa had stayed behind.' Bella must have looked shocked because she quickly went on. 'For Ernest's sake, I mean. I've decided to try and follow your lead and become a little more modern in my outlook. A little less judgmental.'

Now, it was Lucian's turn to leave the dining room and make his way upstairs. The two women watched him go.

'Given the mess we've made of it all,' Lady Latchmere continued, 'we can't blame the young for wanting to squeeze as much out of life as quickly as possible. Who knows how long they'll have to enjoy it?'

'"That it will never come again is what makes life so sweet."'

Lady Latchmere pondered. 'Is that Shakespeare?' she asked.

'Emily Dickinson.'

'My poor boy. He didn't taste enough of life's sweetness.' She held up the vase of flowers, which Bella only just noticed she had brought from the table herself. This was something she could only have done with two hands, which meant she was no longer using her stick. 'I'm very touched, my dear,' Lady Latchmere said. 'That you should think of him.'

'I always shall from now on, your Ladyship.'

'Please, my dear.' The older woman looked at Bella imploringly. 'My friends call me Gertrude.'

*

After his encounter with Plum – and after checking Nish was safely back in his room – Lucian had collapsed onto his bed and fallen into a deep, dreamless sleep. But he had woken restless, unable to stop thinking about Paola.

The first thing he had done after getting back to the hotel last night was go to her room. He had wanted to tell her, without implicating anyone, about the meeting and the raid. In return he wanted sympathy and compassion: the kind he had shown her in the early days of their relationship when they had talked, falteringly but with intensity, about her late husband. The kind she had shown him whenever the thunder at night made him shake and twitch and scream.

He had known she was in because her light was on. He had knocked and called her name several times, but in response the light had gone out. And now, at breakfast, she'd ignored him again – avoiding his eye, moving on quickly to the other tables where before she would have lingered, grinning, and taken a furtive bite of his toast.

What was going on?

He was passing the door to the first-floor communal bathroom when it opened and Rose emerged.

Lucian's first reaction, stupidly, was to frown. 'I thought you had your own bathroom?'

'Mother is using it,' Rose explained. 'And I felt queasy all of a sudden . . .' She did look very pale.

She was about to say more, when the door to her suite further down the corridor opened and a voice called: 'Rose?'

Lucian bundled Rose back into the bathroom and locked the door. The gesture caused Rose's eyes to bulge with shock. Never in her life had she been in a bathroom with a man!

Lucian put a finger to his lips. Footsteps approached, a brisk clip-clopping on the wooden floor. Then the doorknob rattled. 'Rose? Are you in there?'

'It's occupied,' said Lucian, trying to disguise his voice.

'My apologies,' said Julia.

But Lucian could still hear her breathing on the other side of the door.

*

Julia was standing outside the bathroom door when Bella came up the stairs. It was impressive, Bella thought, the way Julia always managed to look composed – and icily composed at that. It all came down to posture, she decided, remembering with distaste her own experience of being taught the same at school.

Bella's first reaction upon seeing her was concern that the suite's private bathroom was faulty or in some other way unsatisfactory. But no, Julia reassured her, taking care not to pay a compliment by accident, all was adequate there.

'Have you seen Rose?' she asked.

'Not since breakfast,' said Bella. 'Although as it happens, I was hoping to have a word with you about her.'

'A word?' Julia looked wary.

'Yes. Perhaps we . . . ?' Bella gestured towards the suite.

'If we must.'

Julia entered the suite first. She went over and stood by the window, staring out at the sea so that she didn't have to make eye contact. 'I'd like to apologise,' she said.

'Whatever for?'

'For the unedifying spectacle that greeted us on our return from dinner last night.'

Bella shrugged. 'It was just a bit of high spirits.'

'More like drunkenness.'

'I was happy to see Rose enjoying herself,' said Bella. 'I was beginning to worry she was having a miserable time.'

Julia turned to face Bella. She looked affronted. 'Is that why you wanted to see me?'

'I just thought it was time we had a talk. Woman to woman, if you like. About Rose and Lucian.'

'I've been speaking to Cecil about the arrangements.'

'The financial arrangements, yes. There are other aspects to consider.'

A cold, condescending smile formed on Julia's lips. 'Matters of the heart, you mean?'

'Of course. Why not?'

'How very sentimental of you.'

'Is it sentimental to want to see your children settled and happy?'

'No. But it is to put happiness ahead of status and security.'

Bella said nothing. She opened the doors to the balcony and walked out.

Julia followed her. 'Have I offended you?' she asked.

Bella stared ahead. 'Not at all.'

'I fear I have.'

'I was wondering whether you thought Rose was ready. That's all.'

'She's a year older than I was.'

'Still,' said Bella. 'She seems very young.'

Julia considered this. 'Is anything to be gained from waiting?'

'A little perspective, perhaps. To see if they are well-matched.'

'Are any of us well-matched? You and I, Bella, of all people ... We shouldn't pretend that love trumps money when it comes to marriage.'

This remark was intended to hurt Bella and it did. The urge to belittle and dominate, so strong in this woman – where did it come from? What sort of childhood had she endured? Julia was like a lump of rock into which a thousand accumulated slights, grudges and disappointments had been compressed.

Without saying anything, Bella walked back into the room and left the suite. She had tried her best. But Julia was grinding her down.

*

Rose sat on the wooden toilet seat, looking flushed and anxious. Lucian was perched on the edge of the bath.

'Are you all right?' he asked. 'You look a bit peaky.'

She shook her head. 'I don't feel well at all.'

'You're well enough to come on our boat trip, I hope?'

She frowned. 'What boat trip?'

'The one we agreed upon last night?'

Rose looked horrified, as if she had no memory of agreeing to anything of the sort. *Fair enough*, thought Lucian. She had been pretty far gone. 'Oh, Lucian,' she said. 'I can't.'

'Can't? Or won't?'

'What does it matter?'

She stood up, agitated. Lucian tried to take her hands in his, but she put them behind her back. 'Look,' he said, 'I know what it's like. To live in fear of a parent's disapproval.' Rose stopped fidgeting and listened. 'My father finds fault with everything. Ever since I became ... damaged ... it's as though he can't bear the sight of me. My mother says I should stop worrying about making him happy, and worry about myself instead.'

Rose nodded.

'I can't believe the Rose I saw last night – the girl who danced with such abandon – is too fearful to tell her mother she wants to go on a boat trip with her friends.'

Rose smiled shyly. 'I could ask?'

'That would be wonderful.'

Lucian unlocked the door and they giggled as they prepared to open it.

But their timing could not have been worse. They emerged just as his mother was leaving Julia and Rose's suite. She didn't see them, but Julia, in hot pursuit of Bella, practically bumped into them.

Rose squealed. Julia gave Lucian a look of cold fury as she grabbed Rose by the wrist and dragged her down the corridor back to her room.

Lucian brought his hands up to his temples and squeezed gently. This whole situation was ridiculous, like some French farce.

Sooner or later, something would have to give.

*

Say what you like, thought Plum, as he pushed lightly on the door of the Epsom Suite, the cook here really knew how to make scrambled eggs.

Lizzie was tucked beneath a quilted bedspread adorned with birds and red flowers. Her face looked tiny behind her dark glasses. The curtains were closed. Plum walked over and looked around for the cord to open them.

'Must you?' she said in a fey voice.

'At least now I know why you're feeling so beastly.'

'Has someone been telling tales?'

'Only the bar bill.' He paused. 'Listen, Lizzie . . .'

'Hmmm?'

He braced himself. 'There's no easy way to say this. So I'll just out with it.'

Lizzie sat up against the pillows, lowering her glasses. 'What? What is it?'

'We're in trouble.'

'Oh, Pelham.' She relaxed visibly, hearing this familiar phrase. 'You always say that.'

'But this time I really mean it.'

'OK, then.' She caught the expression on his face. 'How bad is it?'

'Bad enough that I can't pay the bill.'

'The hotel bill?'

'The bar bill. Any of it.'

Her face froze in bafflement. 'But your father gave you five hundred, not all that long ago. Where's it all gone?'

'I lost it.'

Lizzie's confusion gave way to concern. 'Lost it?'

'I had a wager on myself in Monte Carlo. Rather a sizeable one, I'm afraid.'

She had the good grace not to be surprised. 'Well, can't you ask him for more?'

'I've already written to him. But it's been ten days. Not a peep.'

'He'll come good. Won't he?'

He stared at the floor. 'Not this time, I think.'

She bit her lip. 'Then ... what are we going to do?'

With a magician's timing, Plum produced the stolen banknotes from his trouser pocket. 'I've a plan,' he said, flourishing the notes. He caught Lizzie in his gaze, wanting her to grasp the gravity of the situation. 'But for it to work, you need to be ready to leave. At short notice.'

*

Betty was a wonderful woman. Kind, thoughtful, considerate. Constance owed her everything and genuinely wouldn't hear a word against her. But, goodness, she was nosy.

They were in the kitchen, preparing the picnic for the boat trip. The door was open. The sun was streaming in and the cat, which Betty had christened Victoria 'because she thinks she's the queen' – was slinking around, looking for scraps.

Betty must have stumbled over Constance's cotton drawstring bag on the kitchen floor. Because Constance had left it open, its contents were visible. And before you could say Jack Robinson, Betty was reaching down into it and pulling out the bathing costume Constance had, after much agonising over its suitability, stuffed into the top.

She held it aloft, as if it were something the cat had dragged in. Constance strode over and hurriedly snatched it off her. 'Mrs Turner lent it me,' she said, by way of explanation. Not that Betty was owed an explanation. She pushed it back into the bag before returning to where she had been wrapping sandwiches. She felt Betty's eyes, still on her. 'What?'

'I hope you know what you're doing,' her mother's friend said carefully.

'And what does that mean?' She couldn't stop the words shooting out like darts.

'It means be careful! Wearing a skimpy thing like that! You should know, of all people.'

Constance could hardly believe her ears. She expected this sort of thing from folks back home, but not from Betty. 'What are you suggesting?'

'I'm not suggesting nowt.'

'Are you saying it's my fault? What happened to me?' She looked back over her shoulder to see Betty's face glowering.

'That's not what I said.'

'But it's what you think. You, and all the rest of them.'

Betty shook her head emphatically. 'I don't want you to get hurt again.'

But Constance had been roused to fury. 'I'm sick of it, Betty. Skulking around. All buttoned up. Living in fear that what I do or what I say or how I look gets taken the wrong way. I just want to ... let go.'

'That's just the way it is!'

'Not for Mrs Turner, it's not.'

'Never mind her. They'll cut her down to size soon enough. You watch.' Seeing Constance looking downcast, she held out her arms. 'Pay no heed to me, love. I'm just a silly old fool. Who's forgotten what it's like to be young.'

Constance accepted the hug, then put her hands on Betty's shoulders as she said, 'No you're not. You're the wisest woman I know.' It was true. Constance knew she would be lost without her.

Betty rolled her eyes. 'Get on with you. Go and enjoy yourself.'

Constance packed the last of the sandwiches and slung the bag over her shoulder. Then, flashing Betty a smile, she picked up the hamper and carried it out to the forecourt where the day-trippers were congregating.

She loaded her bag into the luggage rack at the side of the

carriage. In the meantime, Bella and Lucian's conversation was too loud not to overhear.

'Is Rose joining you?'

'It doesn't seem so.' He sounded indifferent.

'Mrs Drummond-Ward must think you're a bad influence.'

'Me and everyone else.' He said this pointedly, observing Claudine and Lizzie emerging from the hotel.

'Well. At least it leaves you free to focus on our other guests.'

Sighing, he helped Claudine and Lizzie up into the carriage, handing their beach things to Constance for loading.

'Is your husband coming along, Mrs Wingfield?' he asked Lizzie.

'He's lying low, I'm afraid,' she said. 'Saving his strength for the big match.'

'And what about Mr Turner?'

Claudine burst out laughing. 'Jack wouldn't be seen dead in a boat.'

Lucian grinned. 'Then Mr Albani and I will have you all to ourselves.'

As he said this, Roberto ran out of the front door and clambered up onto the carriage, taking a seat next to Claudine.

Constance couldn't help noticing that Claudine looked rather unhappy about this.

*

And there was Alice, standing forlornly by the window in the drawing room, biting her thumbnail as she watched the boat trippers depart.

Her father's voice from behind her was familiar and reassuring. 'Aren't you going to the ball, poppet?'

It was a welcome return to the sort of language they'd used when she was small. She had always been his favourite, no question. His princess. Between fathers and sons there was rivalry. But with a daughter nothing got in the way.

'Nobody thought to invite me, Daddy.' She gave him a self-pitying look – part joke, part genuine. 'No one ever does.'

Cecil walked over. He placed his hands on her shoulders. 'Then start inviting yourself. Put yourself out there a bit.'

She laughed. 'You don't want me to be the last chicken on the shelf. Is that it?'

'We've all got to let our hair down, from time to time.'

'I'm too old to go gallivanting.'

'Gallivanting?' He moved round beside her so that she could see his face. 'You're twenty-six, for heaven's sake. You know what they say. All work and no play.'

'Or all play and no work, in your case.'

'Now, now. I get quite enough of that from your mother, if you don't mind.'

She smiled. 'Poor old Daddy.'

Bella's sudden appearance in the room caught them both off guard. 'Why "poor old Daddy"?' she asked brightly. She clearly had no sense that she was intruding.

'He's feeling put upon,' said Alice, after a moment's pause.

Cecil rushed to clarify. 'I was merely trying to suggest to our daughter that she might occasionally allow herself to have some fun.'

249

'And I was telling him I'm too busy!' As she said this, Alice felt a curious mix of emotions. Indignation and fear, but also the pain of someone else pressing on a bruise.

Was this really what she'd been telling her father? Not quite. And was it true? *Was* she really busy? It did feel like it. Of course, if someone uncharitable were to break down Alice's day, it would quickly become clear that for long periods she wasn't doing much at all. So why did she feel this way?

She didn't know. It was one of the questions she never stopped to ask herself.

Until now.

Alice thought: *We all find consolation in different ways. Lucian has his art. And I have God.*

Soon after George's death, when Alice had been at her lowest, her Catholic friend Roberta had lent her a book by a priest. She'd assured Alice that it would answer the many questions swirling around in her head.

'He's marvellous, this man,' she'd told her. 'He knows everything. His book is like a catechism, with each question or statement followed by a response. And when you read the responses ... Well, you realise there's no need to ago-nise anymore. No need to *think*. Because all the thinking is done for you!'

What is the purpose of life on this Earth?
Man is created to praise, love and serve God so that he might attain eternal life.

How old would you declare the Earth to be?
*We cannot know because God has not told us. He alone was
present at the dawn of creation.*

**Can the child of a mixed marriage between a
Protestant and a Catholic go to Heaven?**
*If the child is brought up as a Protestant it has the same
chance as any Protestant. If it is brought up Catholic then
it has a small advantage – though also the poor example of
the non-Catholic parent and the weak faith of the other, who
has chosen to marry outside the Church.*

The book had worked on Alice like an aspirin for the soul!
But it had worried her too because of its tone, which seemed
harsh and judgmental. Until she read it, there had been no
doubt in her mind that George was in Heaven and that she
and Lottie, who had never known her father, would meet
him there.

But the book made her anxious that she was not good
enough for Heaven. How could she be, when she had com-
mitted such a terrible sin?

On the night before George left England for the first time,
when they were not yet married, the couple had shared a bed.

This lapse, for which Alice had always felt guilty, now
gnawed away at her. The book had had strong things to say
about such behaviour. At the very least, it implied, she and
Lottie would end up in Purgatory, that "intermediate state
of purification", even if Alice repented. Yet, everyone knew

it was hard to find fellow lost souls in Purgatory because it was much larger than Heaven, where relatively few people got to go.

Alice might walk around for days, weeks, years – desperately seeking George. Lottie would be clutching her hand all the while, crying and asking, 'Where's Daddy? You told me Daddy would be here!'

Some weeks after George's death, Lucian had come home on leave. Upon learning that Alice had shut herself away, refusing to talk or eat, he had come to her room and found her in tears, reading Roberta's book.

At first soft and sympathetic, his manner had quickly changed after he read some of the passages. He'd become angry and started shouting, saying it supplied 'non-answers to non-questions' and that she was a fool for wasting her time.

'If God exists,' he'd said, face red with fury, 'why isn't he in France and Belgium? Why didn't he stop George from dying?'

His anger had not, however, had the desired effect of making her see the light. Rather, it had confirmed her zealotry. She had shut Lucian out, even after his injury. Even after he'd arrived home from the convalescence centre in France.

By then his atheism had become so entrenched it was painful for her to witness. So she'd resolved not to witness it – and not to show more emotion than she had to. Showing emotion meant making yourself vulnerable to other people's arguments, and she had no wish to do that.

Here in the drawing room, for example, she wanted to cry. But the shame of crying in front of her parents was more than she could bear. And so she swept off, leaving Bella and Cecil standing there staring at each other.

Still, she waited outside the room, listening.

'What brought that on?' she heard her mother say.

'She says she's overlooked.'

'Perhaps she's right. Perhaps it's Alice you ought to be matchmaking, not Lucian.'

There was a pause. Alice fancied she could hear pistons churning and cogs clanking in her father's brain. 'Perhaps it is,' he said finally, and sighed.

Alice knew his sighs well. This one was a sigh of regret – but also of despair.

*

The rest of the morning did not go well for Bella.

She had been on the way to her office when she stopped to talk to Cecil and Alice. Once there, she took out the petty cash box and unlocked it. Counting out the banknotes revealed a predictable shortfall. Truly, it was the same old story. And a particularly annoying one, given what she had to do next.

She had never been to the Municipal Building before. She found it as she expected, drab and utilitarian, but also it was surrounded by Blackshirts, which she hadn't expected. They lolled around, smoking and chatting. A couple of them were play-fighting while a small crowd egged them on. Feeling self-conscious, she had to step round them to get to the front door.

The first door she came to had Danioni's name on it. She knocked, bracing herself for the inevitable charm offensive.

'Signora Ainsworth!' he called out – apparently for someone else's benefit – as he opened the door and invited her in. 'What an honour.' He gestured to a chair. 'A coffee, perhaps?'

Bella shook her head. 'I wouldn't stay long enough to drink it.'

She produced an envelope and put it on the desk. Danioni looked at it, then at her.

'It's a gift, Mr Danioni. From one friend to another.'

He smiled and bowed his head. Then he picked up the envelope and slipped it into his inside pocket. '*Grazie.*'

'And I am afraid it will be the last.' Saying these words gave her an enormous feeling of satisfaction.

His face sank sideways. 'I am sorry to hear that.'

'You imagine I am a woman of means. But every penny I own has been sunk into our hotel. I simply cannot afford to keep paying you.'

Danioni digested this in silence. Then he leant forward on his elbows. In a sharp, malevolent tone he said: 'Don't try to be clever with me, Signora. You are a resourceful woman. You will find another way.'

Shaking, for this was not the response she had been expecting, she said, 'And you are a resourceful man, Signore. So will you.'

*

It was about half-past eleven when Nish spotted Bella emerging from the Municipal Building. He was sitting in the bar at the corner of the square, as he had been for over an hour. In that time, he had drunk two espressos, smoked four Caporal cigarettes and read two chapters of *A Passage to India*, smiling at Forster's clever mockery of Baedeker-style travel writing.

In fact, he had spotted Bella going in too, edging her way past the Blackshirts. She hadn't seen him, thank goodness. But he had watched her closely, imagining how he would view her if he didn't know her. She was a good-looking woman, with her high cheekbones and lilting, percussive way of walking. You knew it was her, even when your eyes were shut.

Once she'd disappeared round the corner, he sat idly watching the Blackshirts, wondering whether they all bought their uniforms from the same shop.

A voice sounded behind him in English. 'Your bill, sir.'

Without looking, he reached for it, but when he unfolded the small slip of lined paper he saw that it wasn't a bill at all.

There was a message written on it.

FOLLOW ME.

Nish looked up to see Gianluca standing a few yards away. They smiled at each other, Nish's heart thumping in his chest, then Gianluca started walking off in the direction of a junction marked by a newspaper stall.

After throwing a handful of coins onto the table, Nish stuffed his belongings into his bag and set off after his friend.

Nish tailed Gianluca along what felt like every street

in Portofino. From Via Roma they turned right, cutting through Piazza Martiri dell'Olivetta to stay on Salita San Giorgio. Nish hung back, trying to look casual, like any other tourist exploring the town.

When Gianluca finally turned into an alley, Nish followed, expecting to find him waiting, but there was no one there except a priest mending his bicycle's inner tube and a couple of bare-footed children filling old tomato tins with water from a standpipe.

He carried on walking, confused – until a hand reached out and dragged him through a half-open door.

Immediately, they fell upon one another, kissing hungrily. And then they were tearing each other's clothes off, desperate for what they had both been wanting for so long.

Afterwards, they lay on the floor on an improvised bed of sacking, propped up by enormous bags of potatoes. Gianluca had his head in Nish's lap.

For the first time, Nish looked around. It was a sort of warehouse, with a high ceiling and shelves on either side. Light trickled in through a single dirty window. Nish saw demijohns of wine, sacks of grain, boxes of fruit and vegetables.

He asked, 'What is this place?'

'It belongs to my father.'

'Is he a farmer?'

Gianluca laughed. 'No. He's a lawyer. And a landowner.'

'He grows all this?'

'He rents the land out. His tenants send him half of what they harvest.'

Nish lit a cigarette as he considered this information. 'A bit bourgeois, isn't it?'

Gianluca lifted his head from Nish's lap. He stared straight at him, his eyes earnest and shining. 'My grandfather bought the land off the church in the last century. I have pleaded with him to give it away.'

'And what does he say?'

'He calls me an anarchist.' Gianluca paused. 'It's why I'm leaving.'

'Leaving?'

'Me and my father. We are not . . . *simpatico.*'

'He wants you to settle down,' said Nish. They both laughed. 'Where will you go?'

'Torino. I am needed there.'

'You're needed here.'

'Not so much.' Gianluca took his hand, stroked it. 'We must take the fight against Mussolini to the cities.' He reached to lift the tip of Nish's chin. 'Perhaps you will come too.'

'What could I do in Turin?'

'That's easy,' said Gianluca, pausing before he leaned in for another kiss. 'You will learn to resist.'

9

Truth be told, thought Claudine as she reclined on her lounger, she was still getting used to Portofino.

It was a beautiful place and she was happy to be here – to see it for herself after everything she'd heard.

But, still.

The anomaly of the previous night's revels, which she had loved, made her realise how much her extrovert side missed the Venice Lido – the way its café-terraces and ballrooms and weird rituals, such as everyone wearing pyjamas all day, contributed to an air of licensed excess: fun you never had to feel guilty about, however extreme it became.

Snaring a pitch or even a cabana on the Excelsior Palace's private beach had involved some serious befriending of important folk. For Claudine that meant putting on a show – and putting on a show was her favourite thing.

One night, on the stone dancefloor of the Excelsior's Chez Vous nightclub, she had demonstrated the Charleston, kicking up her heels to ecstatic applause. On another she had sung 'I'm a Little Old Lido Lady' on Cole Porter's *gallegiante* – a vast raft which floated up and down the canals – accompanied by her old friend Leslie Hutchinson's jazz orchestra.

Afterwards, Lady Diana Cooper herself – dressed as an Italian soldier in a white cloth cloak and a *bersagliere*'s hat plumed with cocks' feathers – had poured Claudine a glass of champagne. 'That was marvellous!' she cried. 'Come and see us, won't you? Duff and I have taken a small *casa* in the Via dei Catecumeni.'

Then Greta Garbo had floated across to her. Garbo! She was wearing trousers and a simple white shirt. Her mousy hair looked matted and unwashed. 'I like you,' she said.

'Why, I like you too, honey.' Claudine nodded towards the man standing behind Garbo. He was wearing a Pierrot costume and an expression of forlorn disapproval. 'Who's that following you?'

The actress looked round. 'Oh,' she said, flatly. 'That's Cecil Beaton.'

'The photographer?' Claudine had heard that they were friends.

Garbo nodded. 'He wants to fuck me.'

Claudine frowned. 'But I thought . . .'

'That he's homosexual? He is. He still wants to fuck me.' And she shrugged, as if to say, 'What can you do?'

It had all been a far cry from this – a genteel day-trip by charabanc to the beach. She tilted her head, the better to observe her fellow day-trippers.

To the left of the tableau was Constance. She had sweated for half an hour coaxing the beach umbrella until it was stiffly upright. Now she was laying out the picnic lunch, arranging exquisite little sandwiches on glinting white plates. Gracious, she worked hard, that girl. She looked so hot and constrained in her heavy English dress. Would she have the courage to change into the bathing costume Claudine had lent her? She was *so pretty*. But she had no idea. None whatsoever.

Claudine shifted her gaze. Lucian and Lizzie were some distance out, taking turns to dive down and pick up shells and rocks from the sea floor. She hadn't had much to do with Lucian, but he seemed a decent sort. Lizzie too, though her drinking worried Claudine. As her mother always said: 'Whatever the question is, the answer is never the bottom of a bottle.'

As for Roberto, well . . . He was splayed lazily in the boat, which was anchored about ten yards from the shore. Why he didn't want to join the party was anyone's guess. Claudine lowered her sunglasses and looked more closely. His body was good, no question. But it had lost its appeal for her in ways she couldn't put her finger on.

Sometimes it happened like that. You had sex. And afterwards, whatever it was that had attracted you to the person just . . . disappeared. Even if the sex had been good, which it had.

Closing her eyes again, she reflected on the past year. Sex with Jack had been good too, at first. Those hot summer evenings at the Hôtel Apollinaire on Rue Delambre, followed by a bite to eat at the Dôme and a stroll along the Seine. As they passed the shuttered-up *bouquinistes*' stalls they'd discussed their plans – or rather Jack's plans. What he hoped to sell to whom and for how much.

It all felt like a lifetime ago.

And yet here they were, still together.

Claudine rose now, smoothing out the wrinkles in her green, V-necked bathing costume, and waded into the sea. She was a strong swimmer and forged ahead, passing the boat which bobbed sleepily in the waves. She noticed Roberto noticing her but thought nothing of it.

Her toned muscles aching delightfully, she followed the curve of the headland to the cave she had spotted on the boat trip out. She'd always resolved to visit it and now she would.

She approached its mouth cautiously, taking care not to chip her pedicured toenails on any hidden rocks. Once inside, she floated on her back, enjoying the steady rhythmic sloshing and the way shards of sunlight bounced off the cave's ceiling.

After a couple of minutes, however, she sensed something. A presence. Someone swimming up beside her.

She lifted her head.

It was Roberto. He was grinning, as if the whole thing – which was to say, the carefully planned infringement of her privacy – was a tremendous joke.

His insouciant manner made her furious. 'Leave me be, can't you?'

She splashed past him, then hauled herself half out of the water so that she was perched on a flat section of rock beside the cave mouth. But Roberto, who clearly thought the strength of his ardour was being tested, swam after her. He followed her up onto the rock and tried to sit beside her.

Claudine kicked at him, pushing him back into the water with her feet.

Roberto evidently hadn't expected retaliation. But then he seemed to decide that this too was a game. He grabbed her leg and started pulling it, dragging her into the water. When her face came within reach he tried to kiss her, rubbing his stubbly chin against her cheek, nuzzling her ear with his nose.

But Claudine slapped him away with all her force. 'I said leave me be!'

At this Roberto stopped, his brow creasing in confusion. '*Cosa c'è?*' he asked. What's the matter?

'Don't you understand? That was only a onetime thing.' Claudine held up one finger. 'One time.'

She shallow-dived into the water and shot past him, torpedo-like, before he had a chance to react.

She was sure he would try to follow her again and was relieved when he remained on the rocks, looking down into the water.

Not being chased meant Claudine didn't have to race back to the beach. So she took her time, pausing every so often to admire the scenery, thinking about Greta Garbo and Cecil Beaton and how nice it would be if, just for once, men stopped wanting things.

*

It seemed to be the Italian maid's turn to serve coffee after lunch today. The way they did it here always annoyed Julia – straight from the stovetop machine rather than a china pot. It was so . . . inelegant. An unnecessary bit of bohemianism. She resolved to have a word with Bella.

She and Cecil had had a pleasant lunch. The hotel's food, at least, was reliable. That she conceded. They had enjoyed catching up with each other's news, but talk had turned – inevitably if fitfully, for they fell silent whenever anyone else entered the room – to the events of last night.

The maid, Paola, spoke no English. Everyone knew that. It was possible she had had no education at all, poor thing. Still, Cecil waited until they were well and truly alone before resuming the conversation.

'You don't think you're being a touch hard on Rose?' He glanced over to where the girl was playing a desultory game of patience on the terrace. As Cecil watched her, Julia thought again how lucky she was that Rose had turned out to be beautiful. Sometimes, she felt ownership of that beauty more keenly than Rose herself. Beauty was an asset that needed tending and protecting – and goodness knows, Rose wasn't clever enough to be left in sole charge of it.

'She acted shamefully,' said Julia.

'But I thought the general idea was to bring the two of them together?'

'Not at the cost of her good name.' She sipped her coffee. 'Besides, nothing's agreed yet.'

'Isn't it?'

'We haven't talked about money, for one thing.'

Cecil shifted uncomfortably. 'What did you have in mind?'

'Well, there's Ivor's mother's house in Bayswater. I rather thought they might have the top two floors. And then the whole thing over time.'

'That's jolly decent of you.'

'But that still leaves the cost of the wedding. And what they're going to live on, of course.'

'I'm hoping the boy will settle down to some suitable employment.'

Julia rolled her eyes. 'You can't run a household on hope.'

'Of course not.' Cecil loosened the knot of his tie. 'Which is why ... I'll be happy to give them an income. Until they get on their feet.'

'Splendid. Have you decided how much?'

'Not yet. I'm, er, waiting. For a few things to fall into place.'

Julia laughed mirthlessly. 'To pluck up the courage to ask your father-in-law, you mean?'

'I wouldn't lower myself.'

'Why ever not? There has to be some benefit to opening up your blood line to the highest bidder.'

'I have other means of raising money.'

Julia drained her cup and rose from the table. 'Well, don't leave it too long.' She looked again at Rose, who had given up on patience and was staring out across the sea, probably pondering her own crude ambitions for herself. 'We don't want to let it get much further. Without knowing the price we both have to pay.'

*

Alice was still poring over the hotel ledger when Bella returned from wherever she had gone. Town, probably, judging by her rather formal clothes.

Alice didn't normally concern herself with accounts, especially when Lottie was in her charge, as she was at the moment, Constance having been requisitioned to help at the beach. But the tea party had been her baby, so to speak, and Lottie was happy playing with her dolls on the terrace. 'We made a profit,' she announced proudly as Bella emerged from her office, where she had been changing her shoes and sorting through the post. 'On our tea party. I thought you'd like to know.'

'Well done.' This was said rather flatly, Alice felt, under the circumstances.

'It will be bigger next time.'

Bella put a package on the desk in front of her. 'This came for you,' she said. The paper wrapping was torn.

'What happened?' Alice asked, inspecting the damage.

'I'm sorry. I opened it. Before I realised it was addressed to you.'

Cautiously, Alice picked it up. She ripped off the remaining paper and stared in amazement at the box which had been hiding beneath it.

'Listen, darling, don't take this the wrong way, but . . .'

Alice turned towards her mother. She felt confused; alarmed, almost.

But Bella was still talking: '. . . with money being so tight, if you have anything left over from your pension or the annuity George left for you and Lottie, well . . . It really should go towards the running of this place. Rather than on buying Bulgari jewellery.'

'But I haven't,' said Alice. She opened the black box to reveal a raised bed of yellow velvet and, on it, an exquisite gold bracelet. She held it up, genuinely bewildered. 'I really haven't.'

'Count Albani,' said Bella, suddenly.

Alice looked at her mother in horror. 'Oh no,' she said and felt herself flushing scarlet. 'No, no. I can't accept this.'

'You *can*,' said Bella. 'The question is whether you *should*.'

'I should have realised. What was happening.'

'What do you mean?'

'He's very . . . solicitous. Count Albani.'

They fell silent for a moment, each pondering the best course of action. Bella spoke first. 'You must talk to him. Now. To clear the air.'

'Do you know where he is?'

'In the garden,' she said. 'He's sleeping off his lunch there, I believe.'

Alice felt sick with nerves. Or perhaps it was more than that – a stealing sense of frustration with herself for not knowing what she wanted, not knowing what was best – for herself or Lottie. Her feet dragged as she followed the path around to where Count Albani was lying on a bench, a Panama hat pulled down over his eyes.

Was he truly asleep? In that case, she wouldn't want to wake him. She waited for a few moments, clutching the box. The lack of movement came as a relief because really, this was not a conversation she wanted to have. She was about to withdraw, when quite suddenly he spoke in that orotund way of his.

'Do not concern yourself. I am only resting my eyes.' He tipped back the brim of his hat and smiled at Alice – a smile of great charm, one he likely used often to light up opportunities for himself. 'My dear Mrs Mays-Smith. It is always a pleasure.'

'Count Albani . . .' she began, her voice breaking.

'May I assist you?'

'I . . . I cannot accept this.' She all but thrust the box at him. 'It's a lovely thing. Exquisite, even. But inappropriate.'

He spoke slowly and with gravity, as if he had been expecting this. 'I am sorry to hear you think so.'

'I would be accepting it under false pretences.'

The Count nodded his head. 'I understand your sensibilities,' he said. 'And I will convey them to Roberto.'

Alice felt herself jolt. 'To Roberto?'

'*Si.*' Count Albani opened the box and looked lovingly at the bracelet. 'It is he who commissioned this gift for you. As a token of our . . . *his* . . . admiration. For you and your family.' He closed the box and, with a sigh, pushed it into his pocket with his thumb.

'I would be most obliged,' she said.

'Good,' said the Count. And with that he tipped his hat before lowering it over his eyes once more.

*

Constance had taken her lunch and eaten it as convention dictated, away from those it was her job to serve. She sat behind the baskets, into which she had packed most of the leftover food and used plates and cutlery. Everyone else had finished their lunch a while ago. Staff always ate last.

They were a friendly bunch, this lot, and she felt comfortable around them – comfortable enough to risk putting a splash of white wine in her water.

Lizzie still had a drink on the go. Claudine was sunbathing. Roberto had come ashore for lunch and was now sitting at the water's edge, sulkily tossing pebbles into the waves. Something had happened between him and Claudine, over on the rocks. Constance wasn't sure what, though she could guess. Meanwhile, Lucian was sketching, wearing a blue and white striped bathing suit that covered the whole of his well-defined torso.

Constance watched him as she gulped the remains of her watery wine.

Nice, she thought.

She took the bathing suit she had borrowed from Claudine and disappeared behind some rocks to change.

The costume was a green-and-yellow Jantzen made of stretchy, ribbed jersey with a little red logo of a diving girl at the bottom of the skirt. Constance had never worn anything like it before. There was something unsettling about the way it clung to her body, emphasizing every curve. When she had finished she stood where she was, frozen with self-consciousness.

'You'll knock 'em dead,' Claudine had said. 'You just need to be confident. Stride, don't shuffle.'

Constance's instinct was not to stride exactly – she wasn't a strider – but to walk confidently, as if this was a normal look for her. Though perhaps with her arms folded in front of her chest . . .

But come on! What was this if not a bid for attention?

With her back straight and her arms by her side, she walked over and stood in front of Claudine. 'Mrs Turner?' she said.

Claudine opened her eyes. 'My, oh my!' she cried, clapping her hands and hooting with delighted laughter. 'Look out, world!'

'I feel silly,' she said.

'You look amazing,' said Claudine. 'Now enjoy it.'

Encouraged by this, she wandered along the beach to where Lucian was sketching. She sensed Roberto looking as she passed by. But she ignored him and went straight to Lucian, who was absorbed in his work, pencil in mouth.

Standing in front of him, she said, 'Will you swim with me?'

'Uh-huh,' he said, without raising his eyes.

She waited there for what felt like hours until finally Lucian leant back and looked up at her. For a second, his gaze slid back to the drawing. But then he did a double take, a proper comedy one like you'd see Charlie Chaplin do at the pictures. It was such a funny face – mouth gaping, eyes lingering on her as if he'd never seen a woman before – she had to stop herself from laughing as she said, 'I thought you might show me the cave.'

He nodded dumbly.

Constance knew where the cave was. Claudine had told her. She swam rapidly, powerfully, enjoying the feel of her muscles pushing against the clear blue water. Every now and then she stopped to check Lucian was following her before continuing. When she got there she climbed up onto the rocks by the entrance and just had time to arrange herself to best advantage before he arrived.

He called out, 'Where did you learn to swim?'

'Scarborough. In the summers.' She gazed around her at the placid expanse of sea, the bouquet of bright umbrellas on the strip of beach from which they had both swum. 'Nothing like this. What about you?'

He hauled himself out and sat a little apart from her. 'At school. We had this terrible lake thing. We called it "the spinney".'

'Is that where you learned to draw? At school?'

'No. I've always just known how to do that.' He followed her gaze towards the play of light on the ceiling of the cave. 'It's a beautiful effect, isn't it?'

'It's lovely. What would you call it?'

'Luminescence, I think.'

They sat in silence, mesmerised; she by the shimmering display, he – she could tell – by her own delight in it.

At one point, she caught him looking at her. She gave him a shy, noncommittal smile, a smile of acknowledgement that offered and demanded nothing. Even so, it was clearly too much for Lucian.

'We ought to be getting back,' he said, breaking the spell.

'I'll race you.' She slipped into the water before he had a chance to respond. As she swam, she thought of him watching her and imagined the expression on his face.

*

Lizzie was filling her glass with what remained of the wine from lunch when she heard Claudine exclaim, 'Well, there's a thing.'

She glanced up. 'What?'

'Lucian. And Constance. Swimming back together.'

Lizzie looked – and was surprised rather than shocked. Nothing much shocked her anymore. 'Goodness,' she said. 'I don't like to use the word "forward" ...'

'But you will, anyway? Come on, Lizzie. Let the girl live.' There was a hint of disapproval in Claudine's voice and Lizzie felt suddenly ashamed of herself. Because it was true. Constance couldn't help being beautiful. She couldn't help being desired.

Perhaps Claudine was worried that she'd been harsh, because she leant up on an elbow and turned her head towards Lizzie. 'You were telling me about Pelham?'

'Was I?' She looked down. 'Only that I've been on at him for ages. To give up tennis. Losing is so bad for his self-esteem.'

'Men and their egos.'

Claudine was so good to talk to. She always understood absolutely what you meant – even when you weren't sure yourself.

'They're such children!' Lizzie gulped at the wine. 'Pelham can sulk for days – weeks, even – over a stupid tennis match.'

Claudine shook her head. 'They're all the same.'

'I'm beyond caring, to be honest. I'd be happy to leave him to stew in his own juices. If he'd only pull himself together long enough to give me what I want.'

'And what would that be?'

'A damned baby!' she burst out, more passionately than she'd intended. She laughed awkwardly and was surprised to feel tears welling up. She'd had no idea she was this upset.

'Oh, sweetheart, have you been trying long?'

'We're not trying at all.' This was the nub. The dark heart of it all. 'He shows no bloody interest.'

Two tears rolled down her flushed face. They felt strangely satisfying and she let them drip to the bottom of her cheeks, before wiping them away with her hand. Claudine climbed off her lounger, came over and gave her a hug. 'You're right. Men are babies. But that does mean, with a little pampering and hectoring, we can teach them to behave the way we want.'

*

The glaring heat seemed to build and build. Constance was tired and thirsty. They had run out of drinking water, though no one had noticed yet apart from her.

She had changed out of her wet costume and packed away the remaining picnic things in the hamper. They were ready now for the carriage, which she hoped would be here soon.

She headed back towards the rocks to fetch her towel and drawstring bag.

But someone else was using the rocks to change behind. She found herself frozen to the spot. It was Lucian. He stood with his back to her, peeling off his costume. It was like watching someone peel an apple, revealing not just his naked body – glazed and sculptural, milky-white where the costume had hidden his skin from the sun – but a thick purple scar running all the way from his waist to his neck.

She gasped in shock – but not quietly enough, because he turned round and caught her watching. She would never forget the shame on his face as he fumbled to cover himself with his hands.

'I'm so sorry,' she said, and hurried away.

*

Bella was just leaving the drawing room when she turned to see Cecil emerging from the library. He was looking uncharacteristically purposeful.

'Bellakins!' he called out when he spotted her. 'Do we have any more crates of Prosecco tucked away? The cellar is bare.'

'I've been keeping back a crate or two. Why do you ask?'

'Well, be a good girl and break out a bottle or three.'

'I've told you, Cecil. We can't afford to drink it ourselves.'

'Not even when we're celebrating?'

'What have we got to celebrate?'

He smiled. 'Let me show you.'

Two hours later, still shocked by what she had seen, Bella found herself back in the drawing room, welcoming guests in a daze. Paola, Constance and Francesco stood beside her, waiting to fill the arrivals' glasses.

Lucian went straight over to her. 'What's this about?'

'Your father is making an announcement.'

'What about?'

'He'll tell you himself. How was the beach?'

Lucian chewed his lip. 'Revealing,' he said.

Once everyone had arrived, Cecil clinked his glass to make sure he had everyone's attention. The room fell obediently silent – even Lottie, who had been allowed to stay up specially. Beside Cecil stood Lucian's easel, on which was mounted an oblong object, covered by a white sheet. Bella stared at it, wondering if this could all really be true.

'Thank you for joining us at this slightly earlier hour,' her husband began, rocking back and forth on his heels. 'I promise I won't keep you from your dinner.' His eyes gleamed with excitement. 'Now, I have to confess that when it comes to art, I'm a bit of a philistine.'

Polite laughter rippled. But Bella sensed Lucian's discomfort and embarrassment. He shot her a look, as if to ask, 'How can he declare such a thing so proudly? Why would he want to?'

Emboldened, Cecil continued. 'I enjoy a good cartoon in *Punch* as much as the next man. But that's the end of it. I leave the appreciation of finer things to my wife and son.'

He gestured towards Bella and Lucian, smiling.

'The rest of the Ainsworth clan are equally lacking in aesthetic sensibility, I'm afraid. So it shouldn't surprise you to learn that we've had a quite extraordinary artefact hanging in our midst for more than half a century, without having the foggiest idea about it.'

He surveyed the room – the rapt, upturned faces. He was relishing his moment, Bella thought, and she realised that in spite of everything she felt happy for him. His wellbeing was something that mattered to her and probably always would. Marriage was like that.

'Thankfully, I've recently made a new acquaintance, a new friend, who does know his art from his elbow.' He threw out a hand. 'Take a bow, Jack.'

Jack did no such thing. But he did raise his glass and look around.

'Not only is Jack a connoisseur, he's also a man of action. It's taken my brother and me a lifetime to realise we own a masterpiece. But it's taken Jack a jiffy to get his man up here to authenticate it.'

There was movement at the back of the room. A soft scraping as the door opened. Bella turned. With horror she saw that it was Danioni. Who had invited him? When she looked back, Cecil was pulling something from his pocket.

'So,' Cecil continued, 'with a letter in my hand to prove it, it gives me very great pleasure to present a previously unidentified work by an Old Master.' He unveiled the painting with a flourish. 'May I introduce Peter Paul Rubens.'

There was some applause, also gasping and shocked exclamations. Everyone clamoured round and craned their necks to get a look at the painting.

Bella overheard Julia get straight to the point with Cecil, when she asked, 'So this is what's saving you from going cap in hand to Old Man Livesey?'

'Jack says we shouldn't settle for a penny less than a hundred thousand,' he replied.

For goodness' sake, Bella thought, watching from the back of the room. *Don't tell everybody.*

Plum looked shell-shocked. She saw him mouth to Lizzie, 'A hundred thousand pounds!'

Just in front of them were Lady Latchmere and Melissa. 'She's certainly voluptuous,' said Melissa.

Lady Latchmere sniffed. 'That's one word for it.'

'Not to your taste, Aunt?'

'I fear nudity is one thing I shall never learn to be comfortable with.'

Bella covered her mouth with her hand to conceal her laughter.

It was no surprise to see Lucian looking at the painting so closely. Rose had been standing by his side. But she soon drifted away, apparently bored. Lucian didn't notice that she'd gone and was keeping up his commentary: 'Such verve in his brushstrokes, but such delicacy at the same time. Just look at the skin tone. It's almost . . .' He turned, clearly expecting to see Rose. Instead, there stood Constance in her maid's outfit, tray hanging by her side.

'Luminescent?' she finished for him. They smiled at each other.

Bella was impressed. A girl like Constance knowing a word like that. Wherever could she have heard it? It just proved you should never underestimate people.

Danioni was in the corner talking to Roberto, wearing

an aloof, faintly superior smile. Then Roberto walked off, at which point Danioni turned and exchanged a look with Francesco, of all people. Something passed between them. Was it Bella's imagination or did Danioni give a nod, as though he was giving or receiving an instruction?

She was about to head over to Cecil to congratulate him on a speech well delivered, when Danioni materialised by his side. She noticed he was carrying a briefcase.

Extraordinary, she thought, shuddering. The speed with which he'd crossed the room. It was almost enough to make a person believe in evil spirits.

*

Danioni coughed into his hand. 'A private word, please, Signore Ainsworth?'

Cecil spun round. 'Oh, it's you again,' he said, wearily. 'Of course. Somewhere quieter, perhaps?'

Frustrated to be dragged away, he led Danioni into the library, closing the door firmly behind them.

He smiled – a formal, chilly smile. 'What a stroke of luck, Danioni. That you happened to be here for the unveiling.'

'Most fortunate,' the Italian agreed.

'What brings you this way?'

Danioni placed his suitcase on Cecil's desk. He opened it with a firm click and produced from it a white towel. Slowly, enjoying the performance, he unfolded it so that the monogram 'HP' in the bottom right-hand corner was visible before handing it to Cecil for closer inspection.

Cecil ran his thumb over the soft cotton. 'Where did you find this?'

'It was recovered from a bicycle. Left at an illegal gathering. Held by enemies of the Italian state.'

'Goodness. How very rum. Any idea how it got there?'

He took out a notebook and pretended to consult it. 'One of the undesirables we arrested has confessed to stealing the bicycle. At the request of . . . William Scanlon.'

Cecil couldn't disguise his shock. 'Billy, you say? The little blighter.'

'He has fallen in with criminal elements,' Danioni said in a regretful tone of voice.

Cecil absorbed this unwelcome, barely plausible information. 'And what exactly do you propose to do about it?'

'I will leave that to you. As master of the house.'

'That's very decent of you,' said Cecil. He clapped his hands. 'Well. If there's nothing else?' He was keen to get back to the party.

'No, Signore Ainsworth. That is all.' Danioni turned to leave. But then he stopped, patting his sides as if he had forgotten something. '*Che stupido che sono!*'

'What is it?' asked Cecil, growing impatient now.

With a flourish Danioni produced an envelope from his inside pocket. 'I remember now. There is also this.'

Cecil plucked the oblong envelope from his long, nicotine-stained fingers. Immediately, he recognised Bella's favoured Smythson stationery. Addressed to a Mr Henry Bowater Esq of 12 Lyndhurst Gardens, Harrogate.

'Where did you get this?'

'It was found in the street,' said Danioni.

Cecil turned it over. It had been opened. 'This is my wife's private correspondence.'

'I fear so.'

'A letter to her father's accountant. I've no head for sums, I'm afraid. I leave all that to her.'

'Very good, Signor Ainsworth.' Danioni bowed before withdrawing again, more emphatically this time. But he stopped at the door to deliver his parting shot. 'A man should always be across his wife's affairs.'

Cecil looked again at the letter. He felt uneasy, slightly nauseous. He was about to open it when Jack appeared in the doorway. 'There you are! I wondered where you'd got to.'

'Jack!' Cecil managed, quickly arranging his face into an expression of pleasure. 'Sorry to miss you in there. I got collared.'

'So I saw. Funny old chap, isn't he?'

'They all are,' said Cecil. He slipped the envelope into his jacket pocket. 'Now, I don't know about you, but I need another glass of Prosecco.'

10

Nish was the last person to examine the painting. He had resolved to wait, put off by the unseemly crush, which reminded him of a particularly hot, tiring trip he'd made to the Uffizi Gallery in Florence a few months ago.

It was so different, being able to look at a painting as impressive as this up close. A person could stand before it for half an hour, drinking it all in. There was no one to say, 'Excuse me, please. My wife wishes to see the painting and you are blocking her view.' Or, 'Are you an Indian, sir? I was not aware that Indians were allowed in here . . .'

The most intriguing thing about the painting was Venus's Black maidservant, hidden away in the top right-hand corner. Her tight curls were flattened by a white cap fastened with a braid, which stretched from one side to the other. The maidservant was gazing in apparent admiration at Venus's long, wavy blonde hair cascading down her shoulders.

What if Rubens had switched things round? What if he had painted Venus as a Black woman? Nish resolved to discuss the matter with Claudine when he saw her next. Had she been there when Cecil was making his speech? He couldn't remember seeing her . . .

So absorbed was Nish by the painting, it took him a few moments to notice that Billy had entered the room. Betty's son was wandering around, collecting empty glasses. He drifted over to where Nish was standing and held out the tray. Nish placed his glass on it automatically, without looking at him. But the boy remained there, as if waiting for something.

'What is it, Billy?' Nish asked.

The boy said nothing, but his eyes dropped to indicate the corner of an envelope just visible beneath the tray.

He'd brought a message.

Checking there was no one else in the room, Nish grabbed the missive and hastily tore it open. It contained a piece of notepaper with an address:

VIA GIOVANNI PACINI, 41, TORINO. G

By the time he glanced up again, Billy was already leaving the room.

Nish rushed after him, trying to be discreet, to look as if he wasn't actually running. After waiting for Billy to deliver the tray to the kitchen, Nish followed him along the corridor and down the spiral iron staircase to the wine cellar. The light was dim, the cold, musty smell a relief after the stuffiness of the drawing room.

Nish waved the note in Billy's face. 'Who gave you this?'

'A friend. I were asked to pass it on.'

'Was that all?'

'There's summat else.'

He produced a stack of pamphlets tied with a linen bow. 'I was told to tell you to bring these when you come.'

Nish took them. He untied the ribbon and carefully pulled out one of the pamphlets. It was advertising an anti-fascist meeting. On its front was a grotesque caricature of Mussolini riding a donkey. He looked up at the boy. 'Did they say where I should go?'

Billy shook his head.

'I don't suppose you read Italian?'

'Not a word. But I can tell these don't say nowt nice about Old Musso.'

Nish shuffled the pamphlets back together, worried that someone might see them. To his right, was a stone shelf laden with casks of wine. He wedged the stack of pamphlets behind one of the casks and started to back away.

Billy was horrified. 'You're not going to leave them there, are you? That's jail time if you're caught.'

'Well, what *am* I supposed to do with them?'

'I could hide them for you. For a price.' Billy grabbed the pamphlets.

Nish was about to ask after the injured boy when there was a sound on the stairs. It was Constance, carrying four empty Prosecco bottles by their necks. When she saw Nish and Billy, she was so startled she almost dropped them. 'I'm awfully sorry, Mr Sengupta . . .'

It was more than Nish could bear. Panicking now, he pushed past her without saying anything, his spats clicking on the perforated iron steps as he ran up them.

The front door to the hotel was wide open.

He needed to be outside. He needed to breathe.

*

Constance was carrying the empty bottles down to the cellar for storage when Francesco passed her on the way up.

This wasn't unusual in itself. Francesco frequently went down to the cellar.

But most of the time, he'd acknowledge her. Smile or nod.

This time he didn't say anything; barely made eye contact. The more she thought about it, it was as if he'd been waiting halfway down the staircase. There were sixteen steps. She had only heard him climb six or seven in his heavy clumping shoes.

What had he been doing down there?

Only when she got all the way to the bottom did she see Billy and Nish and put two and two together. Or maybe three and two, because some things still weren't clear to her. Had Francesco been with them? Or watching them?

They both looked guilty, as if they had been engaged in something furtive. Seeing them had given her a shock. She had almost sworn and dropped the bottles. But she had remembered herself just in time and apologised to Nish for disturbing him.

Nish had left without a word. Rushed off, in fact. Which wasn't like him at all.

Now, she turned to confront Billy. 'What are you skulking about down here for?' He was hiding something behind his back. 'What have you got there?'

'Nowt for nosey.'

She put down the bottles and stuck out a hand. Reluctantly, Billy brought out the brick of leaflets. She took the top one. She looked at it quickly, then handed it back. It was written in Italian, but its meaning was obvious from the picture on the front. 'I don't know what any of this has got to do with Mr Sengupta. But I do know you're asking for trouble.'

'Not if you don't tell on me.' He put the package back on the shelf.

'You can't leave them there!' cried Constance. 'Mrs Ainsworth ... Mr Ainsworth ... They're up and down here all day!'

Billy picked them up again. 'I'm going to hide them under Lady Latchmere's bed. While they're all busy with dinner.'

Constance stared at him, horrified. 'What?' she said.

'Don't get your knickers in a twist. No one will look for them there.'

*

In the afternoon, Constance played with Lottie. The girl had so many toys – toys Constance had dreamed of owning as a child. A yo-yo, a spinning top, several bags of marbles ... But then she was an only child. Her toys were sibling substitutes. Friend substitutes. It was a miracle really, how uncomplaining she was, and how sensitive.

'You're sad,' she told Constance today. 'I can tell.'

'Hush your mouth. I'm nothing of the sort.'

'Has something happened?'

'Of course not.'

Sometimes she had an urge, a strong one, to tell Lottie about Tommy. She felt the child would understand, be sympathetic and interested. But Lottie was Alice's daughter, and thinking this way was madness. A symptom, she was aware, of her broader desire to be both part of and equal to the Ainsworth clan. And the focus of that desire was Lucian.

Dinner passed in a blur of pasta and some weirdly-named cheese. Gorgonzeelia? Gorginzolla? All the while, she couldn't stop thinking about what she'd witnessed in the cellar.

Nish and Billy. What had they been discussing that was so interesting to Francesco? And how could he have understood what they were saying? From the moment she'd arrived at Hotel Portofino, everyone she asked about Francesco had said the same thing.

Ah, he doesn't speak English.

They said it the way Menston folk used to say of old Bill Evans the ostler, 'Ah, don't worry, he were dropped at birth ...'

But what if everyone was wrong?

She felt like a machine. Press me here and I serve food. Push me there and I tell you where the wine is from. Dazed and head-achey, she wandered out onto the terrace to collect more glasses, when she spotted Lucian.

That phrase, 'her heart skipped a beat'. Constance had always thought it was just something people said.

Turned out it wasn't.

He was leaning on the balustrade, looking at the view – for shooting stars, he told her. 'Though it's a bit early,' he added. 'The best time is early August. The nights before and after the feast of San Lorenzo. The sky fills up with them, and the whole of Italy watches.'

She leant the tray against the balustrade. 'Are they really stars?'

He laughed and shook his head, but gently and without condescension. 'It's a meteor shower. Catholics, though – they think they're sparks from the flames that killed San Lorenzo. He was burned alive, you see. By the Romans. On a gridiron.'

'You know so much,' said Constance. 'I wish I knew things.'

'You do know things. You know how to run a household. How to look after a child.'

'Women's things, you mean.' She smiled, sardonically.

'*Practical* things. What I know, it's . . . useless.' He took a drag on his cigarette. 'You liked the painting, then?'

'The painting? Oh, yes. To think Rubens painted that woman more than three hundred years ago. Yet it seems so fresh.'

'So sensuous.'

'So *tender*.'

There was a pause. Then Lucian said, 'You have a good eye, you know.'

Constance shrugged. 'I've never really seen a painting like that before. Least ways, not so close up as I could touch it.'

'It's not the only thing you saw close up today.'

Constance felt herself flush. She looked around for more glasses to collect.

'I'm sorry you were exposed to that.'

She said, 'You have nothing to apologise for.'

'It must have repulsed you.'

'It took my breath away,' she said. It was ridiculous, the idea that she might have been repulsed. 'It made me yearn to know what you must have been through to get it. And what it must be like to carry it still.'

'To be scarred for life, you mean?'

She hesitated. 'We all have scars.'

'I saw none on you today.' He stepped closer. 'I looked and looked. There were no imperfections.'

'Mr Ainsworth . . .'

'Lucian, please. You must call me Lucian.'

Usually, when Constance looked at Lucian she felt reassured. But that was no longer the case. The attraction between them was no longer possible to deny. On one level, they both seemed to welcome this – he as much as her. And hadn't she gone out, looking for it?

There were dangers now, no question.

Constance felt suddenly giddy, as if she had stood up too quickly. The vastness of space was pushing down on her so that her breath came quickly, in short gasps. She was terrified. But she could not show it. The mask must not drop.

Lucian was her employer. Her social superior. What possible use for masks could he have?

She heard herself say, 'I must go.'

'Of course,' said Lucian.

She picked up the tray and carried it unladen into the kitchen.

*

Alice and Melissa were playing Old Maid in the drawing room when Roberto entered tentatively, as if he wasn't sure why he was there.

'Mr Albani,' said Alice, glancing up from her cards.

He gave a little bow. '*Buona sera.*'

'You are looking for your father?'

'*Scusi?*'

'*Tuo . . . padre?*'

'*Sì.*'

'He's gone to bed, I think.'

'*Molte grazie.*'

He turned to leave the room. But before he could step away Alice suddenly put down her cards and stood up. She cleared her throat. 'I wanted to say thank you.'

Roberto turned. '*Sì?*'

'To say *grazie* for the bracelet.' She held up her wrist and pointed to an imaginary accessory. 'It was beautiful. And extremely generous and thoughtful of you.'

He smiled and nodded, though Melissa was sure he didn't understand a word her friend said.

'I hope you understand why I had to refuse it,' Alice continued. 'It doesn't mean I'm not grateful for your interest.'

She held out her hand. Roberto stooped and kissed it. Then he left the room, with a noticeable spring in his step.

Melissa was agog. When Alice sat back down, she said, 'You sent back a gift?'

Alice's face blushed. 'I couldn't accept it.'

'Because he's Italian?'

'I thought it was from his father!'

Melissa pondered this as they resumed their game. 'Poor man,' she said. 'He hardly speaks a word of English. Perhaps he needs his father to speak on his behalf?'

*

Jack had a pretty good idea of what was going on in the library before he entered. As it transpired, he was spot on. Cecil and Francesco were there, packing the Rubens back into its plywood crate.

'We all right to talk?' Jack asked Cecil, flicking his eyes towards the Italian, who was poised with a screwdriver and a handful of long nails.

Cecil looked at him as if he was mad. 'Of course. He doesn't understand a word.'

'Well, then. If you're sure.' Jack reached into his pocket and pulled out a cheque, which he handed to Cecil. It was for fifty thousand dollars. 'Will that do?'

Cecil grinned. 'Very nicely. Let's hope she sells.'

'Don't worry about that. The only question is how much for.'

'Should I keep her locked up in here?'

'I'd prefer to take her with me, if you don't mind.'

'Will she be safe with you?'

Jack lifted his waistcoat to reveal a Colt revolver. 'She'll be well protected.'

'Fine, then. Take her away.' Cecil stepped forward, gesturing to Francesco that he should help Jack carry the crate upstairs. 'But come back down for a brandy and a cigar, Jack. I hate to drink alone.'

*

As she had been instructed, Claudine unlocked and opened the door as soon as she heard Jack's knock. Then she stood by the bed, watching as he and Francesco manoeuvred the crate into the room and propped it against the wall.

'So that's it,' she said.

'That's it.'

'I'll say one thing, it beats Napoleon's sabre.'

This was a private joke, a reference to an old sword of dubious provenance that Jack had managed to sell for a lot of money to an American collector.

Jack stared at the crate, then at Claudine. His eyes were blazing with excitement. 'Trust me, baby. Compared to this painting, Napoleon's sabre is a steak knife.'

As soon as Francesco had left, Jack took out his revolver and placed it carefully on the bed. Then he fixed her with an intense stare. 'Don't let anyone in. And make sure you stay put. I'll be back in a short while.'

'Where are you going?'

'It's better that you don't know.'

Claudine let him out and locked the door behind him. She picked up the gun. After examining it to check that it was loaded – it was, or seemed to be – she put it in the bedside drawer.

She stood for a few moments, contemplating the crate and its contents. It was scarcely credible that something so valuable should be here in the room with her. By rights, it ought to have an aura of some sort. To be radiating light or heat – a clue to let you know how special it was. But, no. It was a simple wooden box.

Once she had decided on a plan of action, she removed a silk negligee from her chest of drawers and stuffed it into her vanity case.

Checking that the coast was clear, she emerged from the room, locking the door behind her.

She padded down the darkened corridor until she reached the communal bathroom and knocked softly on the door.

Lizzie opened it a crack. When she saw it was Claudine, she grabbed her by the wrist and silently pulled her inside.

*

It was unusual for Bella to be up before the servants. But she had woken early, at five o'clock, and felt restless.

She dressed casually in a floral cotton dress that showed off her arms, which she had always been told were shapely, and made her feel young. Leaving her hair loose, she crept out of her room and down to the kitchen.

She liked the kitchen because it was the centre of the house. If Hotel Portofino was a ship then the kitchen was its cockpit, its levers and switches the pans hanging bright and shining from the ceiling and the knives glittering in their racks.

She ran a finger along the smooth, waxy surface of the

table. They had bought it in Lucca at an auction. It had poured with rain, and she had got soaked. Funny to think back.

From a porcelain bowl she took a green fig, so ripe it threatened to burst in her hands. She popped it in her mouth, then lit the range and made herself a cup of tea.

She opened the kitchen door and stood on the threshold, staring out across the courtyard to the green hills and the glinting sea beyond. The scene was as still and perfect as a painting. Already, she could feel the sun's heat. She slipped off her shoes and wandered outside in her bare feet, delighted to find the ground warm.

This is what you always wanted, she thought. *Hold tight to it. Remember it on the days when life feels like a relentless exercise.*

An image flashed before Bella. That poor boy, lying on the floor so helplessly. She resolved to ask after him when she next saw Billy. Not that Billy would know anything – or tell Bella if he did. Hadn't she warned him off any further association with the boy?

She was just sipping her tea, pondering these questions, when she heard something. The soft, accidental thud of someone trying not to be heard.

She checked the kitchen. No one there.

When she went into the hall, she saw Plum. He was dressed for travel in a cream suit, padding down the stairs with a large bag over his shoulder.

She called out. 'Sneaking off without saying goodbye?'

'Mrs Ainsworth! I'm so sorry.' He made a decent show of not being shocked to see her. 'I wasn't sure if anyone was up.'

'Will you have breakfast?'

'I won't if it's all the same.'

'Oh, come on.' Bella kept her voice bright and normal. 'Betty will be horrified if I let you go without so much as a cup of tea.'

'I'd rather get on,' he said.

'You'll need a carriage to the station.'

'It's all fixed, Mrs Ainsworth. All sorted. I spoke to Francesco last night. Managed to make myself understood.'

Did you, she thought. *Did you indeed.*

Plum picked up his pace as he crossed the hall towards the door.

Suddenly, Bella had an idea. 'Will you wait a moment?'

He stopped, looked at his watch. 'Of course.'

Bella ran into her office and grabbed her most recent letter to Henry and a handful of coins.

She gave them to Plum and asked, 'Would you mind awfully posting this for me? Once you get to Milan?'

He looked at the address. 'Harrogate, eh? A lovely town.'

'It is, isn't it?'

'Well, then.' He straightened his shoulders. 'Wish me luck.'

'Best of British!' She put out her hand. He shook it, grinning.

Quite a performance, Bella thought. What was really going on here? And where was Lizzie?

The door creaked as she opened it to let Plum out. Francesco was waiting, checking the horses' shoes. Her eyes sought his. Was she imagining it or was there a tinge of apprehension there?

293

So entranced was she by the soft crunch of the vanishing coach that she almost didn't notice Danioni walking towards her up the drive. Not just Danioni, either – he had another man with him. She waited in the doorway, arms folded, unable to suppress her irritation.

'Oh, good heavens. Not again! Can't you leave us alone?'

'And a very good morning to you also, Signora Ainsworth.'

'What is it now?'

'This is Signor Ricci. From the Inspectorate of Industry and Labour.' Ricci was tall and stooping, with a bushy moustache. He tipped his hat, as Danioni produced a bit of paper. 'And this is the letter that authorises him to carry out an inspection of the working conditions of your premises.'

Bella could hardly believe her ears. 'At this time of the morning?'

Danioni shrugged. 'What is it you English say? "The early bird catches the worm."'

She led them into the kitchen and forced them to wait, standing, until Betty had arrived and made a start on the buns required for breakfast.

The cook's reaction, when she saw them, was entirely predictable.

'What's all this nonsense?'

'It's just a formality,' Bella assured her. 'We need to cooperate. Grit our teeth.'

'I've no teeth left to grit!' Betty protested. And she opened her mouth wide enough for Bella to see that this was indeed the case.

Bella watched as the black-suited Ricci made his dolorous way round the kitchen, shadowed by Betty. At one point, he found a bowl on the worktop. He brought his nose close, wrinkling it, and was about to make a note on his clipboard when Betty snapped, 'It's just batter. There's nowt queer about that.'

Betty kept looking at Bella, appealing to her, as if she had the power to make it stop. Bella felt awful. But she feared making things worse. Not without shame, she realised that this fear was greater than her anger; the fear was paralyzing her, not respect for process.

Ricci ran his fingers over the stove, checking for grease. He stooped, examining the oven's contents through the glass, and was about to open the oven door when Betty could control herself no longer.

'Hey!' she cried, smacking his hands away. 'I don't care if you've orders from the King of Italy himself. You're not opening that!' He squared up to her, arms folded. She mirrored him, daring him to contradict her. 'If my buns don't rise, there'll be hell to pay!'

Afterwards, they went through to the office. Bella sat at her desk, squinting at the report, which was not only written in Italian but in the tiniest, messiest handwriting imaginable. Danioni stood watching her, drumming his fingers.

With some difficulty Bella read, '*Condizioni anti igieniche.*' She looked up sharply. '"Unhygienic conditions"? I've never read such rubbish. You could eat your dinner off Betty's floors.'

Danioni said, 'This report, I did not write.'

'But your signature's all over it.' She handed it back to him. 'So. What does it mean?'

'You have fourteen days.'

'To do what?'

'To comply. Or face closure.'

She was about to retort when there was a sound, a bellow of masculine anguish, from somewhere within the hotel.

She looked at Betty in alarm. 'What on earth was that?'

'I don't know,' she said. 'But I don't like it, ma'am. I don't like it at all.'

*

Cecil woke alone in his own room. He lay in bed for a few moments, listening to the church bells, pondering a fresh mosquito bite on his arm. Then he searched for a light for his first cigarette of the day.

He had thought he had some matches in his jacket pocket. But when he checked, there weren't any. Only the letter Danioni had given him – Bella's letter to her father's accountant. A letter Danioni had been particularly keen to bring to Cecil's attention. Now, why was that?

In his heart of hearts, he knew the answer.

Come on, man. Face up to it.

He felt the anger well up in him as he read. A very deep anger, closely aligned to shame. How long had this been going on? And how many people knew? Had Danioni passed the letter round his office? Of course, he had. So, the whole town knew everything. Not only that Bella was loose, but that she was not satisfied by him. And that he, Cecil, had been passed over for some ... milksop.

He felt energised by his anger. Electrified. Really, it was extraordinary, the way his whole body felt different. Well, he would show her. That bloody woman. He would show her who was in charge.

He got dressed in a daze, not minding for once what he looked like. How his hair was parted, or if his collar was straight. What mattered was the confrontation ahead.

Slamming the door behind him, he stalked down the corridor.

The letter was in his hand. He would not tolerate this behaviour. This ... humiliation.

At the top of the stairs, he stopped.

Something was happening in the hall. Some panic or perhaps an altercation. It was hard to tell. He saw Bella rush out of the kitchen followed by Betty and, for some reason, Danioni. What the hell was he doing here?

Their quarry was Jack, of all people. The American was standing at the foot of the stairs. 'Where is it?' he shouted.

'Where is what?' Cecil watched his wife ask.

He descended the stairs briskly, the letter momentarily forgotten. 'Jack!' he called. 'What's going on?'

Now, Jack was careering around like a madman, pushing open doors and peering into rooms. 'You goddamn crooks. Where is it?'

His tantrum had woken the hotel. One by one, bleary-eyed figures appeared on the landing.

'Jack! Please!' Cecil moved towards him, but Jack held him off.

'You stay away from me.'

'Mr Turner,' said Bella, 'please, calm down. Tell us what the matter is.'

Jack rubbed a hand over his stubbly chin. His eyes were wild, his face as pale and waxen as a corpse's. 'It's the painting,' he said. 'It's gone!'

11

Bella conceded that there was something staged and formal about the current circumstances. They reminded her of the Agatha Christie novels she enjoyed when she had time to read, where a hotel's guests were arraigned in a drawing room very like this one and made to account for their movements at a particular hour on a particular night.

But this alone couldn't account for the mood of resentment that lingered over the assembled company. Bella grimaced as she took in the panorama of blank faces. Guests stood warily apart, oddly vulnerable-looking in their dressing gowns and slippers, their eyes sunken with fatigue.

Danioni had taken charge of the situation and was interrogating Jack with evident enjoyment. *What a horrid little man he is,* she thought. *The very worst of modern Italy.*

'And you are sure the painting – it is stolen, Signor Turner?'

'Of course I'm sure. What kind of jerk do you take me for?'

'You have searched your room?'

'If I say it's gone, it's gone.'

Cecil weighed in, exasperated. 'How could something of that size just disappear? From right under your nose?'

'How the hell should I know? I ain't the guy that stole it.'

'Yet you're "the guy" who was supposed to be keeping it safe.'

'Meaning what, Mr Ainsworth?'

'Meaning whatever you choose to make of it, Mr Turner.'

Count Albani stepped in, to Bella's relief. He looked commanding in his red paisley silk dressing gown. 'We should all try and stay calm.'

Bella turned to him. 'What would you advise, Count?'

'To do as Mr Turner requested. Send for the police. *Pronto!*'

Jack nodded enthusiastically. 'And get them to search every inch of this goddamn place.'

'Perhaps Lucian could go?'

Lucian jumped up. 'Of course. I'll just get changed.'

But Danioni waved his hands. 'No, no. It will be better if everyone . . . if they do not go to their room, Signore. For a little time.'

This instruction did not go down well. From Lady Latchmere and Julia, especially, there was muttered incredulity that they should be expected to wait around for much longer in a state of undress.

But Cecil seemed to agree. 'Danioni's right,' he said. 'That way we can be sure no one's up to any shenanigans.'

'What exactly are you insinuating?' demanded Lady Latchmere.

'No one's insinuating anything,' Bella reassured her, hastily.

'Now is everybody present?' Cecil wondered.

'The Wingfields aren't,' said Alice, glancing around.

'Mr Wingfield left early this morning,' revealed Bella.

Jack looked sceptical. 'Did he now?'

'He's travelling to a tournament,' Bella explained. 'He'll be back in a week at most.'

'Maybe he ain't coming back,' said Jack.

'But his wife's still here,' Alice pointed out.

Jack turned to her. 'You're sure of that?'

Another voice piped up. 'I saw her last night, Jack.' It was Claudine. 'Just before we went to bed.'

Jack looked at her severely and Bella wondered how he hadn't known this; why Claudine hadn't told him before. Had they not been together? Had she forgotten?

'Alice will check on her,' said Bella. 'Constance, will you send Billy out to me? And in the meantime . . . Perhaps a little breakfast might improve everybody's mood?'

*

Betty was unamused by the idea of having to serve so many breakfasts so quickly. But not as unamused as Constance when she saw Billy creeping in through the kitchen door. He looked grubby and dishevelled.

'Where have you been?' she asked him.

'Nowhere.' Immediately, he looked guilty.

'Well, you're wanted.'

'Who's asking?'

'Mrs Ainsworth. She's talking about calling in the police.'

Billy startled. 'Police? What for?'

'The painting's gone missing,' said Betty.

'That's got nowt to do with me.'

'No one's saying it is, Billy. They want them to search the hotel.'

The boy's face drained of all colour. 'But why?'

Betty ruffled his hair. 'Stop worrying, you soft lad. You're to *fetch* the police, not hand yourself in.'

Constance led Billy into the drawing room. Almost all the hotel's occupants were in there, some milling around, others sitting looking bored and cross. Bella was standing with Cecil, Lucian and Jack. They were all in their dressing gowns, talking in low, serious voices to the slimy Italian man – Danioni, or whatever he was called.

'Ah, Billy,' said Bella when she saw them. 'I need you to run into town. Signor Danioni will tell you where to go.'

Danioni was looking hard at Billy with an unusually intense stare. 'This is William Scanlon?'

'Yes, this is Billy,' confirmed Cecil.

'The boy who stole the bicycle?'

'We only meant to borrow it . . .' Billy looked frantically around for support.

'A known associate of criminal elements,' said Danioni.

Constance rolled her eyes. 'Don't be daft.'

But before she could say anything else in his defence, Billy had bolted for the door. Constance willed him to make it, but Jack was faster on his feet. 'No, you don't, kiddo,' he said, grabbing Billy by the arms.

'Let go of me!'

'Quit struggling.'

'You're hurting me!'

Betty must have heard his cries from the kitchen. She came into the drawing room with angry, bustling speed, still wiping her hands on her apron. 'What's all this? Billy?'

Ignoring her, Cecil turned to Lucian. 'Get me the key to the outhouse. We'll lock him in there.'

'Please, Cecil,' Bella pleaded. 'Is that necessary?'

'"The guilty flee when no man pursueth".' He turned to Danioni. 'My man, Francesco. He can go for the police.'

Billy continued to struggle and squirm as Cecil and Jack bundled him out of the room. Lucian followed, she guessed on a quest for the keys. Constance went over to Betty and put her arms around her.

The older woman was in shock, her face pale, her breathing rapid and shallow. 'Billy!' she called out. 'Billy!'

'Mam!' His pained cries echoed briefly in the hallway before fading into the most awful silence.

*

The men dragged Billy to the outhouse, a small stone building hidden away up a rutted track behind the hotel. Francesco used it for storing tools and building materials – and God knew what else, thought Billy. Dirty books? Dead animals? He'd always struck Billy as a weirdo.

Billy had his hands on the window grille and was shaking the door hard, kicking at it for all he was worth. The wood was old, but thick. Not rotten enough to smash through.

'Let me out!' he cried. His side hurt from where that bastard Mr Ainsworth had punched him hard when he thought no one was looking.

How come all the good men had died in the war – all his brothers! All of them! Yet, people like Mr Ainsworth had got off scot free? Anyone could see he was a useless sponger. What did he *actually do*? Sweet Fanny Adams. Just strutted about in his fancy clothes, barking orders at people. A cowardly bully.

They were all out there, chatting about what they'd just done. Mr Ainsworth, Mrs Ainsworth, Danioni and the American with the shiny car. The only one who looked uneasy was Mrs Ainsworth.

'Little blighter's got a pair of lungs on him,' he heard Mr Ainsworth say.

'And a kick like a mule,' offered the American.

'I need a doctor!' Billy called out. 'I can't breathe!'

'The boy's distressed,' said Mrs Ainsworth.

But Mr Ainsworth said he wasn't, he was just panicking because they were onto him.

Billy tried again. 'I've got a pain in me side!'

This seemed to bother Mrs Ainsworth. She turned to her husband. 'Couldn't I ask Nish to take a look?'

'Don't be so feeble,' he snapped.

'Please!' Billy cried. 'It hurts bad!'

'Cecil, please!'

'Oh, for goodness' sake, Bella. All right. But be quick about it.'

Nish arrived about five minutes later. Mrs Ainsworth was with him, Mr Ainsworth and the American having disappeared, perhaps back to the house, or perhaps they were guarding the path. Either way, he could no longer see them through the window.

It was Mrs Ainsworth who unlocked the door to let Nish in. She stood over them, watching the examination, biting her thumbnail.

Billy had considered running for it the second the door opened. But perhaps there was a better way. In any case, if he escaped now that would just get Mrs Ainsworth into trouble. And his beef wasn't with her. She was a decent sort.

As Nish crouched down, they made eye contact. Something passed between them. An understanding, about what needed to happen.

'His breathing is certainly laboured,' said Nish.

Bella asked, 'Can you give him something?'

'Perhaps a sedative. It would calm him down. Ease the constriction.'

'I don't want nowt like that,' Billy protested.

'Maybe something for the pain, then.' Nish looked around. 'But my bag is in my room.'

'Danioni won't let you up there,' said Bella. 'There are aspirin in my office. I'll go and get them.'

Seizing his opportunity, Billy grabbed Nish's arm. 'They're in Lady Latchmere's bedroom,' he whispered.

'The pamphlets?'

Billy nodded. 'Under the bed.'

'Christ, Billy. Are you mad?'

'I thought it were the last place anyone'd look!'

'The police will find them there. They're searching the whole hotel.'

'The keys are in me room. I didn't get a chance to put 'em back.'

'Which keys?'

'The master set. I took 'em from the office.'

The two of them shared a look of desperate complicity.

*

Cecil was standing sentry at the foot of the path back to the house. Bella was forced to pass him on her way to get the aspirin for Billy.

He had been off with her recently. But she knew, because he was always telling her, that she had a tendency to be paranoid. To overread situations. And in all likelihood, that was what she was doing now. So, there was no reason to be nervous as she approached him.

He didn't look at her, pretending instead to be engrossed by a trail of ants on the ground.

Bella said, 'Let's hope the police can get to the bottom of it.'

Cecil said nothing. It was as if he hadn't heard her.

She tried again. 'I said, let's hope . . .'

'I heard what you said,' he snapped. He walked away, towards a bed of azaleas at the edge of the path.

'What's the matter?' She followed him, reaching out, trying to take his hand. 'Cecil?'

He jerked his arm away. He turned and when she saw his face it was white with anger. 'Stay away from me.'

'Darling,' she said, as if to a fractious child, 'don't take it out on me. You said it yourself – you weren't even aware the painting might be worth something until very recently.' She grabbed at his hand again but he put it behind his back, fixing his attention even more directly on the ground.

At this, Bella found it impossible to contain her frustration. 'Really, Cecil! If anyone should be upset, it's me. This sort of incident … Well, it could be ruinous for the hotel's reputation.'

He looked up and met her gaze. 'You haven't a clue, have you?'

'A clue?' Bella's voice shook with bewilderment. 'A clue about what?'

*

The drawing room resembled a station café packed with angry passengers waiting for a long-delayed train. Hardly anyone was talking. They were too tired and agitated.

Claudine certainly wasn't in the mood for conversation. She wasn't in the mood for anything much.

It was funny, she mused. When she first saw Hotel Portofino, she had loved the way it looked, especially the interior: quaint English stylings suggestive of a grand country house. But now she was starting to get restless.

Blame the drama. It could have that effect, even when she had played a part in it – which she had to admit, she had.

Whatever the cause, the outcome was that now, when she looked around at the room – at the low-backed chairs, the immaculately dusted houseplants and that fireplace, with its vast overmantle on which statues of angelic children frolicked behind a row of books – it reflected this restlessness back at her.

She studied the paintings. There were lots of them. Rich, white women in crinoline mostly, painted with a nod to what was going down in France thirty years ago. Some of them, she knew, were Lucian's. She wasn't sure if she liked them. He was good, she could see that. But he needed to move with the times. Be bolder. Paint more like the artist friends she had left behind in Paris.

She was staring at one in particular. It was of a woman who looked disconcertingly like Rose. Then, suddenly, Jack appeared by her side and dragged her into a corner.

'What do you mean you saw the Wingfield woman before you went to bed?' His breath stank of alcohol.

'Exactly what I say,' she said, pulling away.

'But I told you to stay put.'

'You know I don't like to be "told".'

'Oh, cut the crap!'

'What crap is that, Jack?'

'Your Queen of Sheba act. We both know you come from nothing.' Claudine absorbed the insult blankly. She tried to walk off, but he grabbed her again. 'Don't you dare walk away when I'm talking to you.'

She froze. 'Or else?'

'Or else.' He squeezed her wrist.

'Take your damn hand off me.'

'You just back me up. Whatever I say, OK?'

Several options presented themselves. Quite deliberately,

and with her eye on the bigger picture, Claudine chose the most straightforward. 'Whatever you say, Jack,' she said.

*

Amazement at Bella's brazenness was the fuel that sustained Cecil on his walk back down to the hotel from the outhouse. Who did she think she was fooling with her denials? He looked around at the flower beds and lawns, at the immaculate landscaping, and felt a surge of resentment. This was all hers, not his. It had never truly felt like his. And now he was starting to wonder what he was doing here at all. In this place. In this marriage.

His friend Horace had said, when he learned of Cecil's plan to move to Italy, that running a hotel was only ever as easy as the guests. At the time, it had struck Cecil as rather a banal observation. But, dash it – he'd been right.

He arrived in time to catch the end of Claudine and Jack's argument, which Lizzie was watching from the drawing-room doorway.

Cecil went up to her. 'Lovers' tiff?'

She answered without looking at him. 'Seems that way.'

'Trying to get their story straight?'

'If you say so.' Lizzie tried to walk away, but Cecil was not to be deterred.

'Have you spoken to Mrs Turner?'

'Not yet. I've only just woken up.'

'But you saw her last night? Just before bed?'

'I don't recall.'

Cecil closed in on her, sending out more than a hint of

menace. 'Mrs Wingfield, I don't mean to alarm you. But the coincidence of your husband departing just as the painting disappears has been noticed.'

Lizzie held her ground. 'What are you saying?'

'Nothing, my dear lady. Just that if you have any information that might help us establish the sequence of events, then you would be wise to share it.' He paused, the better to deliver his *coup de grâce*. 'I would hate to see one of our most celebrated sportsmen dragged into this murky affair. With all the attendant publicity.'

Lizzie's mouth fell open. But before she could respond, Bella appeared behind them.

'Breakfast is ready when you are,' she said, brightly.

Cecil stepped away from Lizzie. 'Excellent.'

'I'm letting everyone know they should make their way to the dining room.' Bella didn't seem to have noticed anything untoward.

'Then let's go. I'm sure Mrs Wingfield is hungry.'

As Lizzie pulled ahead, Cecil and Bella walked together down the hallway, neither of them speaking. They found themselves accosted by Julia. At any other time, Cecil would have enjoyed the opportunity to flirt. But not now.

'What a dreadful business,' said Julia.

'Quite so,' Bella agreed, flatly.

Julia glanced at Cecil. 'You seem surprisingly calm.'

'It doesn't do to lose one's cool.'

'Do you think the painting really has been stolen?'

Bella said, 'I don't think any of us know what to believe, Julia.'

As he entered the dining room, Cecil observed Jack making his way towards his table. 'Or *who* to believe, more to the point.'

Jack turned on the spot. 'Is that directed at me?'

Cecil felt a flare of satisfaction. 'You surmise correctly.'

'You're calling me a liar?'

'I'm suggesting you're being a trifle economical with the truth.'

'Cecil!' cried Bella.

The room fell silent as the two men squared up to each other. Cecil had the advantage of being properly dressed. Jack's dressing gown kept flapping open to reveal the flannel pyjamas beneath.

'Out with it, then,' said Jack.

Cecil smirked. 'I rather think the onus is on you, old chap. To tell us what *you* know.'

Jack looked around at the sea of expectant faces. 'The painting was definitely in the crate when you handed it over to me. I saw you pack it with my own eyes.'

But Cecil had seized the opportunity for grandstanding. 'What I can't help wondering, is why you were so keen for the exchange to take place last night?'

'After you insisted on showing it to everyone, well ... I thought I was better *equipped* to keep it safe than you.'

Bella said, 'I'm sure you did what you thought was best, Mr Turner.'

Jack looked across at Claudine, who was sitting on her own with a glass of orange juice. 'I left Claudine with the necessary means to guard the painting while I came down to finish my business with you. And then I went back up at about eleven. Either she or I was with it the whole time. Until I went to look at it again this morning and discovered it had gone.'

'Disappeared?' suggested Cecil. 'In a puff of smoke?' He blew on his hands like a magician.

'I don't believe in magic,' said Jack.

'How fortunate,' said Cecil, sharply. 'Because neither do I.'

'So how do you explain it?' wondered Julia.

'I think Mr Turner hasn't told us the whole truth,' Cecil said. 'He's trying to conceal the extent of his negligence.'

The whole room was now alert and involved.

'Darling,' said Bella. 'Is this the time? Or the place?'

Jack placed his hands on his hips. 'You'd better be able to back that up, buddy.'

'Oh, I'm sure your wife can. Isn't that right, Mrs Turner?'

Claudine said nothing.

'Or perhaps,' Cecil continued, 'I should ask Mrs Wingfield to corroborate instead? After all, I distinctly heard you say you spoke to her. Just before you went to bed.'

The two women exchanged a glance.

'I may have left the room,' Claudine admitted. 'But only for a short while.'

'Claudine!' Jack spun round.

'What, Jack? It's the truth.'

'Now we're getting to it,' said Cecil.

'I never let a girlfriend down.'

'I asked her to meet me in the bathroom,' Lizzie clarified.

Julie looked aghast, as if the very idea of meeting in a bathroom repulsed her. 'Whatever for?'

'To help her get ready for bed.'

'And how long did this rendezvous last?' wondered Cecil.

'About twenty minutes.'

'In which time Mrs Turner was away from the painting. And you, Mrs Wingfield, were away from your husband.'

'I'm not denying I was away from the painting,' said Claudine. 'But somebody must have gotten the key. Because I swear on my life . . .' She glanced around at all the onlookers. 'That door was locked when I left.'

*

Nish was nearly out of cigarettes. Sitting on the terrace, looking out at the sea, he pulled his penultimate Caporal out of the packet and sighed. He was hating this – being a key player in a cluster of interlinked catastrophes.

A yacht glided towards the harbour, a thin ribbon of white trailing in its wake. Nish watched it, abstracted. The landscape here could play tricks on you. The infinity of hills, the vapourless sky . . . They hypnotized you, convincing you that you were immune from life's vicissitudes, and that Italy was the place most English tourists wanted it to be – the sun-blessed sum of its paintings and sculptures and medieval buildings.

But Italy was a broken country. And it had been broken, in part, by the Allies, who in the Treaty of London had promised it territory it was not within their power to grant so that it would enter the war on their side. When it was all over the then Italian Prime Minister, Vittorio Orlando, was humiliated at the Paris Peace Conference and had resigned.

In fact, Italy had gained some territories – Istria, Trieste, South Tyrol. But it lost most of Dalmatia, and this was enough to enrage the nationalists and the Fascists, who whipped up indignation, accusing Orlando of presiding over a 'mutilated victory'.

Enter, stage right – Mussolini.

Nish was so deep in thought that it took him a while to register the footsteps closing in behind him.

'Mind if I join you?' said a voice – Lucian's. 'It's pretty poisonous in there.'

'Be my guest,' he said, without looking round.

'What are you up to?'

'Not much.' Nish smiled. 'If you must know, I'm thinking.'

'Oh, yes?' His friend sounded amused.

'Thinking that we can't destroy Fascism unless we try to understand where it came from. And why it appeals to so many people.' He paused. 'It isn't enough to hate things.'

Lucian sat down beside him. 'Heavy stuff.'

Nish offered his last cigarette. 'I wish it were less relevant.'

Lucian must have noticed his hands shaking, because he asked, 'Are you all right?'

Nish looked at his friend. He couldn't find the words.

'What is it?' Lucian asked. 'Tell me?'

Nish shook his head.

'I owe you my life, for God's sake. There can't be secrets between us.'

'Let's just say I've been a bloody fool.'

Lucian laughed. 'No change there then.'

'It's no joke, Lucian. I'm in a jam.'

'Well, let me help you.'

'I'm not sure there's anything to be done about it,' said Nish.

And then he told him – not everything, but enough. About Gianluca and Billy and the pamphlets. Lucian listened without passing judgement. 'It's no good,' he said, after a while. 'We can't keep this to ourselves.' Seeing Nish's face, he added: 'If I can go over the top, you can have an honest conversation with my mother.'

Nish stubbed out his cigarette. 'It isn't your mother I'm worried about.'

*

The atmosphere in the dining room was lighter than either of them had expected; Betty's buns had worked their magic. But their arrival coincided with that of Danioni's new chum – a sombre, rake-like figure in full police regalia, including silver epaulettes and a white cross-belt, which cut diagonally across his jacket.

'At last,' said Bella. She clapped for quiet. 'If I could have everyone's attention please.'

The room fell silent. As the man began to speak in Italian, Count Albani supplied a running translation. This was, he announced, Sergeant Ottonello from the Polizia Municipale and he was here to search the hotel.

'I request your permission also,' Ottonello said, with a

thin smile, but no one was left in any doubt that this was a demand rather than a question.

Danioni stepped forward. 'I am sure this is nothing to worry about, for you fine people.' Then he turned to leave.

Bella was about to follow him out of the door when Lucian rushed across and intercepted her. 'We need to speak in private,' he said.

'What, now?'

'This instant, I'm afraid.'

'Let's go to the kitchen, then.'

The problem with privacy, Nish thought, is that it was relative. For example, it seemed that for Bella a conversation could involve Alice too – in fact, any family members who happened to be present – and still be a private one.

Nish had never liked Alice, though he had kept this from Lucian. She was grudging and bitter, the sort of person who would always think the worst. So it was entirely predictable that, after hearing his story, she became angrier than her mother.

'How could you be so foolish?' she demanded, her freckled face reddening.

Lucian rushed to his friend's defence. 'Come on, Alice. Nish wasn't to know Billy would hide the pamphlets under Lady Latchmere's bed.'

'I meant both of you!' Alice glared. 'What were you thinking? Sneaking about at some secret socialist pow-wow.'

'I was hoping to educate myself,' said Lucian, pointedly. 'About politics. On the off chance it might be something I could learn to feel passionate about.'

'Why is that so important? Feeling *passionate* about things all the time?'

'If you really don't know,' Lucian snapped, 'I'm not sure I can be bothered to tell you.'

He looked at his mother, hoping for a supportive word. But she had her head in her hands. 'Oh, Lucian.'

'Please, Mrs Ainsworth,' said Nish. 'Lucian didn't know anything about the pamphlets. It's entirely my fault.'

'Don't listen to him,' said Lucian.

'I can only apologise,' Nish went on. 'For the difficulties I've caused. After all the kindness you've shown me.'

Lucian was about to say more, but Bella got in first. 'There's no point bickering about how we got into this mess. We need to focus on getting out of it.'

Alice asked, 'Can't we just retrieve the stupid pamphlets?'

Bella shook her head. 'They've already started to search for the painting.'

'The police are everywhere,' added Lucian.

'Is there a chance that they just find the painting and forget about the rest?' Nish wondered.

'My money's on the culprit having scarpered,' said Lucian. 'I saw Wingfield creeping about the other night in a most suspicious fashion.'

'Then why not just tell the truth?' asked Alice.

Bella looked at her. 'Because Danioni is looking for the slightest excuse to close down the hotel.'

'I'll turn myself in,' said Nish, shoulders sinking. 'Tell them I acted alone.'

Lucian shook his head. 'You can't do that. At best, they'll deport you. At worst, you'll go to jail.'

They sat in silence.

Alice spoke first. 'There's nothing else for it. Billy will have to take the fall.'

'Alice!' Lucian was shocked.

'What?' Yet again, Alice couldn't see the problem. 'It was his stupid idea to put them there in the first place.'

The two of them turned to Bella for her adjudication, as they always had as children. But, for once, their mother gave no indication of her thinking.

'I need to forewarn Lady Latchmere,' she said, eventually. 'She won't like her name being dragged into all of this.'

*

Alice trailed after Bella as she went in search of Lady Latchmere.

'You know it makes sense,' she said. 'About Billy.'

Bella kept walking, hoping to shake Alice off. 'Betty would never forgive us.'

'But he's a juvenile. They'll almost certainly go easy on him.'

'We don't know that.' Alice could hear the bitterness in her mother's voice.

'Well, then. He probably deserves what's coming to him. Nish said he has the spare keys to every room in the hotel stashed in his bedroom.'

'We can't throw him to the wolves, Alice.'

'I don't see what option we have.'

Bella sighed. 'We should at least get him a lawyer.'

'I'll speak to Daddy,' said Alice, brightly. She turned away, feeling suddenly full of purpose. It was a relief.

Bella called after her. 'Alice, wait! Has he said anything to you?'

Alice turned back round. 'Billy?'

'No.' Her mother hesitated. 'Your father.'

'I've barely spoken a word to him all day. Why do you ask?'

Bella shook her head. 'He's behaving oddly. That's all.'

'No change there,' said Alice.

'No,' said Bella. 'No, I suppose you're right.'

*

Lady Latchmere sat by the window in the drawing room, a copy of *Country Life* open on her lap. Her face in profile looked so extraordinarily young that Bella did a double take. Could this really be the same Lady Latchmere who had been so awkward when she first arrived? The same Lady Latchmere who, even a week ago, would have made a fuss about the cup of tea now standing cold on the table in front of her and demanded its removal?

We are all capable of change, Bella thought. *Even in middle age, one can live up to youth.*

'Lady Latchmere,' she began.

The older woman's milky blue gaze shifted. 'Gertrude, please, my dear.'

'Gertrude. I need to speak to you. It's a matter of some delicacy.'

As if sensing Bella's nerves, Lady Latchmere took her hand. 'Then you had best come straight out with it, my dear.'

319

Bella's speech was unusually halting. 'I have been informed that the search of the hotel is likely to turn up certain materials of a decidedly political nature. Hidden under your bed.'

Lady Latchmere looked confused. 'Under my bed?'

'I fear so.'

'What kind of materials?'

'Pamphlets,' said Bella. 'To be exact.'

'And what do these pamphlets say?'

'I'm told they express derogatory sentiments. About Signor Mussolini.'

At this, Lady Latchmere broke into delighted laughter. It was so loud that Bella looked around, nervous about being overheard.

'But how simply splendid!'

Bella was taken aback. 'Gertrude?'

'And who, may I ask, is the subversive in our midst?'

'I'm not at liberty to say. For fear of incriminating them.'

'Then I shall claim ownership myself.'

'I'm sorry?' Bella wasn't sure she'd heard her correctly.

'The pamphlets,' Lady Latchmere whispered. 'I shall say they are mine.'

Bella couldn't help smiling. 'Is that wise, Gertrude?'

Lady Latchmere threw back her head. 'Let them do their worst. One look at that awful strutting peacock . . . You can tell he's a thug. I simply can't abide a bully.'

Bella felt a flush of relief. 'Oh, I couldn't agree more.'

'Herbert . . . Lord Latchmere. He bullied my darling

Ernest terribly. Threatened to disown him if he didn't sign up to "do his duty".'

'I'm very sorry to hear that,' said Bella. She really was. 'I know that Lucian too felt under pressure to volunteer. From his father.'

'I only wish I'd stood up to him more. On Ernest's behalf.'

'Those poor boys.' The two women were once again united by grief.

'I can hardly bring myself to speak to him since it happened,' Lady Latchmere admitted. 'I'm not sure things will ever be normal between us again.'

*

Ever since Hotel Portofino opened, Danioni had been desperate to nose around.

He particularly liked the suites that had their own bathrooms. You couldn't ask for greater luxury than that. He ran a hand over the chrome taps, imagining himself immersed in foamy, scented water, shadows from a flickering candle dancing on the wall.

His own bathroom at home was a cramped affair. And his toilet was outside. Yesterday he had gone out to relieve himself and found a dead rat wedged into the bowl.

You never saw a dead rat here – although, he thought with a smirk, he could easily arrange for one to be secreted somewhere. A kitchen cupboard, perhaps. How that peasant of a cook would squeal when she saw it!

This suite, the old woman's, had its own bathroom. As for the bedroom itself, Danioni couldn't see what all the fuss was about. It was big, for sure. But he disliked the subdued, floral wallpaper. And the furniture was so old!

English people liked old things. They liked to be connected to their past. As a consequence, they were scared of the future. Not like Italians. Not like Il Duce.

Danioni drummed his fingertips against his thighs as Sergeant Ottonello searched under Lady Latchmere's bed.

Why was this taking so long?

As Ottonello eased himself up into a standing position, Danioni looked at him, eyebrows raised. '*Trovato qualcosa*?' he asked. Anything?

Ottonello shook his head.

'*Sei sicuro*?' Are you sure?

Politely but firmly, Ottonello suggested that Danioni take a look for himself. Which he did, lowering himself onto his knees and staring into the dusty space.

Ottonello was right. There was nothing there. How could this be?

Just as Danioni was getting back on his feet, Mr Ainsworth entered the room.

'Any luck?' he asked.

Ottonello handed the bunch of keys to Danioni, who held them aloft and shook them so that they tinkled. 'These were found in William Scanlon's room,' he declared.

Mr Ainsworth turned to Ottonello. 'Yes, yes,' he said. 'But what about the painting?'

Ottonello looked blank.

Danioni translated for him: '*Il dipinto*?'

The sergeant shook his head.

'How unfortunate,' said Mr Ainsworth.

*

One of the first things Constance had learned when she went into service was how to do the laundry. It was more complicated than people realised. There were all sorts of annoying rules and rituals, like putting the stockings and socks in to soak the night before, and remembering to soften the water with pearl-ashes.

She had always hated it, and hated it still, but at least out here things dried quickly in the sun — and the pearl-ashes weren't needed as Ligurian water was naturally soft.

The hotel's copper — actually, this one was made from cast iron — was the biggest she had ever seen, and she had worked in some large houses. It dominated the scullery and made her feel like a magician when she was stirring its contents with the washing dolly.

Today she was washing sheets. Sheets got dirty quickly out here for all manner of reasons, but mainly because the nights were so hot. Fishing them out, she wrung the water from them before putting them in the laundry basket and carrying them outside.

From the scullery, a person had to walk through the kitchen to reach the door to the courtyard. She found that Danioni had stuck one of his policemen outside. He stopped her as she passed him. '*Scusi*, Signora!'

She pointed to the sheets and mimed the action of hanging them up to dry.

'Ah,' said the policeman. He nodded and smiled, extending his arm to indicate that she could proceed on her way.

The clothes line was strung between two trees on a dusty patch of grass behind the courtyard, before the turn-off to the outhouse. The basket was heavy. Carrying it even a short distance hurt her arms and her back.

It was a relief to put it down. As she did so, her attention was caught by a line of tiny black ants winding through the brownish grass to their nest a few yards away. Some of them were carrying bits of food on their backs.

Constance wished she knew more about the natural world. Proper, scientific knowledge. For instance, how did ants know to follow each other? Did they have eyes? Or were they following some sort of smell or sound?

It struck her that humans were more like ants than they cared to admit. Too many of them followed each other blindly, in a straight line, always conforming. But then you would conform, wouldn't you, when the penalty for rebelling was so severe?

Life in service was all about conformity. Wear this apron. Wash these pots. Get up at this time. Rebel, and you lost your job.

The solution was to make your acts of defiance small and discreet.

She hefted up the mound of wet sheets. As expected, beneath them, was a flat layer of dry sheets, folded and ironed. She felt beneath the sheets with the flat of her palm and smiled when it came up against a fat ridge.

Good, she thought. The pamphlets were definitely still there.

12

If Cecil had had his way, Billy would have starved to death in that smelly old den. But Betty wasn't going to stand for that. She made up a tray of sandwiches and leftover cold meats and took it up there herself, her calves aching as she climbed the steep gravelly path.

Danioni had put one of his policemen by the door. He wasn't unfriendly. He smiled and winked and opened the door for her, then stood to one side.

Inside, it was hot and airless, lit from the opposite wall by a single casement window. In the gloom, Betty made out a wooden table with a clamp attached to it and, hanging in front of it, an array of different-sized saws. There were screws and drill bits scattered everywhere.

Billy was sitting on the floor on a heap of sacking. He blinked as the door opened, then stood up.

Betty slammed down the tray on the table and rushed forward to embrace him. 'Oh, Billy,' she said. 'What have you done?'

'I've not done nowt.' He was angry and defiant.

'Here.' Betty took a sandwich from the tray and held it out to him. 'Get some of this down you.'

He pushed it away. 'I'm not hungry.'

'You've got to keep your strength up.'

'I said I'm not hungry, Mam.'

'At least drink this, then.' She gave him a glass bottle of water.

He drank it down thirstily, wiping his mouth on the back of his sleeve. 'How long am I going to be cooped up in here?'

'I don't know, Billy.'

'It were only a bike, for Christ's sake. I were going to take it back.'

'They're not bothered about a stupid bike.'

'What, then?'

'The painting.'

'What's that got to do with me?'

'They're saying someone must have taken it. From Mr Turner's bedroom.'

'And?'

'And they've found a set of spare keys. Hidden in your room.'

Billy went quiet. He shook his head, but Betty noticed he didn't deny having the keys.

'Oh, son.' Her voice emerged soft and weak.

'It's not what you think, Mam. I don't know nowt about no painting. I swear on me brothers' graves.'

'I believe you. Thousands wouldn't.' She pulled him close. 'But what about those keys?'

'I were doing a favour. For someone else. I forgot to put 'em back.' He looked up into her face.

Betty asked, 'What favour? And who for?'

But Billy said nothing.

*

Despite the ongoing police search, the day had settled into something approaching normality. Alice's favourite aspect of hotel life was the sensation it afforded of being afloat on a vast liner. That – and having a defined role – made her feel safe and secure.

She was good at ordering others about. If that sounded like a flaw, then that only went to show how little most people understood about the demands of running a hotel.

As a child, one of Alice's favourite novels had been *The Grand Babylon Hotel* by Arnold Bennett. She had dreamed of working in the exclusive Thames-side establishment imagined by Bennett. She loved his description of Jules, the head waiter, commanding the lesser waiters as they glided across the Oriental rugs, "balancing their trays with the dexterity of jugglers, and receiving and executing orders with that air of profound importance of which only really first-class waiters have the secret".

Alice's goal, as she saw it, was to impart this secret to Constance and Paola.

Occasionally, her advice took root. Constance was putting her tips on posture to fruitful use. But goodness, it could be an uphill struggle, to the point where she wondered sometimes if she and Paola respected her at all.

Look at them now, serving refreshments to the guests in the drawing room. Paola was slouching like someone twenty years older, wearing the thunderous expression that seemed permanently stuck to her face these days.

'Come on, Paola!' Alice had said to her only yesterday, clapping briskly. 'Cheer up a bit. *Siate felici!*'

Constance, on the other hand, was doing what she had been told. Standing up straight, with her shoulders back and her stomach pulled in.

Good, Alice thought. *We're getting somewhere.*

She passed the table where Roberto and Count Albani were sitting and stopped to give them a smile. After all, there was no point being embarrassed about that business with the gift. Awkwardness only bred more awkwardness. As she turned to walk away, she heard Roberto comment, '*È una donna bellissima.*' She's a beautiful woman.

Despite herself, Alice smiled. Beautiful? Was she really?

On her way to the door, she caught sight of her reflection and stopped, studying the still-youthful grace of her outline as if it were something alien and unfamiliar. Before the war, it would have been said of her that she didn't look like a widow. But it was a different world now. A widow could look like anything.

Summoning her confidence like a protective cloak, Alice turned back towards Count Albani's table. He and Roberto were talking quietly in their intense Italian way. She leant forward, cleared her throat, and had the agreeable impression of the pair melting into silence. 'I meant to say earlier, that I hope you'll forgive us all this inconvenience, Count Albani.'

The Count looked up at her flatteringly, as if by merely

addressing them she had penetrated to a kind of truth. 'It is I who should be begging your forgiveness. For my country-men. And their rough and criminal ways.'

'We're very grateful for your help,' she said. 'And the excellence of your English.' At this, the Count gave a little bow and Alice laughed lightly. 'It's strange, I suppose, that Roberto here speaks so little of it.'

She turned her gaze on Roberto, who responded with an obscure smile. She guessed he knew he was being talked about but had no idea what was being said.

'My son is young and arrogant, Mrs Mays–Smith,' said Count Albani. 'He thinks there is nothing he can learn from me.'

'Indeed?' wondered Alice. 'Perhaps I might try?'

'To teach him English?' The Count raised an eyebrow. 'What an excellent notion.'

'The basics, at least. Enough so he can speak for himself.'

'We are at your disposal.'

Alice was delighted with herself for taking the initiative. She celebrated by asserting her authority. When she saw Constance hovering with a tray of biscuits, she beckoned her over and indicated that she should offer some to Count Albani and Roberto.

Constance nodded obediently, then walked towards them in the rather clenched, chest–jutting style Alice had shown her. As Constance held out the tray, Alice noticed Roberto giving her a very different look to the one he had given Alice moments earlier.

She barely had to strain to hear him say, under his breath, *'Bellissima.'*

Alice's face fell. She gazed at Roberto with a kind of plaintive bewilderment, then across to Constance, who seemed every bit as perturbed as Alice but for an altogether different reason. Clearly, she disliked Roberto's attention. Constance! A skinny little maid-of-all-work from Yorkshire!

Alice had watched her flirting with Lucian. They thought they were being subtle with their covert little glances, but she knew what was going on. She knew what Constance wanted, the uppity madam.

All Alice's anger and resentment welled up suddenly and she thought she might embarrass herself by crying.

It was her fate, it seemed, to be let down by life. Which didn't seem fair. All she wanted, all she aspired to do, was to live a conventional adult existence – not a fashionable, artistic one like Lucian. An ordinary existence, religious and law-abiding, with a husband to accompany her and . . . not mould exactly, but modify . . . yes, *modify* her. Improve her. Blunt her edges, so that she was less bitter and judgemental.

Once, when she was young, she had found such a man. And then he had been taken from her, quite suddenly, without warning or apology.

With these noisy thoughts blaring in her head, Alice left the drawing room. She went to the cloakroom next to her mother's office and locked the door.

If she was quiet and held her handkerchief against her face, then no one would hear her sobs.

*

In the hall, Bella passed Danioni and three policemen on their way to a cigarette break in the sunshine. As politely as she could manage, she asked if there was any news.

'I am sorry, Signora. A little longer.'

Count Albani sidled over. 'He seems to be enjoying himself. Directing operations.'

'Making mischief, you mean.'

'You speak with great feeling.'

'I loathe people who seek advantage from others' misfortune.'

'He is trying to take advantage of you?'

Bella bit her lip and shook her head slightly.

'My dear Mrs Ainsworth. It is an insult to our friendship that you should choose not to confide in me.'

She looked at him. What information was he angling for? 'He's threatening to close the hotel,' she said.

The Count snorted with laughter, until he saw she was deadly serious.

Bella went on. 'He brought the Health Inspector here at seven o'clock this morning. He claims we are preparing and serving food in unhygienic conditions.'

'But that is absurd.'

'Which is precisely what I told him.' She put her hand to her mouth, suddenly overwhelmed.

'Please,' said Count Albani. 'Do not distress yourself. Where there is a problem, there is always a solution.'

'But how do I solve a problem that doesn't exist?'

'Ah, but it is clearly not this problem he wishes you to address.'

She looked at him askance. He was digging again.

'In Italy,' he continued, 'a great untruth like this, it serves to hide a greater truth beneath. There is some other issue between you and Mr Danioni. One you are not disclosing.'

Bella said nothing. She didn't care for this game.

But then he said: 'I will speak to him.' He had played his ace.

'Oh, Count. Would you?'

He bowed. 'There is no limit,' he said. 'No limit to what I would do for you.'

*

In the still of the lower terrace, Lizzie was agonising. She huddled next to Claudine.

'I hope I haven't caused a problem.' As she spoke, she snuck a look at Jack, who was sitting stony-faced on his own, a glass of brandy in his hand.

'Honey, you aren't the problem,' said Claudine.

'Only, I'd hate to be the source of friction in your relationship. When you've done so much to help smooth out the bumps in mine.'

Claudine smiled. 'You did "smooth out the bumps", then?'

'Oh yes. Twice, in fact.' She dissolved in a fit of giggles. 'I'm sorry. I don't know quite what's come over me.'

'I do,' said Claudine.

'Claudine!' Lizzie shushed her. 'Lady Latchmere might hear!'

'You have nothing to fear from Lady Latchmere,' said Claudine. 'She's a woman of the world, make no mistake.'

The transformative powers of Claudine's negligee, combined with some radical make-up – blood-red lips, lots of kohl – had surpassed Lizzie's wildest expectations. Not that those were *terribly* wild, centring as they did around Plum managing to stay awake for more than five minutes. But, in fact, the whole night had been an education. More than once, she had thought – *Where did he learn to do that?* – and decided she didn't really want to know the answer.

Claudine smiled. 'You seem like a new woman.'

'I feel like one,' said Lizzie.

But was feeling the same as being?

*

Bella had had quite enough of Danioni and Ottonello for one day. But they seemed keen to debrief her and Cecil in the drawing room so she went along obligingly, hoping Cecil would find it in himself to be pleasant.

He didn't.

If anything, the lack of progress in the investigation had only soured his mood further.

'The search turned up nothing, then?' he asked.

Danioni looked at Ottonello, who said, *'Niente.'*

'Nothing at all?' Bella couldn't believe it either.

'No hidden surprises, Signora,' Danioni reassured her. He stared at her meaningfully. 'Your guests, they live . . . *come si dice* . . . without sin, no?'

Cecil jumped in before she could answer. 'And you have no clue how the painting was removed from Mr Turner's room?'

'There is no trace.'

'No fingerprints?'

'The handle? It is wiped clean.'

There was a pause as they all considered where this left them.

'So,' asked Bella. 'What now?'

'We take the boy for questioning,' said Danioni. 'We will make him confess, no?'

Bella frowned. '"Make him confess"?'

'My apologies. My English is not so good. I mean "encourage him".'

'Gently.'

'*Si.*'

'Without intimidation.'

'For goodness' sake!' said Cecil. 'They can do what they like, as long as it gets results.'

Bella turned towards him. 'He must have a lawyer with him. I insist on it.'

'I've already sent for Bruzzone,' said Cecil.

*

Rose had never found it difficult to assume poses. Sustaining them, however, was another matter. As instructed very precisely by Lucian, she had made a pillow of her arms and was resting her head on them, staring into the middle distance while he sat nearby, sketchbook in hand, trying to capture her likeness in charcoal and pencil.

Would he succeed? Was beauty harder to draw than plainness? It shouldn't be – not if he was as good an artist as he thought he was. In which case, she looked forward to seeing how he handled her perfect, dimpled chin; her small, white, unblemished teeth; and her oval, perfectly symmetrical face.

Not that this stopped sitting for him from being exceptionally boring. One had heard stories about models and muses. The romance novels she devoured teemed with them. Across London and Paris they ran, chasing after genius artists; inspiring them with their beauty and devotion before dying of tuberculosis in dingy hotel rooms. What these books didn't tell you was how much *sitting around* was involved.

Then again, sitting around was the order of the day at Hotel Portofino. What a lot of fuss over a stupid painting. Who would want to steal something so ugly?

Trying not to move her face, Rose asked, 'How much longer will this go on?'

Lucian pointed to his notebook with his pencil. 'This?'

'No. This whole situation.'

'I've no idea. Until they find the painting, I suppose. Or complete the search. Whichever comes first.'

'I'm awfully bored. I think I may have to move soon.'

'Just a minute or two longer.'

Bella came out onto the upper terrace. 'There you are,' she said.

Taking this as a signal to relax, Rose dropped her feet to the ground and sat up straight. 'Lucian asked if he could draw me.'

'Did he?' Bella walked across and looked over Lucian's shoulder, surveying his work. 'It's not your best.'

'I know. There's something about Rose I find difficult to capture.'

Well, that answered her question. It was harder to draw beauty. And after all, she was so lithe, so fluid and energetic in her movements – she must be an artist's worst nightmare!

As if to prove her own theory, Rose felt herself growing restless. 'I must go,' she announced. 'Mama will be wondering where I am.'

'Of course,' said Bella, smiling. 'You must do what you want, child.'

*

Bella watched Rose skip inside. Then she turned to Lucian. 'I thought you'd like to know. The search turned up nothing.'

He stopped shading and frowned. 'Nothing at all?'

'Not a shred.'

'My word. That's a relief.' He paused. 'So, where the hell are they?'

'I don't know. But they're not in the hotel.'

Lucian put his arm around his mother's waist and pulled her close. 'I'm sorry to have to put you through all this.'

Bella stroked his hair. 'Don't be silly. I'm sorry, too.'

'For what?'

'For being at all impatient with you. It will take as long as it takes.'

'What will?'

'Everything. Or maybe nothing.'

'What do you mean?'

'I don't know, Lucian. I'm not sure what I mean about anything at the moment.'

She felt heavy, so oppressed by worries that an apparent triumph, such as the police not finding the pamphlets, had none of its expected capacity to soothe. At such times, everything lost its lustre so that when she looked around she saw not the remarkable world she had created but a flat, featureless terrain peopled by ... Well, they weren't even people, not really. They were like trees, walking.

Her left hand was hanging by her side. Lucian squeezed it. He could clearly sense the change in her; the strained, grudging adjustment to a new reality.

'It will pass,' he said. 'How you're feeling now. I feel that way often. Almost every day, to be honest, for a little bit. The trick is to keep breathing.'

From the hall drifted the sounds of argument and distress. Low male voices raised in anger; women crying and consoling.

Lucian asked, 'What's happening?'

'Billy,' said Bella, with a gasp. 'They've come for him.'

It felt like a public execution; the whole hotel gathered outside the front door. But suddenly the funereal silence was punctured by excited murmurs. A carriage had been spotted at the end of the drive – a carriage containing Signor Bruzzone, the lawyer who would be acting for Billy, and a much younger, very good-looking man.

Cecil pushed through the crowd to greet them. 'Signor Bruzzone?'

'*Sì*.' The older man bowed and mopped his brow. He was long-legged and long-bodied, with a prominent nose and sharp grey eyes.

Cecil turned to his companion. 'And this is?'

The other man introduced himself. 'I'm Gianluca Bruzzone, Signore. My father asked me to come. In case there is translation needed.'

'There certainly will be,' said Bella, who had moved herself into position next to Cecil. 'How fortunate you speak English.'

'Forgive me,' said Gianluca. 'It is not well used.'

'It seems exceptional to me,' said Bella. 'Where did you learn it?'

'At university, Signora.'

'We must be going,' said Cecil.

Count Albani stepped forward, shrugging on his jacket. 'I will accompany them,' he announced. 'To help instruct Signor Bruzzone.'

'And I'll go too,' said Nish. 'I'd like to make sure Billy is all right.'

Bella put a grateful hand on Nish's arm as he came to stand beside Gianluca. She noticed the pair exchanged the merest of glances. They couldn't know each other, surely?

'I'll keep you company,' said Lucian, and walked across to join the others.

They waited by the carriage while Cecil and Francesco went to get Billy from the outhouse. Bella's first impression when finally they emerged was that Cecil had gone wildly over the top. Not only had he tied Billy's hands together behind his back, but he was leading him with one hand while pressing down on his head with the other.

She opened her mouth to protest, then shut it again. There was no point enraging Cecil. Not now.

Betty looked stricken. She was trying to hide her tears with her hands. Constance had an arm around her shoulders.

Bella went over to her. 'We'll have him back in no time, Betty, I promise. I'm sure it's all just a dreadful mistake.'

*

That was that, thought Cecil. One less thing to worry about.

The show over, guests dispersed across the hotel. Cecil followed the crowd, thinking idly that it might be time for a drink, when he said aloud to no one in particular, 'What utter tripe.'

Jack was ahead of him. He heard Cecil and turned round. 'You have something else to say?'

'I do. It's balderdash.'

'What is?'

'The idea that little Billy Scanlon is a criminal mastermind. He and his peasant friends. It's frankly incredible.'

'From where I'm standing,' said Jack, 'it's the only possible explanation.'

'No quite, old boy.'

'You have another one?'

'I rather think I do.'

'Well, then. Enlighten us.' Jack folded his arms, striking a defiant pose.

'You arranged for the painting to be stolen yourself, Jack. I don't know how, but I do know why. To cheat me out of my share of the sale price.'

Jack drew back the corner of his jacket to show the revolver in his waistband. 'Say that again and I'll kill you.'

Bella must have been watching from the other side of the hall because she came forward now and said, 'Gentleman! Please!'

Cecil produced the cheque from his pocket and held it up for Jack to see. 'Don't expect to see a red cent of your fifty thousand back. Let's call it an insurance payment.'

'It isn't worth a tenth of that.'

'What? A genuine Rubens?' Cecil gave him a look, daring him to elaborate.

Jack rolled his shoulders. 'You'll be hearing from my lawyers.'

'You'll hear from mine first.'

'Come on, Claudine.' Jack looked around for her, expecting to find her by his side. But she stayed where she was, standing by the reception desk.

'I said come on,' Jack repeated.

'Uh-uh.' She shook her head. 'I'm not going anywhere with you.'

He strode over to her and tried to grab her hand, but she pulled away. 'Don't touch me!'

'Claudine!'

'Go back to your wife, Jack.'

He stared at her as if he had only just realised how much

he hated her. 'Dumb fucking whore. Who else here is going to pay for you?'

'I've got my own money.'

At this he stepped in close, menacingly so. He said softly, 'You trash.'

The whole room froze.

Claudine gave a brittle, empty laugh. 'Aren't you missing a word, Jack?'

It was odd, Cecil thought, how much this comment provoked Jack. His hand went straight for his gun and there were gasps from the gathering crowd of onlookers as he pulled it out and pointed it at Claudine.

Someone, it could have been Melissa, screamed.

Cecil felt his own heart race – rapid, admonitory knocks – as if his very body were asking him, *What are you going to do?*

The truth was he didn't know, and while he was wondering Bella did an extraordinary thing. She moved across and interposed herself between Jack and Claudine.

Then the old woman, Lady Latchmere, did the same, fixing Jack with one of her steely stares. 'One man's trash is another man's treasure, Mr Turner. It's how a person behaves in life that defines them. Not where or what they come from.'

Jack held his ground for a few moments, not wishing to cede authority. But then, recognising that he had no support, he slipped the gun back into his belt and, summoning the last scraps of his dignity, turned on his heel and climbed the stairs to his suite.

Cecil summoned Francesco, who was watching the show from the kitchen doorway. In fractured Italian he said, 'Help Mr Turner pack his bags. And be sure to see him off the premises.'

*

Of course, Danioni could see Albani for what he was. A member of the old elite, the old papal nobility.

People like him were prisoners of the past.

They didn't understand the need for a strong man who would lead Italy back to order and legality, or what looked like legality from a distance. In this post-war world, there was a new aristocracy: the *trincerocrazia* or aristocracy of the trenches. What equivalent sacrifice had Albani made?

Blood, tradition, heritage. These things were important, yes. But Albani and his kind had no appetite for revolutionary struggle. Which was why Mussolini had talked about putting an end to the widespread misuse of titles like 'count'. He had wanted to abolish all papal titles bestowed since 1870 and had appointed a commission to look into the matter. In the end, nothing had come of it. But only because he needed to keep the church on his side.

Still, Albani had a residual power and influence. Which was why, despite his contempt for the man, Danioni felt a nervous fluttering in his chest when the Count entered his office in the Municipal Building: a passing visit, unsolicited and frankly unexpected.

Danioni quickly tidied his desk and rearranged his plants so that they were evenly spaced.

The first thing the Count did after greeting Danioni ful-somely was offer him a cigar: a good Cuban one, for which Danioni was grateful.

The pair spoke in Italian, Danioni softening his strong local accent so that he sounded more refined.

Albani watched Danioni as he performed the time-honoured rituals of cigar-smoking – cutting off the cap, then toasting the foot to warm the tobacco so that it was easier to light. 'I see you appreciate the finer things in life, Mr Danioni.'

'I rarely get to experience them.' Danioni filled his mouth with smoke. Then he removed the cigar from his mouth and examined it. 'Where did you get these?'

'In London.'

'You are a great lover of the English.'

'And you, also.'

Danioni pulled a face to convey the opposite.

'And yet,' Albani observed, 'you have bothered to learn their language.'

Danioni looked at him. He decided to be honest. 'I thought once I might emigrate. To America.'

'You should practise more. The way things are going over here ...'

Danioni chose to overlook the comment. Albani was goading him. And he would not be goaded. 'Would I like it in England?' he asked.

Albani laughed. He got up and walked over to the window, taking in the view of the *barbiere* opposite. 'The people, the weather ... They are too cold for a man of your sensibilities. Although the women can be warmer.' He turned, offering up a conspiratorial smile. 'And there are many things about their culture that an Italian may admire. For example, they have few of the superstitions that hold our people in their grip.'

'Ah, yes. *Empirismo Inglese.*'

'And, of course, they love Italy. More than many southern Italians.'

'Damn peasants.'

Turning, Albani came over to Danioni and stood behind him, looking down. His tone became sharper as he asked suddenly, 'Why do you want to expel the English from Portofino?'

The question took Danioni by surprise. 'Who says I do?'

'You have threatened to close their hotel?'

'Not I.'

'I am relieved to hear it. I have made a recommendation to Senator Cavanna to stay there.'

Danioni shifted uncomfortably. 'Cavanna? There has perhaps been ... a misunderstanding.'

'I'm glad to hear you say so. There was a report, I think?'

Danioni went over to the metal filing cabinet in the corner. It took a matter of seconds to find a copy of the Hotel Portofino health and safety report. He took it out and brandished it like a broken glass. 'It is only a draft. But please, assure Signora Ainsworth that this ... impertinence has been consigned where it belongs.' He ripped up the report ostentatiously and dumped it in the waste-paper basket beside his desk.

Albani watched him carefully. Then, as he put on his hat and picked up his gloves, he posed a question. 'Why don't you come and tell her yourself, Danioni? I am sure she will be delighted to hear it.'

'Of course,' said Danioni, uncertainly. 'It would be a pleasure.'

*

'Look.' Lucian nudged Nish. 'Coming out of the door.'

Lucian and Nish were in Portofino town, sitting on a wooden bench. From where they were, the door to the Municipal Offices was clearly visible; so too the band of Blackshirts joshing and bantering outside it. Nish was reading a book, but glanced up at his friend's command. What he saw surprised him. 'Well I never,' he said.

Danioni and Count Albani were leaving the building together and crossing the square.

'I don't trust Count Albani,' said Nish.

'You've got to trust someone.'

'I trust you. Isn't that enough?'

Lucian laughed. 'Probably not.'

'I thought I trusted Gianluca. Now, I don't know what to think.'

It was uncanny, thought Lucian, the way Gianluca sloped out of the Municipal Offices at that exact moment. They all noticed each other at the same time, Nish and Lucian rising slowly to their feet as the Italian approached.

Lucian spoke first. 'How's Billy?'

'He is scared,' said Gianluca. 'But my father will do his best to protect him.' He paused. 'I must apologise. I have put you in danger.'

'It's true,' said Nish, with a ferocity that surprised Lucian. 'Not just us, either. The people we most care about.'

Gianluca looked chastened. 'I could not know the hotel . . .'

'Would be searched?' Lucian finished his sentence.

Gianluca nodded. 'But do not worry yourselves. I will return tonight. To take back the pamphlets.'

'There may be a problem there,' said Nish, wincingly. 'I no longer have them.'

Gianluca's face hardened. 'I don't understand. Then, who does?'

'We don't know,' said Lucian. 'I've come here to tell Billy they weren't hidden where he said he had hidden them.'

'My father will give him the message,' Gianluca said. 'You will find him inside.'

*

While Lucian wandered off to find Bruzzone, Nish and Gianluca stayed in place. The awkwardness had vanished, but in its place was pragmatism rather than passion. Perhaps it was better this way, Nish thought. Better for both of them.

He asked Gianluca, 'Are you still going away?'

'Tomorrow. Perhaps the day after. I must.'

Nish smiled ruefully. He shook the hand that Gianluca was holding out. 'Then *addio*,' he said.

'*Arrivederci.*'

'Until we meet again?'

Gianluca nodded. He started to let go, to pull away, but Nish clung tightly to his hand and nodded towards the Blackshirts, who still seemed not to have noticed them. 'Are they worth it? Worth turning your back on your family? Your friends? Worth putting yourself in danger?'

'You think they are a joke. Strutting like cockerels. In their ridiculous uniforms.'

Nish said nothing, but the expression on his face must have confirmed Gianluca's view.

'Do not fool yourself,' said Gianluca. 'They are people who seek to exploit the worst in us – our greed, our self-ishness. Our capacity to hate. They care nothing for what makes us individuals, different, uniquely lovable, human. They only understand the mentality of the mob.' His weary eyes fixed on Nish's. 'There is no place in their world for people like us.'

*

There was no rule that said momentous news had to be delivered slowly. It had taken Danioni less than a minute to tell Bella about the hygiene report – that it had been found to be full of errors and misconceptions. Signor Ricci had been reprimanded and might even lose his job as a result.

'It is a disgrace,' he said. 'The challenge is to be sure it never happens again.'

While he spoke, Count Albani looked on approvingly.

Bella scarcely knew what to say, so she settled for

platitudes. 'I am grateful to you, Signor Danioni. You have put my mind at rest.'

Danioni bowed obsequiously.

'We have had to close the kitchen, I'm afraid, so I cannot offer you anything to eat. But you will find my husband on the terrace. He will be happy to pour you a drink.'

Danioni slunk off.

Bella turned to Count Albani and smiled wearily. 'Thank you. I don't know how I can repay you.'

'To see you smile again is all I ask.'

'It's as if a weight has been lifted.'

'Then I am happy. And I have done my job.'

'I must tell Betty the good news.'

She turned to go, but he stopped her with a hand on her shoulder. 'Mrs Ainsworth.'

'Bella, please.'

'Bella. And *bella*.' He smiled at his little joke. 'This is difficult for me to say.'

Bella felt suddenly unnerved. 'Go on. Speak freely. As friends do.'

'Today I have managed to relieve your difficulty. With Vincenzo Danioni. But tomorrow it may return.'

'Why do you say so?'

'One day soon, the summer will be over. And I will return to Rome.'

She considered this prospect with alarm. 'You will come back?' she asked, hoping she didn't sound too desperate.

He shrugged. 'Next year, perhaps. But it does not matter

so much because your husband – he will be here to protect you, no?'

'Of course.'

'And yet, for some reason, you have asked for my assistance. Not his.' He raised his eyebrows.

'It is true,' she said, then covered her mouth, to stop any further revelations.

'I know a thousand men like Danioni. They believe they are owed something. And they are determined to take it.'

'But you have warned him off.'

'For now, maybe. I have pretended to befriend him, flattered him, threatened him a little. But he will be back. Unless you break whatever hold he has over you.'

Bella remained silent.

'I do not ask you to tell me,' Count Albani went on. 'In truth, I would prefer not to know. But as your friend ...'

She looked up, lured by his warmth, his apparent desire to help her without wanting anything in return.

'As your friend, I advise you – whatever it is you fear, it cannot be worse than letting Danioni bite you. Again and again, like a rabid dog.'

She thought for a moment. 'Yes,' she said. 'Yes, I see.'

*

The last thing Cecil wanted was to entertain Danioni. His heart sank when the odious chap materialised on the terrace, nose quivering like a beaver.

Cecil had been trying to distract himself with his newspaper. But again and again his thoughts returned to Bella's letter and the sordid desires it expressed. It was one thing for men to engage in such activities. Quite another for a woman to do it.

This was modernity, was it? Evidently so. It was also the predictable outcome of such mischievous doctrines as suffragism, Cecil's views on which he had always made abundantly clear.

He offered Danioni a cigar and poured him a grappa. He was about to pour himself a whisky when Danioni asked, 'Where is your anger, Signore?'

'My anger?'

'*Si*. If I had lost a thing of value, I would . . .' He struggled to find the right phrase. '. . . *avere un diavolo per capello*. Be mad as hell, as you people say.'

Cecil stared at him, impassive. 'Just because I'm not shouting and waving my arms about the way you Italians are so bloody fond of, it doesn't mean I'm not angry.'

'Ah! So, it lies beneath?'

'My father taught me to manage my anger. Because other people are so bad at managing their stupidity.'

'But it is ready to explode, no?' The man was goading him, Cecil could see that. 'Like Vesuvio. When you discover who has stolen your painting?'

'You know what they say about revenge, Danioni.'

The Italian laughed and took a pull on his cigar, filling his mouth with smoke. After savouring it for a few seconds, he blew it out in a fat cloud. 'And yet who will you take your revenge on? Signor Turner? Your English tennis champion? Poor William Scanlon?'

At the mention of Billy's name, Cecil spun round. 'Has the boy said anything?'

Danioni shook his head. 'He is true to *omertà*.'

'But the police are following up with those associates you mentioned?'

The Italian nodded. 'And with Mr Wingfield also. To check he is not hiding anything in Milan. With his balls and his rackets.'

'What about Turner?'

'His name has been given to the *Guardia di Finanza*.'

'So, they can keep track of his dealings?'

'If Signor Turner tries to sell the painting, they will know about it.' Danioni paused before trying a different tack. 'Sergeant Ottonello ... He believes the painting will return to you.'

'I pray he is right.'

'I do not have the heart to tell him he is "chasing wild geese", as the Americans would say.'

'Now, listen here,' said Cecil. 'What the hell do you mean by that?'

'That he wastes his time, no?'

'I don't need a lesson in English, you fool. I want to know what you're driving at.'

'Come Signor Ainsworth. We both know the truth.'

'I'll be damned if I do.'

'You wish me to say it?'

'Spit it out, man.'

'You know exactly what has happened to your painting.'

Cecil felt something give inside him. 'Why, you filthy dog.'

Danioni smiled, enjoying the slur. 'Really, Signor Ainsworth . . .'

'How dare you come in here and abuse my hospitality with your greasy little insinuations? If you know so much about the theft, perhaps that's because you're in on it. You and your bloody useless police force.'

Danioni drained his glass and slammed it down.

'I shall report you to the British Consulate,' Cecil warned.

'Will you, indeed?' Danioni removed his cigar from his mouth, then dropped it on the floor. 'I may be a dog, Signor Ainsworth. But in Italy we have a saying.' He ground the butt beneath his heel. '*Cane non mangia cane.* Dogs don't eat other dogs.'

*

For some reason, Lottie was hard to settle that night. First, she complained of a mosquito in her room, then that her toy rabbit Bouncy had a stomach-ache.

'Hush your fussing,' said Constance, fondly. 'Shall I lie with you until you're sleepy?'

Lottie nodded.

Consance settled down beside her and together they lay in silence, listening to the distant hiss of the sea. It was comforting, to both of them.

'I haven't liked today,' Lottie said.

Constance stroked her hair, feeling a pulse of affection. 'Nor me.'

'Will Billy be all right?'

'Of course, he will. He's done nothing wrong.'

Well, nothing *much*.

Constance had been so busy in the kitchen and helping Paola with the cleaning that she had forgotten about the pamphlets. Impatient now for Lottie to fall asleep, she tried to hurry the process by singing her old Yorkshire folk songs. They also helped to calm Constance herself as she mused on where Nish might be so that she could return the package to him.

In his room, she decided.

She headed there first, having stopped off in the scullery en route. She put on one of the bigger aprons, the blue one she used when she was cooking, and stuffed the package into the front pocket.

She knocked loudly on Nish's door, to no effect. She was about to knock again when Melissa's wispy form materialised at the end of the corridor. 'He's in the garden,' she called. 'With Mr Ainsworth.'

'Mr Ainsworth?'

'The young one,' Melissa clarified, coming closer. 'Master Ainsworth, I suppose I should say, but that makes him sound like a schoolboy. I say, are you all right?'

'Perfectly all right. Thank you, ma'am.'

'You look flushed.'

'I've been running,' said Constance. 'Up and down stairs.'

'Yes,' said Melissa. 'There *are* a lot of stairs here, aren't there?' Her eyes drifted down to the bulge in Constance's apron. 'Is your stomach hurting?'

'No, ma'am. Why do you ask?'

'You're clutching it with your hand.'

Constance gave a brittle laugh. 'Oh, I always do that. It's a habit I have.'

'Hmmm.' Melissa looked uncertain. 'Well, I'll let you get on.'

'Thank you, ma'am.'

Constance bobbed a curtsy and raced down the stairs, not knowing whether to laugh or be alarmed by the conclusion Melissa appeared to have drawn.

She followed the glow of hurricane lamps to the bench nearest the house. Lucian and Nish were staring out at the sea, chatting companionably, glasses of grappa in their hands.

The crunch of her shoes on the gravel made them turn.

'It's only me,' she said. 'I'm sorry to interrupt. But I didn't know when I'd get a better chance to return these to Mr Sengupta.'

Checking first that no one else was watching, she pulled out the package, wrapped in linen. She handed it to Nish.

He looked at Lucian, then at Constance. 'Is this what I think it is?'

She nodded.

'Where on earth did you find them?'

'Under Lady Latchmere's bed.'

'But how did you know to look there?'

'Billy told me where he planned to hide them, sir. I knew it was a bad idea. So, I moved them.'

'Where to?'

'Somewhere no man would ever think to look for them.'

She told them about the washing basket and the police-man. About how, afterwards, she had transferred them to an old tin pail and covered them up with clothes pegs.

Lucian and Nish burst out laughing. Constance felt a surge of triumph. But then, Lucian put his head in his hands.

'To think we spent the whole afternoon agonising over them.'

'I'm sorry, Mr Ainsworth. I would have spoken up earlier. But I didn't want to get Billy into any more trouble than he's in already.'

'You have nothing to be sorry for,' said Lucian.

Nish was more effusive. 'You're my guardian angel,' he said. He stood up and, quite suddenly, Constance felt herself enfolded in a tight but unthreatening embrace. She was struck by how nice he smelled – delicate and floral.

'I could kiss you,' Nish declared.

Lucian smiled at the two of them. 'Steady on.'

*

Constance had headed back to the house to finish up in the kitchen. Nish had followed her in order to update his journal.

Now, Lucian sat by himself, listening to the cicadas singing in the moonlight, wrestling with his thoughts. His demons, he nearly called them, but that was overdramatic. His demons were in abeyance for now – thanks largely to Paola and her sympathetic magic.

Paola. He wanted and needed her. But she had detached herself from him. She had noticed what he was trying not to notice – that he also wanted and needed Constance. And then there was Rose . . .

This is a mess, he thought. *A mess of my own making.*

He got up and started walking towards the courtyard. At the very least, they could talk about it. They were good at talking, despite the language barrier. You didn't need a lot of words to make yourself understood.

There was light glowing through the shutters. Lucian knocked at the door. But there was no answer.

'Paola!' he called. 'Come out! Please!'

The door opened a crack, showing a sliver of Paola's tired face. 'Stop,' she said. 'Please.'

'You and I,' he said. 'We must talk.'

She kept the door as it was. Closed her eyes.

'What's wrong? Tell me.'

'Go! Here. You come no more.'

Her words were like a slap in the face. 'But I need you,' he said. 'I need you, Paola.'

Her voice broke and tears came – angry tears. '*Perché mi rendi tutto questo così difficile?*' Why must you make this so difficult for me?

'I don't understand.'

'You are not for me. Go! Now!'

And she closed the door.

*

Bella sat at her dressing table, holding a pile of Henry's letters. She didn't mind admitting she was scared – actually scared.

There had been times in the past when she had been

scared of her husband. But that was a long time ago – a year at least. For the most part they'd managed to exist peaceably; to make the marriage work well enough for it not to be a lie when friends asked Bella how it was and she replied, as she usually did, 'Very well, thank you.' When Cecil was proving especially trying, she might observe, 'No marriage is frictionless, is it?' There would follow a conversation in which friction was equated with passion. And the friend, who was invariably a woman, male friends being frowned upon by Cecil, would squeeze Bella's hand in silent solidarity.

Earlier, she had witnessed Cecil and Danioni having a huge row, standing and shouting at each other on the upper terrace. Having hurried upstairs to avoid detection, she had been waiting here ever since for Danioni to leave and Cecil to come upstairs.

She had been formulating a plan – one which involved exposing herself and her desires to such a degree that she no longer had anything left in reserve. It was a gamble, no question. But there was nothing else for it. Count Albani had been right. She had to break the hold Danioni had over her. And that meant being honest with Cecil, however much it pained her, and however savage the consequences.

She heard his footsteps in the corridor and then listened to him enter the adjoining bedroom. She gathered up the letters in her hands and walked through the connecting door.

He turned and looked at her. Through her, really.

'I have something to tell you,' she said.

His eyes were blank and glazed. 'Save your breath. I know everything.'

He produced a letter from his pocket and threw it in her face. She grabbed at it and saw at once what it was and to whom it was addressed.

Mr Henry Bowater, Esq.

She stood frozen.

Cecil walked towards her, coming close – close enough for her to smell the alcohol on his breath.

Then he raised his hand and struck her.

13

As the first rays of sun pressed against the shutters, Bella lay awake.

How long had she been asleep? Perhaps for an hour or two. There were birds singing and bells and other bright morning noises. But all she felt was solitude and desolation. All she could think of were the events of the previous night.

The jolt of Cecil striking her. The spinning blur as she fell to the ground.

How odd, she thought, *to be me*. To have so much, irrespective of all that she had lost along the way. To present to the world most of the attributes of wellbeing and success. And then, for this to happen. Although it had happened before, of course – several times.

As someone whose belief in God was muted and automatic, Bella had often wondered what religious conversion might feel like. Now, she thought she knew. It would be a sudden lurch into awareness. She felt a version of that awareness now, but directed towards herself, not some sleepy, unheeding deity.

Gingerly, she eased herself upright. Her fingers went to

her cut, swollen mouth and the bruise above her right eye. Both were tender and painful to the touch.

Her glance travelled blankly over the dancing, twirling flowers on the wallpaper. In the low light they looked brown and rotten. She imagined insects crawling over them.

A memory surfaced, of her face being pressed into the bed, the overwhelming weight as Cecil's body bore down on hers. She'd fought with all her strength to move onto her side, to free her airways so that she could breathe, plead, resist.

First, she ran a bath. She poured a trickle of scented oil, thinking it might soothe her, then sat in the water until it was lukewarm. She hugged her knees and watched the swirling silvery patterns on the surface, too stunned to cry.

Beyond the hotel's walls, she could imagine the day continuing as normal. Tourists rising early for health-giving early swims. Bar-owners wiping down their tables. Just now, in the distance, she could hear the soft chug of a motorboat. How could that be? She had felt the same after Laurence had died: the same incredulity that life had not stopped for others as it had for her.

But with Laurence there had at least been a before and an after.

With Cecil, it was a different kind of trauma. Now, things were different. They were clear and true. Irrefutable.

Once she had dressed, she eased herself down to sit before the mirror and tried to cover the bruises with make-up. After several minutes of dabbing and smearing, she stopped to assess her handiwork, noticing a broken blood vessel in the corner of her eye which no amount of artifice could camouflage.

For some reason, this enraged her. But it was a spiky, nervous anger she suspected might dissipate quickly. She understood instantly that she must make use of it while it was still there.

Steeling herself, she went over to the connecting door and tried to open it. It was locked, which surprised her. She twisted and shook the handle, then listened for a response.

Nothing.

So he had locked the door. Well, she had a key too. She found it in her bedside table drawer. Yet, she discovered that he had left his key in the lock on the other side of the door.

Wound up to snapping point, she stormed out into the corridor and tried to open the main door to his room. That was locked too.

She knocked and shouted. 'Cecil? Open this door, please.'

Nothing.

Her anger subsided, as she knew it would, to be replaced by worry and a bold, callous curiosity. Bold because, she realised, she would do anything to satisfy it. Callous because she no longer cared about the outcome.

If the reason for Cecil's silence was that he was lying dead on his bed, then so be it.

*

As Lucian headed into the garden with his pencils and sketch-book, he forced himself not to glance towards Paola's room.

This was a shining world, after all – green and fragrant. A

place of transformation. Important not to lose sight of this, whatever else was going on.

Perhaps he should move here permanently? Not *here* necessarily, but Italy. His friend Keane had moved to Pantelleria – an island in between Sicily and Tunisia with hot springs and sturdy stone buildings called *dammusi*. Keane was staying there while he painted the vineyards. He had written to Lucian: 'You must come! One can live cheaply and well here.'

Would Constance like it there?

The question burst upon him out of nowhere.

Some of his fantasies were embarrassing in their banality. Constance in a floral dress, harvesting grapes. Constance bathing a small child, the house echoing to the sound of splashing and laughter. Constance frying bacon on a stove.

Some of them were salacious. Constance in bed beside him, naked. Constance on top of him, straddling him, leaning forward to kiss him while he stroked her breasts . . .

For God's sake, man. Pull yourself together.

What was happening here?

Constance, Paola and Rose. They formed the three points of a triangle, with Lucian at the centre – the stark geometry of desire.

He was starting now to understand that he had not treated Paola at all well. He had not been abusive or violent, quite the reverse: their relationship had been tender and loving. But he had ignored the inequality at the heart of it. Or rather, he had assumed it didn't matter – which it didn't, for him. For Paola, though, it mattered a good deal. She was employed by his parents, and while Lucian didn't think of himself as her master – and he was confident Paola didn't think of herself as his servant – that was nevertheless the reality of the situation.

And then there was Rose, about whom he was finding it increasingly hard to have any opinions at all.

A small breeze tickled Lucian's face, puncturing his reverie.

He perched on the wall between a Judas tree, with its heart-shaped green leaves, and a row of Italian cypresses. The Judas tree had looked beautiful in the spring when it was covered in clusters of purple flowers. Now, it only absorbed the sunlight, priming itself for next year.

He had just started to sketch the hills and the coastline when the sharp, chirruping alarm call of a rosy starling caught his attention. He swivelled round, trying to find it – and saw Constance making her way carefully down the path to the seafront promenade. She was wearing Claudine's swimming costume, the one she had worn to the beach, with a towel wrapped around her waist.

After allowing enough time for Constance to reach the promenade, he packed up his drawing things and followed her. When he reached the gateway that gave access from the grounds to the seafront, he peered around it, trying to ascertain Constance's whereabouts without giving his own away.

She had already got as far as the water's edge. Letting himself out of the gate, he watched as she eased herself into the sea. She was a strong, confident swimmer and in no time at all she was a good hundred yards from the shore.

Above the beach ran a low parapet wall. Lucian sat down behind it. It didn't conceal him from view, but he was less obviously visible than if he'd gone all the way down to the beach. And when Constance turned around to swim back towards the shore he ducked down until he was certain she was out of the water.

The next time he looked, she was lying on a rocky outcrop with her eyes closed and her face tilted upwards, luxuriating in the weak morning sun.

Lucian opened his sketchbook and started to draw her. His eyes flicked between his subject and the drawing as his hand swept across the page. But as the minutes wore on, he found he was spending more time looking at Constance than he was at the sketch.

All right, he thought. *So, I am openly staring at her. What's wrong with that?*

You know very well, countered his conscience. *It's rude and lecherous, as well as an infringement of her privacy.*

Suddenly, as if she had been aware of Lucian's gaze all the while, Constance looked straight at him. A shock went through his body. For what seemed like the longest time they gazed at each other, nakedly acknowledging the attraction they felt for each other, until finally Lucian was overwhelmed by the intensity of her gaze and dropped his own.

Almost immediately, he regretted it.

He glanced up again, seeking to reaffirm the bond.

She had closed her eyes and turned her head away. But even from where he was sitting, he could see that she was smiling.

*

Cecil had left the hotel early, looking immaculate. Pulling on his gloves, he examined a scratch on his wrist, then wandered off down to Portofino, where he proposed to find a carriage to take him to the station. Francesco was otherwise engaged and he didn't want to involve Lucian.

As he walked, he thought about the events of the previous night. It was unfortunate, of course, when these things happened. Nobody enjoyed fights, least of all him. But as with children, so with wives. When they misbehaved, they needed to be taught a lesson.

So many times, at both prep and public school, he had been beaten – sometimes by teachers, sometimes by prefects; sometimes with a slipper or gym shoe, which didn't hurt too much, and sometimes with a cane, which did.

What Bella had done was unacceptable and she had to take responsibility for it. His job as her husband was to assist her in this.

He arrived at the station with twenty minutes to spare before the train to Genoa. He bought some cigarettes and smoked a couple of them with a tiny coffee at the station bar. Every so often, he felt in his inside jacket pocket for Jack Turner's cheque. Sometimes he brought it out and looked at it, just to make sure.

The train journey passed quickly. He had read the most recent English newspaper cover to cover and they only sold Italian ones at Mezzago. But he had brought a book with him. He wasn't what anyone would call a reader, but he did love *Three Men in a Boat*, which he had first read as a young man and which never failed to make him laugh – especially the bit with Montmorency and the dead water rat.

Once in Genoa, Cecil took a carriage from the palatial station to the appointed meeting place, a *caffè* just around the corner from the British Consulate on Spianata dell'Acquasola. It was only late morning, but grizzled card-players had already colonised the rickety tin tables on the pavement.

Removing his hat, Cecil ordered an espresso.

Godwin was there already – sitting at the bar, chewing carefully on a *brioscia*. He was small and rotund and the little hair he still possessed was combed neatly across his balding pate. He looked up. 'Ainsworth?'

'Mr Godwin. It's a pleasure to meet you.'

'You, too. After our correspondence of recent days.' Godwin looked at his wristwatch. 'Your man's late.'

'Give him a minute. He's very dependable.'

In the event, Godwin saw Francesco before he did. 'Is that him?' he asked, pointing to the stooped, wiry figure in the doorway.

'The very same,' said Cecil, waving to attract Francesco's attention. He had suggested Francesco drive him to Mezzago in the carriage. Then they could take the train to Genoa together. But Francesco had thought it was safer to travel separately.

Francesco nodded. After easing his way apologetically past the other customers, he gave Cecil the piece of paper he was clutching in his right hand.

'Francesco has been a great help to me in packaging the painting,' Cecil explained, 'and arranging its transportation. Not to mention handling the paperwork associated with its delivery.'

Francesco nodded again. He liked praise, Cecil had noticed. Then again, who didn't?

It had been a clever scheme. Its ingenuity lay in its obviousness. Like a magician's trick, it was all about distraction, about where you were and weren't looking.

Jack Turner had watched Francesco hammering nails into the crate when he and Cecil were packing up the painting. But he had only seen one nail go in, after which he had been so busy talking to Cecil that he hadn't noticed the other nails that Francesco had slipped quietly into his pocket.

Then, Francesco had waited for Claudine to leave the room, as Cecil had assured him she would at some point. No sooner had she padded down the darkened corridor and disappeared into the bathroom, than Francesco had stepped out of the shadows. He'd been hiding in the walk-in laundry cupboard, pretending to stack bed linen.

Closing the door behind him, Francesco had crossed to the crate and quickly removed the side, which was only secured by a single nail. He'd removed the painting, cut the paper at the rear and rapidly separated the canvas from the frame. He'd then replaced the frame in the crate and resealed it before crossing back to the door and exiting with the canvas, taking care to wipe the doorknob clean.

The whole operation had taken less than a minute.

Later that evening, through the bars of the locked gate, he'd handed a large, square object wrapped in oil cloth to his friend, Alessandro, who had volunteered to take it to Godwin's most trusted point man, Lorenzo Andretti.

'As you can see,' said Cecil, 'the paperwork is very much complete.'

Godwin squinted. Then, in Italian, he asked Francesco, 'Did Andretti give you a message for me?'

Francesco produced another folded document which he handed over. 'I speak English, Signore,' he said, in a heavy accent.

'Although sometimes it's beneficial to pretend he doesn't,' added Cecil, grinning.

'You don't find many who do,' observed Godwin.

'Only the ones who've emigrated.'

'And been sent back.'

Cecil ignored this. He nodded at the document. 'All in order?'

'Andretti attests that the painting has been handed over in perfect condition.'

'Excellent.' Cecil turned to Francesco. 'So, I shall see you when I get back.'

Cecil watched Francesco leave. When he was sure he was

gone, he turned back to Godwin, who produced an envelope from his briefcase. 'Your receipt.'

Cecil ripped it open and examined its contents greedily.

'I've included a reserve price of fifty thousand pounds, as agreed,' said Godwin. 'Although we are clearly expecting a great deal more.'

'I'm relieved to hear it.'

'And of course, your advance in the form of a bank cheque.' He handed a second envelope to Cecil. 'Twenty-five per cent of the reserve price, less our commission.'

Cecil opened this, too. 'Looks about right.' He tucked it into his pocket. 'And I have your assurance the sale will be handled privately?'

Godwin gave him a disappointed look. 'Please, Mr Ainsworth. Discretion has always been our byword.'

He held out his hand and Cecil shook it firmly before pushing back his chair and collecting his hat. He was about to walk out, when Godwin cleared his throat ostentatiously. Evidently, the transaction was incomplete.

'Ah,' said Cecil, 'how foolish of me.' He reached into his pocket and produced an envelope.

Godwin examined the certificate of authenticity.

'There you go,' said Cecil. 'Proof that you now have in your possession a one-hundred-per-cent genuine, cast-iron, copper-bottomed Rubens.'

Godwin put it in his briefcase before rewarding Cecil with a thin smile. 'Do you have anything planned for the rest of the day?'

Cecil replied that he might take in a bit of culture.

'I can give you an address,' said Godwin, 'of a place where the culture is especially seductive.'

Cecil gave the offer some thought before scrunching up his nose. 'Do you know what? I think I'll pass.'

'As you wish.'

In fact, Cecil had planned a straightforward, respectable day.

After leaving Godwin, he strolled in the sunshine to Via Dante where, in the cathedral-like hush of the Banco Popolare, he paid in two cheques. Godwin's for £12,000, signed on behalf of the British Italian Art Company, and Jack Turner's, for £50,000. The clerk, a sweaty old fellow with a pince-nez, made a face and blew out his unshaven cheeks when he saw them – as well he might.

Then he went to the telegram office, a little further up the same street opposite the police station. Finding himself a quiet perch, he wrote on the form:

```
SORRY - stop - SCHOOL OF RUBENS
NOT RUBENS - stop - WORTH A TRY -
stop - SOLD ANYWAY - stop - ONE
THOUSAND POUNDS - stop - WIRE YOUR
SHARE - stop - CECIL - stop.
```

He sat back and examined his work. Yes, that would do.

Now for some sightseeing.

More to impress Bella than to please himself, Cecil trudged through Porta Soprano, the towered gate in the ancient city wall, following Via di Ravecca until he reached the old Gothic church of Sant'Agostina. He considered going inside but couldn't face it – all those candles and frescoes and plaster saints bored him to tears. Instead, he explored the square it gave onto, Piazza Sarzano, dirty and full of pigeons.

There, he found fruit and vegetable vendors and stalls selling lace – more bloody lace! – and leather bags. A sharp-eyed girl of about sixteen with black corkscrew curls smiled at him as he passed her stall, selling bedraggled flowers.

His purchase of a single bunch of roses – at least, he *thought* they were roses – seemed to thrill her. Probably, he thought, it had been the highlight of her day.

It never ceased to amaze Cecil, the drab lives some people led.

As the girl wrapped the flowers in paper, he watched the shape of her breasts beneath her too-small brown dress and wondered what it would feel like to kiss her.

*

Alice was full of suspicion. She had been at the window, brushing and pinning her hair, looking out at the hotel grounds, when she saw Constance making her way up from the seafront, her ridiculous borrowed swimsuit covered only by a towel.

Craning her neck, she followed the girl's progress to the kitchen door at the side of the house, and was about to turn away when she saw Lucian following the same route up from the beach.

No one needed to be a genius to work out what was going on.

Later, at breakfast, Alice kept a wary eye on Constance as she flitted between the guests. More than once, she approached the table where Lucian and Nish sat eating. Each time, Nish looked up at her and smiled. But Lucian studiously avoided eye contact. He didn't even glance in her direction.

It told Alice all she needed to know.

But now, there was something else.

She always went into the drawing room after breakfast to straighten the furnishings. Many guests liked to migrate there with their final cup of coffee and read or plan their day. She was about to remove a pile of books from one of the occasional tables, when she spotted Lucian's sketchbook.

Usually, he was very protective of it. It was clearly an accident that he had left it balanced on the arm of the sofa. Perhaps he had come in here with Constance before breakfast, before she went off to get changed?

Perhaps they had ...? No, no. She felt embarrassed just thinking about it. Embarrassed on Lucian's behalf, that is.

After checking that there was definitely no one else in the room, she opened it.

As she flicked through the heavy, slightly yellowy pages, her gaze rested on a sketch of Constance – it was clearly Constance – at the seafront.

A burst of childish laughter came from somewhere. Lottie, being entertained by Constance. Alice quickly snapped the book shut. But then she waited and, after a minute or so, reopened it and studied the sketch again.

Something about the intensity of Lucian's focus on the girl

disturbed Alice. It wasn't just that the drawing was exquisite and sensual. She had seen enough of Lucian's work over the years to know the kind of effects he strove for, especially when his subject was the female form. But here he seemed ... obsessed. Enraptured.

She followed the trail of laughter out onto the terrace. Peering over the parapet, she saw Constance and Lottie running around, playing some sort of chasing game while Lucian sat nearby sketching them.

Alice stood and watched them, until she could no longer bear the dry, sultry heat. Then she went across to the reception desk, where the master set of keys was kept.

Really, Lucian had left her with no choice. Constance was her daughter's nanny. Everyone seemed to forget that.

Alice climbed the stairs to Constance's room and let herself in. She stood with her back to the door, listening. Then she relaxed, letting her eyes sweep the tiny room. Even with the window open it was hot and stuffy, but not a bad room, though its wallpaper was more basic than in the guest suites and the rug on the tiled floor rather threadbare. Constance kept it tidy, which was a point in her favour.

Alice's first target was the old pine chest of drawers. Opening each drawer in turn, she rifled through Constance's meagre possessions. How did she manage with so little? It didn't take long, nor did it reveal anything interesting beyond Claudine's expensive bra, which stood out among the otherwise threadbare and muted undergarments.

Likewise, the only item of interest on the bedside table

was a shiny tube of lipstick that must also have come from Claudine. Alice frowned as she pondered the nature of that relationship. Was this another instance of Claudine forgetting her place? Mind you, Claudine wasn't exactly high-class. Where was she *really* from? Alice was desperate to know.

The sense that she was missing something nagged at her. Where did people normally hide things? Where would *she* hide things? She felt under the pillow and, when that turned up nothing, slid an exploratory hand under the mattress.

And there she found them. A pile of letters addressed to Constance.

Alice's heart raced, more with excitement than nerves. She wiped her clammy hands on her dress, then took one of the envelopes and carefully pulled out its contents – a letter and a cheap silver locket. Her eyes skimmed the contents, which were barely legible, then quickly turned it over to check the signature.

Ever yours, Mam X

Her mouth was dry, her breathing quick and hungry.

Putting the letter down, she undid the clasp on the side of the locket and prised open the hinge with her thumbnail.

When she saw its contents, she froze. Then she extended her little finger and touched them to make sure they were real.

There was a photo of a small boy – and with it, tied together with cotton, a lock of brown hair.

*

Lottie was holding a tea party for her toys.

Constance was trying to focus on Lottie and her game,

but she kept being distracted by Lucian – by the way he was watching her, as if she were the sum of her stretched-out legs and tilted head. She was dimly aware of the need not to be aware of it, or not to show that awareness, but it was impossible.

Lottie was trying to get her teddy bear to sit up behind a doll's cup and saucer. But he kept falling over and she realised she needed another pair of hands to steady it.

'Lucian?' she asked.

'What is it, Lots?'

'Will you play with us?'

'In a minute.'

Lucian added some last detail to the drawing and leant back to evaluate it before putting it to one side and shuffling forward to join the party.

He gave a little salute. 'Reporting for duty, ma'am!'

Constance smiled. Lucian was so good with his niece.

'You can be teddy,' said Lottie.

She showed him where to sit and how to hold the toy, with the teacup held to its paw. She took the handle of the toy teapot between the hands of the doll she was playing with and pretended to pour.

Then she said, 'Teddy likes Annabelle.'

'And which one is Annabelle?'

Constance held up the doll assigned to her and Lucian smiled. 'Teddy has excellent taste,' he said.

'But he can't be her sweetheart,' said Lottie.

'Just because he's a bear?'

Lottie was unimpressed by Lucian's logic. 'Because it's "too soon", silly.'

Lucian reached out and stroked his niece's hair. 'And why's it too soon, Lots?'

'I don't know. It's what Mummy says.' At this Lucian and Constance found their eyes drawn haltingly to one another. 'But,' the girl added, 'they can still sit together.'

She indicated to Constance and Lucian that they should bring their toys together so that their hands were almost touching. As they did so, Lucian stroked the back of Constance's hand with his little finger.

It was the first time he'd touched her in this way and the effect was electric. She froze, scarcely able to believe it had happened. She kept her head down until she forced herself to look up and found he was staring at her. He was smiling and she felt herself blush.

But then a voice called out. 'Lucian!' cried Alice.

The two of them snatched their hands away.

She called again. 'Lucian!'

He scrambled to his feet as his sister came striding across the grass.

'There you are,' she said, as if he had been deliberately hiding from her.

'We were having a tea party.' He held up the teddy bear as Alice surveyed the scene. Constance noticed that the woman's gaze did not include her.

Alice turned to Lucian. 'Could I have a word?' Her tone was clipped and peremptory.

'Of course.' He waited, expecting her to speak.

'In private,' she said.

'Righto.'

'Aw,' said Lottie.

'I'll be right back, Lots. Promise.'

Constance sensed him trying to send a glance of apology her way. But she knew better than to acknowledge it.

She didn't like or trust Alice.

*

Alice led Lucian into the house and up the stairs to her room before she gave him one of Constance's letters.

He read it in silence. When he had finished, he said, 'Where did you get this?'

'That doesn't matter. What it says does.'

He looked at it again. 'And why are you showing it to me?'

'Oh, Lucian.'

'I mean it, Alice. Why?'

'To stop you making a bloody fool of yourself. And the rest of us.'

For a moment they stared at each other. Before she could speak again, he let the letter fall to the floor and walked out of the door.

*

On her way out of the kitchen Bella saw, through the open front door, Cecil striding across the forecourt towards the house. His face was shiny with sweat. He was carrying a meagre bouquet of flowers and his demeanour was jaunty.

She had been dreading this moment all day. Even now,

when some sort of confrontation was inevitable, she wished to postpone it further. She hurried towards the stairs to escape him. But she was too slow and too late.

'Bella!'

She carried on walking up the stairs. But then she got to the landing and didn't know what else to do, because he was bound to catch up with her. And so he did, climbing the stairs three at a time, hoisting himself up with the bannister, which creaked under his weight.

As he walked towards her, she walked backwards.

He was out of breath. Panting. 'Why the hell are you running away? I have the most marvellous news!'

*

Claudine was on her way out for an early-evening stroll when she heard Cecil's booming voice. The door to the Goodwood Suite, which she had just opened, gave on to the landing so she could see everything.

She saw Bella, her arms hanging limply, edging backwards.

And she saw Cecil, out of breath, advancing towards her, a straggly, half-dead bouquet in his hand.

She was experienced enough in the world to know immediately what she was seeing. But to be of any use, she needed to see more.

Quickly, before either of them noticed her, she closed the door and placed her eye to the crack.

'I spoke to Heddon,' Cecil was saying. 'It seems the painting was insured after all. So, I stand to make quite a tidy sum from the payout.' He was talking quickly, with a grating false bonhomie. 'It'll be enough to put a bit towards Lucian's wedding. And pay off a few ... debts that I've accumulated.' He paused, clearly giving time for this revelation to sink in. 'I might even have a few hundred to bung your way for this place. But only if you promise not to use it to pay back your father.' He forced out a laugh, but it met with stony silence from Bella. Cecil looked confused. 'I thought you'd be happy.'

'I can't be happy while poor Billy is locked away.' Claudine just managed to catch the sound of her voice.

'Quite. Well, perhaps I'll go and see to that. And maybe when I come back ...' His glance dropped to the bouquet, but he evidently decided against giving it to Bella. 'Then, we can talk.'

His wife looked at him, but otherwise did not react.

His tone grew wheedling and winsome. 'It was a nasty shock you gave me, Bellakins. I mean, how's a chap supposed to react? When he finds out his wife's been canoodling behind his back. And the whole town seems to know about it ...'

So that's what this was all about, Claudine thought. *Good for Bella.*

'Of course, I see now that I may have been heavy-handed. A little more so than was necessary.'

He could no longer hold her gaze. Claudine had seen this so many times. Men like Cecil never wanted to confront the reality of what they had done or who they really were.

Look at him – turning away and hurrying off down the stairs, like a child at a party caught stealing cake.

As soon as he was out of sight, Bella crumbled. She slid down the wall like a broken marionette. Claudine opened the door fully and rushed forward to comfort her.

'Hey,' she said, softly. 'Come here. Let me help you.'

She led Bella into the Goodwood Suite and locked the door.

Bella sat on the side of the bed as Claudine examined her grazes and bruises. She was agitated, anxious to explain. 'It's not what you think . . .' she began.

'Hush, now. There's no need to make up excuses for my benefit.'

'But I provoked him.'

Claudine tutted. 'Don't give me any of that "I blame myself" horseshit. Most kinds of men don't need much provoking. And I know most kinds of men.' She paused, indicating the marks on Bella's face. 'Do you want me to cover them up?'

'Thank you, but I can do it myself.'

'Well, at least let me put something on that cut.' She searched in her vanity case. 'You know you're stronger than him, don't you?'

'I'm not sure my face would agree.'

'I don't mean that kind of strength. Any fool can use his fists.' She dabbed cream on Bella's lip, which looked worse than she had originally thought. 'I see the way everyone in this hotel looks to you. For guidance and wisdom. For support.'

Bella rose. She went over to the dressing table and

examined herself in the mirror. 'Thank you,' she said. 'Mrs . . .' She paused.

'Please.' Claudine curtsied. 'Call me Claudine. Ms Claudine Pascal.'

'Then thank you, Claudine. For being so sisterly.'

The American woman smiled. 'Now, there's a fine word.'

*

As children, Alice and Lucian had had an Irish governess called Miss Corcoran, who wore a black merino cloak and a bonnet. She was thin and spectacled, but not as old as she looked, though of course to Alice she had seemed ancient. Her trick was to be calm and quiet at all times. She never raised her voice and, unusually for a governess, never resorted to corporal punishment, even though she had on occasion sent them to bed without any supper.

Even more unusually, Miss Corcoran was an excellent teacher – though her chief interest was in art, which meant Lucian benefited from her more than Alice.

Now, in the cool of the library, the business with Constance temporarily banished from her mind, Alice closed her eyes and channeled Miss Corcoran as she prepared to give Roberto his first English lesson.

She hadn't thought he would take her up on her offer. He hadn't seemed all that enthusiastic when the subject was first discussed. But after lunch, Count Albani had crept up on her in the kitchen and asked if this evening would suit her – because it would suit Roberto, who was thrilled, really thrilled, by the idea of learning English.

'Perhaps,' he suggested, 'the first lesson could be about making introductions?'

Alice said she thought that was an excellent idea.

When Roberto appeared – freshly washed, smelling of cologne – he didn't look thrilled exactly. But he was here at least and must be reasonably keen, or why would his father have suggested it?

She held out her hand for him to shake, as Miss Corcoran had done, and said, 'How do you do?'

Roberto mimicked her. 'How do you do?' He took the proffered hand, but kissed it instead. Alice flushed and smiled. He smiled back, letting go of her hand only with the greatest reluctance.

She said, 'My name is Alice.'

Roberto repeated, 'My name is Alice.'

'No, *your* name.'

Ah. *Mi dispiace.* Your name is Roberto.'

'No. *My* name is Roberto.'

'*Sono confuso.*'

'Imagine how I feel.' Alice sighed.

'*Cosa stai dicendo*?' What are you saying?

'You send me an exquisite gift,' said Alice, 'yet you can't even introduce yourself properly. I could say anything I like and you wouldn't have a clue, would you?'

She shook her head at him. He shook his head back.

She went on: 'I could tell you you're frightfully good-looking. But really just a boy.'

'*Riproviamo.*' He gestured that she should stand.

'And that I wouldn't be wasting time on this fool's errand if there were any half-decent Englishmen left to marry.'

Roberto bowed low. 'Your name is Roberto,' he said.

*

Cecil was resigned to Bella's mood remaining low for some time. Some of it was his fault.

He hadn't behaved impeccably, he appreciated that. But there were other factors to consider, such as the stress of running Hotel Portofino; the business with the painting; uncertainty over Lucian and Rose; Julia's habitual dissatisfaction with everything; and – of course – the change, which loomed over Bella as it loomed over all women of her age, making her tetchy and hysterical.

The more Cecil thought about it, the more compelling his 'change' theory seemed. It was the reason Bella never wanted to sleep with him. Her affair with Henry Whateverhisnamewas was plainly a romantic passion, not a sexual one, whatever the letter suggested to the contrary. Because why would she sleep with that idiot – who was probably homosexual, let's face it – and not Cecil, whose prowess as a lover had been remarked upon by every woman he had ever been with?

The solution was to give Bella a wide berth. Hence this visit to Luigi's, his favourite Portofino bar. Not the most salubrious place, to be sure – it overlooked a patch of scrubland directly opposite the back door to the Municipal Offices – but it sold tolerable pastries and a person could always get half-tight on grappa for next to nothing.

Cecil was about to head home when the door in the wall opened and no less a person than Danioni emerged, followed by Francesco.

Cecil did a double take. It couldn't be, surely? And yet it was. What's more, it was clear from the men's relaxed, chatty demeanour that they knew each other well.

Cecil called, 'Francesco?'

Francesco froze, alarmed to have been caught out. He was obviously thinking: *Do I run? No, there's no point. Better to ride this out.* 'Signore!' he said, and bowed.

Cecil looked from Francesco to Danioni and back again. 'What the devil are you doing here?' He turned to Danioni. 'What's the meaning of this?'

Danioni looked supremely unbothered. 'Just one cousin, Signor Ainsworth ...' Grinning, he clapped a hand on Francesco's shoulder. 'One cousin, paying a call on another.'

'I'd like to talk to you,' said Cecil. 'Now, if you don't mind.' To Franscesco he barked: 'And I'll see you back at the hotel.'

Danioni led Cecil up the stairs to his office. 'I expect a visit, yes, from the British Consul. But from Signor Cecil Ainsworth? Not so much.'

'All right, you've had your fun.'

'I am surprised you wish to speak to me.'

'Not as surprised as I am to discover we've had a spy in our midst all the time.'

'Ah, yes.' Danioni puckered his lips. 'It is a sadness for you, I see. And so, you wish to be friends again?'

Cecil sat down. Apologies did not come easily to him, but he was determined to do his best. 'Perhaps some of the language I used the last time we spoke was a little . . . Look, in the heat of the moment I may have accused you of one or two things that . . .'

'Your "greasy little insinuations"?'

'In the light of what we now know we don't know, those details don't stand up to scrutiny.'

'You wish to say sorry?'

'I can do better than that.' From his jacket pocket, Cecil produced a wad of banknotes. 'Given your knowledge of my intimate dealings . . .' He peeled off a number of them, then added a few more before putting them on the desk. 'This is the price I'm willing to pay. To bring an immediate close to the police investigation.'

Danioni reached forward, but Cecil kept his hand on the notes.

'And to secure William Scanlon's release.' He took his hand away. 'As well as make reparation for any hurt feelings.'

Danioni swiped the notes. Licking his thumb, he counted them carefully before pocketing them.

'And this?' Cecil continued, peeling off another bundle of notes. 'Let's just call this a gesture of goodwill.' He threw them on the desk. 'From one dog to another.'

*

Alice was still hard at work with Roberto, when through the open door she saw Bella crossing the drawing room. Excusing herself, she rose quickly and rushed after her.

'What is it, Alice? You look flushed.'

'Is there somewhere we can speak? Somewhere private?'

They walked through the kitchen to Bella's office. Bella locked the door then sat behind the desk. She gestured to Alice to sit down but she shook her head.

'I thought you should see these,' she said. She produced a bundle of Constance's letters from her handbag and placed them on the desk.

Bella stared at them but made no attempt to pick them up. 'What are they?'

'Letters. To Miss March.'

'You intercepted her mail?' Bella's harsh, reproving eyes met her daughter's.

'I found them in her room.'

'What were you doing there?'

Alice tutted with impatience. Surely this was the wrong question to be asking? 'I've known for ages that something's not right with her,' she said. 'And now we have the proof.' She crossed her arms, proudly.

Bella paused, as if taking stock of the situation. Then she said, 'Put them back, Alice.'

'What?'

'Put them back. This instant.' Her mother's voice was calm but ice-cold.

'Aren't you going to read them?'

'Of course not.'

Alice frowned and scratched her temple with her little finger. This was not the outcome she'd envisaged. 'But don't you want to know the kind of girl she is?'

'I already know what kind of girl she is.' Bella's voice

swelled in volume. 'Anyone can see that. She's honest, kind, conscientious—'

'And the mother of an illegitimate child!' Alice interrupted. 'At fifteen years of age!'

Silence fell as the two women stared at each other. Alice could feel her pulse racing, her chest rising and falling. She couldn't remember when she'd last felt so thwarted – so *angry*.

Eventually, Bella said wearily: 'Where did I go wrong with you?'

'With *me*?'

'How could I have raised a daughter who is so utterly unfeeling? So utterly *unsisterly*?'

Alice flushed scarlet. '*Unsisterly*? What sort of nonsense word is that? I'd sooner be unsisterly than ungodly.'

'Somehow, you're managing to be both.'

'This is absurd.'

Alice leaned in to pick up the letters, but Bella snapped, 'No you don't. You leave them there.'

'But . . .'

'Go, Alice. Go now. And shut the door behind you.'

It took a few moments for Bella's command to register. Once it did, Alice obeyed it to the letter, storming out of the room, then slamming the door so violently that the whole hotel seemed to shake.

14

It was odd, Lucian thought. How the way you looked at something changed what you were looking at. You saw the world through the prism of your mood. And his mood now was bleak and cynical.

He felt trapped. Out-manoeuvred.

He had come to this grand garden, with its formal paths and manicured beds of exotic shrubs and flowers, to think over his situation. But these thoughts were all over the place, and the heat insufferable.

The villa seemed to loom over him. Turning, he appraised it neutrally. With its shady loggias and soft lemon sheen, Hotel Portofino demanded to be seen from the front. It wasn't – like the other villas stacked further up the hill – hidden away behind a thick screen of cyprus trees.

No, the reason for building a house like this in a place like this, on a hillside overlooking the sea, was to show off. To dominate the seascape. The garden had been designed with the same aim.

Wiping the sweat from his brow, he turned back and surveyed the panorama. Only thirty years ago, his mother had told him, this area was hardly developed at all. Portofino had been a pretty fishing village, known only to the discerning few, with a reputation for being hard to reach because of the terrible roads.

The railways had changed all that. These days, even though the trains stopped well short of Portofino and Santa Margherita and Rapallo, every year they brought tourists in their thousands. And, of course, there was reverse flow too, as labourers from the old farming communities drifted towards the cities, particularly Genoa where there was work at the port and in construction – better and more reliable work than growing olives and oranges.

Incomers, often foreigners like the Ainsworths, had transformed the Ligurian rivieras. If you'd asked them, they would have said their goal was achieving harmony with nature. And yes, of course, gardens were about nature, taste and beauty. But they were also about *taming* nature. Imposing your will. Replacing chestnut trees that had stood for centuries with Lebanon cedars and cypresses because, well, why not?

Some of these gardens were ridiculous. Lucian had seen them for himself. They had lakes and grottoes, waterfalls and Gothic pavilions. At least his mother knew the meaning of restraint.

The truth was, he had loved this view when he had thought Rose loved it too – when he had thought she was the kind of person who liked the things he liked.

It turned out she wasn't.

But was that a meaningful impediment? Did it necessarily mean they couldn't be happy together?

He turned and there she was, gliding across the lawn with her parasol. As always, she looked beautiful. And as always, he sensed her mother's guiding hand in her wardrobe – a modish sleeveless shift dress that emphasized her slight physique.

But Julia wouldn't be around forever. Rose would change over time. They both would. They might end up growing together, in parallel. Lots of couples did, despite having started out from very different places.

'I thought you'd be painting,' she said, approaching him. She had her hands behind her back, as if she were hiding something.

'Did you?' He turned back to the view. 'I'm not really in the mood.'

Already, he had created an awkward atmosphere. He cursed himself. Try harder, for goodness' sake!

'It's our last day tomorrow,' she said.

'Gosh. So soon?'

'These three weeks have flown by.'

'Haven't they just.'

'We may not have a chance to speak again properly. So, I wanted to say thank you. For all you've done to look after me. To make me feel at home here.'

It was a sweet little speech and Lucian was genuinely touched. 'It's been a pleasure,' he said.

'And I wanted to give you this.' She produced from behind her back the thing she had been hiding. It was a small, rectangular piece of cardboard and on it a painting – a neat but simple coastal landscape. 'I've been working on it. In secret.'

Lucian took it from her. 'Oh, Rose. It's . . .'

'. . . not very good, I know.'

'I was going to say wonderful.'

She smiled. 'You don't have to pretend.'

'But, I mean it. The very fact that you've created it. For me. When painting's not your thing.' He tried to supply in his own manner all the confidence that was lacking in hers.

She laughed. 'It's *really* not my thing.' She stepped closer, shedding her reserve. 'I've tried, really I have. To like painting, for your sake. But, I don't see what you do in it. It's all just colours and shapes to me.'

He shrugged. 'Better to be honest. In any case,' he went on, risking a too-clever joke, 'most art these days is *obsessed* with colours and shapes. You might revise your judgement after you see a Paul Klee painting.'

'I might.' She sounded uncertain. Of course she did. 'So, you're not upset?'

He shook his head. 'I'd be more upset if I thought you were pretending to like art. Just to please me.'

'But that's it! That's all I do. Try to please people.'

A crack had appeared in the golden bowl. Before today, Lucian could have imagined her murmuring such a thing to her reflection in an unguarded moment, but not saying it out loud, to someone else. That she had found the courage to do so, he took as a sign of progress.

He pushed further. 'Please your mother, you mean.'

'And everybody else as well.' Rose turned away. She

started to walk back towards the villa. There was a catch in her voice, when she spoke next. 'I try so hard to be interesting. When really I'm not.'

'You *are* interesting,' Lucian heard himself insist.

She shook her head. 'I'm not sure I'm even very likeable.'

'How can you say that?' He moved forward, tried to embrace her. But she shook him off.

'I'm not stupid, Lucian. I can see that people don't warm to others who can't be true to themselves.'

'No,' he said. 'It's not as simple as that.'

But Rose was already walking away.

*

Nish had been watching Lucian and Rose from a bench on the other side of the garden. He had chosen his position carefully to ensure he was hidden. His was a partial view, impeded by an oversized ornamental hedge.

He hadn't been able to hear them, but it looked as if they had had a row, or at least a tense, testy conversation. As he followed Rose's progress back towards the hotel, he became aware of Claudine standing beside him, wearing her trademark sunglasses and a wide-brimmed straw hat. She was watching too, but much more blatantly.

'I can't see it myself,' she said.

'Can't see what?'

'That little love match.'

'They'd have fine-looking children,' said Nish.

'So would we.'

They both laughed.

Claudine sat down beside him. She lit a cigarette. 'She isn't his soulmate.'

'Do people have soulmates?' he wondered.

'All the time. But not if they're too damned scared to admit who they really are. And what they really feel.'

Nish felt an unpleasant tingling sensation. His weakness – and he knew this because it had been an issue once before – was that he believed himself to be in control of the image he projected. It was a kind of arrogance. Yet now, he understood that Claudine had seen beneath the carapace.

'Is it that obvious?' he asked, warily.

'To me it is.'

He looked at her, suddenly scared. 'You won't say anything?'

'Of course not. It isn't anyone's business but yours.'

'How did you guess?'

'I didn't guess. Call it an intuition. A sixth sense.' She took a deep drag on her cigarette, then exhaled lustily. 'Lots of my friends in Paris are like you. All my favourite people.'

Before he could respond, Nish noticed that Lucian was watching them. He raised a weary hand.

Claudine asked, 'Have you ever tried telling him?'

'God, no! And I never will.'

'I don't mean how you feel about *him*. Just how you feel in general.'

'Why ruin the best friendship I've ever had?'

'It isn't much of a friendship if that would ruin it.' She took his hand. 'So, you're just going to let it eat away at you?'

'What choice do I have?'

'That's the saddest thing.'

Something in Claudine's tone annoyed Nish. 'I don't need your pity.'

She smiled, ignoring the barb. 'It's not just you I'm feeling sorry for. I wrote the book when it comes to loving where it isn't allowed.' Her hand moved to his shoulder. 'You need allies, Nish. Everyone does, out on the margins. They don't all have to be like you. In fact, it's better sometimes if they're not.' She shrugged. 'So Lucian likes women. That doesn't mean he won't understand. Or that he won't be receptive.'

Nish was about to respond when he heard the distant sound of a carriage coming up the driveway. He looked at Claudine.

'Billy,' he said. 'Mr Ainsworth was collecting him today.'

Claudine nodded slowly. 'Lucky old Billy.'

*

Cecil was almost impressed. They had held Billy in a cell at the police station on Piazza della Liberta. A bit rough and ready and smelled like a *pissoir*, but they hadn't beaten him. Besides, Billy was young. He might be looking rather disconsolate, but boys of his age could cope with anything, and should be encouraged to.

It was with this in mind that, just before they reached the kitchen door, he grabbed Billy and pushed him against the wall. No harm in reminding him who was boss. 'Not so fast, Master Scanlon.'

Billy struggled, twisting his body, pushing Cecil away. 'You're hurting me!'

Cecil tightened his grip. 'Listen to me, you little bastard. I've paid to release you. And I can pay to get you put back inside just as quickly.' He gave Billy a playful slap on the cheek. 'I have Mr Danioni in my pocket. Which means I have you in my pocket as well.'

Billy nodded dumbly.

'So, from now on, if I say jump, your only question is, "How high, Mr Ainsworth?" Do you understand?'

Billy nodded again. 'Yes, Mr Ainsworth.'

'Good.' He released his grip. 'Now get on with you.'

He opened the door and steered Billy inside, keeping his hand on his shoulder as they entered the kitchen.

The air was heavy with the smell of rich, raw foods and perspiration. Not for the first time, Cecil wondered how anyone could possibly work in such a dim, stuffy room.

Betty turned when she heard the door. She called out Billy's name and ran forward to embrace him in her thick, white arms.

Cecil smiled benignly. 'The return of the prodigal son.'

'I've been worried to death,' said Betty. She stepped back to get a closer look at Billy. 'You've lost weight.'

Billy rolled his eyes. 'I've not been gone twenty-four hours, Mam.'

'I'll make you a sandwich. A nice bit of salami.'

'I don't like salami.'

'Egg, then. You like egg.'

She pushed him down onto a chair, then set to work cutting slices of bread.

Bella had emerged from her office on hearing the commotion. 'Is he out on bail?'

'Released without charge,' Cecil declared. 'They were happy to accept my word that I don't believe Billy has anything to do with the disappearance of the painting.'

Betty looked up from her bread-buttering. 'What about the bike, Mr Ainsworth?'

'I've persuaded them to overlook it. It has now been returned to its owner. And a small payment made in lieu of its loan.'

'Oh, sir. I don't know how I can ever repay your kindness.'

Cecil loved it when people said things like this, especially servants. He looked at Billy. 'Just keep the boy's nose clean from now on,' he said. 'That's all I ask.'

'But that's just it,' said Betty. 'How can I? I've got me hands full here.'

Bella came forward to comfort her. 'Don't distress yourself, Betty. We'll work something out.'

But Betty was on a roll. 'Maybe it's better if I take the lad home, ma'am. You know, hand me notice in.'

Was she saying this for effect? Cecil couldn't tell.

'I won't hear of it,' said Bella. 'We'd be absolutely lost without you.'

'Bless you, Mrs Ainsworth.'

Sentimental scenes like this bored Cecil and he drifted off for a moment. But when he looked up, expecting to see Bella still standing beside Betty, she had disappeared.

Damn and blast it.

Where had she gone? Her office?

He heard the click of her shoes on the hall floor. So, she was heading up to her bedroom. Good. He would follow her.

He ran out of the kitchen and up the stairs after her. He could see her now on the landing, holding up her dress so that she could walk faster.

But the moment he reached the top of the stairs, Julia emerged from her suite.

This was not good timing. On the other hand, Cecil could never pass up the opportunity to talk to Julia. There was something bracing about her spikiness, something reassuring about the reliability of their rapport after so many years. In addition to which, he still found her decidedly attractive.

'Cecil!'

'Julia.'

'You're in a frightful rush.' She followed his gaze along to the end of the corridor. 'Are your creditors chasing you?'

'Very droll. But the joke's rather on you, I'm afraid.'

She raised an eyebrow. 'I'm intrigued.'

'Shall we?' Cecil signalled that they should go back into her suite, which was cluttered with open suitcases and bags in the process of being packed.

'You've caught me at an awkward moment,' said Julia.

'Indeed.' Cecil considered a pile of petticoats on a chair.

He followed her out onto the balcony. They stared in silence at the placid blankness of the sea.

Cecil asked, 'Have you enjoyed your stay with us?'

'Tolerably.'

'Oh.' He tried not to sound disappointed.

'I would like to have seen and heard a little less of some of my fellow guests . . . and a little more of you.'

'That might still be possible.'

Julia looked at her watch. 'In the eighteen hours we have left?'

'I don't mean here necessarily.' He lowered his voice. 'I intend to be in London rather more than I have been of late.'

She frowned. 'Has something changed?'

'My circumstances. And, of course, there's this wedding to arrange.'

'You have the means to go ahead?'

'I do.'

Julia burst out laughing. 'Oh, Cecil. I've waited so long to hear you say, "I do".'

He smiled and took her hand, raising it to his mouth. 'And do *you*?'

'Oh yes,' said Julia. 'I most certainly do.'

*

The last thing Lucian wanted was a conversation with his father. But here he came, practically skipping down the steps towards the bower where Lucian was hiding, trying to read a John Galsworthy novel which Nish had recommended. Trying and failing. He had never been much of a reader.

He put the book down and braced himself.

'There you are! Playing hide and seek?' Cecil's face was flushed and he seemed out of breath.

'If you like.'

'Who are you trying to avoid?'

'I'm not sure. Myself as much as anyone.' Lucian knew this kind of reply would wind his father up.

'Don't be such a misery,' Cecil snapped. 'I've something to show you.' He handed Lucian a piece of paper.

He opened it out and read what his father had written in his usual burgundy ink:

The engagement is announced between Lucian, son of the
Right Hon Mr and Mrs Cecil Ainsworth of Portofino, Italy,
and Rose, daughter of Mr and Mrs Jocelyn Drummond-
Ward, of London.

It wasn't a surprise, exactly. He and his parents had spent months discussing the wedding, so long that it had assumed an abstract, hypothetical quality. Seeing it written down punctured all that. The starkness and formality of the phrasing left no doubt that this was an actual intended event – unignorable, so best approached head on.

'I thought we might stroll down to the telegram office tomorrow,' his father said. 'Get the message out.'

Lucian nodded dumbly.

'Of course, that means you'll have to get your skates on.'

'My skates. Yes. Of course.'

'Will that be a problem?'

Lucian said nothing.

'Is it Rose you're trying to avoid?'

'Not exactly.'

399

'What's the issue, then?'

'I'm not sure.' He handed the paper back to Cecil.

'Not sure what?'

'That Rose and I are . . . sympathetic.'

Cecil frowned. 'I don't even know what that means.'

'We're not *well matched*.'

'But our families have been marrying into one another for generations.'

'I mean emotionally.'

Cecil's bloodshot eyes registered disbelief. 'Now, listen here. All this womanish malarkey has to stop. Yes, you've had a rotten go of it and got a nasty scratch. But the war's been over now for more than eight years.'

'I know.'

'Well, then. Pull yourself together. You're alive, aren't you? Capable of breathing, thinking, walking? Millions weren't so lucky.'

Lucian felt his anger rising. 'You don't think I'm aware of that? You don't think I spend every day and night in that shadow?'

'Then step out into the sunlight, man. Start to live a little.' Cecil paused. 'You're being offered the hand of a beautiful girl from an excellent family. And a house in London. And an income of fifteen hundred a year to go with it. Most young men with a drop of blood in their veins would be champing at the bit. Not mooning around worrying about *emotions*.' He held up the paper. 'This will be in the *Times* next week. So do your duty.'

'Yes, father.'

'Just as I did mine.' He pressed the paper against Lucian's chest, obliging him to take it.

As he walked off back to the house, Lucian looked down at his father's spidery writing, which had always hovered on the threshold of legibility. He folded the paper in half, then in half again, then in half again. Then he put the tiny square in the pocket of his trousers so that it would annoy him whenever he thrust his hands in – and remind him to take action before it was too late.

*

The afternoon dragged on monotonously. Nish felt anxious and unable to settle. He tried reading, but the words refused to rise from the page. He tried writing, but the results were flat and uninspired.

He found Lucian in his room, changing into a smarter suit. He must have recognised Nish's playful rap on the door because he called out 'Enter!' in the pompous, stentorian voice that was one of their old jokes.

Nish was relieved. He gazed musingly at his friend as he fastened his cufflinks. 'I was wondering where you'd got to.'

Lucian rolled his eyes. 'Not you as well.'

'Is something wrong?'

'Only that my father's given me an ultimatum.' He nodded towards the paper, open on the bed. 'Marriage to Rose it is.'

'Congratulations.' Nish kept his voice bright.

'Thank you. I haven't even spoken to her yet.'

'When do you plan to?'

'No time like the present.'

Nish opened his mouth to speak but nothing came out. *We think we're so modern*, he thought. *But really, we're still Edwardians.* A line from one of his favourite novels, *The House of Mirth*, floated into his mind. 'The situation between them was one which could have been cleared up only by a sudden explosion of feeling; and their whole training and habit of mind were against the chances of such an explosion.'

Lucian looked across. 'Did you want something?' There was irritation just below the surface.

Nish shook his head. 'Nothing important.'

'You're sure?'

'It can wait.'

There was a long pause, then Lucian said, 'Do you ever wish we could go back?'

'To when?'

'Trouville. After the war.'

'The Convalescence Depot?'

'Yes. We were so giddy that it was all over.'

Nish chuckled at this nostalgic distortion. 'Those bloody Nissen huts. It was all right for you. You just lay in bed. Some of us had to work.'

'I remember troughs full of flowers.'

'Good for you. I remember boxing matches and stupid beach games. Enforced swimming. Lots of pale, skinny bodies.' He shuddered. 'Every day was like a school sports day.'

Lucian laughed and Nish's heart leapt at the thought that

he had cheered him up. 'You're forgetting how happy we were. That we were still alive.'

'Things were simpler,' Nish conceded. 'In some ways.'

Lucian made some final adjustments to his suit, straightening the lapels. Then he combed and waxed his hair. He looked wonderful, like a Greek god.

'Right, then,' he said. 'Wish me luck.'

*

Constance had come to the drawing room on the off chance that Lucian might be there. But, of course, he wasn't – nor in any of the other public rooms. He would be in his own room, which was out of bounds to servants unless it needed cleaning.

On one of the tables, she noticed the copy of *The Iliad* that she and Lucian had been reading together. She picked it up and flicked through its pages, remembering.

A noise through the French doors startled her. Someone was on the terrace. Two people. A man muttered something. A woman laughed lightly and cleared her throat. There was the pony-trot clicking of heels on tiles. Then silence – a lingering, weighty silence.

It was Lucian who spoke first. 'I need to speak to you.'

Rose replied, 'But I have to pack.'

'Packing can wait.'

'Try telling my mother that.'

Frustrated that she couldn't hear better, Constance tiptoed across to the wall beside the open French doors and pressed herself against it.

She ought not to be doing this. It was sly and furtive. Nosey. What would her mother say? *Curiosity killed the cat.*

But she would find out eventually. So, she might as well hear it now, from the horse's mouth.

Lucian again. 'I've been thinking about what you said. About how difficult you find it to be true to yourself. And the thing is, I feel exactly the same.'

'You do?' Rose sounded shocked.

'Absolutely. I've spent my whole life trying to live up to everyone else's expectations of me. And not liking myself much as a consequence.'

'But ... all the time we've spent here, you've seemed so sure of everything ...'

'Maybe this place, Italy, allows me to behave a bit more freely. A bit more honestly. Though not honestly enough.'

There was a pause. Then, in her sing-song voice, Rose asked, 'Why are you telling me this now?'

'Because I want you to know we have more in common than you realise.'

'Do you think so?'

Constance's heart lurched. What was about to happen? She had a feeling of dread, as if she were at the edge of a cliff, looking down into the foaming sea.

'You never need to worry about being yourself with me,' Lucian continued. His voice was so reassuring that Constance felt her heart would break.

There was a shuffling sound, then Rose said pleadingly, 'Get up, Lucian. Please.'

It was like being at the pictures, the final devastating reel; but this time it was actually happening.

Rose said, 'You don't need to do this.'

Wise girl, thought Constance. *You tell him.*

But Lucian ploughed on. 'I don't need to, Rose. I *want* to.' A pause. And then he asked it. The question Constance had been hoping against hope he would never ask any other woman but her. 'Will you marry me?'

*

Cecil wanted everyone together – family, guests and all employees – to celebrate the engagement. He seemed determined to create a buzz. Bella heard him whistling in the corridors, clicking his fingers as he skipped out into the garden to round up stragglers. 'Have you heard? . . . Marvellous news, isn't it? . . . I had a feeling it was going to happen today . . .'

At reception, he stuck up a gnomic notice that left space for him to break the full story:

Formal reception: 6 pm, Drawing Room

Though, of course, he had been telling anyone he came across for the last two hours, Bella included.

'Exciting stuff, what?'

He used it as an excuse to get close to her. She felt herself contract away from him, pressing her back against the wall of the dining room where she was laying the tables.

'I'm glad you're happy,' she said, edging sideways like a crab, her hatred of him stronger at that moment than her interest in anything else.

Of course she was happy – for her son. What mother wouldn't be? At the same time, it was obvious to her that marriage to Rose was, for Lucian, an invidious compromise.

The reception was awkward before it even began. Cecil had neglected to check the hotel's stocks of sparkling wine or inform Betty of the need for *hors d'oeuvre*. She sent up some hastily assembled platters of olives and mixed nuts, which he rejected as inadequate until Alice intervened, telling him it wasn't fair, Betty needed more notice to provide food for an event such as this. Meanwhile, Francesco was dispatched forthwith to buy Prosecco.

At the appointed time, a crowd gathered, as instructed. Most people had dressed up, though Bella hadn't had time. Cecil stood at the front, by the doors to the terrace – the self-appointed Master of Ceremonies. He seemed to be enjoying himself immensely, yet again. When would it ever end?

'Julia? You come and stand by me.' He glanced around. 'And where's the happy couple?'

Rose was located at the back, looking shell-shocked in that funny shift dress that made her look all skin and bone. Glancing around for support, she raised a limp hand then shrank back into her chair.

'And has anyone seen Lucian? Don't tell me he's done a runner already?'

A ripple of nervous laughter greeted Lucian's appearance in the doorway.

'I'm here, father.'

Bella watched as he steered his way through the watching

crowd, past Paola and Constance, who were standing mutely with trays of drinks.

Standing awkwardly beside Rose, he looked around at the throng of encouraging, smiling faces – though Paola was scowling, and Constance seemed on the verge of tears.

'Now,' said Cecil. 'Does everyone have a glass of something wet and bubbly?'

Bella gestured to Paola and Constance to start serving the Prosecco.

But then, an extraordinary thing happened. Constance put down her tray on one of the occasional tables and ran from the room. Paola started to go after her, but Bella stopped her. 'No, Paola. You're needed here. I'll go.'

Bella followed Constance up to her room. The girl had closed the door. Bella put her ear against it and could hear the sounds of sobbing.

She stood there, waiting for Constance to calm down. Then she heard a rummaging, as though Constance were looking for something that might console her. The hunt became increasingly frantic. Bella heard drawers opening and closing. The slam of a wardrobe door. She heard Constance say, 'Where the hell are they?' and then, a note of keening desperation in her voice, 'They've gone. They've all gone. Oh, Tommy . . .'

Quickly, Bella went back down to the office and took the letters from the drawer she had locked them in.

Then she went back upstairs and knocked softly on the door.

*

Melissa was standing beside Lady Latchmere, watching Cecil propose the toast. 'To Lucian and Rose!'

It was all terribly exciting. She had known it was on the cards, of course. But she hadn't expected it to be announced now, or for it to involve her in any way.

They made a beautiful couple; no one could deny that. She hadn't spent much time around either of them, so she couldn't say for certain how well matched they were. Alice, who had become a good friend, never had much to say about Lucian. And yet Melissa sensed an underlying competitiveness. That was often the way, wasn't it, with siblings?

Melissa sipped her Prosecco and clinked glasses with Lady Latchmere, who was on her second Limoncello. 'I do so love a good wedding,' she said. 'Don't you, Melissa?'

'I've not been to very many,' Melissa admitted.

'Well, never mind. There's only one that really matters.' Lady Latchmere tilted her head. 'You have suitors, my dear?'

'Goodness me!' Melissa giggled. 'What a question!'

'No need to be coy. I'd turned down half a dozen at your age.'

'Please, Aunt. Might we change the subject?'

But the older woman was not to be deflected. 'If it's a matter of money . . .'

'It's a matter of inclination.'

'I'd be willing to pay for it.'

'But I'd much rather be allowed to continue with my education.'

Lady Latchmere frowned. 'Education?'

'University,' said Melissa, warming to her theme. 'Perhaps even a doctorate.'

'Are you sure?'

'I'm absolutely certain.'

Lady Latchmere took a moment to digest this news, which Melissa had delivered with a firmness that had surprised even her. 'Very well, dear,' she said. 'I only want to see you settled and happy.'

'I *am* settled and happy.'

'If you say so.'

Melissa kissed her on the cheek. 'I'd rather be wedded to a good book.'

*

Lizzie stood with her glass of sparkling water – for once she wasn't in the mood for Prosecco – when she saw Plum through the open door of the drawing room. He dropped his bag as she rushed to throw her arms around him.

'Oh, Plum darling! You're back.'

Plum pulled her arms away from around his neck to observe the chatter and bright laughter. 'Awfully decent of them to throw me a victory party.'

'You won?'

'Not quite, old girl. Lost to some Frenchie in the third round.'

Lizzie frowned. 'You don't seem very put out.'

Plum patted his pocket and winked. 'I had a little wager. On the other chap.'

'Oh.' Realisation dawned. 'So does that mean we're OK?'

'We're OK, sweetheart.'

'Well,' she said. 'I may have some even better news.'

'Oh, yes?'

'I've been feeling very strange these last few days. And it's probably far too early to tell, of course ... But I think I may be, well, you know ...'

Plum's eyes widened in an unspoken question which Lizzie answered with a nod and a shy smile.

*

A hoarse, tear-thickened voice called out, 'Who is it?'

'It's Mrs Ainsworth. Bella.'

The door opened. The girl's eyes were red and swollen, her face tear-stained. 'I'm sorry,' she said.

Bella's heart went out to her. 'What is it, Constance? I hate to see you so distressed.'

'I've lost something very dear to me.'

Bella entered the room. Then she took Constance by the arms and folded her in a motherly embrace. 'Hush, hush.'

'Oh, ma'am.' The crying began again.

Gently, Bella lowered her onto the bed. 'I fear this is a complicated business.' She produced the letters from her dress pocket. 'Are these what you've lost? What you're looking for?'

Constance's startled eyes flicked from the letters to Bella and back again. Shock, embarrassment and anger collided on her face. Wiping her eyes, she grabbed them and quickly opened the top envelope – to look, Bella presumed, for the locket, which was still there. Relieved but concerned, she turned to Bella. 'You've read them?'

'No. Though someone else has, I'm afraid.'

Constance absorbed this for a moment, the horrible implications. 'You know everything?'

'I know of your misfortune, yes.'

Constance stood up. She looked frail and thin, but resolute. She pushed the strands of wet hair off her face. 'Then I am dismissed.'

'Dismissed?' Bella sat back. This was not what she had expected.

'Of course. You cannot want me here, looking after Lottie. Knowing what you know.' The girl started to look around, presumably for her suitcase, but Bella stopped her. She gestured for her to sit down again. 'I can't think of anyone better than a mother to look after a child.'

'A mother who never had a husband?'

'But who is doing her utmost not to let that define her.'

Constance opened the locket and stared at the photograph. 'Who has abandoned her son.'

'But holds him close to her heart.'

Constance sniffed and looked up. 'I thought you would judge me. Most people do.'

'I've learnt not to do that,' said Bella. She paused. 'We all deserve a chance to make amends. Until we prove ourselves unworthy.'

Constance's eyes shifted to the photograph once again. 'I don't know where to start.'

'You can start,' said Bella, 'by telling me something about your boy.'

*

Cecil wondered where Bella had gone in such a hurry. He asked Lady Latchmere, who happened to be standing next to him. She replied 'Servant trouble' with the air of someone who had endured many such inconveniences in her time.

So, that was all right. As long as it was nothing to do with him.

He wandered through the party, dispensing bonhomie and ordering Paola to keep everyone's glasses topped up, never mind the low supplies of Prosecco.

Then he got a shock. Plum Wingfield, back from the dead. With Lizzie, who looked unexpectedly pleased to be talking to him.

He bounded up to them. 'Ah, Wingfield! You're back!'

'So, it would seem.' His manner was cold and offish. Generally, he seemed less than completely pleased to see Cecil. Which only increased Cecil's desire to humiliate him.

'Has your wife been filling you in on all the drama you've missed?'

Plum bobbed his head. 'Bits and pieces.'

Cecil turned to Lizzie. 'And did you tell him he was almost implicated?'

Plum reddened and glanced at his wife. 'Implicated?'

Cecil guffawed. 'In the theft of the painting, man!'

'I was just getting round to it,' said Lizzie, flatly.

'I don't mind telling you,' said Cecil, leaning in conspiratorially, 'there were one or two here who were ready to try you *in absentia.*' He leant back, enjoying Plum's discomfort. 'But I said, "No, he's an Englishman! And a sporting hero to boot! Plum

Wingfield is beyond reproach!"' He took a sip of Prosecco. 'It would be awful if that turned out not to be true. Wouldn't it?'

*

Slowly, the drawing room began to empty. Guests drifted back to their rooms. A few of them loitered, chatting, at the base of the stairs. The hall echoed with laughter and the hiss of whispered gossip.

A part of Alice wished she could be out there, joining in. But it was her job to oversee the tidying of the empty glasses, the sweeping of the floor. In any case, there was dignity in labour. Hadn't Jesus continued working as a carpenter until he was thirty?

The Bible was always a help and a solace. Whenever she felt aggrieved by the amount of work required of her, Alice remembered Genesis 2:2: 'And on the seventh day God ended His work which He had done, and He rested on the seventh day from all His work which He had done.'

Only one day's rest in every seven! If it was good enough for God, it was good enough for her.

That said, where on earth was Constance when she was needed? Snivelling in her room. Musing on past misdeeds. Alice felt strongly that Lottie's contact with the girl should be limited; though not to the point where Alice herself would have to step in and look after her.

She saw Count Albani approach her from across the room, dark-suited and eminent as always. She stopped what she was doing and smiled, for one must always be courteous.

'A happy occasion,' he said.

'My brother is certainly a happy man.'

'Miss Drummond-Ward is very charming. Very English.'

As he said this, Paola swept past with a trayful of empty plates. Was it Alice's imagination or was there a certain hostility in the look she gave the Count? As if his observation had been pointed in some way? Italians and their feuding! It was hard, sometimes, to tell what on earth was going on.

'You are leaving tomorrow?' Alice asked.

'At nine.'

'I hope we will see you again, Count Albani. You and Roberto.'

'I very much hope so too.'

Alice was about to disengage from the conversation when he spoke again.

'Before you go, I would like to clear up a misunderstanding.' He fumbled in the inside pocket of his jacket and produced the jewellery box. 'I hope you will reconsider.'

He opened the box, his perfect nails forming a claw on the plush blue velvet.

Alice had forgotten how beautiful the bracelet was. 'May I?' she asked.

'Of course.'

Gingerly, she plucked it out and held it up to the light. 'It *is* very pretty.'

The Count swallowed, as if he had been building up to this. 'As are you, Alice.'

It took a few seconds for Alice to process the remark. A nervous agitation swelled in her chest, threatening to overwhelm her. She felt herself start to shake as she said, more quietly but also more fiercely than she intended, 'Count Albani . . .'

'Forgive me. But I must speak what is in my heart.'

'What about Roberto?'

'I speak on my own behalf,' said Count Albani. 'You will grow old waiting for him to speak on his.'

Alice shook her head. 'No,' she said. 'It is not appropriate.'

'For a man of experience and means to wish to marry again?'

'To marry? Please!' She dropped the bracelet back in the box. Then she backed away from him. 'Do not ask me that!'

'Alice . . .'

'No. I am not Alice to you. I am Mrs Mays-Smith.'

Before he could protest, she fled from the room, barely giving herself a chance to wonder if she'd left her heart behind.

*

Journeys home were always boring and dispiriting. But as Julia made her way along the platform with Rose, a porter wheeling their luggage behind them, she felt an unusual sensation – sadness, tinged with regret.

She quashed it quickly, of course, because you couldn't become a slave to sensations like that. Better to focus on what had been achieved: the engagement. Though about that topic, Rose seemed less ecstatic than Julia had expected. Her daughter had barely said a word in the carriage on the journey to Mezzago.

Julia had had nothing to do except sit with her hands in her lap, watching the dreary scenery roll past and Francesco spitting in the road. Disgusting creature.

415

When, finally, they reached the waiting room, Julia was more than slightly dismayed to find Nish already sitting there, his single suitcase lying at his feet. Of course, India was British and Indians were our people and some of them had fought bravely and marvellously in the war, despite the impediment of their turbans – most of them wore turbans, didn't they? – but really, it was best to keep close contact to a minimum, even with the educated ones. It only made them uppity.

Bella's indulgence of characters like Nish was, she thought, regrettable. Who knew where it might lead?

'Mr Sengupta,' she said.

'Mrs Drummond-Ward. Rose.'

'I wasn't aware we would be travelling back in your company.'

'You won't be, I'm afraid.' Nish indicated a wrapped pile of pamphlets on the bench next to him. 'I'm heading for Turin. To distribute these. And to meet a friend.'

'A friend,' said Julia, smiling. 'How nice.'

*

She didn't much like the man, but Bella couldn't help feeling sorry for Francesco. No sooner had he returned from dropping the Drummond-Wards at Mezzago, than he was preparing to make the same journey for the third time that day, loading bags onto the carriage and checking the horses while his next batch of passengers said their goodbyes.

Lady Latchmere sought reassurance that she and Melissa would have the carriage to themselves.

'You will,' said Bella. 'The Drummond-Wards, Count Albani and Mr Sengupta have already left.'

Alice added, 'And the Wingfields and Ms Pascal are staying on another day.'

'Do you have other guests arriving?' wondered Melissa.

'A party of eight from Zurich,' said Bella. 'We have a few days to get organised.'

'Well,' said Lady Latchmere, smiling. 'It has certainly been ... eventful.'

'We try our best,' said Bella.

This was true, she realised – and she felt exhausted from the effort.

'My aunt and I have both grown very fond of Hotel Portofino,' said Melissa.

'I shall tell all my friends about it,' added Lady Latchmere. 'And the genteel lady who runs it.'

Bella grasped the older woman's outstretched hand. 'And might we see you again?'

'Who knows, dear, at my age.'

Melissa asked, 'But Alice, you will come to visit me in London?'

'I hope to,' said Alice. 'Actually, there's something I wanted to ask you ...'

She led Melissa away for a private word, leaving Bella and Lady Latchmere together.

'I do appreciate how understanding you've been about everything,' said Bella.

'Oh, I wouldn't have missed it for the world,' said Lady

Latchmere. 'It really has been like one of those Agatha Christie novels.'

'Indeed,' said Bella. 'Though I'm not sure even she could dream up *quite* so motley an assortment of characters.'

'Nonsense, my dear! It is the 1920s, you know.' She squeezed Bella's hand. 'The world is changing. For the better, I hope.'

Bella smiled thinly. 'I wish I had your confidence, Gertrude.'

It was unusual for Bella to feel any great attachment to hotel guests after they left. But as the carriage rattled through the gate and turned right, she felt a pang of sadness, a little like the homesickness she used to feel at school – a weight in the pit of her stomach and an ache in her throat that never, or almost never, resolved itself into actual tears.

On her way up to her room, she stopped in the hall and looked around. This was all her dream. Her handiwork. She had chosen the green shade of paint for the wood panelling on the stairs. She had commissioned the chandelier with its hundreds of sparkling crystals. She had picked the flowers which adorned the top of the reception desk and painted, in gold leaf paint, the words 'HOTEL PORTOFINO' onto the sign set on the wall behind it.

She had selected the paintings on the walls, including several of Lucian's. She had decided on diaphanous muslin curtains for the drawing room rather than lace because they made the room feel cooler, diffusing the sunlight into a gorgeous, dreamy haze. She had made sure there was a gramophone for the young people and back issues of *Country Life* for the older ones so that they would feel at home.

All of this was for everybody else. But now she had a little time to enjoy it herself before the next wave of guests. A little time just to *be*.

As she padded upstairs she sang to herself – some silly music-hall song from her childhood, she couldn't remember its name. It was funny, she thought, how powerful songs were. The emotions they were capable of provoking.

He had left the door of her room open. Which is to say, he had opened it. Bella could see into the room, but the violation meant it no longer felt like hers. How dare he colonise her bedroom as he had done her body? Still, she stepped forward and looked around. What was different? What had he done? What did he *want*?

She started to cross towards her dressing table, being careful not to slip on the Persian rug, when she noticed an envelope on her bed, addressed to her in too-familiar handwriting.

She picked it up and opened it.

Inside was a cheque made out to Mrs Arabella Ainsworth for the sum of £1,000, signed by the Right Hon Cecil Ainsworth.

She turned and he was there, in the doorway, watching.

'I thought it might help,' he said.

'Help what?' She came over and stood in front of him, the cheque in her hands. 'Help *this*?' She pointed to the marks on her face, concealed with make-up but still visible.

He squirmed – that was the only word for it. 'No,' he said. 'Even I wouldn't be that crass. Help make us friends again.'

Bella said, 'I don't want to be friends.' She tore up the cheque and scattered the pieces at his feet.

He watched the shreds fall across the floor. 'What on earth are you doing?'

'I won't take a penny from you. I've played by your rules for too long, Cecil Ainsworth. It's time to start making some of my own.'

Placing the palm of her hand against his chest, she pushed him gently backwards across the threshold and into his room. He had the good grace not to resist. Then she shut the door and locked it, dropping the key into the waste-paper basket in the corner. Whatever her future held – and she had plans, grand plans – it would have nothing to do with Cecil. Not anymore.